THE SOPHOMORE

THE SOPHOMORE

MONICA MURPHY

Cover design: Letitia Hasser
R.B.A. Design

Editor: Rebecca, Fairest Reviews Editing Services
Proofreader: Sarah, All Encompassing Books

CHAPTER 1

ELLIE

The text notification shows up every night at approximately the same time. I anxiously wait up for it, anticipation racing through my veins. Anything to do with him leaves me giddy with nervous excitement, which is ridiculous.

He doesn't feel the same way about me. It's clear. It's been clear for a while, since he graduated high school and went off to college. My friends tell me I'm wasting my time on him, but I can't help it. My heart won't let him go no matter how hard I try. I care about him.

Too much.

I lie in bed with the lights off, my phone in my hand as I scroll TikTok. I work mostly nights during the summer anyway, so I'm usually up till the early morning hours, still wide awake. He knows this. He's currently traveling the West Coast and has a hard time sleeping too.

Jackson: **You around?**

I smile, my heart rate kicking up. I decide to make him wait until the two-minute repeat notification pops up, and then I'll answer him. Not like he's sitting around waiting for my reply anyway. I get this image of him living this glamorous, bohemian life. Traveling in a tour bus, his dad actually bought for him, writing beautiful lyrics inspired by his travels and having spontaneous jam sessions with his newfound band members.

What I don't try and think about are the groupies who he could be getting with on a nightly basis. The girls go crazy for him, and I understand why. I go crazy for him too. I have for a long time.

Too long, according to my closest friends.

His social media has blown up since he's gone on tour this summer, and most of his followers—and fans—are women. They blatantly flirt in the comments. They blow up his DMs with blatant propositions and even naked photos. I'm sure they say all sorts of dirty, lewd things to him, what they'd do to him, for him. What they want him to do to them.

I'm not like that. Sure, I want him to do dirty, sexy things to me, I can't lie. But I could never say those things to him. I'm too shy. I don't think I could ever be that bold, even with Jackson.

Besides, he always keeps me at an arm's length when we're in public together, the asshole.

In private? Via text? We're as close as two people can be—as friends. He shares his hopes and dreams and worries with me, and I do the same. It's not one-sided. He listens to me. He makes me feel like he cares.

And that is the most wonderful thing in the world, to be cared for by Jackson Rivers.

Now that he's gone, I miss him fiercely. I'm scared he'll find so much success, he won't come back here.

Worse, I'm scared I'll never see the real him again. The version of himself that he only shares with me.

This is why I live for our nightly text conversations. Just like we used to have when we were in high school. Back then, they meant so much more to me than they did to him, and that secretly devastated me. Especially when we'd be together at a party or whatever, and sometimes, he'd act like I didn't exist.

He doesn't do that anymore, thank goodness. We're friends. He's friendly toward me, always careful not to lead me on though. And there's something about him that's just so damn appealing. He's charming. A natural charisma you can't help but be drawn to. Male or female, it doesn't matter. You either want to be his friend or *be* with him, if you know what I mean.

I fall under both categories. I'm sure plenty of others do too.

Oh, and then there's his face. Gorgeous. Blue eyes. The blond hair. The cheekbones, the lips and the little curve upward they always have when he's performing. The way he looks at me when he sings his songs.

As if he's singing them to me.

According to my best friend Ava, I let him take advantage of my kindness. She's probably right. I'm a nice person. Too nice. Tony Sorrento's girlfriend Hayden has been giving me lessons lately in standing up for myself and learning how not to take any shit. I'm trying my best to stand by what she says, but it's so hard. Especially when it comes to Jackson.

I do love Hayden, though. We've spent a lot of time together since she started dating Tony, and when our friend group gets together, us girls always gravitate toward each other. I call her my mentor. I hope to be just like her when I grow up. I mean, she's only around three years older than me, but still. She's strong and smart and she doesn't back down from anything. While I'm quiet and shy and sometimes a little scared of trying something new.

Ava doesn't take any crap either. She stands up for what she believes in, no matter what. I'm going to miss her. She's going away to college. Her boyfriend isn't too happy about it either, but we can't convince her to stick around. If we try that, it'll push her to leave even more. She's kind of stubborn.

I wish I was more like her.

Jackson's text pops up again and I tap it, contemplating my reply. I decide to keep it simple.

Me: **Hey! What's up?**

The gray bubble pops up immediately, surprising me. Maybe he was waiting for me to respond.

Jackson: **Nothing much. Tired. Homesick.**

Me: **Getting tired of traveling already?**

He's been gone over a month. He said he'd come back at the end of July, so he could be back at school in time for football practice, which is about three weeks before classes start. He claims he's going to be on the team again this season, but I don't know. How is he going to do that? His entire life is changing, and he's currently split in two directions. Something will have to give. He'll have to make a choice soon, and I'm thinking he'll let go of football.

Jackson: **Yeah. I miss sleeping in my own bed.**

I wish for once he'd say he misses me. He misses my smiling face. Something, anything like that would send me over the moon.

Of course, it would also send my expectations soaring sky high and I'd end up sorely disappointed when I realized, yet again, that Jackson isn't interested in me like that. In his eyes, I'm a friend. Nothing more. Even if I desperately want there to be.

That. Is. It.

Shoving all negative thoughts aside, I focus on our conversation.

Me: **Where did you perform tonight?**

Jackson: **At an outdoor music festival on the outskirts of Seattle. It was so fuckin cool, E. We went to the place where Kurt Cobain killed himself.**

Me: **Uh, that's gruesome.**

Jackson: **He's my fuckin idol, you know this. Anything that has to do with him, I want to see. Fuck, I want to** absorb whatever I can, wherever I'm at. Seattle is an amazing city.

I've never been there. I haven't been many places, really. Grew up in the same small town. Never traveled out of the state. My parents don't have a lot of money, though we're not what I would call poor. I feel poor though, compared to all the people I hang out with. They mostly all come from money.

I didn't even bother applying to colleges anywhere else. I chose Fresno State because it's close and not too expensive, and thank God I got in. I'm not adventurous. Not even close.

Me: **I can see you living in Seattle.**

Jackson: **I would've moved to Seattle in a heartbeat if it was the 90s. But it's not. The music scene is cool here, but not like back then. Those were the good days.**

Me: **I think you were meant for another time.**

Jackson: **I think you're right.**

We talk a little more about his travels. Where he's going next. When he's coming home. He says record executives are still chasing after him, trying to get him to sign deals, which has been going on for a while, ever since he started performing regularly at one of the local venues in Fresno. But he's not ready to tie himself down with anything. He claims he's not sure if this is what he really wants.

Me: **You're going to have to make a choice sometime.**

Jackson: **I'll keep up the dual life as long as I can. I'm only nineteen. I want to go party with my friends too, you know? This is starting to feel like a grind. Like a job.**

Me: **Are you performing at Strummers when you come back home?**

Jackson: **Yeah. I have a performance lined up for July 31st. Didn't I tell you? Though I'm coming home on the 27th so I can have a little time to relax. I can't wait.**

My heart cracks wide open. He'll be home in less than three weeks. I can't wait to see him.

Me: **It'll be nice to have you back.**

Jackson: **Can't wait to see you.**

He sends me a heart emoji.

Don't read too much into that. Don't do it. Don't.

Me: **I'm sure you have plenty of female company.**

Jackson: **They're not you though.**

He doesn't deny he's with other girls, which I'm sure he is. Can't focus on that though. That's a downward spiral I don't want to experience right now.

Me: **I'm glad we're friends.**

There. What can he say to that? We are friends. And that's all we're gonna be. That's all he'll allow.

He doesn't respond and I keep scrolling TikTok, my eyelids growing heavier and heavier. I'm tired. It's already past two. I need to go to sleep. I work at eleven tomorrow, so I won't get to sleep in as much as I usually do when I close.

Jackson: **Sometimes I wonder why we're not more than that, E. Why are you always so good to me? I don't deserve you.**

I stare at what he wrote, reading it again and again. He's right. He doesn't deserve me. And he probably doesn't mean it when he says he wonders why we're not more than that. He's said that type of thing to me before, when we were younger and he'd flirt with me, always getting my hopes up.

I'm trying to not let that happen anymore.

Me: **Because we both know it would never work.**

Jackson: **Right. I'd mess it up.**

Me: **You would. Oh, and you're right.**

Jackson: **What about?**

I contemplate telling him the truth. Will he get angry? Do I care if he does? For once, I should stand up for myself. Call him out for his crap. He needs to hear it.

He needs to hear me.

Me: **You don't deserve me.**

Me: **You never really have.**

CHAPTER 2

ELLIE

O *ne month later*

I'm at the front of the growing crowd, my gaze on the darkened stage directly in front of me and nowhere else. The air is thick with anticipation, and it settles just beneath my skin, making it buzz. I can't help but smile at people I don't really know, considering we're all here for the same thing. They smile at me in return, nodding their heads to the faint music playing in the background. Everyone else is buzzing too. We can feel it.

Feel *him.*

I arrived at Strummers early, saving a spot near the front of the stage for our group of friends. A group that has completely embraced me and made me feel a part of them, even if the boy I want to embrace me the most is totally blind to my loyalty. Not that he's been around to see it lately, considering he's been on tour for the last two months.

If my friends were here, they'd all tell me he was an idiot for not seeing me for what I really am. They'd be on my side, though they adore him just as much as they like me. Maybe even more so.

But no one adores him as much as me. I'm his biggest fan. None of these girls in this room can say they've personally spoken to him. They've held him in their arms. They've kissed him.

Well, it was a kiss on the cheek but damn it, I'm counting it.

A sigh leaves me and my butt buzzes. I reach for my phone, pulling it out of my pocket to see I have a text from Ava.

We're coming inside right now! Where are you?

I text her a response.

At the very front of the stage, more on the right side. Good luck fighting the crowd to get to me.

Ava: **We have Caleb with us. He'll bully his way through the pack of girls.**

I shove my phone back in my pocket, glancing over my shoulder to see if I can spot my friends. But it's no use. I'm surrounded by nothing but girls.

Overly excited, mostly teenaged girls who are wearing their most revealing clothes, hoping to catch Jackson's eye when he comes on stage.

Good luck. He definitely doesn't like them underage. I know that for a fact.

I hear a loud male voice that I recognize—Caleb's—and the whiny protests of about a bazillion teenage girls who are pissed he's shoving past them. He doesn't care. Anything to make a path for his friends. When I feel hands settle on my waist, I glance over my shoulder to see it's Ava standing there, and she wraps me up in a hug.

"We made it!" she squeals near my ear.

"Thank God," I say, squeezing her in return before she shifts away. I'm surrounded by everyone who's a part of our group. The boys. The girls. They're all here tonight, in support of our beloved Jackson Rivers.

AKA that 'soulful motherfucker'—that's what Eli always calls him.

Eli is Jackson's best friend, and he's missed Jackson so much while he's been on tour. He even went to Portland and hung out with him for a couple of days. Ava went too. I was so jealous, but I had to stay home to work. I've worked all summer, trying to save my money for college this fall. I got a few scholarships and community awards, but that won't cover everything.

Compared to everyone else in our group, I'm a broke ass joke. Well, Diego doesn't come from money either, but he has Jocelyn and her dad is a lawyer so they do pretty well.

Me? I'm scrambling for everything I've got. It was a big deal that I took today off, but this performance is special.

I want to be here, in support of Jackson. After not seeing his face for the last couple of months, I miss it.

Terribly.

"Ellie. Baby." Caleb wraps me up in his arms and squeezes me, lifting me up so my feet are dangling off the floor before he sets me back down. "You nabbed us the best spot in the entire place."

"You know it," I say, my cheeks turning pink at the flirtatious way he talks to me. Looks at me. I'm not interested in Caleb. He's naughty. There are no other words to describe him. He was a player in high school and he's remained much the same in college.

I've remained much the same so far too. I'm the girl all the guys view as just a friend. The one they can always count on, but never the one they're interested in.

"Leave her alone," Ava says, slapping Caleb on the arm. "It feels like I haven't seen you in forever."

I've been working a lot, that's why. And okay, I've been

avoiding her a little bit too, because though I don't blame her, and I know she has to do what's right for her, I'm sad.

Because Ava is leaving us. She's going to San Diego State. Eli is suffering mostly in silence too. We don't want her to go.

But we understand. This is what she wants. We can't stand in her way.

"Yeah. My work schedule has been really heavy with my new job. All the training," I tell her when she pulls away.

Ava frowns. "You're working too much."

"I have to. I can't afford tuition like the rest of you," I say, immediately hating how…bitter I sound.

"I'm with you on that," Caleb says, holding out his hand for a high five.

I give it to him, my slap and my smile weak, Ava's careful gaze tracking my every movement.

"We need to get together," she tells me, her voice firm. "What's your schedule like this week?"

"Busy," I say automatically.

Eli magically appears, wrapping his arms around Ava and pulling her into him. These two have been together for almost two years, and they're madly in love.

"When is this concert going to start?" Eli asks me, as if he doesn't know.

Jackson and Eli are roommates. They play on the Bulldogs football team together. They spend almost all of their time together, though Jackson was sneaking around, performing at Strummers secretly, never telling any of us. We only found out thanks to Tony's girlfriend taking him to a concert here where Jackson opened up for another band.

Despite the secrecy, Eli wasn't fazed. He loves his bro Jackson with his whole heart, and has missed him this summer almost as much as I have.

"It should start at eight-thirty," I tell him, glancing at my phone. It's eight-fifteen now. "We're getting closer."

The lights suddenly shut off, and the teenagers start

screaming. I suppose I shouldn't think of them as *teenagers* like it's a bad word, considering I'm one too, but I feel so much older than them. Graduating high school changes you. Having to work full-time the summer before you start college changes you too.

I'm tired. And wondering if this is all my life will be for the next four years. Constant school and work? I'll fry my brain completely by the time I graduate. If I even graduate, considering I have no idea what to do with my life after college…

There's movement on the stage. I can hear it. And just as quick as the lights went out, they come back on, and there's a giant wooden throne sitting in the middle of the stage. The girls start cheering, and Caleb whoops it up as he usually does. He even gets everyone to start chanting our star's name.

"Jack-son! Jack-son! Jack-son!"

Over and over and over again, we yell. Until it's a rumble, a force growing within the room, ready to spill out everywhere. I'm caught up. We're all caught up, until someone turns up the volume on the music being played in the background. We go quiet and I frown at Ava as I listen to the opening chords. They're familiar. I know I've heard this song before.

Jackson's voice starts singing and I smile. So does Ava. The groupies start screaming their joy at hearing their young god's voice and Caleb cups his hands around his mouth to shush them loudly.

I sway to the beat, caught up in Jackson's words as usual. There's nowhere I'd rather be. Lost in his lyrics. He switches to the chorus, the words that always get me.

Only for you, I'd hesitate
  Only for you, I'd stand and wait
  It's only you that can change my mind

And only you would leave me behind

Yet again I wonder who he's talking about. Me? I couldn't be so lucky. He doesn't wait for me. He barrels ahead with his life without regard for anyone else. It's not that Jackson is insensitive...

Okay, if I said that out loud to Hayden right now—who's currently swaying her hips to Jackson's song while Tony watches her with appreciation in his dark eyes—she'd tell me I was making excuses for him and I need to call him out for his bullshit.

She's right. Jackson is a bit of a selfish asshole. I have been waiting for him to see me for over two years, yet he doesn't. I'm the friend. The original groupie. The one who gushed over his talent and hung on to his every word, glance and touch. The idiot who believed he was secretly in love with me, but didn't know what to do with his feelings.

Ugh. Yes. So embarrassing when I look back on it now.

Diego and his girlfriend Jocelyn show up to join our group, and I study everyone's faces, grateful for each one of them. Ava and Eli. Tony and Hayden. Caleb. Hayden's best friend Gracie. I've grown closer to all of these people over the last year, and now we're all going to college together.

Well, except for Ava.

The music stops and the lights dim once more, but don't go completely out. It's still dark enough that you can't make out much, but I'm close enough to the stage to see Jackson come out. He settles onto his throne like the king he is, his acoustic guitar in his lap. There's a full band performing behind him tonight, which is a new addition, thanks to the tour he's been on this summer.

A single spotlight shines upon his golden head and Jackson leans toward the lowered mic. "Good evening. My name is Jackson Rivers."

The crowd screams.

"HAVE MY BABIES, JACKSON!"

That last bit is from Caleb.

Jackson grins and gives Caleb the finger. The crowd swivels their heads in unison, all of them glaring at Caleb, who only smiles and waves in return.

"My friends are here tonight, so I have to make this performance extra special, don't you think?" The crowd responds with enthusiastic cheers, my friend group especially. "Okay, let's do it."

He launches into a Nirvana song. They're his all-time favorite band, which would be incredibly cliché if it wasn't so genuine. He loves Kurt Cobain. He loves all the grunge bands from the nineties. He wants a grunge revival, wants to bring that type of music back but with a new spin on it, and I told him he could do it. He can do anything he sets his mind to.

I believe in him that much.

His set goes on for ninety minutes, playing a combination of original songs along with plenty of covers, and all of those he makes his own. It's so good. *He's* so good. His smooth, sexy voice. The full band backing him only accentuates his talent and—

I'm gushing. Even if it's in my own head, I can tell I'm going on and on and I need to chill the hell out.

He ends the set with the song they played over the sound system before the concert started. Only You. As he's building up to the chorus, he sweeps his gaze over the crowd before it settles on me.

Just me.

His lips curve upward and he leans in closer to the mic, his lips brushing it as he sings the chorus, then launches into the second verse. His gaze never leaves mine as he croons.

Finally got you in my bed

Not sure why it took me so long
Since you've been living in my head
Before I started writing this song

Everything inside of me melts, despite the fact that I know this song isn't about me. He hasn't got me in his bed—not even close. But the way he looks at me in this moment, as if he's singing this song just to me, makes me wish he had.

I glance to my left to see Ava watching me with a knowing look on her face, though I can see the concern in her eyes too. I can only smile weakly at her in return, too giddy to worry about what she thinks. I'm too busy having a total moment of realization.

It feels like Jackson is finally seeing me. Really seeing me for the first time.

My entire body buzzes with excitement at the thought. There's an afterparty tonight. Eli is hosting it at their apartment. Maybe something will…happen between Jackson and me. Something real. Something magical.

A girl can only hope.

The song ends and Jackson grins while the crowd cheers uncontrollably. I glance around, spotting girls with tears streaming down their faces as they scream their heads off for him, and I'm blown away. He's touched so many. I wonder if he can see it. The power he wields over people with his performance, his songs, his words, his smiles.

Oh God, the smiles.

"Good night," he says into the mic, and the lights fade, shrouding him in complete darkness. The concert is over.

The girls are still going wild.

"Let's go backstage and talk to him," Eli yells at us over the screams. "He told me our names are on a list."

I nod eagerly, a different kind of anticipation thrumming

in my veins, in my head. The excitement of finally getting to see Jackson in the flesh is making me anxious.

Nervous.

We make a human chain and work our way through the crowd, all of us connected by hands or hanging on to the back of someone's shirt. We head for the backstage area, Eli and I leading the pack, until we're stopped by a burly looking man with a menacing expression on his face.

"We're friends of Jackson's," Eli says and the guy rolls his eyes. I'm sure he's heard that before. "No man, I'm serious. Look up our names. Eli Bennett."

The bodyguard grabs a clipboard that's hanging on the wall and checks it before lifting his head. "You're good."

We each give him our names and he finds every single one of us on the list. I can tell he's surprised as he opens the chipped black painted door. "Right this way."

We file through the open doorway. Excitement licks at my skin. It's been way too long since I've seen Jackson. I don't care how sweaty or smelly he might be after that performance, I want to hug him.

Truthfully? I want to rub myself all over him. Don't know how he'd react to that, so I'm reminding myself, yet again, to calm down so I won't act like a groupie.

Within seconds of coming backstage, we find ourselves in a narrow hall with closed doors on either side.

"The dressing rooms," Gracie announces. She's dated a few musicians who've performed at Strummers in the past, so she should know. "His name should be on the door."

We find his room with the small chalkboard sign hanging on the wall with his name on it. Eli knocks on the door and tests the handle to find it's unlocked so he barges in, all of us following behind him.

"Congrats on a fucking awesome performance tonight, bro!" Eli yells, stopping short when he sees what's happening.

I go still too, my mouth popping open in shock.

Jackson is sitting in a chair in front of a mirror with a very beautiful woman on his lap. She's clad in a crop top and tiny denim shorts, miles of bare skin on display. Her arms are wound around his neck, her hands in his hair. His arms rest casually around her bare waist, one hand grasping her butt and holding her to him.

Their mouths were fused. He breaks the kiss when he hears us, his wide, slightly wild eyes meeting mine for the briefest moment before he tears them away.

My heart drops. Crashes to the ground, shattering into tiny, jagged pieces.

"Oh. Shit." He smiles, not the least bit ashamed to be found with a woman on his lap practically humping him. She glances over her shoulder to look at us, a sultry expression on her beautiful face. "Thanks, guys. Didn't, ah, expect you all to show up back here."

"What did you expect then? You did leave all of our names with the doorman," Ava reminds him, sounding pissed.

God, I love my best friend. I'm too shocked to say or feel anything. I'm numb.

And stupid. So, so stupid.

Jackson practically shoves the girl off his lap and rises to his feet, going to Eli so they can perform some complicated, ritualistic handshake they've perfected over time before they quickly embrace. "So glad you're here."

Eli pulls away, Ava snagging his arm so she can stand directly beside him. "Who's your friend, Rivers?"

"Ah, this is…" He gestures toward the woman, who glares at him before telling us her name.

"I'm Brit." She waves. Wipes at the corners of her lipstick-smeared mouth.

My stomach pitches and rolls, like I'm in the middle of the

ocean and about to puke my guts out. I can't stop looking at Brit, wondering what she has that I don't. She's tall. All legs and arms and tits and ass. I'm short. And not much in the tits or ass department, especially compared to her. Her hair is blonde, her makeup is perfect and she looks older than us. Definitely older than me, and I'm the youngest one here besides Ava. While we're the same age, she's still got me beat by a couple of months.

So that's what she's got. Beauty and age and experience. She's bold and not afraid to go after what she wants.

Basically, the complete opposite of me.

Jackson ignores Brit, which I take no satisfaction in. He's too busy hugging everyone, and he saves me for last. As if he knows.

Of course he knows. I've been the obvious, ridiculously dumb groupie girl for months. Almost two years, if we're being super specific.

FML times one hundred million.

"Ellie. Baby. You're looking good." He wraps me up in a smothering hug that I revel in for only a second.

Okay, fine. Maybe a couple of seconds. I can't turn off my feelings for him that quick.

He smells like Jackson and a hint of sweat. His body is lean and even more muscular, I swear. And when I feel his lips press against my forehead in a sweet, chaste kiss, I pull out of his arms quickly, not wanting his mouth on me after he kissed Brit—the sexier, far more experienced groupie.

Ugh, I hate him. I'm in love with him, yet I can't stand him right now.

"I'm so glad you came," he says, seemingly clueless to my distress. "Did you like the last song?"

"Yes," I bite out, and that's all I can say. If I part my lips again, I might let forth a stream of curses and bitter words just for him.

Why are men so oblivious?

He smiles, his expression tender. Just like it always is when he deals with me. "I'm glad. You know I wrote it for—"

"We need to get going, don't we, Eli?" Ava asks in an extra loud voice, purposely interrupting Jackson. "We have to finish setting up for your party. You're still coming to the party right, Jackson?"

"Definitely. For sure." He nods enthusiastically, ignoring her dark tone. It's so obvious she's disgusted with him, but he's not acknowledging it. "Give me some time though. I need to wrap up a few things here first before I can leave."

His gaze slides to Brit for the briefest second and I want to die.

I know what he's going to wrap up. Whatever he started with Brit. I'm sure he'll have sex with her in this skeezy dressing room that's probably seen plenty of action in the past. At the very least, he'll get a blowjob from her.

God. I'm so desperate to leave, I can feel my entire body vibrating with the need to run. Just run and never look back.

"Okay, well take your time—*oof*." Eli glares at Ava, who just jabbed him with her pointy elbow. "Yeah, just get back to the apartment as soon as possible okay, bro? We can't really party until the guest of honor is with us."

"Yeah. I'll head over there in a few. Thanks again for coming tonight." Jackson's dark blue gaze meets mine and I stare back, letting my fury be known. But it's as if it flies straight over his head. He doesn't see it.

How does he *not* see it?

Oh, I know. He just doesn't see everything else I throw his way. My undying love and devotion—he's never noticed that. My endearing friendship? Nope, doesn't realize that either. I've given him hours and hours of my time. I think about him every single day, worried, happy, curious, yearning. All of the emotions, they hit me when it comes to Jackson.

Yet he doesn't think about me at all. Not at all.

Wait. I take that back. He does think about me. As his

friend. As the one girl who's always just sitting there, waiting to lap up whatever scraps he tosses my way.

Well, I'm done. I can't be that girl any longer.

Jackson Rivers is dead to me.

And I mean it this time.

CHAPTER 3

JACKSON

I fucked up.

When do I not fuck up when it comes to Ellie? It's almost as if I want to get caught. Maybe I do. I'm not good enough for her. I never have been. She's just so damn sweet, always there, always willing to talk to me, give me advice, encourage me when I need it the most. And I need that support a lot.

Deep down, I'm an insecure asshole who's scared to take it to the next step with the pretty girl who's been waiting in the wings for me to get off my ass and actually do something for far too long. And what happens? I start kissing some rando woman I don't know and I get caught.

By Ellie.

If looks could kill, I'd be dead thanks to the glare Ava's shooting my way as Eli grabs her arm and escorts her out of the dressing room. Always protective of her best friend. Gotta love that. Eli knows I got busted and I see the sympathy there in his eyes, though he'd never say anything in front of Ava and Ellie.

He's not stupid.

All of my friends are currently looking at me as if I've lost my damn mind, which maybe I have. Well, with the exception of Caleb, who grins and flashes me two thumbs up as he nods in Brit's direction before Diego shoves him.

They offer up muffled goodbyes as they exit the tiny dressing room and the minute the door is shut and they're all gone, I breathe a sigh of relief.

Brit—I didn't even realize that was her name until she introduced herself to everyone—is on me the second that they're gone, her mouth finding mine as she grinds her tight body against me.

"I thought they'd never leave," she murmurs against my lips before she dives her tongue into my mouth.

I kiss her for a while and then push her away, taking a couple of steps back for some much-needed space. "Don't know if I want to do this."

Huh. When do I not want to do this? I'm all about the quick fuck in a dressing room, hotel room, on the tour bus. Hell, wherever I can get it. I've lost track of how many women I've been with over the summer.

Too many to mention.

But now I can't get Ellie's face out of my mind. The flash of pain in her eyes when our gazes met. Seeing me with Brit hurt her.

I don't know if she'll forgive me for what she witnessed.

"What do you mean, lover?" Brit rests her hand over my dick, giving it a squeeze. "You seem ready to go to me."

I remove her hand from my crotch. "Yeah. Not right now."

Anger lights up her eyes. They're pale blue and a little freaky. "So when? A few minutes? You want to change? I get it. You're all sweaty and worked up." She rests her hands on my shoulders, letting them roam over my chest. "I can help you burn off all that energy rumbling inside of you."

Her words are tempting. She's describing exactly what I'm

feeling. I guess she's done this before. How else would she get backstage when I didn't invite her? Security must know who she is.

A groupie. It doesn't matter what band you're in, she'll do you just for the clout.

"I don't know…" My voice drifts.

She drops to her knees.

And I don't stop her.

———

I show up at my apartment an hour later, freshly showered and without a lick of Brit's cloying perfume on me. When she was finished, we shared a bottle of Jack, though I drank most of it. Kicked her out of the dressing room when I realized she wasn't going anywhere. Cleaned up, then got an Uber home because I didn't drive to Strummers, knowing I would get fucked up when my performance was over.

This is it for me this summer. My rock star moments are finished—for now. I still want to produce music. Write a few songs. Plan for a tour next summer. Maybe even put together a record—independently of course.

I don't want some asshole in a suit telling me what to do.

The Uber driver drops me off in front of my apartment building and I climb out of the car, staring at my door. I can hear music coming from inside. The sound of raucous laughter. My heart immediately lightens and I feel like I'm home. With my friends.

Where I belong.

I march up the walkway and barge in through the door, throwing my arms up as soon as I enter. "The party can begin!" I yell.

There are at least thirty people crowded in my living and dining room, if not more, and all of them roar in approval when they spot me. I see members of our football team. Faces

I don't recognize whatsoever. Lots of pretty girls eyeing me up and down. And scattered among them all, my closest friends.

"You made it," Eli says as he approaches me. He pulls me in for another hug and murmurs close to my ear, "Just a warning, but my girl and her best friend are plotting your death."

"Noted," I tell him with a firm nod, pulling away from him. "I should avoid?"

"At all costs," Eli says seriously, which is not a normal look for him.

I knew Ellie would be sad. A little mad. But plotting my death?

I bet I can convince her what I did wasn't so bad. I have in the past.

God, I'm such a dick. She should run screaming from me.

Forgetting Ellie for a moment, I let myself be embraced by our guests. So many people offer their congratulations. Tell me how glad they are that I'm back. I didn't play much on the Bulldog football team last season, but we're sophomores now, and I can tell my teammates are ready to embrace me.

It feels good. I feel welcomed. Missed.

Loved.

Diego finds me a beer and we all sit in a circle outside, on the back patio, in the only chairs available out there. People leave us alone, as if they know we need the time to talk. It's me, Diego, Eli, Tony and Caleb.

"Why haven't you signed a record deal yet?" This is from Diego, who's looking at me as if I'm crazy. "I'm sure they're offering you all the damn money in the world."

I'm privileged AF and I know it. Diego comes from a middle-class family. A single mama who raised her two sons as best she could. He became a dad when he was eighteen, but he's doing shit right. Sticking with his girl Jos while they raise their baby girl, Gigi. But he's all about the money. He hustles during the off-season, trying to provide for his family.

So when he sees me squandering what looks like a good deal, he thinks I'm an idiot. And he's probably right.

"Is it the money?" Caleb asks. He also comes from a middle-class family. Solid, hardworking parents. "Is it not enough?"

"It's plenty." I hesitate, not sure how to word it without sounding like an asshole. But too late. I am an asshole, so I decide to just say it. "But it's not enough for me to take the deal."

My dad is fucking rich. He is the manager of one of the most expensive hotels in the Yosemite Valley. Plus, he comes from money. My grandparents were rich too. I've had access to whatever I wanted, whenever I wanted, my entire life.

Since my parents divorced, it's been just me and Dad. Mom lives in Oregon. I used to visit her more, but life got busy—for her and for me. Dad has a girlfriend who's only a few years older than I am, and they like to party. They've almost always been my source of booze and weed.

Until I went on tour, and everyone else became my source for booze and weed—among other things.

"How can you turn them all down and settle for this bull-shit, when you could be doing so much more?" Diego asks, his voice incredulous. "You're talented, man. Just—go for it and take the deal."

How can I explain to them that I don't want to give up what he calls 'this bullshit'? I like going to college. Hanging with my friends. Meeting girls. Being on the team. Belonging to something. I have no siblings. Growing up, I spent a lot of time alone, and I hated it. This is why Tony and I bonded so quick last year. We have similar backgrounds.

I look around at all of my friends, and I realize quickly how much they mean to me. How much they won't judge my ass for telling the truth.

"I'm not ready yet," I admit quietly, staring at the beer bottle in my hand. I'm buzzing hard. Actually, I'm fucking drunk, and when I have this much alcohol in me, it makes me melancholy sometimes. "I want to play football."

Caleb makes an exasperated breath. "Rather sit on the bench than get pussy every night?"

"He gets pussy every night whether he's on a bench or not," Eli jokes.

They all laugh, with the exception of me.

And Tony.

"I get what you mean," he says to me, his voice quiet. When Tony talks, people lean in to listen. Because he always has something good to say. "Do your own thing, man. Do what makes *you* happy."

I smile at him and hold my beer up, offering him a silent cheers before I slug half of it down.

Soon, I'm blindingly drunk, telling stories about being on the road. We're laughing as I describe one of the many desperate chicks who snuck onto my tour bus. How I found her in my bed, buck naked, save for a pair of fire-engine red panties.

"Did you fuck her?" Caleb asks excitedly.

"Hell no." I shake my head. "She was *sixteen.*"

They all groan in disappointment.

Jailbait is to be avoided at all costs.

"What are you boys doing out here?"

We glance up to find Ava standing there, looking pretty as can be, her gaze scanning over all of us. When her eyes meet mine, they narrow the slightest bit, and I know she's not happy with me.

Not much I can do to change her mind, so I just grin at her in return.

"Jackson's telling us stories about his summer," Eli answers, slapping his hand against his thigh. "Come here."

She plops down on his lap, wrapping her arms around his

neck and leaning in to give him a kiss. I watch them unabashedly, wondering what that would be like. To be with someone permanently. To have a steady girl in my life, one I could count on, one who would always be there for me, no matter what. Would I get bored of the same old pussy every night?

Probably.

I think of Ellie. How easy she is to talk to. How she accepts me no matter what. I can't lie—I've been tempted to try something with her. See if there is any magic between us. I bet there would be. But she'd eventually have expectations and I don't think I could meet them. I'm not the commitment type.

This is why it's best I don't try anything with her at all. No matter how much I want to.

"Where's Ellie?" I ask Ava once she's done kissing on my friend. The words leave me without thought, and I realize my mistake when Ava glares at me.

"Inside. Like you fucking care though," she tosses at me.

"Whoa, whoa, whoa. Calm down, princess. Don't be hostile to my friend," Eli says, running his hand up and down her back in a soothing gesture.

"Don't tell me to calm down, Eli. He's the one who had his tongue down another girl's throat when we walked into his dressing room." Ava points at me.

"He didn't know we were coming." This is from Caleb, who sends me a bro nod.

I nod at him in return. "And may I correct your assessment? She had her tongue down my throat, not the other way around."

"Po-tay-to, po-tah-to, it doesn't make a damn difference," Ava says, rising to her feet. "You fucked up, Rivers. That girl has been pining away for you all summer. Living for your texts at night. Dying for you to come home. First night she gets to see you, and she witnesses you with someone else."

"We're just friends," I start, but Ava bursts out laughing.

"Please," she says, shaking her head. "That's what you think. That's not what she wants."

"I can't control her," I say morosely, hating how shitty Ava's making me feel. I don't need this right now.

I don't want it.

"Then tell her how you really feel. End her misery once and for all. You're just stringing her along. Using her."

"I'm not using her."

"This is getting way too heavy." Caleb rises to his feet, stretching his arms above his head. "I'm gonna go find Baylee."

"Another girl who's getting strung along," Ava says as Caleb starts to walk away. "Stop messing with her head, Caleb! I mean it!"

"Girl, you need to calm down," Eli says when Caleb's gone. "You're pissing off all my friends."

"Funny how you used to hate Caleb, back when he flirted with me," she reminds him.

"Ava. Babe. You're on fire tonight." Eli shakes his head. "Why you starting so much drama?"

This is turning heated. The rest of us look at each other, silently communicating as we rise to our feet.

And get the hell out of there.

"Why are they fighting?" I ask Tony once we're a safe distance away. As in, in my kitchen.

"Things are tense between them. She's leaving soon," Tony explains.

I knew this, but forgot. "Where is she going again?"

"San Diego State."

"Damn. That's a long way from here." I scrub the side of my face. Eli and Ava are solid. Things might be tense now, but they'll make it. I have all the faith in them.

"I know. Eli's not happy about her being that far. And I think Ava feels guilty." Tony glances toward the sliding glass door, watching Ava and Eli duke it out in conversation. "They'll be all right."

"Sure they will," I say with a nod, glancing around the room. My gaze snags on a dark head, and I know even though I can't see her face that it's Ellie. She's talking with a gorgeous blonde, and I realize it's Tony's girlfriend, Hayden.

They glance over at me at the same time, averting their heads quickly when they spot me already staring, and I wonder...

"I think your girl and Ellie are talking about me," I tell Tony.

"Oh really?" His voice is casual, like it's no big deal. "Hayden is a huge fan of your music."

"You don't say?" I try to take a sip from my beer bottle but realize it's empty. Damn it. "I'm thinking Ellie is filling her in on how much she hates me, and I bet your girlfriend eventually won't like me anymore."

"Hayden's not like that," Tony says. "She gives everyone a fair chance. Trust me, she's a total fan. If she wasn't so into me, I'd be jealous of the way she talks about you."

I start to laugh. "You just made my night. Maybe Hayden could be the president of my fan club."

"I think that's more Ellie's thing," Tony says, sending me a knowing look.

"Not anymore." Her catching me with that groupie in the dressing room ruined everything, I bet. I set my empty beer bottle on the kitchen counter. "I think I'm gonna go talk to her."

"Who? Ellie? That's probably not a good idea." Tony frowns.

"Nah, I need to talk to her. It's the right thing to do. Y'all are giving me shit for what I did. I need to acknowledge her." Maybe even apologize to her, but shit. I never said we could end up together someday.

Tony yells at me as I make my way to the two women

huddled together on the couch, but I ignore him, too busy concentrating on putting extra swagger in my step. So much, I nearly trip and fall on my fucking face since I'm so drunk.

The girls witness my near fall and don't even crack a smile as they watch my approach. They just stare at me blankly.

Huh. Maybe this isn't such a good idea after all.

CHAPTER 4

ELLIE

"Stay strong," Hayden murmurs close to my ear as we watch Jackson stagger toward us. How much did he have to drink anyway? "Don't let him sweet talk you into removing your panties."

"Ha, in my dreams," I mutter, not even bothering to smile when he stops directly in front of us, his body swaying as if he's being blown by the wind.

"Ladies." He beams, and my heart flutters. I tell it to stop. "Talking about me?"

"Arrogant as ever, Jackson," Hayden says, her voice light. Teasing. I need to do more of that. Be light. Teasing. But I'm too mad to be anything but a pissed-off bitch toward Jackson.

"Well, I couldn't help but see you two looking over at me earlier." He plops down onto the couch beside me, so close his warmth seeps into me. Slinging his arm around my shoulders, he leans forward so he can look at Hayden. "Tony tells me you're a fan."

"I'm going to kill him," she mutters under her breath as she smiles pleasantly at Jackson. "Yes. I've enjoyed your performances."

"Cool, cool." He nods, his arm squeezing my shoulders as he tugs me closer. "Ellie here is my most devoted fan."

"You don't say." The sarcasm in Hayden's voice is heavy. "I had no idea."

"Yeah, she's been loving my music since my senior year in high school." He gazes down at me, his perfect lips curved into the faintest smile. "I can always count on Ellie's unwavering support."

"Um, I'm going to go find Tony." Hayden glances at me. "You going to be okay?"

I nod, ignoring the flare of panic lighting up my insides at her leaving us alone. "Yeah, I'm fine."

"I'll come back and check on you in a few." She stands, pointing at Jackson. "Be good."

"Me?" He rests his free hand against his chest, seemingly offended. "Always."

We watch her go, both of us quiet. I brace myself for what he might say. Or worse, for someone to approach and draw him away from me. I'm mad at him, but I'm also basking in his presence because, come on. It's not easy for me to turn my feelings for him on and off. When he shows me those vulnerable little pieces of himself, pieces he doesn't share with anyone else, I feel so connected to him, it's hard to break free.

Like right now, while I stare at him like a lovesick fool.

"Did you enjoy tonight's performance?" he asks me, his voice low. Intimate. It touches something deep inside of me, turning my legs to jelly and making me grateful I'm not standing right now.

"You were great, as always," I reassure him, wishing he wasn't touching me. Wishing he wasn't sitting so close. I can't think when he does these things.

"I've missed you." He drops his head, his mouth right at my ear. "Did you miss me?"

I close my eyes for the briefest moment, wishing my 'tangled up in him' emotions away. This is what I've longed for all summer. Jackson paying attention to me and no one else.

I nod, unable to find the words. Too overwhelmed by his nearness. His voice.

It's a weapon. One that shatters my defenses every time I hear it.

"You shouldn't though," he says, his fingers drifting up and down my arm, lulling me into this false sense of security. "I'm a prick. You saw me with that girl."

"I don't want to talk about her." My voice is flat. I refuse to go back to that moment.

Even though it's burned into my brain forever.

"I don't either, but she's right there, sitting in the forefront of your mind. Am I right?" When I nod again, he continues, "She means nothing to me. Not like you do."

I lean back so I can stare into his beautiful blue eyes. I see nothing but sincerity in his gaze. "Are you just saying that?"

His mouth drops open. "No. You mean a lot to me, El."

"Just as a friend, though. Right?"

He blinks at me, as if he can't believe I'm calling him out for his shit. He deserves this. No matter how badly I'm quaking inside, scared I'm going to make him mad and push him out of my life for good, I have to do this.

"What are you asking me?" He seems genuinely confused.

"If you care about me so much, why do you get with other girls?" Why can't he see me as more than a friend?

He makes a face. "Come on. I don't want to have a heavy conversation with you tonight."

He never wants to have a heavy conversation with me, period.

"Wanna go to my room?" he asks, quickly changing the subject. His smile is charming. Devastating. "I have something for you."

"What do you mean?" I ask warily. If he says it's his dick, I'm going to hit him.

But he's not Caleb, so I doubt that would be his response.

"I have a gift. Something I bought you on my travels. Come on." He removes his arm from my shoulders and pushes up from the couch to stand. He offers his hand to me and I stare at it like it's a snake about to strike. "Ellie. Come on. Let's go."

I follow his command and slap my hand in his, gasping when he pulls me up so fast, I nearly crash into him. He doesn't let go of my hand as he leads me through the throng of people congregated in his living room, all of them calling his name because he is the man they're all here to see tonight.

He smiles and waves like a damn celebrity, but doesn't stop. Just drags me down the hall and into his bedroom, hitting the light switch and shutting the door, cutting off all sounds coming from the apartment.

It's quiet in here. And an absolute mess. He's only been home for a couple of days, but his shit is strewn everywhere. There's a giant suitcase sitting open on the floor with all kinds of stuff in it still.

"You're still a slob I see," I tease.

"I just got home," he says defensively, dipping down toward the suitcase and rummaging through the items in there before he pulls a small, flat brown paper bag out. He turns toward me, thrusting his hand out. "For you."

I take the bag from him with a small smile, anticipation making me shaky. I peek inside the bag to find a smaller, black velvet drawstring bag. I pull it out and untie the string, the weight of his heavy gaze on me as I reach into the bag and pull out a delicate silver chain with a tiny charm on it.

It's a sand dollar.

"Found it in this little shop on the Oregon coast and it made me think of you," he says. "I hope you like it."

"I love it," I say softly, my heart turning over itself. He thought of me. He bought me a gift. This has to mean something. "Thank you."

"You really like it?" He looks so eager, so hopeful. He reminds me of a little boy.

Nodding, I smile. "I do. It's beautiful."

"Let me help you put it on," he says, taking the necklace from my hand and undoing the clasp. "Hold up your hair."

I do as he says, lifting my hair up as he stands close behind me, looping the chain around my neck, his fingers fumbling with the tiny clasp and brushing against my nape. I can feel the gooseflesh rise from his touch.

I wonder if he sees it.

"There you go," he says when he closes the clasp. I turn to face him. "It looks good on you."

Jackson reaches out, tracing the charm, his finger coming awfully close to my chest. I hold my breath, waiting for what he might do next, but disappointment washes over me when he turns away so his back is to me.

"You're right," he says as he surveys his room, his hands on his hips. "I'm a fucking slob."

"No, I shouldn't have said that. You just got home," I start, but he turns on me, his expression...

Angry.

"Why do you always do that?" he asks, his tone vaguely hostile.

"Do what?" I blink at him in confusion.

"Defend me. You shouldn't." He runs both hands through his hair, clutching the back of his head, his biceps bulging. "I'm a shit, Ellie. And I shit all over you on a daily basis."

He does, but I don't call him out for it. Instead, I reach up, tracing the edge of the silver sand dollar. "I love my necklace."

"It's not enough for what you do for me though," he says, dropping his arms to his sides. "What do you want from me?"

Irritation floods my veins. I hate how he's suddenly putting this on me. "I don't know what I want."

Liar. You know exactly what you want from him. You're just afraid to say it out loud.

"You know," he says, his voice low. "Admit it. What do you want from me?"

I remain quiet, refusing to let the words leave me. If I say them, that gives him the opportunity to reject me, once and for all.

And I don't think I could handle that. Not tonight.

"Whatever it is you want, I don't think I can give you," he says after a long minute of my silence. "I'm a fuck-up who can't commit."

I roll my eyes. "I hate your excuses."

"They're not excuses."

"They are." I take a couple of steps toward him, until I'm practically standing on top of his boots. "You know what you are? A chicken shit."

"I'm a chicken shit?" He raises a brow. "You're the one who won't confess your feelings."

"Right back at you, asshole," I toss at him, anger filling me as I turn and head straight for his bedroom door.

I'm fast, but he's faster. He's got me pinned to the door before I can even open it, his hot, hard body pressing into mine. I lift my chin, glaring at him, and he dips his head, his alcohol-tinged breath wafting over my face.

He's drunk. I need to remember that. He's not in the right frame of mind.

"You want me to confess my feelings?" he asks. "Here we go. I need you in my life, Ellie. And I want you. I want you so damn bad, it's all I can think about right now. But I can't take it to the next step with you, because I *will* mess it up. I guarantee it. Whatever expectations you have of me in your head? The reality will not meet. I'm a mess. I make mistakes. And I'm not loyal. Not to women."

His words leave me confused, but he also said he wanted me. He wants me.

I need to stand strong. "You're just afraid to commit. You can't even take a record deal when they're throwing them at you like candy."

His eyes narrow as his hand comes up to touch my cheek. My skin burns where his fingers press. "You have no idea what you're talking about."

"Uh, I think I do. We're pretty close, Jackson. You've told me a lot of stuff over the years," I remind him. "I think I have you pretty well figured out."

"Oh yeah? Well, I've got you figured out too," he says, his voice taunting, despite the gentle way he touches me. Such a contradiction. Typical Jackson. "You're just a lonely, scared virgin who puts all your hopes and dreams on a guy like me who keeps you at arm's length because it's safer that way."

My mouth drops open and I jerk away from his stroking fingers. His description hurts. Only because it's too close to the truth. "You're such a prick."

"I warned you." His grin is faintly menacing, and I wonder if he's acting like an asshole on purpose. It's like he wants to prove a point. "I'm not good enough for you, Ellie."

"That is the worst excuse ever," I tell him, annoyed. He's said that time and again, and I'm tired of hearing it.

"It's the truth. And the truth always hurts." He leans in close, his mouth a whisper away from mine. "Doesn't it?"

A trembling breath leaves me and I swear he swallows it. I stare at his lips, willing them to touch mine. Yes, he's an asshole. Yes, I will probably cry over this conversation later, but right now, all I can focus on is Jackson.

And his deliciously full lips only inches from mine.

"You want me?" he whispers.

I don't say a word. I don't freaking move.

"I've been curious." His face shifts, his cheek pressed against mine, his mouth at my ear. "What would little Ellie Jessup do if big bad Jackson Rivers took her to his bed?"

I reach up to shove him away from me, but instead, my

hands land on his broad shoulders and my fingers curl into his soft T-shirt. "You won't do that."

"Why not?"

"You're too afraid of the repercussions if you did," I answer. "The responsibility. You'd feel too guilty."

"I'm not feeling real guilty at the moment," he drawls.

I tilt my head back to find him watching me with an unfamiliar gleam in his eyes. Is this what it's like, to truly be ensnared in Jackson's web? Because this is heady stuff. Having him pressed against me, his hands braced on either side of my head, his face still so close to mine. I could rise up and fit my mouth to his, no problem. I have a feeling he'd respond without hesitation.

But where would that lead us? Past the point of no return?

Yes. I know it would. And I don't want to risk it.

That's my biggest problem, right? I'm not a risk taker. And Jackson Rivers is the biggest risk of my life.

I have a feeling he'd be the biggest mistake of my life too.

"Jackson," I say, my voice a warning.

"Just one kiss, El. Give me one," he murmurs. "You know you've been dying for it since the first time we met."

I want to hit him. I want to kiss him. Not only is he a contradiction, he is *my* contradiction. I hate him.

I love him.

I don't want to be near him.

I can't help but come back for more.

Jackson reaches for me, his fingers cradling my chin as he lifts my face up so our gazes meet. "Kiss me."

I slowly shake my head, denying myself what I've wanted for so long. "It'll be a mistake."

"No, it won't. Come on." He smiles, his straight, white teeth almost blinding.

"You'll regret it," I whisper.

"I will?" His brows shoot up, his thumb stroking my jaw. "You so sure about that?"

I nod, his fingers never slipping from my face. "You'll kiss me once and want to keep kissing me."

"Is that such a bad thing?" He touches the corner of my mouth with his finger and I want to melt, damn him. "Maybe you'll feel the same way." He frowns. "You'll kiss me once and never want to stop."

He smiles. Leans in closer, his mouth so close to mine, I feel it move when he speaks. "Let's test this theory then."

I should let him kiss me. Consequences be damned. I'll survive. I've lived through all of his torture before. What's one kiss? And what if he's terrible at it? That would end my suffering once and for all, and besides, it's the perfect time for him to be terrible at it.

He's drunk. He'll be sloppy. Unskilled even.

I don't think too much about it. Instead, I tilt my head back, lift up and press my mouth to his. He goes completely still, I think from shock, and nothing happens for a second. Two. Three. I'm about to pull away, mortified that he doesn't react, when he cradles my cheek with his hand and moves his mouth against mine.

Oh God. He's kissing me. Jackson Rivers is actually kissing me. And it's not sloppy at all. He's just as skilled as I was afraid he'd be.

He tilts his head to the side, his mouth soft, his lips tugging on my lower lip. I open for him, his tongue sliding in, dancing around my own. My entire body turns to liquid at the first touch of his tongue and my fingers clutch fistfuls of his T-shirt as I anchor myself to him, drowning in his kiss.

It's so good. Too good. Everything I was afraid of. How will I go on if all I ever get is this one kiss?

Jackson ends it first, pressing his forehead to mine, his breaths ragged. As if he's just run a marathon. I swallow hard, trying to find the right words to say, but what can I do after a kiss like that?

Demand more, that's what.

I edge closer to him, just about to press my lips to his again when he says, "That was—nice."

I pull away, dread settling low in my stomach. "What did you just say?"

"Ellie. Come on. You know we can't do this, right?" His hand drops from my face and he takes a step away from me.

I'm immediately cold at the loss of his warmth. Oh, and furious. Coldly furious.

"Right," I bite out. "We can't do this."

"It was a great kiss though." He smiles, though it doesn't quite reach his eyes. Why is he acting like this? Why is he pushing me away? "You'll be hard to resist."

His compliment feels like a smack in the face. The smack of reality I need. "You're an asshole, Jackson." I reach behind me, my fingers fumbling with the door handle before I grasp it tight. "Looks like you proved your point."

"What point is that?" He sounds genuinely confused.

"That you can have me whenever you want me." I open the door and am halfway out of his room before I say, "But that was your last shot. Hope you enjoyed it."

I slam the door in his face before he can utter another word.

CHAPTER 5

JACKSON

ne month later

"Fuck me, it's hot out here." I grab a water bottle and drain it in a couple of swallows, glancing around the field as I wipe my mouth with the back of my hand. We've been running drills all week at football practice and I'm fucking sick of it.

But I'm also happy as hell to be back out on the field, all the trappings of Jackson Rivers, teen dream rock star behind me.

At least temporarily.

"Yeah," Eli says, squinting into the sun as he watches our defense run their asses across the field. "Sucks. Glad to be here though."

"Same."

He sends me a look. "Are you really? You don't miss performing?"

"This is performing too, you know. A different kind of performance," I tell him, gesturing toward the field. "Some-times I think I enjoy this more."

"Really?" Eli sounds baffled. "I think it would be pretty awesome getting so much attention focused on you from all the girls. The record execs wanting to sign you. People wanting autographs and shit. That's cool as fuck."

"It's cool, but it's also a lot of pressure." So much lately, I don't like talking about it anymore. "I prefer being part of a team."

"Even when we're a shitty team?" Eli grins and shakes his head. "I don't miss high school football at all."

"We weren't that bad back then," I defend, because we weren't. We just played teams that were so much better than us.

"I understand where you're coming from with the pressure," Eli says, changing the subject. "With Ash gone, coaches are looking at me to carry this team."

"What about Jerry?" He was Ash's second-string last year. He's a senior this year and can throw like a motherfucker. And by motherfucker, I mean pretty great.

"He's been messing up. Throwing a lot of interceptions lately." Eli sends me a look. "Haven't you noticed?"

I shrug. "It's still early days."

"We've been practicing for a month. Our first game is this Saturday."

Nerves flare within me at his words. "Shit."

"Yeah. You forgetting dates or what?"

We've been in class for a week. I haven't forgot. But then again, I sort of have. I'm just going with the flow, and not really paying attention to what's going on around me, I guess. Too busy always looking for Ellie.

Haven't spotted her on campus once. Is she even here? I don't know. I'd love to ask Eli about her, but that's opening a can of worms I don't want to examine right now.

So I keep my mouth shut instead.

Ever since our kiss that night, I haven't really seen her. Definitely haven't talked to her. Girl said she was blowing me off and she's stuck to her word. I deserve her abandonment. I give her a gift and tell her I can't be with her. I kiss her, after letting another girl suck my dick, all in the same night. Ellie is right.

I'm a complete asshole.

But I'm also right.

I don't deserve her.

I miss her though. So damn much. I miss her smiling face and laughing eyes. I miss her encouragement and the way she makes me believe I can do anything I set my mind to. I miss just being in her presence, whether it's in person or virtual. She hasn't even Snapchatted my ass, not once in the last month, which is some sort of record for us. It also hurts.

Her rejection stings, but I suppose I asked for this, acting like I did that night.

Pushing all thoughts of my shitty ways out of my mind, I change the subject.

"How's Ava?"

"She's good." Eli rubs his chin, his gaze filling with longing. He misses his girl something fierce. "Meeting new people, having fun with her roommate. Checking out San Diego. Hanging out at the beach every weekend. Having the time of her life without me."

"Bro. Get a grip. She loves you," I tell him, hating how sad he sounds. A depressed Eli is no fun, let me tell you.

"I know. I just—it sucks that we're living separate lives. Though you'd think I'd be used to it by now. We've pretty much always lived separate lives for the entirety of our relationship," Eli says, exhaling loudly.

Ava went to a different high school than us. She's a year younger than us too, and he was at Fresno State while she was a senior in high school. He's right. Their lives have always been fairly separate.

"You'll get through this." I punch him in the arm, needing

to lighten up the moment. I hate heavy shit. "Stop being such a pussy."

He grins. "Dick."

"Sweet talking each other as usual."

We both turn to find Tony standing there, sweaty and with a tired smile on his face.

"You know it," I tell him. "How's it going?"

"Good. Feels like I'm standing on the edge of hell." Tony takes a long drink from his water bottle. "This weather sucks ass."

"Yeah, it does," I say with a nod. "Can't wait to play Saturday night's game out here."

"It's at seven so it'll be a little cooler," Tony says, trying to be optimistic.

"Right. It'll only be ninety instead of ninety-nine," I say drolly, making Eli laugh.

"We should grab something to eat after this," Tony suggests. "You guys down? I'm sure Caleb would go too."

"What about Diego?" I ask, glancing around. I spot him in intense conversation with one of the offensive coaches on the sidelines. "Think he'd want to come with us?"

"He mentioned having to head straight home after practice to take care of Gigi. Jocelyn has a night class," Tony says.

"It'll just be the four of us then," Eli says with a nod. "Let's do it. I want tacos."

"You always want tacos." I shove Eli's shoulder and he staggers backward with a laugh.

"I want someone's taco, but she's not here right now," Eli says with a leer.

Sick fucker. Though he doesn't say that kind of shit about Ava usually. He keeps the details of their relationship pretty much to himself. Which to me is always a sign that he loves her and doesn't want to disrespect her.

Tony is the same way. He's quiet when it comes to his girl. Diego is as well. These guys and their steady relationships. I don't get it. We're young, we're in college, we should be fucking as many women as we can before we have to grow up and be responsible.

The only one who agrees with this thought process is Caleb. That guy is insane for all women, and I love him for it. He will bang whoever he wants, whenever he wants to. I aspire to that. I did do that while on tour. It was a sing fest and a fuck fest. A bit of a drug fest too, if I'm being real.

And now, I'm doing nothing. Playing football. Going to class. Having a few beers on the weekend, smoking a little weed. We're back to playing Call of Duty in the evening too.

Honestly? It's kind of boring, compared to what I was doing over the summer. Singing and touring and meeting new people. Seeing new places, performing for new crowds, reveling in their adulation. That was some cool shit.

It was lonely though too. Being on the road. Traveling constantly, having no one to share it with beyond my band-mates. We grew closer. They're cool, but they're not my friends.

Not like these guys.

Once we're done with practice and showered, we head over to a Mexican restaurant not too far from Tony and Caleb's condo. We order our food at the counter and go find a table, which is a fight considering how many people are currently in this place.

"Everyone loves their tacos," Eli says after we finally snag a table.

I take a sip from my soda, wishing there was a splash of whiskey in it. "They have damn good food."

"The girls are hosting a party at my place tomorrow," Tony says conversationally. "You guys are invited, of course."

"What girls are you talking about?" I ask.

"Hayden, Gracie, Joselyn, Ellie," Tony says. "The usual gang."

"I hate that Ava's not here," Eli says. He looks down in the dumps.

"Bro, you planning on visiting her during our bye week?" Caleb asks.

"She wants me to," Eli says. "Though I told her she should come here. See her family and her friends."

"You should go there. And I'll come with. Check out the babes." Caleb grins.

"Do not take his ass," Tony says, jerking his thumb in Caleb's direction. "You want private time with your girl. Not to have to entertain this guy the entire weekend."

"I can find my own entertainment," Caleb says, irritated. "I don't need a babysitter."

"I'll be your babysitter," I tell him with a sly smile.

Caleb lifts up his hand for a high five and I give it to him. "Sounds like a plan," he says.

"You two will be up to no good," Eli mutters, shaking his head.

"That's the idea," I say, already looking forward to the change of scenery. "When's our bye week again?"

They laugh at me, and I laugh along with them, but I'm serious. I don't remember. I'm caught up in my head most of the time, and it's not the best place to be right now.

"You know we play San Diego State in September," Tony says. "You can see her then too."

"It's great that they're on the schedule," Eli says with an enthusiastic nod. "When football season's over, I'll be able to see her even more."

"Then maybe you won't be such a pouty baby," I tell him.

He glares. "Whatever. You don't get it."

I ignore Eli's anger toward me because I know he's right. I don't get it. I'm not in a relationship. Don't have a girl that means that much to me—with the exception of Ellie, and she's mad at me so I blew that. I don't really have many people that mean that much to me in general, besides the ones who are sitting at this table.

A server shows up with our food and we dig in, conversation forgotten as we each devour a plate full of tacos.

"What's up with Ellie anyway?" Caleb asks when he's on his last taco and finally comes up for air. "Haven't seen her much lately."

At least I'm not the only one.

"She's around," Tony says mysteriously, sending a meaningful look in Caleb's direction.

Caleb snaps his lips shut and shoves his last taco into his mouth.

And that's it. That's all they've got on that particular topic.

Ellie is around...where? What's she doing? Who is she hanging out with? How are her classes? Does she like Fresno State? Who is she living with? Is she at the dorms? Is she happy? Has she made any new friends?

My questions are endless because I'm genuinely curious. I miss her. I miss her more than I want to admit. She was my touchstone throughout the summer. The one constant I could count on. I kiss her once—and what a kiss, I still can't stop thinking about it—and now she's gone. I fucked up.

What else is new?

CHAPTER 6

ELLIE

I am totally in my element. Being at college, on campus, and away from the only home I've ever known, is downright liberating. I've remained in one place my entire life, and I thought I would miss it. Be homesick. I was scared at the thought of not having Ava beside me. My sidekick, my constant companion for the last four years. Gone, just like that. At first, I felt untethered. A little lost. Like a balloon let go. Adrift, climbing higher into the sky.

But it turns out…I'm okay. In fact, I'm more than okay. I'm taking a heavy class load—all general ed classes this semester and next, trying to get those out of the way. I still don't know what I want to be. My major is undeclared, and that scared me at first too, but you know what?

I'm eighteen. How the hell am I supposed to know what I want to do for the rest of my life? Some people have it all figured out, but I am not *those* people. I'm not even close to those people.

I exit my Intro to Statistics class with a vague headache. While I like school and do well at it, math is not my thing. Stats is a really intimidating subject, and I'm worried I'll bomb the class, but I don't have a choice. I have to take it.

I'm walking with my head down, trying to shove my note-book into my backpack so I can zip it up, when I collide with someone.

And not just someone, but a male someone. I know this because he's tall, solid as a rock, and is wearing cologne. Oh, and he speaks, and his voice is super deep.

"Sorry, you okay?"

I glance up to find an attractive guy studying me with concern. His hair is dark, as are his eyes, and he's wearing glasses.

Oh my God, he's cute.

"I'm fine." I quickly zip up my backpack and hitch the strap up higher on my shoulder. "Sorry. Wasn't watching where I was going."

"It's okay." He smiles. It's nice. He seems nice. He's got this pleasant, open aura about him that I'm immediately drawn to. "Aren't you in my statistics class?"

"The one we just came out of?" I gesture toward the open doorway, not too far from where we're standing, and he nods. "Yes. Here's where I confess I hate math."

"Here's where I confess I'm actually really good at math." He smiles, revealing straight teeth. He's not some gorgeous, untouchable boy like Jackson, but he's definitely pleasant to look at. "I'm a finance major."

"Of course you are," I say, laughing. When he frowns, I realize I need to make myself clearer. "Trust me, that's not a bad thing. I'm just—I was feeling really dumb while walking out of that class right now, and I'm sure you know exactly what you're doing."

"If you need help, I don't mind," he says, holding out his hand. "I'm Carson."

"Ellie," I say weakly, shaking his hand before letting it go. I didn't feel a zip of attraction up my arm like when Jackson touches me, but I'm not discounting this guy. Not at all. "Are you a freshman too? Please tell me you just started here."

"I just started here," he confirms with a faint smile.

We both start walking down the hall. I don't have class for another hour, so I'm taking my time, and so is he.

"Do you like it here so far?" I ask.

"I do. I'm not used to this hot weather, though. I grew up in Morro Bay," he explains.

"Oh my God, I would kill to live in Morro Bay! I love the ocean," I say a bit too enthusiastically. I tell myself to calm down. "Why didn't you go to Cal Poly?"

"I wanted out of there," he says, grimacing. "I've lived in that area my entire life. I needed a change."

"I totally get it. I've lived in the same town my entire life too," I say.

We exit the building and head toward the quad. He doesn't leave my side, and we keep talking about Fresno State. Our classes. Turns out we're in the same sociology class too, though we didn't see each other. Not surprising, considering how big the classroom is.

"Do you have class right now?" I ask him.

"Oh shit." He pulls his phone out of his pocket to check the time before lifting his head to look at me, his eyes wide behind his glasses. "I'm late."

I laugh. "Better get going, Carson."

"It was nice meeting you, Ellie. I mean it about helping you with stats," he calls before he takes off.

"Bye!" I watch him go, smiling to myself. That was nice. I ran into a boy and we flirted. A cute boy too. And I didn't think of Jackson once.

Wait, that is a complete lie. I compared Carson to Jackson in just about every single way possible, which sucks. I need to stop doing that.

I need to stop thinking about Jackson Rivers, period.

Scowling, I stomp my way toward the quad near the library, eager to meet up with Hayden and Gracie. We all have a break at this particular time and we decided to make a date of it.

I am so grateful for these girls and their friendship. They're older than me. They didn't have to take me under their wing, yet they did anyway. I soak up every bit of advice they give me, which is a lot. Both of them are so completely different than me. They're fearless. They go after what they want, and don't let stupid things like their insecurities hold them back.

I could take more than a few lessons from them, I know this.

I spot them, one dark haired with golden highlights, the other one a bright blonde, sitting next to each other at a picnic table under a tree. They're talking and laughing and I stride right up to their table, plopping my backpack on the bench before I slide in next to it.

"What's so funny?" I ask, genuinely curious. I want in on the joke. I need some laughter in my life.

"Gracie was telling me about her latest boy toy," Hayden says, a wicked smile curving her lips. Gracie gives her a shove, irritation flitting across her face. "What? It's true."

"He's not a boy toy," Gracie tells me. "That's so crude."

"What is he then?" Hayden asks.

"A boy I'm talking to," Gracie says, sounding prim and proper. "I take that back. He's not a boy. He's a *man*."

"How long have you been talking to him?" I ask.

Gracie shrugs. "A couple of weeks?"

"Where'd you two meet?"

"On Tinder," Gracie says.

"Oh. I could *never* do that," I say with a shake of my head.

"Don't dismiss dating apps without giving them a try first. You really should give Tinder a chance. It's such a great way to meet people who go here, live around here. Whatever," Gracie says. "It's how I've met the majority of the guys I've been with since I started college."

"And how's that working out for you?" Hayden says sarcastically.

Gracie shoves her again, making Hayden laugh. "Shut up, you. I remember you doing the same thing until you met Tony."

"True, true." Hayden nods, her gaze coming to mine. The smile on her face is sly. "Tell Ellie about your new man."

Gracie bounces where she sits, clasping her hands together. "Gladly. He's tall. Blond. Curly hair. Big Adam's apple."

I frown. "You like his…Adam's apple?"

"It's so cute when he swallows! I don't know. I'm weird sometimes." Gracie waves a hand dismissively. "Anyway, his name is Franz."

I send a questioning look to Hayden, who's watching me carefully. As if she's waiting for my reaction.

"Franz?" I unzip my backpack and grab my water bottle from it, popping open the lid and taking a sip. "What's up with the name?"

"He's from Germany. He's a transfer student," Gracie says with excitement. "His accent is sexy."

"Really? We had a German foreign exchange student at my high school when I was a freshman. He was really nice, but whenever he spoke German, it kind of…scared me."

Gracie frowns. "What do you mean?"

"I don't know. It's a very intimidating sounding language," I say with a shrug, not wanting to upset Gracie. She seems really excited by this guy.

I've come to realize quickly that she's excited about every new guy who comes into her life. And that lasts a few weeks before she's ready to move on. I'm guessing this Franz is on the tail end of his journey with Gracie.

"Well, he's coming to our party at Tony's tomorrow so you'll get to meet him then," Gracie says. She must see something on my face because she frowns. "You *are* coming to the party tomorrow, right?"

"I don't know." I shrug, suddenly wanting to evade this conversation.

Hayden rests her arms on top of the picnic table and leans across it, reminding me of a stern teacher. Which is perfect since that's her major. "Why are you even considering bailing out on this party? We're the ones in charge of it, and that includes you. Tony's just being kind enough to let us have it at his place."

"Yeah. I don't know." I shrug, trying to play it off.

Hayden sends Gracie a knowing look before blasting me with her intense gaze once again. "Does this have anything to do with a certain Jackson Rivers possibly showing up?"

"Not at all," I say too quickly.

"Bullshit," Hayden says on a sigh, shaking her head. "Ellie. Don't let him scare you off."

"Will he be there?"

"Probably," Hayden says.

"Then I don't want to be there," I say firmly.

"Girl, you can't let him control your social life," Gracie says. "I hate Caleb with a passion, yet he's always right there. In my face. I've just learned how to ignore him."

"You don't hate him," Hayden reminds her.

"Yeah you definitely don't," I say. "But has Caleb kissed you? Led you on and then told you he just wants to be your friend?" I ask. They know what happened that night after the concert. How much he humiliated me after giving me the most spectacular kiss of my life.

I still can't forgive him for it.

"Caleb propositions me pretty much every time we run into each other," Gracie says. "He wants in my pants. Badly."

"And she wants in his pants," Hayden adds. "Badly."

"I do not," Gracie says irritably.

"I don't want in Jackson's pants," I say.

"Liar," they say at the same time before they start laughing.

I can't help but laugh too, because they're right. I'm a total liar. I would love to get in Jackson's pants. But I'm not going to keep throwing myself at him. I can only take being rejected a couple of hundred times before I want to wither up and die.

His rejection that night was like having a hammer banged on top of my head. Knocking sense into me and making me see exactly what he was doing.

Using me. I made him feel good. Puffed up his ego, whatever. Yes, he had adoring fans at his concerts every night, but I was the one constant in his life who didn't let him down. Who was always there to pick him up.

Well, screw that. I'm tired of picking someone up who doesn't want me. Lesson learned, the hard way, but at least I didn't get in too deep.

Okay, that's a total lie. I got in way too deep with Jackson. I'm still there, treading water in the deep end. But I'm trying my best to get out, and Carson might be just the distraction I need.

"I met a boy," I tell them, which silences their laughing almost immediately.

"Tell us more," Hayden says, her eyes twinkling.

I explain my literal run-in with Carson. How cute he was. How he said he'd help me in class.

"I hate math," I say, wrinkling my nose.

"How kind of him to offer," Gracie says, waggling her eyebrows.

"It was nothing like that. He was kind of nerdy in a cute way. He wears glasses."

"I love a cute boy in glasses," Gracie says with a wistful sigh.

"He's in my sociology class too," I add. "Hopefully I'll see him tomorrow."

"If you see him tomorrow, you should invite him to our party," Hayden says.

I slowly shake my head. "No way. I'm not going, remember?"

"Ellie!" Hayden sounds completely frustrated with me. "You're going. Who cares about Jackson? Ignore him the entire night. It'll piss him off."

"That's my plan with Caleb," Gracie adds. "I love nothing more than to piss him off. He makes it so easy."

"I don't think I'm as strong as you two," I say morosely. "Besides, you'll have Franz with you." I point at Gracie.

"And you could have your cute, nerdy Carson with you," she says with a smile. "That will make Jackson so jealous, he won't be able to see straight!"

"He doesn't get jealous of anything I do."

"Because you haven't given him a reason to be jealous yet," Hayden says, ever so logical. "Your boy shows up at the party tomorrow night, just for you? Jackson will lose his mind."

"Doubtful," I say, though maybe…

Maybe they're on to something? I don't know. Jackson doesn't give a crap about me. That much is clear. I gave him clear *stay away from me* vibes and he did exactly that. If he really cared, he would've reached out by now.

Right?

And I don't want to use Carson to get back at Jackson. That's mean. I like him. He seems nice. I need to move on with my life and try to actually live it, versus sitting around, waiting for Jackson to notice me.

Forget that. Forget him. I'm going to move on from Jackson.

Even if it kills me.

"Ellie, please go. Invite whoever you want. All of your friends. Let's make this thing a rager," Gracie says, her voice soft and pleading. "You need to let loose and have a good time. You're so uptight, worried about a guy who clearly doesn't care."

Ouch. Her words hurt. But they are also the slap of reality I need. Jackson has proven he doesn't care. It's been a month. No calls, no texts, not even a glimpse of him on campus. I don't hang out at his apartment anymore since Ava left. I'm not hanging out at Tony and Caleb's condo either because I know I'll run into him. Plus, I've been busy with work and school. My new job at the restaurant near campus is practically full-time, because I need the money.

It's a lot. I don't have time for him. Though he haunts my thoughts still.

Constantly.

Ugh. Whyyyyy?

"Fine," I say, sitting up straighter. "If I run into Carson again, I'll invite him to the party."

"Good," Hayden says with a firm nod. "Come over early and we'll glam you up."

"Glam me up?" I ask cautiously. "I don't like wearing a lot of makeup."

"Don't worry about that. We want you to look your absolute hottest. You're so cute, Ellie, but you don't emphasize it." Gracie points directly at my chest. "You have good boobs. You should show them off."

I glance down at the front of my very plain, very boring T-shirt. "How do you know?"

"Look at them!" Gracie rolls her eyes. "Girl, you need to work it, and work it *right now*. You will have two men potentially vying for your affection tomorrow night. Give them something to think about later when they're jerking off in the shower."

"Ew!" I say with a laugh.

Hayden and Gracie laugh too. "The way you just said that makes it sound like they're jerking off in the shower together," Hayden says in the middle of her laughter.

"Ooh, I watched some male/male porn a few weeks ago," Gracie says, fanning herself. "It was hot."

"Whaaaat?" I am so sheltered, I swear.

"Yes," Gracie says, nodding and grinning. "Super hot."

Hayden giggles. My mind wanders.

Whoa.

"What time is your last class tomorrow?" Hayden asks.

"Two o'clock," I answer.

"Perfect. Come to our place first, say around three? We'll have fun picking out an outfit and doing your hair, and then we'll head over to Tony's and set up for the party," Hayden says with a firm nod.

"Okay." I nod, excitement fizzing in my veins despite the fact that we're a full twenty-four hours away from me arriving at their apartment.

It's fun to think about though. Of getting ready. Of actually making real changes when it comes to myself. I'm tired of being sweet, dependable Ellie. I want to be something different.

I want to be more.

CHAPTER 7

JACKSON

"Are you really not even going to consider taking the phone call?"

I pull the phone away from my ear with a grimace. The booming sound of my dad's voice is sometimes a trigger. Reminds me of when I was younger and I did something stupid, like break that expensive vase in the living room, or wrecked his car when I wasn't even sixteen yet.

Yeah, that last one is true, and I paid for it dearly. But that all happened before we moved to California. Half the reason we came here, I think, was for me. Dad wanted me in a new environment. He doesn't realize, to this day, I'm still up to no good. I just got smarter and know how to hide it.

"I don't want to sign a record deal right now," I tell him for what feels like the thousandth time.

"And why the hell not?" he retorts. Jeffrey Rivers is a force to be reckoned with. Most people cower when he talks normally. When he barks like the ferocious dog he can be? Forget it. They all fall at his feet—or run away screaming.

Except for me. I'm used to him. The yelling. The bark is worse than his bite. Plus, I'm his only son, his only child. He has expectations for me, and he's fully embraced the rock star thing, which is surprising.

While I'm the one over here fighting it.

"I'm in school," I remind him. "I want to get my degree."

"Why? When you have the chance to make it big? Look, I'm not one to discourage my child from going to college. I went. And I used my degree to get myself where I'm at today. It works. College is not a waste of time."

He pauses and I wait for the giant but following this statement.

"But—" There it is. "You are on top of your game right now. There are multiple labels clamoring for you. Throwing money at you. You could become a household name in a matter of months, Jackson. Why wouldn't you jump on that?"

Because I'm terrified of failure? Of the fame? Of the attention and expectations and agony that comes with it? Being a household name is great, but it was never a goal. Not originally. I just liked playing my guitar and singing songs. I enjoy writing songs. The more I performed, the better I got. The more attention I got.

This has been a wild ride, but right now, I need a break.

"You take the call," I tell my father. He grunts in response, so much frustration in that one noise. "Tell me their offer. I'll let you know whether I want it or not."

I won't. I can already guarantee it.

"You're being ridiculous," he mutters. "They probably won't talk to me."

"Then that's their loss."

"More like your loss." I hear the creak of his desk chair. I can envision him leaned back, staring out the window at the Yosemite Valley spread out before him. He's got the best view in the house, but he deserves it, considering he's the one who runs that hotel. "You need to talk to them. Listen to what they have to say."

"I'll consider it."

"It's Friday. Take the weekend. Think about it good and hard, son."

He ends the call before I have a chance to say anything else.

I toss my phone on my desk and plop down on my bed, resting my hands over my face. Everyone's pulling me into different directions, demanding this or that. Wanting me to be something I'm afraid I'm not. I'm tired of it.

I'd rather focus on football.

There's a game tomorrow, and I'm nervous. I didn't get much field time last season. When you're a freshman, and so many of us are fighting for the same position, it's normal. Plus, last year I didn't take football too seriously and I paid the price by getting benched.

Some of those guys who started with me gave up, and they're no longer on the team. Some of them were released. Kicked off. One of them got arrested last spring for drugs and made the entire team look bad. It was a PR nightmare. The seniors graduated in May. Ash Davis got drafted. All eyes have been focused on our team for months. Since the bowl win in January.

This game is a big deal. Feels like all of Fresno shows up for our games, wearing their red T-shirts, tailgating in the parking lot before the game. It's a party, and everyone is invited.

If I get a chance on the field, I can't fuck up. None of us can. We want the win.

So bad, I can taste it.

Speaking of parties, I think of the one Hayden and Gracie are hosting tonight at Tony and Caleb's. Ellie will be there. I'd bet money on it. But no one else would bet on it because they'd know I'd win.

She's that reliable.

I want to see her, but I also know she's still pissed at me. I can't blame her. We kiss—and it was a fucking good one, I cannot lie—and then I hit her with the friend zone shit. She had full on heart eyes when the kiss ended and by the end of our conversation, the hearts were replaced by little orange blazes of fire.

They should make an emoji that looks like that. I bet it'd get used a lot.

I drop my hands from my face at the same time I hear a knock on my door. It swings open before I can say a word, Eli standing there in just his boxer shorts and nothing else.

"You're going to the party tonight, right?"

I nod, not saying a word.

"Want to ride over together?"

"Yeah. You driving?"

"Fuck yeah. That'll ensure I won't drink too much. I need to be on top of it for the game tomorrow." He sounds nervous. He's starting tomorrow, and that would leave me a quaking mess.

"Perfect. This means I can get wasted while you're my sober driver," I tell him.

"Aren't you starting tomorrow too?" He frowns.

"Nope. I'm not as fancy as you."

Eli makes a noise. "Bro. Give me a fucking break. You're on the verge of breaking out and becoming the next big thing."

"Right." I flick my chin at him. "Why the fuck are you naked?"

"I'm not." He glances down at his boxers. "I just wanted to make sure you were here."

"My car is in the parking lot," I tell him, sounding like an asshole.

He frowns at me. "I know. I just—what the fuck ever man. Be ready to go in an hour."

Eli slams the door before I can respond.

I was a dick just now. I'll apologize to him later.

Sitting up, I pull open my bedside table drawer and rummage around inside until I find what I want.

A little baggy of weed. Another bag of a variety of pills. Got those while on tour and have been saving them for a special day.

Looks like tonight is gonna be pretty damn special.

CHAPTER 8

ELLIE

"You look like a goddess," Gracie breathes as she turns me toward the mirror.

I blink at my reflection, trying to take it all in, but it's difficult. I look…like me. But different.

Older.

After class, I ended up at one of those walk-in haircut places and took a risk by asking for a trim. And curtain bangs.

"Oh honey, with your big brown eyes, you can totally pull that look off," the hairstylist reassured me as she sat me down in the chair.

She took off four inches and gave me curtain bangs, just as I requested, and the perfect length too. I don't hate them. Not at all. When I showed up at Gracie and Hayden's apartment, they squealed when they saw me, pulling me inside with grabby hands and telling me how fantastic I looked.

It did my battered ego some good.

Now here I am in their bathroom after Hayden curled my hair into gentle waves and Gracie applied makeup, mostly to my eyes.

"What do you think?" Gracie asks, bringing me back to reality.

"I look…"

"Older," Hayden says as she worms her way into the tiny bathroom. We're standing shoulder to shoulder. Well, Gracie is standing above us, because she's pretty damn tall, while Hayden is average height and I'm a freaking shrimp. "Your eyes, El. *So* pretty."

I turn to the left, then the right, checking myself out. "Gracie did a fabulous job."

"I only emphasized what was already there," Gracie says. "This is all you, babe."

My heart warms. Not having Ava around has left me feeling lonely, but I don't know why. I have good friends. Ava is my very best friend and no one can replace her, but I'll be all right.

"Let's pick out clothes for her now," Hayden says to Gracie, like I'm not even there.

"I want to stick with my shorts." I point at them. I bought them on clearance last week at one of my favorite stores and they make my butt look good.

"They meet my approval," Hayden says as she thoroughly checks me out. As in, she's staring at my chest, and then my butt. "But you need something different up top." She plucks at the shoulder of my pale blue T-shirt. "Too bland. We're going to spice it up tonight."

Worry makes my stomach clench, but I fight the feeling. I want to dress to impress. Not only for Jackson, but for Carson too.

Yes, both my boys, as Gracie and Hayden call them, will be there tonight. Hopefully. I invited Carson after our sociology class was over, and told him to bring a couple of friends with him. He seemed pleased by my invite, his eyes sparkling behind the glasses, reminding me that he is really cute. I shouldn't dismiss him so easily.

And of course, I assume Jackson will be there. We share the same friend group. Eli is definitely coming. I figure he'll bring Jackson with him.

He's bound to be there. He's never one to miss a party.

The girls drag me into Hayden's bedroom and she starts thumbing through her closet. She has a lot of clothes, that's for sure. Way more than I do. But she's rich. Her dad is loaded. I'm used to this sort of thing. When Ava Callahan is your best friend, you're surrounded by money, thanks to her very rich and successful father.

A lifestyle I will probably never have, but it's fun to hang on the fringes of it. Pretend that you're rich too.

Though I don't care about that. Not really. I just want to be comfortable. Safe. Happy. I don't ask for a lot. I'm not a demanding person. I'm quiet and prefer to hang in the background while surrounding myself with big, over the top characters.

I'm drawn to big personalities, what can I say?

"What about this?" Hayden pulls a black tank out to show me.

"It looks...really small." I frown at the scrap of fabric.

It's cropped. Low cut neck, snap buttons down the middle.

"It's cute," Gracie says encouragingly. "You'd look good in it."

Hayden slips it off the hanger and tosses it at me. I have no choice but to catch it. "Try it on."

I take off my T-shirt, a little self-conscious, but they're not even paying attention to me. Too busy responding to whoever's on their phones, their fingers moving rapidly over the screens. Maybe Tony and...Franz?

I can't even with that name.

I pull the tank over my head, careful not to mess up my hair. I tug the shirt into place, quietly horrified that the tops of my boobs are basically on full display, along with my stomach.

"It's definitely small," I say, still pulling on it, trying to cover up some skin.

"Stop messing with it." Hayden slaps my hand away before taking a step back, contemplating me with her head tilted to the side. "What do you think, G?"

Gracie comes to stand right beside Hayden, studying me with a narrowed gaze, tapping her index finger against her lips. "Looking good, Ellie."

"I'm too exposed." I wave a hand at my chest. "Look at me."

"You look fabulous. Like I said, your boobs are spectacular. Not too big, not too small," Gracie says.

"Just right," Hayden adds.

I roll my eyes and walk over to the full-length mirror that hangs on Hayden's wall. Oh shit. I am all legs and arms and tits, and normally I would never think of myself like that. I'm short for the love of God, and my legs are kind of stubby.

I don't look stubby right now though. I look...older. On display, but not in a bad way.

"You don't think it's too much?" I frown at myself in the mirror, hating how insecure I suddenly feel.

I don't want to look like I'm trying too hard.

"No, I definitely don't think it's too much. You're adorable." Hayden comes up behind me and gives my shoulders a squeeze. "Adorably sexy."

"I'm not used to showing so much skin," I admit, pulling the waistband of my shorts up to cover my stomach.

Hayden slaps at my hand again before grabbing the denim at my hips and tugging them back down.

"It's hot. You're going to be burning up with all the people coming tonight. You'll be grateful for this outfit later, trust me," Gracie says.

"If you say so."

"Jackson is going to swallow his tongue when he sees you," Hayden says.

"I don't care what he thinks," I say, lying through my teeth.

"Uh huh. Well, then precious Carson will think you're a not-so-secret hottie," Gracie says with a laugh. "I'm so glad you invited him. He better show up."

"Definitely. Jackson is going to get so jealous if there's some guy sniffing around you," Hayden says.

"Sniffing around me? Gross." I put my hand in her face, but she just laughs harder. "I'm not trying to make him jealous."

"Keep telling yourself that," Hayden singsongs. "I need to figure out an outfit for me."

"Let me find you something!" Gracie runs to the closet and shoves Hayden aside. "I want it to be a surprise."

My phone buzzes in my back pocket and I pull it out to find a text from...

Jackson?

Frowning, I tap my phone to read it.

You going to the party tonight?

I stare at his message, contemplating my reply. So grateful I didn't reach out first. Does that make me a petty person? Probably.

But I don't care.

"What's got you frowning?" Hayden asks me.

I blink her back into focus and hold my phone out to her. "This."

Gracie leans in to read the text too. "When was the last time you talked to him?" she asks through narrowed eyes.

"The night he kissed me." They know all the details. There was no point in keeping it a secret. Plus, I wanted their input.

Like I do now.

"Don't respond," is Gracie's advice. "Keep him wondering."

"Nah, that's not it," Hayden says, slowly shaking her head. "Tell him you'll definitely be there. With your new *friend*."

Gracie cackles evilly. "I like that."

"What if Carson doesn't show up?"

"It doesn't matter. Jackson will be curious, wondering about your friend. Male? Female? He'll think female, because he's just that arrogant," Hayden says.

"You're not wrong," I tell her with a little laugh.

"Right. So he'll show up, perfectly prepared for fangirl Ellie to hang all over him," Hayden continues.

I wince. "Was I that bad?"

"You were kind of bad," Gracie says, not unkindly. Just very matter of fact. I see the sympathy in her gaze and it's reassuring. "I've been there. I feel you."

"What will be great is you won't give him any of that. Not an ounce of fangirl behavior. You will ignore him," Hayden says.

"I will?"

"Yes." She nods. "Ignore him the entire night, but make sure you're always standing nearby. Close to him, but not too close. Always in his peripheral."

This sounds silly. Why avoid him, but also make sure he can see me?

"Don't frown. This kind of shit works," Gracie says.

"It's just a bunch of game playing," I say, throwing my hands up. "I don't like playing games. I'm more the straight-forward type."

"Yeah, but that's not how it's done. Look." Hayden comes to me, grabbing my shoulders and gently turning me so I have to face her. "I hate playing games too. Not every rela-tionship has to be that way. And yes, there are people out there, that's all they do. But sometimes, you have to work the system to your advantage. You have to play the game for a little bit. You need to do that with Jackson, if you want to be with him."

"I don't know if I want to be with him," I say, my voice soft. Almost as if it doesn't exist.

That's how I feel when it comes to him. Online, on the phone, whatever, I exist. I'm in his world. In reality? Face to face? He runs. Avoids. Or says something shitty to make me run and avoid.

It sucks.

"Then maybe you shouldn't respond to him at all," Hayden says. "Maybe Gracie is right. You should ignore him."

"I don't know what I want," I admit with a sigh.

My phone buzzes again and I glance down at it to find another text from Jackson.

I'll be there. I want to talk to you.

"Oh. My God!" Gracie squeals when she sees it. "Maybe something will happen between you two tonight."

"Do not get my hopes up," I warn her.

"Yeah, G. You know how he is," Hayden adds.

Ouch.

Oh well, it's true.

"Tell him you'll be there with your new friend and leave it at that," Gracie encourages as I tap out my response.

Me: **Hey! Yes, I'll be there with my new friend. Can't wait to see you.**

I read the reply out loud before sending it.

"Get rid of the last part," Gracie says.

I erase it and send this instead: **Hey, yes, I'll be there with my friend.**

"Better," Hayden says with a nod.

"He's already typing," I tell them, staring at the screen. That little gray bubble sits there forever, driving me mad with curiosity. Gracie resumes choosing Hayden's outfit for the night as they discuss Franz the German and how much Gracie hopes he's down for a make-out sesh.

Jackson: **Hopefully you'll get a chance to talk to me. I miss you.**

I read his words out loud.

"Do not tell him you miss him! Don't do it!" Hayden is practically screaming.

"I won't, I promise." I tap at the phone. Erase letters. Rewrite my sentence. God, it's the worst.

Me: **See you later!**

That's all I say.

And I think that's enough.

———

The party is in full swing by the time Carson shows up, and we're only about an hour in. I run to him the moment I spot him, the two friends he brought with him looking at me with shock on their faces. I don't know what their deal is, but I give Carson a big hug, and he very carefully wraps his arms around me before they spring away from my body.

"I'm so glad you made it," I say with way too much enthusiasm.

I might've had a couple of White Claws. So I'm buzzin'.

"We almost didn't show," Carson admits with an embarrassed smile. "These two didn't want to come." He jerks his thumb toward his friends standing behind him.

"What are your names?" I ask them, swaying a little bit on my feet. I need to keep my stuff together. Not act like a drunken fool.

"I'm Jonah," one of them says.

"Danny," says the other.

"Jonah and Danny, don't crush your friend's spirit," I tell them, wagging my finger in their direction. "Let's go find drinks for you guys."

I lead them into the throng of people crowding the living room, making our way to the kitchen where all the alcohol is. Once we're in there, the crowd lightens up a bit, and I find Tony sitting at the counter on a barstool, Hayden standing in between his spread legs with her arms around his neck.

"You two are cozy," I say with a sly smile.

Hayden checks out the three dudes following me. "Hey, Snow White. Who are your friends?"

I laugh. "Carson, Jonah and Danny."

They smile uncomfortably and nod toward Tony and Hayden. I can tell they're not the partying type. Kind of nerdy.

Kind of adorable. Especially Carson.

"Let's get you guys some beer," I tell them. "You want cans? Or there's a keg out back."

"It's almost out," Tony says. "Give them cans."

I dole out the beers and they all say thank you like the polite boys their mamas raised. I spot Caleb in the far corner of the kitchen, leaning against the sliding glass door and talking intently to Baylee. She's waving her arms every once in a while, like she's mad at him, and I wonder what they're up to.

They've been off and on since high school. I once predicted they'd get married, but I don't know…

Gracie bursts into the kitchen from the patio, leading a tall, pale, blond guy by the hand. She sends a disgusted glance in Caleb and Baylee's direction before she spots me. "E-dog!"

I frown. "E-dog?"

"Just go with it," Hayden whispers as Gracie drags her blond boy with her toward us.

"You look so good," she says, crushing me in a hug and whispering in my ear at the same time. "Which one is yours?"

"Gracie, this is Carson," I tell her once she's released me.

She crushes him in a hug too. "And his friends, Jonah and Danny."

"Well, aren't you two cute as a button," Gracie drawls to the friends, who both turn red cheeked. She swivels her head in my direction. "This is Franz."

"Franz. I've heard so much about you," I tell him as he reaches out his hand and I shake it.

"Nice to meet you, E-dog," he says with the utmost sincerity in his German accent, making me laugh.

"It's Ellie," I correct.

We chat and drink, and the conversation flows easily. Franz is nice. Quiet. Polite. So are Jonah and Danny. A couple of girls I don't recognize stop to talk to our group, the two of them sidling up to the boys and engaging them in more one-on-one conversation.

"Looks like they've made friends," I tell Carson.

"Good. They were both so reluctant to come with me," he says, rolling his eyes. "They're both total homebodies."

"Are you a homebody?" I ask him.

"Yeah, kind of," he admits, sounding bashful. "But I really wanted to see you tonight. Couldn't believe you invited me to your party."

My heart pitter patters in my chest. "What do you mean? Why can't you believe it?"

"Well, look at you." He waves a hand in my direction, his cheeks ruddy. "You're—hot."

"You think I'm hot?" I'm stunned. No one has ever, in my entire life, called me hot.

"Don't act like you don't know it," he says, taking a step closer.

I smile at him, appreciating his nearness. His compliment. He's taller than me, but probably not six foot. More like five-nine maybe? But that's okay. I don't need some towering giant like all the rest of the guys I know.

Like Jackson.

I shove him out of my mind and smile at Carson, who smiles at me in return.

"I don't hear that word much to describe me," I admit. When he frowns, I clarify, "Hot."

"Oh. Well, that was probably rude of me to say." His cheeks turn even redder, poor guy. "You're pretty. And nice. I like your smile."

"Aw, thank you. I like your eyes," I say.

"Even with the glasses?" He touches the rims, and I can tell he's self-conscious of them.

"Especially with the glasses. You look cute in them," I say, my voice flirtatious.

See? I can do this. I can flirt with another boy. A stranger. I can have fun at a party and wear a tank top that's a little too small. I can have a couple of drinks and not make a fool of myself for a guy who doesn't give a shit about me.

Carson likes me. I can see it in his eyes. Read it in his body language. He's leaning toward me, and I know if I asked him to take it slow, he'd take it slow. He'd respect my wishes. He'd respect *me*.

He's definitely more my speed. Not as risky.

Jackson just takes. He'd crash into me and demand whatever he could. My time, my adoration, my utter devotion. I gave it to him willingly, I always did, but I was blind to his selfishness. Always believing he would eventually return my feelings. How could he not? What we shared was amazing. We were connected. I'm realizing I was too dazzled by his aura, his face, his stupid voice to see what was really going on.

That he was just using me. I was a convenient crutch. The girl he could always count on being there for him. The girl he could never see beyond as a friend.

I was so blind.

"Thanks," Carson says, tipping his head toward mine.

"Maybe we could, uh, get together sometime? Go to a movie?"

Giddiness rises inside of me and I tell myself to remain calm. He's asking me on a date. I'm definitely going to say yes. For sure. I need to give him a chance. Remind myself I don't need to be starstruck in order to get with a guy. There are perfectly average, attractive guys out here in the real world waiting for me, eager to spend time with me. Like this one.

I part my lips, ready to say yes, when I spot him.

Jackson. Entering the kitchen. Alone. No girl hanging on his arm. His expression determined, his gaze sliding to mine.

I freeze, the words sticking in my throat. His eyes seem to almost bug out of his head as he makes his way toward us, staring only at me.

Oh. Shit.

CHAPTER 9

JACKSON

What the hell did Ellie do to herself?

I'm not complaining. Hell no. She looks… gorgeous. Sexy. All I see is skin. Her shoulders, her arms. Jesus, her tits. There's a lot of her on display tonight, and I like it.

Eli and I showed up late, because that's how we roll. He was on the phone with Ava for God knows how long. Probably jerking off to the sound of her voice, but whatever. I get it. He misses her something fierce and she misses him, and when he came out of the bedroom after their call, he told me he didn't want to go to the party.

"Fuck that, you need to go," I stressed when I saw the hangdog expression on his face.

I finally got him to agree. And now we're here. The moment he walked through the door, Diego snagged him up and they're neck deep in conversation. I let him go, knowing he's also stressed about the game tomorrow.

I'll probably only play the second half, if I get any field time at all. Meaning I'm a little nervous about tomorrow's game, but not as much as Eli is. What's funny is I didn't pre-party like I originally planned. I pulled out the weed and the baggie of pills earlier, when I was still in my room. I even took a couple of pills out and held them in the palm of my hand.

Then I tossed them back into the bag and shoved it, along with the weed, into my bedside table drawer, irritated with myself. No alcohol is currently coursing through my veins either. I realized I'm tired of doing the same ol' thing, day in and day out.

For the first time in a long while, I'm stone-cold sober.

Look at me. Acting like a grownup and shit.

I make my way to where Ellie is, only realizing at the last second that she's with a guy. Who's currently looking at her as if she created the moon and the stars just for him.

Considering what she's wearing, and how gorgeous she looks, I can't blame the dude.

"Hey." I stop directly in between them, looking from her face to his. I thrust my hand toward him. "Jackson."

"Carson," he says, giving me a quick shake. "Nice to meet you."

"How do you know Ellie?" I ask with a frown.

She sends me a look. One that says, *get the hell out of here.*

I return my own look, and it says, *not a chance, babe.*

I need to know who this guy is. Size him up. Is she interested in him? I hope to hell not. I don't have a claim on her but damn…

Can she move on from me that fast?

Check your ego, Rivers. It's a little out of control.

"We have two classes together," Ellie answers for him, her gaze cold. "What do you want, Jackson?"

"Whoa, so unfriendly." I send a cajoling smile in Carson's direction and he smiles back, appearing confused. Poor dude. He has no clue. "Just wanted to say hi. You're looking extra— good tonight."

Her cheeks turn pink. "Thanks," she bites out.

"You do something different to your hair?"

She immediately touches it. "I got it cut."

"I like it, El. You're looking fine, for sure." I nod and smile, like I'm an easily agreeable, straight-up homie.

I'm not though. I can tell she wants to get rid of me, and I know why. She's probably interested in this dude. I can tell he's definitely interested in her, by the way he's looking at her right fucking now.

I don't like it. Not one bit. I bet she only just met this guy, and I can't help feeling overprotective of her.

"Your friends are outside," she tells me.

"Really?" I glance around, spotting almost every single one of them. "Yeah, I don't think so."

"Maybe you should go find them." She tilts her head to the side.

"Unfortunately, they're all engaged in other conversation. Tony's currently lip-locked with Hayden. Caleb is getting his ass handed to him by Baylee. Diego and Eli are talking about tomorrow's game. Jocelyn is with Gracie and some giant blond guy with a huge Adam's apple. And...I think that's everyone."

Ellie scowls at me. Carson is completely unfazed. Just keeps sipping from his can of beer, never taking his gaze off of her.

Probably can't believe this fine ass chick is talking to him tonight. I understand where he's coming from. He seems young—probably only a year younger than me, but sometimes I feel like I've aged about ten years in the last twelve months—and kind of dorky looking. Pale. Like he doesn't get much sun because he's inside all the time. I bet he's a smart motherfucker who's majoring in business and is really good with numbers.

Meaning, he's the complete opposite of me.

"You're talking about Franz," Ellie says with an exasperated sigh.

I frown. "What do you mean?"

"The giant blond guy with the Adam's apple," she says. "His name is Franz."

"And who the hell is Franz, exactly?" I ask.

"Gracie's new guy," she answers. "He's from Germany."

Ah. Gracie. Of course she would go out with a guy named Franz.

"I've been to Germany," Carson says with a smile. "Went to Berlin when I was fourteen."

"What did you think of it?" Ellie asks, her eyes wide. "I've always wanted to go."

"It's beautiful. I liked the city. Clean. Lots of cool buildings. Modern mixed with old. Most of the city was blown up in World War II," Carson says.

"I've always wanted to go to Europe," Ellie says to him, reaching out to touch his knee. "Have you been to any other country over there?"

"We went to France too," Carson says, his gaze dropping to his knee, where Ellie is still touching him.

My gaze is there too. She's not usually so forward. At least not with me. Seeing her touch this guy, a guy she doesn't even really know, makes me want to get all caveman and grab her.

Tell this asshole that she's mine.

Wait a minute. I need to calm the hell down. She's not mine. She never really was. I can't make a claim on her. I'm the asshole who pushed her away after we kissed. What she's doing right now?

I deserve every bit of it.

"That is my ultimate dream, to go to Paris," Ellie says, her expression dreamy. As if she's imagining herself standing beneath the Eiffel Tower. "I've always wanted to see the Eiffel Tower."

Called it.

"It's even nicer than Berlin," Carson says, clearing his

throat. He seems visibly uncomfortable, and I have no idea why.

Ellie gives his knee a squeeze before she drops her hand and glances around. "Oh, I think Diego and Eli want to talk to you, Jackson."

I glance over my shoulder to see them both staring at me. They make *come here* gestures with their hands and I scowl before swinging back around to face Ellie and Carson.

I don't want to leave these two alone. They're too cozy. Something's happening here, and I don't want it to. I may have been the one who stupidly friend-zoned Ellie, but I don't necessarily want to see her with some other guy either.

Meaning, I am one hundred percent a selfish asshole.

"How do you know Ellie?" Carson asks me out of nowhere.

"How do *I* know her?" I rest my hand against my chest, my gaze going to hers. She's watching me, her expressive eyes telling me all sorts of things. Like how she much she doesn't want me here. Chatting with this guy who she is clearly interested in. But is she really? Only a few weeks ago, she was hanging on my every word. "We lived in the same area. Went to rival high schools. Her best friend is dating my best friend."

"Cool, cool." Carson nods, his gaze going from Ellie to me. Can he feel the tension brewing between us? Because I sure as hell can.

I hear Eli call my name and I wince, determined to keep talking.

"I'm a musician. A songwriter," I add, and Carson appears dutifully impressed. "Ellie is one of my biggest fans."

"I am not," she retorts.

"Don't lie, babe." I smile at her and she scowls in return. "She's one of the most supportive people I know," I tell Carson, leaning into him as if I'm sharing a secret.

"Not anymore," she throws at me.

"Don't ever piss her off," I say to Carson. He frowns, his dark brows pulling together. "She holds a mighty big grudge."

"Oh my God, *Jackson*. Go away. Now," she spits out at me, at the same time that Eli calls my name yet again.

"That's my cue to go." I offer both of them a smile. "Nice meeting you," I say to Carson.

"You too."

I saunter away, and I can literally feel Ellie watching me go. Her gaze is hot. Angry, for sure. But probably something else too. It's always been there between us, growing and growing, while I maintain my normal 'in denial' status.

Awareness. We are always so damn aware of each other. In tune with each other. It's annoying sometimes. I can't shake her, even when I want to.

Now is not one of those times.

I head toward Diego and Eli, who immediately pull me into a conversation about tomorrow night's game. They're all worked up while I'm as casual as can be. Being on the football team right now is like a freaking vacation compared to touring this past summer. When everything was on my shoulders. They all looked to me for decisions, for directions. If I fucked up, I was solely responsible, and let me tell you, that shit is intimidating.

With football, we're in it together. And I'm still mostly on the bench. This team shit is a no-brainer. I'll be cruising through the season with no pressure on me, I'm sure of it.

Eli goes in search of Tony, leaving me alone with Diego. I used to hate this guy. Mostly everyone did. But he's mellowed out, especially this last year. Plus, he's really fucking happy living with his girlfriend and their baby.

"Who's the guy with Ellie?" Diego asks me.

"Oh, that kid?" I glance over my shoulder to see they're still talking. Shit. At least she's not touching him any longer.

"They have a couple of classes with each other. His name is Carson."

Diego watches them for a moment before his gaze shifts to me. "I always figured you two would end up together."

"Nah." I shake my head. "She's not my type."

He laughs. "I thought anyone in our age group with a vagina was your type."

"Why you gotta use technical terms?" I grimace, and Diego laughs harder. "Ellie is cool. She's a good girl. Nice. Sweet. If we were to do anything though, I'd break her heart. And I can't do that. I don't want that responsibility."

Meaning, I'm not prepared for that responsibility.

"I get it," Diego says with a nod. "That guy can't stop staring at her."

If Diego is trying to make me jealous, he's succeeding. "I mean, look at her," I say, my voice nonchalant. "She's got a lot on display tonight."

"She looks good," Diego says casually, taking a swig of the beer he's holding. "Older."

Unable to help myself, I glance over my shoulder, once again, just in time to catch her throw her head back and laugh. My heart trips over itself as I watch her, and I wonder what that asshole said. I wonder if I could ever make her laugh like that. Or maybe I just ruined everything and we won't even be friends again.

I turn my attention back to Diego, annoyed with my thoughts. With myself. "There are a lot of girls here tonight," I say, desperate to change the subject.

"Any of them interest you?" Diego asks.

I scan the room, yet not a single female face leaps out at me. I can only think of Ellie. Laughing with the guy like she used to laugh with me. I curl my hands into fists. "All of them."

Diego laughs. Slaps my shoulder. "I can only imagine the stories you have from your tour."

"I have some good ones," I agree. "Got about two hours so I can go into vivid detail?"

"Since I won't ever be living the rock star life, guess I'll have to live through you instead," Diego says, shaking his head.

I wouldn't want to have his life, though he seems perfectly content. He's not even twenty and he's already a daddy. That's some crazy shit. I don't know if I even want to be a father, have a wife, the traditional life.

That sounds so fucking boring.

Or more like fucking scary.

I don't know what I want, and I feel like my mind changes on the daily. I'm only nineteen, for fuck's sake. I have options still.

Plenty of options. I could tour again. Rent out a studio and create my own album. Produce it. Make it all mine. Or I could cave and accept a record deal. But then I wouldn't be able to make music on my terms. And right now, that's the most important thing to me.

My gaze goes to Ellie one more time like I can't help myself and she's smiling. Beautiful. The prettiest I've ever seen her.

An idea forms in my head, and I shove it away. But it keeps coming. In a string of words. Lyrics.

Pulling my phone out, I start typing in my notes, getting the words down before I forget. But soon, it's as if I forget everything happening around me, and I'm lost in the song. The melody. Imagining the chords. The chorus. The entire song.

For Ellie.

CHAPTER 10

ELLIE

Jackson: **I wrote a new song.**

That's what I wake up to. A text from Jackson on Sunday morning. It's almost nine, which is irritating because I'd wanted to sleep in, but my internal clock didn't let me.

I check when Jackson sent the text. 7:48 a.m.

What the hell? He had a game last night too. Not that he played. I went with the girls to watch and Jackson didn't step foot on that field once. I was disappointed. He's so much fun to watch play, both music and football, but the coaches don't seem to ever give him a chance. They keep this up, and he'll eventually quit.

Music has to be calling his name. He can make money from that. Big money. Football? I don't see him going pro. Not even close. Not that he's bad—he just never plays.

A sigh leaves me. I'm still mad at him over how he acted at the party Friday night, interrupting my conversation with Carson. Jerk. He acted faintly territorial over me, though I don't think Carson even noticed.

We're going to the movies tomorrow night, Carson and

me. My one night off this week, since I'm working so much. I'm excited.

Me: **What's it called?**

The gray bubble pops up, telling me he's responding, and I'm shocked. Why is he up so early?

Jackson: **Prettiest I've Ever Seen You.**

Me: **Sounds romantic.**

Jackson: **It's a little dirty.**

Me: **Really? Is it about one of your hookups over the summer?**

Ugh. I don't want to know. But I say that because we both know hookups happened. I need to acknowledge them, cling to them, so I can remember why I'm not interested in Jackson any longer.

Because he's never really been interested in me. He gets with other girls all the time. While I'm sitting at home, waiting for him. It's pitiful.

Pathetic.

I refuse to be that girl. Not anymore.

Jackson: **No. It's about a mythical girl.**

Me: **Mythical?**

Jackson: **Unattainable.**

Me: **A figment of your imagination then?**

Jackson: **What do you mean by that?**

Me: **You can have pretty much whatever girl you want, J. Quite a few guys too if you were interested.**

Jackson: **Not everyone wants me, Ellie.**

Oh please. They all want him. I saw the way the girls flocked to him as the party went on Friday night. At one point, before Tony kicked everyone out, I think they were about eight deep, watching Jackson with adoring eyes as he told a story. I sort of wished I could have gone over there and listened to the story too, but Hayden put a stop to that.

"No way," she said, shaking her head. "Let him come to you."

Of course, after our initial conversation, he didn't speak to me for the rest of the night.

Jerk.

Me: **What are you doing up so early on a Sunday morning?**

Jackson: **Couldn't sleep. Was too excited about the song. Wanna hear it?**

Me: **You've already recorded it?**

Jackson: **No, but I can play it for you on FaceTime.**

He's played songs for me before on FaceTime, and like the sap I am, I listened to them, praising the lyrics, the melody, the whatever when he finished. Like the good little fangirl I used to be.

This time, I don't respond. No, I don't want to hear it. I'm sure it's amazing and I'll get all dreamy-eyed watching him play his guitar while listening to his voice, because he's addictive. I can't lie. I also can't turn my feelings off for him that fast, though I wish I could.

My phone starts to buzz, saying I have a FaceTime call from Jackson. Like I can't help myself, I take the call, and his face appears. He smiles.

"Good morning," he says cheerfully, looking sexy as ever in a white tank, his hair an artful mess, his jaw and cheeks covered in stubble. I want to feel those cheeks press against my face. My stomach. The inside of my thighs.

Oh holy shit, I just went there. Why do I always go there with him?

"Morning." I wish I could tug my comforter over my head. I'm sure I look a mess. Oh, and I'm just wearing a tank top too. No bra. Skimpy panties that I would never dare show him. It gets hot in this stupid, stuffy apartment that I share with roommates who are basically strangers, and I barely want to wear clothes when I sleep. At least I'm living in student housing with reasonable rent that I can pay myself, thanks to my job and student grants. Otherwise, my parents were probably going to make me stay at home and commute to school.

"Ready to listen?" He fumbles around with his phone, setting it on top of some furniture and giving me a better view of his bedroom. Of him. He's wearing gray sweats, his feet bare, and he's all rumpled and pretty and annoying. He's sitting in a chair with the guitar in his lap, strumming it.

"Sure," I say weakly, bracing myself.

Don't fall for it. Don't fall for him. Don't fall for it. Don't fall for him.

"Okay. It still needs some work." He hums, and the sound smacks me right in the chest before dropping, settling between my legs.

Oh my God, I am ridiculous.

In a crowded room, you won't look my way
  All I can do is stare
  I'm captivated, lost in your eyes
  Thinking about your secrets
  What's between those pretty thighs
  And wishing you weren't so far away

My skin grows warm and I laugh a little when his fingers fumble over the strings. He sends me a look. "Still needs a bit of work."

"Yeah," I say faintly, thinking of how he kept staring at me Friday night. How he told me I looked good.

No. This isn't about me. I'm sure I'm reading too much into this, as usual.

You're a goddess
  A woman divine

A siren
And now we're entwined
Together
Wrapped up in my arms
Lost to your lips
Lost in your charms
I fill you and you cry out my name
It's so fucking good
Life will never be the same

"This is the chorus."

The prettiest I've ever seen you
  Wishing you were with me
  The prettiest I've ever seen you
  Wishing I was the only one you see

"That wasn't too dirty," I tell him when he finishes.

"Oh, there's more. I'm just not sharing it with you yet." He frowns.

"Why not?"

"Still needs some work." He sets the guitar to the side, leaning it against his bed. "What did you think?"

"It was—good," I say.

His frown deepens. "Good? That's it?"

"It was great," I say softly. "I wish I knew who you were singing about."

His gaze never strays from mine as he says, "That one girl who is completely unattainable."

I wonder what this girl looks like. Who she is. He may say she's made up, but I don't know. I get the sense that she's real, and I sort of hate her. Even though I don't know her.

"We all want that one person we can't have, right?" he asks when I still haven't said anything.

"Yes," I agree as I stare at his pretty face with longing. "We do."

———

I enter the coffeeshop with my laptop in tow, ready to order my favorite drink—an iced white chocolate mocha with lavender and vanilla infused milk. The lavender, at first, made me avoid the drink, and I always ordered something else. Eventually, though, I gave in.

And never looked back.

The coffee shop is local. Beautifully decorated, with a massive dark gray wall and gorgeous, vibrant pink and white flowers painted on it. Music plays softly in the background and there are a lot of people sitting at the tables scattered about. It's a popular place, one I only just discovered when I moved here.

I order my drink and head for the pickup counter, nearly running into someone on my way.

"I'm so sorry," I say, glancing up to find Carson smiling down at me.

"We keep doing this," he says, his voice light. Teasing.

I laugh. "Yeah, we do. Are we both klutzes?"

"Probably. I know I am." The smile never leaves his face. "I'm glad I ran into you. Again."

"Me too. Though I'm really here to do homework." I pat my laptop bag. "What about you?"

"I was just stopping by for a drink real quick." He hesitates for only a moment. "Mind if I join you?"

"Yes. You should." I like Carson. Talking to him helps me forget about Jackson.

We get our drinks and find a table, right up against the wall of windows that are at the front of the building. We discuss what we like to drink here, and how much he hates the lavender drink, which I get since it's an acquired taste.

"What are you up to today?" I ask, once we're finished squabbling over superior coffee drinks.

"I was just at my parents' house," he says. "They live not too far from here."

It's a nicer part of town. Lots of older, larger houses in quiet, tree-filled subdivisions. "I love the neighborhoods around here. Do you get along with your parents?"

"Oh yeah. They're all right. My dad can be tough sometimes. He has all of these expectations," he says, rolling his eyes.

"I get that," I say, smiling at him.

"What about yours?" he asks.

"They're very supportive, but they don't have a lot of money, so I had to really work to convince them I wanted to go to Fresno State. They'd rather I go to community college first, which I totally get, but I wanted the campus-life experience, you know? So I worked hard, maintained a solid grade point average, got into Fresno State, won some grants and community scholarships, and now here I am," I explain.

"You're the type who doesn't hesitate to go after what you want, huh?" he says, his gaze full of admiration.

I would never, ever describe myself like that but when he puts it that way…

"Yeah. I guess you're right," I say softly, my mind turning his words over and over again.

"Are you from around here?" he asks.

"I grew up in the foothills above Fresno," I say. "Close to Yosemite."

"Nice. It's beautiful up there," he says, nodding. "We went up to Yosemite a lot when I was younger. My parents like to hike and camp."

"The park is amazing," I agree. "But we rarely visited.

When it's in your back yard, you let the tourists have it. At least, that's what my parents always said."

He chuckles. "Figures. When I was little, I wanted to live there."

"Ugh, no you didn't," I tease, making him grin.

"Do you have brothers or sisters?" he asks.

"I have two sisters. They're a lot older than me. They already have kids and stuff," I answer, taking a sip of my drink.

"Why such an age difference? Were you an oops baby?" He grimaces. "Maybe I shouldn't have put it like that. Or maybe that was too intrusive of a question?"

"No, not at all. It's fine." I don't want him to be afraid to ask me questions. I'm a freaking open book. "My mom was previously married. They got a divorce, and she met my dad. They got married and I was born less than a year later. So it's basically like I'm an only child. I love my sisters, but we're not very close."

"It's hard when you don't grow up together," he says.

"It is," I agree. "What about you?"

"I have an older brother and a younger sister. I'm the middle child."

"Do you have middle child syndrome?"

"Nah, I don't think I do. But isn't that half the problem with a middle child? They're not aware they have a problem?" We both laugh. "My parents are cool. Sometimes Dad comes down harder on us guys. I'm not what he wanted."

"And what did he want?"

"A jock, like him. Someone who always has a ball in his hands. Football, baseball, basketball, it didn't matter. My brother is exactly like him. Really good at sports. Broke a couple of records when he was on the varsity baseball team at our high school," Carson explains. "My dad tried with me, but I'm totally uncoordinated. And I kind of don't care, you know? I'm not into it."

"Yet I bet you played sports for years," I say.

His smile is bashful. "I did, but I was never very good at any of them. I finally put my foot down right before I started high school. Besides, I probably would've been cut from the teams."

"They cut players on the teams at your high school?"

He sends me an incredulous look. "Well, yeah."

"Our high school was so small, they practically had to beg people to join teams. Sometimes we wouldn't even have a JV team." I frown. "Except for volleyball. We had four teams one year. Varsity, JV, fresh and frosh."

"That's crazy."

"I know."

"Did you ever play volleyball?"

"Only when I was forced to in P.E." I wrinkle my nose. "I'm not very good at sports either."

"What are you good at, Ellie?"

"I'm an excellent organizer." When he starts to laugh, I protest. "Hey, that's a solid life skill."

"It is, I'm not disagreeing."

"I was in leadership all four years in high school," I say. "I was senior class vice president."

"That's awesome," he says. "I was president of the video game club my senior year."

I burst out laughing. I can't help it. "Tell me you don't play Call of Duty."

"If I did, that would be a lie." He laughs too before grabbing his drink and sucking most of it down. "I should probably go. I need to get back to campus. I have to meet my study group at three."

"I'm glad we got to hang out for a little while," I say with a shy smile.

"We'll get to hang out even more tomorrow night. At the movies," he reminds me, his smile a little bolder than mine.

"Right." I nod, wishing he made me feel all giddy and

nervous and excited for our date. I mean, I'm excited about my date with Carson tomorrow. I like him. A lot.

But if Jackson never came into my life, becoming such a major presence, it would've been so easy to be completely dazzled by Carson. He's the type of boy I would've crushed on hard when I was in high school my freshman and sophomore year. Sweet and cute and a little nerdy. Smart. Shy. Boys like that don't intimidate me as much.

And then I met Jackson Rivers.

That bastard ruined everything.

CHAPTER 11

JACKSON

I'm chilling at Tony and Caleb's condo, playing video games by myself. Tony is coming back soon with lunch for us. Caleb is still in class. Eli is too. We'll all meet up at practice later.

Right now, I'm just kicking it here, when there's a knock on the door.

Pausing the game, I rise to my feet and go to the door, peeking through the peephole. Shock courses through me when I see who's standing there, and I unlock and throw open the door as quickly as possible.

Ellie turns, her eyes widening when she sees me. "What are you doing here?"

"What are you doing here?" I toss back at her.

She presses her lips together, glancing around. As if she doesn't want to look me in the eyes. What the hell? "Is Tony home?"

"No," I say carefully. "I'm the only one home." I don't bother telling her he should be back in a few minutes.

"You don't even live here," she says, her tone accusatory as she brushes a few sweaty hair strands away from her face.

"I may as well, since we're always hanging out together," I

say, leaning against the doorjamb and crossing my arms. I watch her, noting her messy hair, her shiny face. Her T-shirt looks damp around the neck and I frown. "You okay? You look a little…overheated."

"I, uh…oh God, this is so embarrassing." She finally meets my gaze, wincing. "I ran out of gas."

My mouth drops open. "No shit?"

She nods, her expression miserable. "I walked almost a mile to get here."

"What the fuck, Ellie? That's dangerous." The street Tony and Caleb live off of is busy. Cars always speed down the straightaway, and a lot of accidents happen out there. "Where's your car?"

"On the side of the road, parked in front of another apartment complex." She wipes at her forehead. "It's so hot outside."

"Come in," I tell her absently, opening the door wide before I head back into the house so I can turn off the TV and grab my wallet.

"Thank you. It's so nice and cool in here." Ellie wanders into the apartment, lifting her hair off the back of her neck. "Think I could grab a water?"

"Go for it," I tell her. "And then we'll head out."

She walks into the kitchen and opens the fridge, pulling out a bottle of water. "Head out where?"

"To the gas station. Well, we'll need to stop off and buy a gas can first," I say.

"Wait a minute." She pauses in the doorway of the kitchen, watching me very, very carefully. "You're going to *help* me?"

"I'm definitely going to help you," I tell her, my voice firm. "You ready to go?"

"Uh, okay." She frowns, not moving an inch. "You sure you don't mind?"

"Ellie. Of course I don't mind." I pull my phone out and

send a quick text to Tony, telling him I have to leave and help Ellie with her car. He responds fast, letting me know he'll be home in less than three minutes, so I can go ahead and leave the door unlocked. "Let's do this."

We walk out to the parking lot, me going straight to my Mercedes, Ellie trailing behind. I hit the key fob and unlock the doors, making my way to the passenger side first, so I can open the door for her.

I'm a gentleman, even if she doesn't think I am.

"Thank you," she murmurs before she slips inside my car. Breathing deep, I inhale her sweet scent, trying to catch it as I shut the door for her.

Damn, she smells good. How could I forget that?

I jog around the front of the car and settle into the driver's seat, hitting the button to start the car. "You lucked out that I was here. Both Tony and Caleb aren't around."

"Yeah. Really lucky," she says, her voice laced with sarcasm.

What the fuck?

Putting the car into reverse, I back out of the parking spot quickly, my tires squealing when I shift into drive and punch the gas. Ellie grips the handle on the inside of the passenger door, sending me a glare.

"Show off," she mutters.

Who is this stranger and what did she do with my Ellie?

"You're the one who's being kind of rude," I mutter under my breath as I pull into the drive, coming to a stop. "Left or right?"

"What?" she snaps.

"Which way is your car? Left or right?" I say the words slowly, as if she might not get it.

In other words, I'm being a complete prick.

She glares. "Left."

I hit the blinker, check both ways for traffic, and when it's finally clear, I pull out onto the street, hitting the gas hard, the tires squealing again. Even my car's back end gets a little squirrely.

"You're driving like an asshole," she accuses me.

"You're kind of acting like an asshole." I let those words sink in for only a few seconds before I continue. "Not cool, considering I'm helping you."

"I didn't ask for your help."

"As if I'm going to tell you no, El. If you need help, I'm going to help," I say, my voice a little gentler.

She turns her head, staring out the window as we drive. Not saying a word. Which only makes me angrier. What the hell is her problem? Why is she being so hostile toward me? I thought we were cool yesterday. After I played part of my new song for her. She seemed to like it. She was supportive, which was what I needed yesterday. I was feeling a little low, but talking to Ellie always picks me up.

Always.

Until now.

I send her a quick glance, staring at the back of her head, willing her to look my way, but she doesn't. A loud, long sigh leaves me, but I get nothing.

"Tell me when you see your car," I say.

Her head moves. The most subtle of nods.

What the fuck ever.

We drive for a few minutes, hitting every single red light along the way. We're approaching a major intersection when Ellie sits up straight, pointing to the right. "There it is!"

On the opposite side of the road, of course.

I check the roads and, at the last second, swing an illegal U-turn, so I'm on the other side of the street, parking so our cars are nose to nose.

A car speeds past us, making my Mercedes rattle, the driver's hand thrust out his window, giving me the finger as he honks repeatedly.

"Jackson, oh my God," Ellie says, sounding frazzled. "That was crazy."

"I took my shot when I could," I say with a shrug.

And if those words don't accurately describe me, I don't know what else does.

"I thought we were going to get a gas tank first," she says.

"I wanted to check out the car, see what's up."

Her head swivels in my direction, her dark eyes meeting mine. She's mad. Frustrated. I'm guessing it all has to do with her car situation, but maybe she's mad at me too. For what, I don't know. I'm her knight in shining armor right now. Maybe she'd prefer it was her precious little nerd boy, Carson?

Nah, I can't take my frustration out on him. He seemed perfectly fine.

Perfectly boring, but yeah. A decent human being. Ellie's type, I'm sure.

A decent human being, I am not.

"You don't believe me?" Ellie asks, pulling me from my thoughts.

"Believe you about what?"

"That I ran out of gas," she says tightly. "I know that's what happened. I feel really stupid right now, trust me, but I was trying to stretch it out as long as possible. Gas prices have gone up so high lately, and I don't get paid until tomorrow…"

She clamps her lips shut. I immediately feel like shit. I don't struggle for money, thanks to my dad. I'm not as rich as the Callahans or even the Bennetts, but my dad does really well at his job. The fancy ass car I'm currently driving used to belong to him. He got tired of it after only two years and gave it to me.

Must be nice.

If I stay on my rock star path and actually get a record deal, I could afford a hundred of these cars for my closest and dearest friends. I could buy Ellie a lifetime supply of gas for her car. She'd never run out of gas again. If I hit it big, I could end up with the world at my feet, and I could do whatever the hell I wanted, whenever I wanted to. I would be set for life—if my over-the-top dreams come true.

And here Ellie struggles, driving on fumes, crossing her fingers that she won't have to fill up her tank until she gets paid.

While I live on my daddy's dime, able to fill up my gas tank, no problem.

"You're not stupid," I say gently, glancing over at her to find she's already watching me. "I just wanted to make sure there's not some other problem with your car before we go get a gas can and fill it up."

She nibbles on her full bottom lip, her eyes wide. Trusting. She shouldn't trust me. I don't know jack shit about cars, but I want to help her. She's helped me so much over the last couple of years, and I give her nothing in return.

This is the least I can do.

"Okay," she says, nodding, her teeth still working her lip.

"Can I have the key?" I hold my hand out.

She reaches inside her purse and pulls out the keychain, handing it over to me. "Here you go."

"Why don't you get out of the car while I do this," I suggest.

She frowns. "Why?"

"It's not safe to sit on the side of the road in a car. Someone could smash into it—and you," I explain.

"Isn't it just as unsafe to stand on the side of the road?" she asks.

"At least you'd be on the other side of the car, and not in it," I say with a shrug. This was advice my father gave me when I was first learning to drive.

Guess it stuck.

"Okay," she says with a sigh, reaching for the door.

I go to her car while she finds some shade under a tree, watching me as I settle behind the steering wheel of her old Saturn. This car is ancient, at least fifteen years, maybe older? It's definitely seen better days. Nice and clean inside though. Of course it is. This is Ellie we're talking about, after all.

She takes care of her shit.

I stick the key in the ignition and try to start it. It doesn't even try and turn over. Just makes a clicking sound. I try again, but nothing.

And I've got nothing either. Sure, this could be a simple run out of gas situation. But maybe it's something else. Ellie bought the car the summer before her senior year for cheap. It already had over one hundred thousand miles on it. But it ran and she only paid around fifteen hundred bucks, which was a lot of money for her. I always worried about her driving around in this car. Figured it close to falling apart at any time.

I climb out of the car and make my way over to her, standing beneath the tree. It's as hot as a bitch outside, and I see she's sweating despite being in the shade.

"How old is the car again? 2005?"

"2003," she admits.

I frown. "It's eighteen years old."

She nods.

"The same age as you," I say, as if she needs the reminder. I'm sure she doesn't.

She rolls her eyes. "Ooookay."

"Weren't you born in '03?"

"Stop." She shoves my shoulder, but I don't really move. "Do you think it's just out of gas? Or something worse?"

"Has it been acting up?"

"What do you mean?"

"I don't know—engine stalling? Having trouble starting? Lights flickering? When was the last time you replaced your battery?" I'm throwing questions at her and she looks overwhelmed. And I don't even know if I'm asking the right questions.

"I haven't replaced the battery since I bought it," she admits.

She's only owned it a year, so that's not too big an issue. I suppose I could look under the hood. Don't batteries have a purchase date on them?

Feeling like a macho asshole who secretly doesn't know what he's doing, I pop the hood and check the battery, squinting at the faded letters and numbers engraved on top of it. Ellie watches me from her spot under the tree, her brows furrowed, as if she's confused by what I'm doing.

I get it. I don't know shit about cars. I'm not dressed for what I'm doing either, clad in black basketball shorts and a torn, faded Tame Impala T-shirt with Nike slides on my feet.

"It might be your battery," I tell her once I slam the hood down. "Do you have an emergency tow service? Triple A?"

She slowly shakes her head.

I get pissed. Why wouldn't her parents give her something like that? She's all alone down here, driving a shitty car, working at a restaurant until late at night. She needs some extra protection.

"I have Triple A," I tell her. "I could have them tow it to a mechanic."

"I don't know," she says warily. "How about we test the gas theory first?"

We drive to a Pep Boys close by and I buy a gas tank for her. She insists on paying, but I won't let her, which irritates her.

I don't really care.

We go to a gas station next, and she literally pushes me out of the way at the pump, shoving her debit card into the reader before I can manage to pull out my credit card.

"You shouldn't use a debit card at the pump," I tell her as she punches in all her information.

"Why not?" She glances over her shoulder at me.

"People put skimmers on those things. Scam card readers so they can make new cards out of your number and charge it up."

"They won't get far. I don't have a lot of money in my account," she says, her voice wry.

"Yeah, but they could wipe you out fast and then your bank won't replace it for a couple of weeks while they investigate it," I point out.

She turns to face me. "Guess it's the chance I have to take."

"You should try and get a credit card," I say, remaining outwardly calm. Inside, I want to scream at her, *why doesn't anyone explain these things to you? Why doesn't anyone take care of you?*

Like I want to be the one to take care of her, but sometimes I can barely take care of myself.

"I tried. I didn't get one." She shrugs. "I don't make enough. Or they want me to pay two hundred dollars so I can have a four-hundred-dollar credit limit or whatever. I can't afford to have two hundred dollars just tied up in some weird credit card that feels like a scam."

I unscrew the top of the gas can before inserting the nozzle inside. "Wait a few months. You can probably get a credit card on campus. The companies always seem to have booths in the quad, trying to get you to sign up. The student offers are pretty good."

Diego got one and they gave him a fifteen-hundred-dollar credit limit. He couldn't believe it.

"Yeah. Maybe. I don't know. Credit cards scare me. What if I run up a balance that I can't afford?" she asks, frowning.

"Then you make the minimum payment and pay it off," I explain.

"Right and pay sky high interest on stuff that I don't need." She shakes her head.

"Sometimes we need things we can't afford," I point out.

"I'm sure you know so much about that." Her tone is laced with faint hostility.

As calmly as I can, I finish filling the plastic can, put the lid back on it and set it carefully in the trunk of my car. If that thing spills, that'll suck major ass, but like precious Ellie just said, it's the chance I'll have to take.

It's only when we're finally back in my car do I speak again.

"What exactly did you mean by that?"

"Mean by what?" she asks, sounding genuinely confused.

"When you said I know so much about needing things we can't afford?" I start the engine and pull away from the gas pumps, turning onto the street and stopping at the intersection, waiting for the light to change.

A sigh escapes her. "Jackson, you never have to wait for anything. You get whatever you want, whenever you want it."

Not true, I think to myself. But I don't bother correcting her.

"You don't know what it's like to struggle financially. Your dad pays for everything. And I'm not jealous, or mad about it. I've been around that sort of thing since Ava and I became such good friends. I'm used to it. I benefit from my friends' good fortune. But I wasn't born into a wealthy family. Not even close. I have to work and save and sometimes struggle a little bit. It's not fun, but I also know my life isn't so bad. I have a lot of things to be grateful for," she says, sounding so logical. Downright content, even.

She goes silent for a moment and I absorb her words. I never really thought about Ellie's financial circumstance before. I mean, it's obvious. The old Saturn is what finally tipped me off and made me realize she comes from a middle-class family. Nothing wrong with that, of course. Though I wonder if Ellie realizes that.

"So no, I don't really want you to tow my car to a mechanic shop, because I won't be able to afford fixing my car. My parents can't either. I'm praying all it is, is a gas problem and that's it," she further explains, sinking into the seat with a soft sigh.

I'm quiet as I drive back to her car, hoping that it's only a gas problem.

Wishing I could solve all of her problems with a snap of my fingers. A worried, stressed out Ellie worries and stresses me out.

Not that she'll let me ease her burden. She's too proud. Too stubborn. I'm sure she'll think I'll want something in return. I can admit I'm selfish, but when it comes to Ellie...

I just want to help her. That's it. No strings attached. When Ellie's okay, all is right in my world.

And I don't know how to feel about that.

CHAPTER 12

ELLIE

My little car issue turned into an all-afternoon endeavor.

Adding gas to my tank didn't help at all. The car still wouldn't start. Kept making this weird clicking noise every time I turned the engine. Jackson went on YouTube—no joke—did a little investigating and figured out it could be the alternator.

After waiting for a tow truck to show up, which took over an hour, we followed the driver to a local mechanic shop. I absolutely did not want to go that route. I can't afford fixing my car right now, but Jackson insisted. He was kind of a dick about it, really. Gave me no choice but to go along with *his* decision, and I finally gave in.

Eventually.

We're still sitting in the waiting room of the mechanic shop around three o'clock; Jackson texts one of his coaches and says he can't make it to practice.

"Oh my God, you can't miss practice," I protest after he tells me.

He shrugs his broad shoulders, not seeming too bothered by it. "I don't mind."

"Will they be mad?" I really, really hope they won't be mad. I don't want him to get in trouble because of something that happened to me. Last year he skipped a couple of practices with Tony and the coaches came down hard on both of them.

"This is legit. I explained everything to them and they understand," he says. "It's not like I'm skipping just to be a prick."

"What did you tell them?"

"I said I was helping out my girlfriend." His cheeks turn red.

And my heart soars.

Stupid heart.

"Your girlfriend, huh?" I jab him in the ribs with my elbow, trying not to read too much into this whatsoever. "Didn't realize we were in a relationship."

It would be my every secret wish come true if we were in a relationship, but I know that won't happen. And even if it eventually did, he would break my heart into a million tiny pieces and destroy me.

No thanks. I need someone safe. Like Carson.

Oh shit.

Whipping out my phone, I send him a quick text.

Me: **I'm having car trouble right now. At a shop, waiting to hear the damage. I don't know if I can make the movies tonight.**

Carson: **Oh no. What happened? I wondered why you weren't in class.**

It really killed me that I had to skip class. That is not something I ever do.

I explain via text to Carson everything that happened, that my afternoon has been really stressful so far, and how I don't think I'm up to going out tonight.

Though honestly, if he would've tried to convince me that he still wanted to take me out and treat me right, I'd go for it.

Silly but true.

Of course, he does none of that. He's not insistent or commanding, like Jackson is. Walking around as if he can solve all the world's problems—at the very least *my* problems —with a snap of his fingers.

Carson is more…sensitive. He's understanding of my feelings, and doesn't want to push.

That's all Jackson does. Push, push, push.

Carson: **Maybe another time then?**

Me: **Probably not till next week. I'm working every night for the rest of this one.**

Carson: **Sorry we can't get together. See you tomorrow?**

Me: **For sure.**

Jackson hovers over my shoulder, trying to see who I'm talking to and I dodge away from him, sending him a glare. "So nosy."

"Carson, huh?"

That's all he says. And oh my God, I am probably reading way too much into this, into his reaction, the look on his too gorgeous face, but…

He seems a little jealous.

"We were supposed to go to the movies tonight," I admit.

"Did you just cancel on him?" He raises a single brow.

I nod.

"Did you tell him what happened?"

I nod again.

"And he didn't try and make shit better by offering to buy you dinner?" He shakes his head before waiting for my response. "What a chump."

I had the same thoughts. Jackson would've tried to make my day brighter because I'm feeling low. I know he would've. That's just how he is.

The mechanic comes out, wiping his dirty hands on a red rag as he talks to us.

"Afraid it's the alternator," he says. "It went out."

My heart sinks. "Oh no."

"How much to fix it?" Jackson asks.

"Probably around eight hundred bucks. I'll go draw up an estimate so you can look it over." The mechanic leaves us to go to the counter, where he starts tapping away on an old desktop computer.

"I can't afford that," I whisper to Jackson. "That's over half what I paid for my car."

"I know. I'll take care of it." He reaches over and pats my knee.

"Jackson." I settle my hand over his, ignoring the sparks that ignite between our hands. They're all one-sided, those sparks. He doesn't feel it. Not like I do. "I can't let you pay for that. Fixing my car. It's too much."

"I don't mind. Let me do it. You need a car, El. To get to school, to work, whatever. I want to help you. Let me help you." His voice is soft, as is his gaze when it settles on my face. We're sitting so close to each other in this cramped waiting room. Our shoulders brushing, his leg pressed against mine. I can feel his breath on my face. If I lean in and tilt my head just so, his mouth could end up on mine….

"Here's your estimate."

We jerk away from each other at the sound of the mechanic's gruff voice above us.

Jackson takes the piece of paper, scanning it briefly before meeting the mechanic's gaze once more. "Go ahead and fix it."

He didn't even give me a chance to say anything. To argue. To protest. He's just going to do it. I'm a little irritated by him taking the situation completely over, but then again…

I'm also glad. I didn't know what to do, or how to make this work.

"I should have it finished in about two days," the mechanic says.

"Two days?" I jump to my feet. "But I need my car back tonight."

"Might be three." He shrugs, not giving a shit about my problems. "Have to order the part. Sometimes that takes a while, especially with cars as old as that one."

Ouch. Okay.

Jackson stands, looming behind me. "You'll keep us posted on what's going on with the car?"

"Let me get your information and I'll definitely keep you up-to-date," the mechanic says.

Jackson follows after him, rattling off his personal info as the mechanic enters it into the computer. I watch him, admiring his confidence. How he sweeps in to rescue me without hesitation. I know I'm supposed to be mad at him. That I'm supposed to ignore him and move on with my life, but he makes it pretty hard when he steps in and helps me so readily.

"All right, we're good to go." Jackson comes up beside me and slips his arm around my shoulders, giving me a gentle shake. "You ready?"

I nod. "Yeah."

We exit the waiting room, the hot air outside hitting me like a wall and I immediately break out into a sweat. Jackson drops his arm from my shoulders as we walk toward his car, and I miss his touch. His closeness. But when we climb into his car, I feel like I'm wrapped up in a Jackson-made cocoon, and all is right in my world again.

I am such a sucker.

His unique scent fills the space. And he's so big, so broad, he physically fills up the space. He glances over at me with a faint smile, and I smile weakly at him in return.

What am I doing? I'm supposed to be mad at him. Cutting him off for good. Yet here I sit, indebted to him financially after he sweeps in and rescues me.

Jackson starts the engine and pulls out of the parking lot,

headed in the complete opposite direction of his apartment. And mine too, since we all sort of live in the same area.

"Where are we going?" I ask, my voice low.

He sends me a quick look before returning his gaze to the road. "I don't know about you, but I'm fucking starving."

My stomach growls at hearing his words. "Same."

"Let's grab a late lunch. Or an early dinner. Whatever you want to call it." Jackson checks his dashboard. "It's already past five. We can call it dinner. My treat."

I glance down at myself. "I'm not dressed the best." I bet I smell bad too. I was sweating up a storm when I had to walk to Tony's condo complex.

"Me either," he says with a chuckle. "We won't go anywhere too fancy."

He takes me to a Mexican restaurant near downtown Clovis called 559 Taqueria.

"Ever been here before?" he asks as he pulls into a parking spot behind the restaurant.

"No, but I've heard of it."

"You're going to think you've died and gone to taco heaven. Trust me." He sends a grin in my direction before he climbs out of the car.

I'm left sitting in my feelings for a moment, stunned stupid by the look on his face. Sometimes I really hate how attractive he is.

Though most of the time, I love it.

I follow after him as we enter the restaurant, and we have to stand in line to place our order. It smells delicious in here. Like…mouthwateringly good. My stomach growls nonstop, reminding me that I never ate lunch and had a really crappy breakfast, and I think about my options. I just want a couple of tacos. Maybe some chips?

"What do you want?" Jackson asks, his eyes on the menu board on the wall.

I tell him my simple request and he nods.

"I'll order for you. I know what you like."

Frowning, I stare up at him, at a loss. He does?

He tilts his head down, lowering his voice. "I know you think this has been a one-sided thing between us the last couple of years, but I've been paying attention to you, Ellie. I know you love Mexican food, but you don't like tomatoes. And all the other girls drink Diet Coke, but you prefer root beer. Though you're not a big soda drinker at all. You'll eat salsa, but you dunk your chips in it without scooping anything up. I'll make sure there's no pico de gallo on your tacos."

Jackson's right. Every single thing he just said is correct when it comes to my Mexican food preferences. And while I usually feel silly over how I eat chips and salsa, and that I don't like Diet Coke like my other friends, he just made me feel as if everything I do and like is perfectly natural.

Perfectly me.

Out of nowhere, he grabs my hand and brings it up to his mouth. As in, his lips are on my knuckles, and what the hell is he doing?

"Trust me?" he asks with those blue, soulful eyes.

I nod, unable to speak. As if I'm in a trance.

"I got you, El." He kisses my hand. "More than you know."

His words stick with me as I listen to him order for us, and I want to pick them apart. Analyze them. Turn them over and over in my head. Have him explain to me exactly what he means by that.

But I will never ask. I'm too afraid of the truth. That he really only likes me as a friend. That he's 'got me' in a friend-ship way and that's it. Coming to my rescue with my car. Paying for the repairs.

He's just being kind.

Jackson finishes paying for our order and we each grab our drinks before going outside to sit on their covered patio.

Spanish music plays softly in the background and a new song starts—that one that's on TikTok. "Telepatia." The song about being in tune with your lover so strongly, you don't even have to speak. It's also about being in a long-distance relationship.

I might've looked up the meaning behind the lyrics a couple of days ago, curious because I really love the song.

A breeze blows through the space, making the vines covering the lattice walls rattle. A beam of sunlight shines upon Jackson, outlining his face in gold, making his hair look blonder than usual.

I stare at him, unable to look away. He's ridiculously good looking. Painfully so. Even doing something as mundane as scrolling through his phone, which is what he's doing currently. His hair hangs over his forehead, so long it has to be in his eyes, and I'm tempted to lean over the table and push it out of the way. Run my fingers through it. His hair is soft. I've only really touched it once…

"Oh my God, are you Jackson Rivers?"

We both glance over to see a group of four teenaged girls sitting at the table next to us. Their eyes are comically wide, and they all have braces on their teeth. I'd put them no older than freshmen in high school, and I'm probably pushing it. More like middle schoolers.

They're definitely dressed better than I am. A table of really pretty, soon-to-be knock out beautiful girls. And they're all looking at Jackson with stars in their eyes.

Jackson smiles, his expression turning bashful. "Maybe."

One of them squeals. So loudly, every person sitting on the patio looks up and over in our direction. "OH MY GOD CAN WE TAKE A PHOTO WITH YOU?"

"Sure," he says, rising to his feet.

The girls lose their damn minds. There is no other way to describe their reaction to finding Jackson in the same restaurant as them. They flutter around him, giggling uncontrollably as they each individually take a photo with him. They lavish on the praise, telling him how much they love his music, his lyrics, his performances, their adoring gazes never leaving his face once. As if they're afraid if they look away, he'll disappear.

I'm thinking they love more than his music, but they're keeping that part quiet.

"Could you take a photo of all of us with Jackson, please?" one of the girls asks me with hope shining in her eyes.

"Of course," I say as I stand and take the phone from her hand. I wait for them to position themselves around Jackson, noticing how they keep looking at me with frowns on their faces. As if they can't believe their beloved idol is hanging out with a commoner like me.

Or maybe that's my own personal complex coming out in full force.

I snap what feels like a million photos so they have plenty to choose from. I'm a girl, I know what it's like to take group photos with a bunch of other girls. It's so difficult to find a photo where every single person looks good.

"Thank you," the girl says when they're done and I hand her back her phone. "We appreciate it."

"When are you performing next?" one of the girls asks Jackson.

He smiles. Shrugs. Playing it cool with that warm gleam in his eyes, like there's nowhere else he'd rather be but with those girls. He knows how to put it on, making people feel alive in his presence. "Don't have anything scheduled at the moment."

"Too busy playing football?" She bats her eyelashes at him, trying to flirt.

It's cute and all, but she's wearing braces. She's terribly young. But I guess this is good practice for her.

"Yeah," he says with a smile that doesn't quite reach his eyes. "You coming to the Bulldog games?"

"Yes!" they all say in unison as they jump up and down, like the little girls they truly are.

Though, technically, I'm not that much older than them, I feel much older. And wiser.

Wait a minute. Not so much wise. I am the idiot, after all, who's in love with a boy who only thinks of me as a friend.

Once they're gone, as in they've left the restaurant, and we have our food in front of us, Jackson sends me a wry smile.

"That was wild," he says, seeming in a daze.

"Happens a lot to you when you go out?" I take a bite of my taco and holy crap, it's delicious.

"Not really. That was kind of a first," he admits right before he takes a big bite of his own taco.

"They were true fangirls. They even knew you were on the football team," I point out.

"Yeah. I mean, that's public knowledge. I don't hide it," he says, his gaze thoughtful as he stares off into the distance, his taco forgotten. "But I have to admit, it was kind of—overwhelming. Having them recognize me and freak out. Talking to me as if they know me. They don't. Not at all."

I frown. "You didn't like their attention?"

"Sometimes, I don't know how I feel about it," he admits. "I've played a lot of shows at Strummers, so I get why I have fans here. I've built up a following, I guess. It's just really weird."

"I thought this was what you wanted," I tell him, settling my taco onto my plate as I study him intently. He seems a little shaken by the encounter, which is not like Jackson.

He embraces this kind of thing usually.

"Maybe." He shrugs. Grabs his half-eaten taco and shoves the rest of it into his mouth.

"Maybe not?" I arch a brow.

"Not sure," he says once he's swallowed. "Honestly? I don't know what I want. And do I really need to make a decision right now?"

"Is that why you haven't signed a record deal?"

Jackson nods. "I'm not ready to give up control yet. Not ready to have it all rest on my shoulders. I just want to have fun while I still can, you know?"

"Being a rock star won't be fun?" I tease.

"After a while it won't be. It'll become a job, and I don't want to kill my spirit, my love for music." His expression turns distant, a faint smile curling his lips. "I could totally write a song about this."

"You seem able to write a song about pretty much anything," I say softly.

His gaze meets mine, his eyes a deep, dark blue. "You have no idea."

CHAPTER 13

JACKSON

Having those girls freak out over me kind of freaked *me* out. Their enthusiasm was overwhelming. They fluttered around me like hyped-up bees. Buzzing and jumping, talking in overly high-pitched voices in the middle of a restaurant, where I least expected it. I certainly didn't think they'd recognize me, yet they totally did. Chatting me up like we're old friends. They knew a lot of things about me, and it felt strange.

I know I have fans. I've performed enough to know that they're out there. They come to my shows and scream my name. Say obscene things. Flash their tits at me while in the audience. Some of them even come backstage and proposition me after a performance, and we hook up.

There were a lot of hook ups over the summer. Quick, frenzied sex in a dirty bathroom. A dimly lit hallway. A cramped dressing room. On the tour bus. A lot of blow jobs. More than the actual sex. I was drunk. High. Whatever. Alcohol, weed, pills.

Coke was readily available while I was on tour, but I only did that a couple of times since it made me feel too out of control. And downright exhilarated, like I couldn't jump off the roller coaster ride no matter how hard I tried. That's a feeling I know I'd want again and again, which scared me. I laid off the shit after the second time I tried it.

The ultimate high though?

Being wanted. Adored. Screamed over. Your name on their lips as they chant it over and over again. And when you're some low rent, wannabe rock star and they still lose their shit over you? It's heady fucking stuff.

The younger fans, though? Not so much. They're a little scary. Rabid in their adoration. A bunch of little detectives, searching for you on the internet and finding out all your private information. That shit worries me. I don't know why. Losing my privacy is a precarious thing. You want people to find out who you are and listen to your music. I'm not just writing songs for myself. I want to share my songs with the world.

But sharing them with the world, and the world loving them, that all comes with a heavy price.

Having Ellie there while those girls lost their shit over me calmed me down. She's a touchstone. *My* touchstone. Someone who's been supportive of me from the start. Who's always adored my songs, yet also calls me out on my shit when I act like a dick, which is most of the time. She's real.

Just about as real as a person can get.

We finish our food mostly in silence. Me still thinking about what happened, her probably realizing hanging out with me comes with a lot of baggage. By the time we're back in my car and I'm pulling out of the parking lot and onto Clovis Avenue, the tension between us is thick, and I don't know why.

I decide to break it first.

"Are you mad I took over your car situation?" I ask.

A soft sigh escapes her, and it's like a sock to the gut. A straight hit to my dick.

I can deny it to myself all I want, but I'm still drawn to this girl. And as more than just a friend, too.

But she's moved on. Found someone else already. Right?

"I was mad at first," she admits. "But not anymore. I know you just want to help."

"I was kind of bossy about it," I say.

"You totally were." She sounds amused. "Which made me mad. Not gonna lie. I'm over it now, though. I appreciate your help. And I want to pay you back."

"No. I don't want your money."

"Jackson…"

"No," I repeat firmly. "It's a gift."

"Like for the next five years?"

"Nah, you'll be indebted to me for maybe only two years." I laugh when she sends me a look. "Seriously, I expect nothing in return. I want to help you. You need a car that runs."

A better car than the one she currently has, but I keep that opinion to myself.

"I definitely need a car. Not sure how I'm supposed to get to work the next couple of days. Public transportation?" She makes a face. "I suppose I could take the bus."

"That late at night?" I shake my head. "No fucking way."

"How else am I supposed to get home, hmm?"

"I'll pick you up."

"Come on, Jackson. You've already done enough," she says. "I can find a ride from someone else. Maybe one of my roommates."

She barely knows those girls. I haven't met them yet, and I'm sure Ellie wouldn't ask them because she doesn't want to impose on people. Even those she's known for years.

"It's no big deal. Though I probably can't take you to work because I'll be at practice when your shifts start," I say.

"Yeah. I start work at four."

"I can definitely pick you up after though," I say.

"Won't you have plans?"

"With who?"

"I don't know." She shrugs.

"Video game sessions with the boys? Yeah, that's about all I've got going on this week," I say, chuckling.

"No dates with random girls?" She says this to her lap, as if she's afraid to look at me.

I'm quiet for a moment, letting her words sink in. My mind immediately goes to the kiss we shared. When I was a drunk dick and said shitty things.

It was a good kiss.

Fuck that, it was a great kiss. But I shoved her away because she scares the hell out of me. She makes me want more.

So much more than I deserve.

"Like your date with a random dude?" I throw back at her. I'm suddenly feeling hostile about her date with that guy.

"Carson isn't random," she says, defensively.

"Random enough. You don't know him that well."

"We had a coffee date over the weekend," she says.

"Oh really?" A foreign emotion rises up inside of me, settling in my throat. Threatening to choke me.

"Yes, we talked a lot. He's nice," she says.

"Is that when he asked you to out?"

"No, he asked me at the party Friday night," she admits.

Carson moves fast, the asshole.

"What do you even know about that guy?" I clear my throat, hating how irritated I sound.

"He's perfectly polite."

Perfectly boring if you ask me, but what do I know?

"And I want to get to know him better," she adds.

I frown. I'm frowning so hard, I can feel my forehead wrinkle. "You're actually interested in that guy?"

"Why else would I agree to go on a date with him?" She glances over at me.

"I don't know. Because you felt sorry for him?"

She laughs. "Um, no. Why would I feel sorry for him? I do actually like him. He's sweet and funny."

"Uh huh."

Whatever. He sounds dull as shit to me, but I'm not the one who has to date him so…

"You're not dating anyone right now?" she asks.

I actually scoff. "When do I ever date anyone?"

Her smile is small. "Never."

"Exactly. I'm not going to start now."

"I want a boyfriend."

Her voice is so low, I almost didn't hear her. "You what?"

Okay, I heard her. I'm just making her say it again. But why? So I can torture myself? I can't be her boyfriend. I can be her friend and that's about it.

"I want a boyfriend. I've never really had one," she says, her voice louder, her gaze sliding to mine. "So I want one. But I don't know exactly how to get one."

"What do you mean? Carson seems interested in you," I say. Little fucker definitely seems interested in her. Probably not worthy of her though.

No one really is.

"I'm the girl who's always the friend to guys," she stresses. "They never see me as anything beyond that. I'm terrified he's going to think the same thing."

"Then you have to do something about it," I tell her.

She frowns. "What do you mean?"

"I mean, if you think he's interested in you as more than a friend, you have to give him non-friendly vibes." I shift uncomfortably in my seat. I don't want to encourage this. If she gets with this guy, our friendship will fade fast. He won't want her hanging around me, and I wouldn't blame him.

If I lose her to some other guy, I'll miss her so damn bad. More than she'll ever know. Can I risk that? If I tell her she shouldn't date this Carson dude, then I have to give her a reason why. Because I don't want her to—because I want her to be with me. But am I ready for that responsibility?

"What do you even mean, send him non-friendly vibes? I told you I'm not good at this thing. I'm kind of hopeless at it, actually," she says, her voice getting stronger. "I don't know why guys can't see me beyond being a friend to them. You do that. You put me in the friend zone all the time."

"Ellie—"

"Don't bother arguing. You know it's true. You kissed me once and then shoved me back in the friend zone corner, where you keep me at all times. You talk about how much you need me in your life. How you can't imagine me not being there for you, yet you won't give me what I want," she says.

Her words are terrifying. Only because I want to give her what she wants. I'm desperate to, but I know in my heart, I would ruin everything.

I always do.

"And don't give me those excuses about you fucking it up. I know how you operate. How you think you're this giant piece of shit who can't be loyal. Who can't commit. You think I'm a scared little virgin? Well, you're a scared little boy pretending to be a rock star who's terrified of responsibility. It's called being a grown up, Jackson."

She crosses her arms in front of her chest, making a little harumphing sound that is decidedly not grown up.

I got so caught up in our conversation, Ellie's apartment complex is suddenly right in front of us. I turn into the parking lot and pull into a space, throw the car in park and turn to look at her.

Ellie keeps her head averted, as if she doesn't want to look at me.

I'm heated. I could continue this argument, but she's right. And I don't feel like fighting with Ellie right now.

I decide to switch gears.

"You've really never had a boyfriend?"

She turns her head slowly in my direction, her gaze meeting mine. The interior of my car is lit by an outside light, casting her pretty face in an orangish glow. "Yes, Jackson. I've really never had a boyfriend."

A thought occurs to me and my eyes nearly bug out of my head. "I wasn't your first kiss, was I?"

She looks vaguely horrified. "No."

"How many guys have you kissed?"

Ellie chews on her lower lip. Something she does when she's nervous. "Uh...three."

"Three." I nod, thinking of my own number. Way more than that. Though my hook ups over the summer didn't involve much kissing. Feels too personal, lips on lips. "That's a decent number."

"Don't mock me."

"I'm not." I send her an earnest look. "I swear."

I don't know if I necessarily believe her, but I'm going to get her to tell the truth.

Any way I can.

CHAPTER 14

ELLIE

I lied.

Jackson definitely wasn't my first kiss. But I inflated my numbers. I've kissed someone before. But only one someone. Technically, that makes Jackson my second kiss.

Well, the second person I've ever kissed. The first person was during my sophomore year in high school. He was a year older. Played on the drumline in band. Marshall. Kind of cute, super nerdy, but not in a bad way. More in that shy boy who has potential way.

I asked him to the Sadie Hawkins dance, and we went out a couple of times after that. We kissed at the end of every date. Nothing earth shattering, but it was good practice. His lips were kind of dry though. And he did this slightly creepy thing with his tongue—it reminded me of a flickering snake tongue, ew—and yeah.

That was it.

Jackson, of course, kissed like a master. I can't dwell on how many girls he might have kissed in his life. Just last summer alone. It's too many. This is why he's so good at it. Our kiss might've been brief, but it was by far the best kiss

I've ever experienced. He knew just what to do with his lips. And his tongue.

Especially his tongue.

Now here I sit in Jackson's car, and he's looking at me in this funny way, asking me really personal stuff. Face-to-face, which is not normal for him. He keeps all the personal stuff for over DMs or texts.

The little chicken shit.

"So these three guys, how were they?" he asks.

"What do you mean?"

"Kissing-wise. Too much tongue? Not enough?" He raises his brows.

"Not enough," I say immediately, thinking of Marshall's flickering tongue.

Gross.

"All of them weren't enough?"

"Most," I say with a shrug.

"Okay, okay." He nods. "Too much slobber? Too dry?"

"Slobber?" I repeat.

Jackson chuckles, and the gravelly sound wraps all around me, settling right between my legs. "I gather you haven't kissed someone who slobbers all over your face."

"Um, no." I grimace.

He's quiet for a moment, contemplating me. Studying me a little too closely, probably searching for the lie. I keep my face as impassive as possible. "Are you sure you've kissed three other guys?"

"Are you calling me a liar?"

He shrugs.

I bristle at that shrug. At the fact that he knows me so well, he can probably tell that I am, in fact, lying. "You're being really rude right now, Jackson."

"I want names, El."

"I'm protecting their privacy."

"Ha!" He laughs. "Come on. Give me names."

"Marshall, Bobby and Justin." Bobby was the kid I adored when we were in the first grade. He was so ridiculously cute. I just wanted to hang all over him and kiss his rounded cheeks. He moved away when we were eight.

I wonder whatever happened to Bobby.

And Justin is a general enough name that it feels safe. Yeah, of course I kissed a Justin. We all know about a bazillion Justins, it seems.

"Justin who?"

Damn it. He thinks he knows him. Of course he does.

"You don't know him."

"I might."

"You went to another school," I remind him. "This guy was older."

"How much older?"

"A year older than you," I answer.

"So you were kissing a guy who was two years older than you. When you were a sophomore," he says, his voice flat.

"Yeah. I was. Justin was super-hot. The only one out of the three who was good with his tongue." I nod. My lie just keeps growing.

He pins me with a look, his gaze serious. His entire demeanor serious. "Ellie."

"It's true! We hooked up at a party," I tell him, exasperated. More with myself because I'm a complete liar, and I don't lie. Not ever.

Well, I lie to Jackson on a consistent basis because I hide my feelings and pretend I don't care about him. Which isn't true. I care about him too much and if he asked me to be with him forever right now, at this very moment, I would say yes without hesitation.

I'm that much gone for him.

Deep down, I think he knows it. That's why he keeps me around. Why he helps me out. He probably feels sorry for me.

Oh God, that's the worst thing ever.

"Okay. Cool." He's nodding repeatedly, going along with my story. "So it's true. You hooked up with a senior at a party your sophomore year. Meaning you two probably did—other things. Am I right?"

I fold in on myself like a flower closing when the sunlight disappears. "That's none of your business." My voice is prim.

"Aw, Ellie. Come on. We're close. You're like one of my best friends," he says, his voice extra deep as he studies me. "You can tell me the truth. I can keep a secret."

It's the best friends comment that's like a douse of cold water, waking me up. Reminding me that's all I'll ever be to him. A friend. "I don't need to let you in on all of my secrets."

His gaze drops to my mouth, lingering there. "Really."

My lips part. He leans in. What is he doing? "Yes. Really," I say shakily.

"So when this Justin guy kissed you at the party, did he touch you anywhere?" He reaches for me, his hand settling on the outside of my thigh, his fingers perilously close to my butt. "Like here?"

"Yes," I whisper, sucking in a breath when he tries to drag me closer.

It's a little awkward in the front seat of his car, the console in between us, but he's managing.

"And I'm guessing he didn't just kiss you here." With his other hand, he touches my lips, his index finger dipping in between them for the briefest moment before he removes them. If I were quicker, I would've bit him. "But maybe... right here?"

Jackson leans into me, and I go completely still when he presses his face against my neck. I can feel him inhale, his mouth moving against my sensitive skin, feather light.

"Y-yes," I say, because I can't stop continuing the lie.

He kisses me, his damp lips clinging to my neck, making about a million shivers course through me. What is he doing?

"Did he touch you here?" he whispers against my neck, his hand coming up to gently cup my breast.

I close my eyes, falling under his spell. I have him all over me. Right where I want him. His fingers tighten around my breast, his thumb lightly tracing along the top edge of my bra, over my T-shirt. This is by far the most intimate a guy has ever had his hands on me. And it's Jackson.

Of course, it is.

"Ellie," he whispers, close to my ear. "Did he do this?"

He releases his hold on me to slip his hand beneath my shirt, his fingers skimming up my bare stomach. A jolt runs through me at first contact of his fingers on my skin, and I brace myself for more.

"Jackson." My voice breaks. My breath quickens.

"Did he?" His fingers trace the underside of my bra slowly, back and forth. Putting me in a trance. "Tell me. What did he do next? After he touched you here?"

"He kissed me," I say because that's what I want Jackson to do. What I want to feel.

Jackson's mouth on mine. His tongue sliding against mine. I want to swallow his groans and feel him press his body against me. I want all of that.

Even if he ignores me the next day, or treats me like I'm the same ol' Ellie for the rest of my days, right now, that's what I want.

I want it.

I want *him.*

He lifts his head and is so still, so quiet, I have no choice but to open my eyes to see what he's doing.

Watching me, his hand still under my shirt. "Has anyone ever made you come before, Ellie?"

I slowly shake my head, my gaze never straying from his. My body starts to tremble at his words, at the promise in them. It's in his eyes too. I know he could make me come. He just does it for me. I am completely caught up in him. No other guy has this kind of effect on me.

No one else.

Just him.

"Then you've been with some real shitty guys." He removes his hand from beneath my shirt and shifts away from me, plastering his back to the driver's side door. As if he needs the space.

From me.

"Yeah," I say, staring right at him, anger slipping into my veins, making my blood boil. "I have."

I'm referring to him. He's the shittiest one of them all.

"Want me to walk you to your door?" he asks.

I gape at him. What the hell was that just now? Feeling me up and then pulling away like he never touched me in the first place? I don't understand him. He toys with me because he knows he can get away with it.

"I can manage," I say tightly, reaching for the handle to open the door. I climb out of the car as fast as I can, slamming the door with extra force because damn, that felt good.

Jackson immediately rolls down the passenger side window. "Don't forget your stuff in the back seat."

When I left my car at the shop, I took out everything that was important to me. As if I might not see that car ever again. Which is silly and dramatic, but I couldn't help having that thought. What if my car is unrepairable? I'll be screwed.

Like, totally screwed.

I jerk open the back door and grab my backpack and the rest of my stuff. "Thanks again," I bite out.

I turn away from his car and march toward my apartment building, trying my best to fight my jittery nerves from having Jackson's mouth and hands all over me.

God, he's the worst.

He can decimate me with a few whispers, his mouth on my neck and his hand on my boob. He's deadly.

Awful.
I hate him.
Okay. Fine.
Not really.

———

I work at the Doghouse Grill. It's one of the most popular restaurants close to campus, if not the entire town. Customers spill into the place all day, all night. The parking lot is small and cramped, so it's a constant fight out there for parking. The line to order is always out the door, and we never seem to have enough seating for everyone.

We're slammed from the time we open until we close, and this means time passes really, really quickly. I got the job thanks to my experience working the fountain at one of the lakeside resorts in my hometown for three summers in a row. Most of the high schoolers work at the various resorts and restaurants that surround the lake. At the height of summer, we'd get slammed there too.

I'm used to a fast pace, and I'm super-efficient. I got hired here easily, and I love it. I make decent tips too. The only thing I don't like? The hours. We stay open pretty late, especially when management doesn't like to turn customers away. Only when the grill is completely closed will we finally stop serving food. Though the bar is always open way longer than it should be.

Most nights we close at nine, but sometimes I don't get out of there until around eleven. I don't like being out alone that late. Yes, I'm a big girl, but the crime rate is up in this part of town. I can't help but be a little nervous.

I'm a small-town girl, what can I say?

I never talked to Jackson about picking me up after work. Hayden dropped me off when my shift started—and then came in and ordered her and Gracie some food with my employee discount.

That's what friends are for, helping each other out.

It's a Tuesday, and we're still busy. A stream of students mixed with regular folks come in and out the doors all night. By the time I'm taking my break, sitting at a table near the back, close to the kitchen, my feet are aching, and it feels good to be off of them for a bit. I check my phone to see I have a text from none other than Jackson.

The jackass tease who felt me up and then essentially kicked me out of his car.

Jackson: **What time should I come pick you up?**

Me: **I already have a ride.**

Jackson: **From who?**

Me: **Why do you always think I'm lying?**

Jackson: **Maybe because you are.**

Irritation fills me and I hit the button so I can call him. He answers on the first ring.

"Who's picking you up?"

This is how he greets me.

"Hayden," I tell him, which is the damn truth. "She took me to work too."

"Tell her I'm picking you up instead."

God, he's so demanding. And annoying.

"You don't have to. You've done enough," I tell him.

"I'll text her and let her know," he says, cutting me off. "What time are you off?"

"Around ten or so," I say. "But really, Jackson. I'm fine. I don't need you to pick me up."

"See you then." He ends the call before I can say anything else.

Annoyed, I immediately call Hayden and tell her what he said.

"Hmm. Why is Jackson acting like this?" Hayden sounds suspicious.

I didn't tell her about my interaction with Jackson last night in his car. She only knows about my car breaking down and him coming to my rescue. The other stuff...I'm not ready to share yet.

"I don't know. I'm sure I'm reading too much into it," I say, deciding to be truthful.

"Yeah, but it's weird, ya know? Is it one of those, *I don't want you, but no one else can have you either* situations? If that's the case, he's a straight-up douche," she says.

I'm quiet for a moment. "We already know he's a straight-up douche."

"True." She sighs. "I think he has a hero complex when it comes to you."

"What do you mean?"

"He wants to be your hero. Run to your rescue. Fix your problems so you'll be indebted to him forever," she explains.

That actually makes a lot of sense. "Maybe so."

"It might give him a sense of power over you. I don't know. I should've been a psychology major," she says. "That kind of thing fascinates me."

It fascinates me too, but only when it comes to Jackson. Most of the time I don't understand his motives. And he doesn't explain himself at all, which makes it worse.

"Should I still come and get you?" she asks when I haven't said anything.

"No." I sigh. "He sounded pretty determined about being my ride."

"If he makes you mad, text me and I'll come get you, okay? It's not a big deal," she says.

"I hate to ask you to do that when it's so late." I chew on my lower lip, glancing around the still very busy restaurant. It's almost nine. Don't these people have somewhere else to be?

"I don't mind. I'm not that far and I'd probably make Tony go with me. He's at my apartment right now," she says.

"Oh, I don't want to interrupt you guys. I'm fine. Really."

"Text me if you want. I mean it."

We end the call and I glance toward the front doors, just in time to see Carson walk through them with one of his friends.

Well, well. If that doesn't make things even more interesting. I never told him I worked here, so he didn't do this on purpose. This is again one of those random meet ups that we keep having.

Makes me wonder if he's the guy I'm supposed to be with. Fate playing a part, maybe?

I sit up straighter, willing Carson to see me. Remembering what Jackson said to me last night. How I need to show some non-friendly vibes. More like some flirty, *I want you* vibes.

Now I'm not exactly sure if I want Carson, but I definitely can be flirty.

Carson is too busy looking at the menu board on the wall above the order counter, so I rise to my feet, making my way over to them. As I draw closer, I see he's with one of the guys he brought with him to Hayden and Gracie's party. He's the one who notices me first. He jabs his elbow in Carson's ribs, who glances in my direction.

And breaks into a giant smile.

"Ellie. We've got to stop meeting like this," Carson says.

I laugh. "I know, right? How are you?"

"Hungry. Glad this place is still open." He scrutinizes me carefully. "Do you work here?"

I nod. "I do. I've only been here a month."

I'm suddenly okay with us still being open and customers still walking in.

"Nice. We've never been here, but heard it's good," Carson says, glancing over at his friend who nods in agreement.

"It's really good. And I'm not saying that just because I work here." I smile. "Get the tri-tip sandwich."

"Is that your favorite?"

"I love their salads too. And their fries."

"Thanks for the recs."

The girl working behind the counter sends them an irritated look. "Are you finally ready to order?"

"Uh...yeah," Carson says as he steps closer to tell her what he wants.

I wave at them and take off, a little giddy. I need to get back to work. I've been assigned bussing tables tonight. Helping customers out if they need anything. We rotate on the schedule. A lot of the time I'm at the register taking orders, but not tonight.

Tonight, I have more freedom. This is my least favorite task, but I do get to move around a lot, which is good, especially now that Carson is here.

Once they place their orders, they get their drinks and find a table. I walk over to them with a fresh, damp rag and clean the table quickly.

"How are you?" Carson asks. "How's your car?"

I saw him in class earlier today, and he didn't ask me about it. Though I did arrive to class with little time to spare once the professor launched into his lecture, so I suppose that was part of the issue.

"It's in the shop. It needs a new alternator," I answer with a frown.

"Ah, that's too bad. They can be kind of expensive," he says.

"Yeah, they can. And my car is old, so they had to special order the part. It's this whole process I really don't need in my life right now," I admit.

"That's tough." Carson's expression is sympathetic. His friend appears bored out of his skull. "You remember Jonah, don't you?"

"Yeah." I wave at him and he smiles back. "Hi Jonah."

"Hey." He tips his head toward me before returning his attention to his phone.

"I should get back to work," I tell them. "It was nice seeing you."

"Yeah, you too, Ellie," Carson says.

I head for the patio outside and grab one of the tubs that's kept behind a counter out there that we use to clear tables. I stack up the empty baskets and glasses inside before I wipe down the tables, breaking out in a sweat as I work. It's still really hot outside, despite the hour and the fans whirling overhead. September in Fresno is still pretty miserable, temperature-wise.

In fact, it's downright awful.

I grab the tub full of dirty dishes and push my way through the double doors, back into the restaurant. I stop short when I see who's sitting at the bar, chatting up the bartender as if he's an old friend.

Freaking Jackson.

His gaze finds mine immediately. Of course he does. We're aware of each other, even when we're pissed at each other. And I am. Pissed.

At Jackson.

I send him a small smile as I march through the restaurant toward the kitchen with my chin held high, trying my best to look dignified but probably failing miserably.

Once I'm in the kitchen, I drop the tub off by the dish-washer and wipe a hand across my brow, pushing aside the flyaway hairs that always come out when I'm working. Why is Jackson here so early? And why is he sitting at the bar? He's not even twenty. He can't drink.

It sucks that he shows up at the restaurant when Carson is here too, but Jackson wasn't aware of his presence. So I guess I can't be mad at him.

You know what? Yes, I *can* be mad at him. He wasn't the one who was supposed to pick me up in the first place. That was Hayden's job tonight. And she wouldn't screw up anything I potentially could have with Carson. More like she would encourage it.

If Jackson knows that Carson is out there? He will do his damnedest to sabotage it. Sabotage me and Carson. Which is a total jerk move, but guess what?

Jackson can be a jerk. Especially when it comes to me.

Frowning, I push my way through the kitchen's double doors, my gaze falling to Carson's table. They already have their food and they're digging in, too preoccupied with eating to notice me. Or Jackson.

Who is currently also watching them with a faint sneer on his face.

I glare at him, and as if he can feel my eyes, he lifts his gaze to mine, one brow shooting up. I slowly shake my head, not afraid to show him just how annoyed he makes me feel.

He smiles in return and turns his back on me, chatting up our friendly bartender, Chuck.

Ugh. Jackson Rivers is absolutely infuriating.

Putting extra swing in my step, I make my way to Carson and Jonah's table, my voice extra loud as I ask, "How's the food, boys?"

Jonah nods, giving me a thumbs up since his mouth is full.

"Really good," Carson says with an easy smile, his appreciative gaze streaking down the length of me. I must look a mess since I've been working for five hours straight, but he doesn't seem fazed by my stained T-shirt. "Thanks for the recommendation. The tri-tip sandwich is delicious."

"Right? It's my absolute favorite, though after a while when you work here? You get sick of the food," I admit.

"Yeah. That would kind of ruin it for me," Carson agrees.

I laugh, as if he told a fantastic joke. Which, you know, he didn't, so I'm being extra over the top. Trying to be flirty.

Doesn't come naturally but I'm giving it a whirl.

"Are you ready for the math test tomorrow?" Carson asks me.

I nibble my lower lip and shake my head. "I'll need to study for it after work."

"Burn the midnight oil?"

"You know it," I say with what I hope is a flirty grin.

"If you need help or have a question, you should text me," he says. "I'm here for you with whatever math needs you may have."

I blink at him, realizing he's flirting right back. If I really knew what I was doing, I'd invite him to my apartment so we could study together. But that might send the wrong message, and I barely know this guy. He seems perfectly nice and normal, but I still don't know him well enough.

"I totally will," I say, smiling. "You know I'm not great at math."

"Oh, I remember," he says before shoving a couple of fries in his mouth.

"I should get back to work," I tell him.

"Yeah, we're almost done," Carson says, picking up his sandwich.

I leave them be, trying to ignore Jackson over at the bar. But there are a couple of tables in that area that need clearing, and that's my job for tonight, so eventually I'll need to go over there.

May as well make it now.

Thinking I can sneak past Jackson unnoticed is silly of me. Of course, he spots me. And of course, he has something to say about it.

"Putting some of my tips to use, huh?"

I come to a complete stop, glaring at him. "What do you mean?"

"Flirting it up with ol' Carson over there. How convenient that he showed up tonight," he says.

I absorb what he just said. The look on his face. My gaze goes to the drink in front of him. Looks like iced tea. Maybe he does know Chuck. Maybe he thought he could come in here and kill time before I'm off work. Maybe I'm overre-acting about him showing up when I don't necessarily want him around.

But then again, maybe it's a good thing he did show up. I don't think I'm overreacting when I think this but...

Pretty sure Jackson Rivers is jealous.

CHAPTER 15

JACKSON

I showed up at Doghouse Grill a little early in the hopes I could just hang out until she's ready to go. Maybe talk to Ellie for a little bit, watch her in her element. Plus, this is a favorite spot for me and my friends to come eat. The food is good. The atmosphere is fun. You always run into someone you know here, like it's one big party.

Pretty dead tonight, though. And I already ate dinner, so I'm not hungry. Chuck the bartender is a Bulldog football fan, so he's easy to talk to. I've chatted him up before, and he knows I'm on the team. He waved me over when he spotted me walk in and offered me a free iced tea so I'm not going to turn him down. Wish it was laced with something else, but I'm underage, which sucks major ass.

What I didn't expect was to see Ellie's potential new love interest here with his dorky friend. Making eyes at her as if she's the prettiest girl he's ever seen.

Here's where I'm getting real.

I have been with beautiful women. Talked to them. Kissed them. Had sex with them. I moved around a lot when I was younger. I have seen a lot of parts of this country and done a lot of things. The summer tour only reiterated my feelings about my life, and what I can do with it.

As in, I don't want to settle down. Especially not now. I'm young. There are plenty of women out there I haven't met. Beautiful, gorgeous, down for anything women.

My favorite type.

Here's where it gets tricky.

There is something about Ellie. She's pretty. No, more than that. She's beautiful. On the outside, as well as the inside. She's got that sweet, girl next door vibe going for her, and I can't help but find it attractive.

As in, I'm attracted to her.

There. I admitted it.

But.

Isn't there always a but?

I am not good enough for her. I will only disappoint her in the end. What I want, she can't give me. She'll get too involved, because she cares too much, which is one of her best traits. And while I will do whatever I can to help her, to be there for her, to be her friend, that's *all* I can do.

I realized this last night, after I went home and jerked off in the shower to thoughts of fucking Ellie in the back seat of my car. I don't know what possessed me to say those things to her. To touch her like that. It's been a while since I've had sex. I need to rectify that.

I need to get laid.

Watching her talk to Carson just now, though, did something to me. Twisted me up inside. Filled me with this weird, unfamiliar sensation that I can't quite describe.

I think it's jealousy.

I turn around on the barstool and watch her blatantly flirt with Carson. Well, as blatant as Ellie can be. She's not that great at it. This is why guys treat her as a friend. She's cute, but she's not particularly flirty. She's nice. Sweet.

Damn it, she's beautiful and even though her T-shirt is stained and her hair is a bit of a mess, she's got denim shorts on that make her legs look endless and I wonder what they would feel like circled around my hips while I drove myself into her...

I snap to attention when she makes her way over to the bar area. Turn around on my stool so I'm facing Chuck once more.

"You playing this weekend?" he asks me.

"I hope so," I tell him. "Though I'm more of a pro-bench-warmer right now."

Chuck laughs. "You'll eventually get your chance."

"Sure." I sound doubtful because I am. Feels like I will never get my chance, which I'm okay with because swear to God, right now it feels like being on the football team is a break from real life. From making decisions that only involve me.

The hairs on the back of my neck stand straight up. I can smell Ellie. Her delectable, unique scent. I can also feel her anger. It's a palpable thing. Aimed straight at me.

"Putting some of my tips to use, huh?"

The words fall out of me before I can even think.

She comes to a complete stop, glaring at me. "What do you mean?"

"Flirting it up with ol' Carson over there. How convenient that he showed up tonight," I mutter.

Ellie comes right up to the bar, standing to my left. I glance up at her, noting the shrewd look on her face. I think she has me all figured out.

Fuck, I hope not.

"Didn't expect you to show up either," she says.

I lift a brow. "I am your ride, after all."

"You're early."

"I wanted to chat up Chuck." I wave a hand toward him. He laughs.

"Right." She draws the word out, like she doesn't believe me.

This is the game we're currently playing. We're lying to each other. I'd bet major money that she hasn't kissed three other guys. The story about making out and getting felt up with the fictional Justin?

All bullshit.

Gave me the excuse to feel her up though. Her tit fit perfectly in the palm of my hand. She shivered when I kissed her neck, and slowly but surely melted beneath me.

I'd also bet major money that it would be good with her. I could make her come easily with a few strokes of my fingers. What would she do if I put my mouth on her? Damn, what would she look like on her knees in front of me, her mouth stuffed full of my cock? Holy shit, that would be a sight to—

"Have fun talking to Chuck," she says to me. "I still have a least an hour left before I can clock out."

She walks away and I watch her go, appreciating the little twitch her butt makes with her every step.

"She's a good girl," Chuck says once she's out of earshot.

"Yeah, she is," I say miserably as I turn to face him once more.

"Your friend?"

I nod.

"She wants more though?"

I nod again.

"If she were my daughter, I'd tell you to stay the fuck away from her," Chuck says, not holding back whatsoever.

"I get it," I say morosely. What he speaks is the truth.

Ellie should stay the fuck away from me.

"She's the type who goes all in. You'd probably break her heart," he continues.

"I know."

"She's also the type who'd do her damnedest to please you for the rest of your life. Which would have you wanting to do the same, just to earn that sweet smile of hers again and again," he speculates.

"You're probably right." There are girls you fuck around with and girls you revere and put on a pedestal, because you know they're not built for that.

And that's Ellie. She's not the girl you have a casual thing with. She feels too much. She'd fall too hard.

"Don't mess with her head," Chuck says, his voice stern, reminding me of my father. "Don't be telling her you want something more when you don't."

"Relax. I've got it under control," I say, flashing him a smile.

He scowls at me in return.

Guess that charming smile only works on the ladies, not middle-aged bartenders who know what I'm all about.

I turn and watch Ellie unabashedly as she works. Carson and his friend eventually leave, and of course, Ellie talks to them before they go, but they're too far away so I can't hear what they say. She watches them go, a wistful look on her face and I remember when she used to look like that over me.

Seeing her face, watching her with that Carson dude, reiterates what I already know.

I messed up with Ellie. Big time.

The front doors are eventually locked and the open sign turned off. Management lets me stay because Chuck vouches for me. I keep out of the way as the remaining employees wipe everything down. Ellie and another girl hurriedly mop the floor—what a shit job. Chuck does a thorough clean-up of his bar space.

I sit there like a prince and watch the servants work, like the spoiled brat I truly am. I've never had to hold down a job such as this in my life. I worked the dock at one of the resorts on the lake back home the summer between my junior and senior year, but that wasn't hard work at all. I was taking in boats and flirting with old ladies and getting tips. Working with a couple of guys who turned into my friends, having the best summer ever. I was tan as fuck and looking good. By the time I arrived at school my senior year, girls were literally falling at my feet.

It was a good time.

Around ten, Ellie is finally ready to go.

"I clocked out. You ready?" she asks as she approaches me.

Nodding, I slide off the barstool and leave a ten-dollar bill in the tip jar for Chuck. "Let's do this," I tell her.

We walk out into the arid night, the heat still lingering. There are only a few cars left in the small lot, and Ellie follows me to mine, not saying a word.

I don't speak either.

Not until we're inside the car and I've finally started the engine does she say something.

"Thanks for coming to pick me up, even though you didn't have to."

Well. That was a shitty thank you.

"You're welcome," I bite out, hating how annoyed I sound.

Also hating how annoyed I get when Ellie isn't happy with me. Which is most of the time, nowadays.

"Have you heard anything about my car?" she asks.

I shake my head. "I'll call him tomorrow and see what's going on."

"I hope it's ready soon."

"I hope it is too."

Then I won't have to give her a ride anymore or see her as much. I really wouldn't have to see her at all, save for when our friend group gets together. Even then it's not like I'd have to talk to her.

I should probably cut her off, even though I'll miss her. She's a good listener. A thoughtful friend.

But right now, sitting in my car, filling the air with her

unique scent, her essence, the last thing I want to do is talk to her. I'm not having friendly feelings toward her either whatsoever.

What the hell is wrong with me?

I clutch the steering wheel tightly, trying to keep myself preoccupied with other thoughts. Like school. I have a psych test tomorrow and I'm not even close to being ready for it. I should go home and study, but who wants to do that? I think of football. Practice. It was tough today, and I'm starting to feel like a failure. Like I'm not measuring up. I'm a third string running back, and there's a fucking freshman who's gunning for my position.

I need to step up my game, but why bother?

"Is there an away game this weekend?" she asks me, as if she's in my head. Knowing Ellie, she probably is.

"Yeah. San Diego." At least we're going somewhere cool. Not that I'll get to enjoy it like I want to.

"Do you think you'll get a chance to play?"

"Probably not," I immediately say. "I'm not that great."

"Jackson," she chastises, her voice soft.

"I'm serious, El. Just keeping it real with you. For whatever reason, I can't get my shit together on the field, and the offensive coaches are noticing. I don't know what my problem is," I say, frustration filling my voice. Filling my head.

I'm irritated on almost all counts right now. I don't know what's up.

"Is there anything bugging you?" she asks, sounding generally concerned.

She blows my mind. Girl will hold a grudge and treat me like garbage—which I deserve—and then I tell her I'm having trouble with something, and she goes straight into nurture mode. What is her deal? Why does she care so damn much?

She shouldn't care about me. I don't deserve her worry or concern.

Wonder what she would do if I told her what was really bugging me right now.

It's her. *She's* bugging me. My feelings for her bother me. Confuse me. I don't understand them.

"Did you plan another date with Carson?" I ask, switching the subject.

I can feel her gaze on me, but I refuse to look at her.

"No," she says softly. "He didn't ask."

"You're going to wait for him to ask then?"

"I think so."

"You shouldn't. Grow some balls. Take the reins. Ask him out," I say, sounding like an asshole.

"Jackson, what in the world is wrong with you?" she asks, exasperated.

I say nothing. Just clutch the steering wheel tighter, hitting the blinker and turning onto her street. I'm so close to getting rid of her. I need to. She's fucking with my head. My thoughts. My libido. I'm an Ellie-induced mess.

By the time I'm pulling into her apartment parking lot, she's undoing the seatbelt, eager to get the hell away from me. I park the car, ready to say something, but she's already opening the door.

"Thanks, bye," she says hurriedly as she climbs out of my Mercedes, shutting the door behind her.

I throw the car into park and cut the engine, ready to chase after her. Though I shouldn't.

Yeah. I totally shouldn't.

I do though. I exit the vehicle and make my way after her, calling her name.

She literally turns around and holds her finger to her lips, shushing me.

"My neighbors are sleeping," she whisper-yells.

I can't help it. I laugh.

And keep following her.

Ellie stops in front of a door on the ground level, which

doesn't thrill me. She should be on the second floor at least. I haven't been to her apartment yet, so I had no idea. At least the complex is quiet. Gated. Newer, and in a decent part of town.

I still worry about her safety though.

"This your apartment?" I ask, already knowing that it is.

"You didn't have to follow me to my door," she says, sounding irritated.

"I wanted to."

"Okay. Whatever. Thanks again for the ride, Jackson." She sticks her key in the deadbolt at the same time that I approach her, stopping just behind her.

"Can I come in for a little bit?"

She shakes her head, keeping her back to me. "I have roommates. I don't want you to wake them up."

"I can be quiet. Do you have a room to yourself?"

She nods. "You can't come in, Jackson."

I press my hand against the door, crowding her from behind. "Why not?"

"I don't want you to," she admits.

We're quiet. I can hear her breathe. There's a warm breeze outside, and it stirs the wild strands of her hair. All I want to do is smooth them down. Run my fingers down her neck. Kiss her there. Pull her into my arms and not let her go for the rest of the night.

But I can't. I can't do it.

I'd fuck everything up.

"I never did tell you what's bugging me," I murmur, giving in to my urges and tucking a few strands of her silky soft hair behind her ear.

She goes completely stiff. "What is it?"

Leaning in, I whisper close to her ear, "It's you."

Ellie turns to face me so fast, I rear back a little, giving her the room she needs. She shoves at my chest, her face screwed up in anger, her eyes blazing with fury.

"Don't give me that bullshit, Jackson. I'm so tired of you acting like a possessive asshole yet you won't do anything about it."

I frown. "What the hell are you talking about?"

"You act like my boyfriend, yet you won't touch me. Or you will touch me, but you never take it too far. Afraid you might break me or whatever," she says, her words hot. Girl is mad. I kind of like it. "I won't break, Jackson. I'm tougher than I look. I can handle you. I've been handling you for years."

"You haven't handled all of me," I boast, unable to resist.

She socks me right in the chest again, and this time, it kind of hurts. "See? It's shit like that. You flirt with me. You've kissed me. You freaking felt me up in the car last night, yet you won't do anything else. I don't understand you. Glaring at Carson like you want to rip him apart when he talks to me. It's stupid! You're being really, really stupid right now, and you need to stop. Or—"

Ellie presses her lips together, cutting off whatever else she was going to say.

"Or what?" I ask when she remains silent. I press both hands against the door, caging her in, standing so close to her you probably couldn't slip a piece of paper between us. I can feel her heat, her chest rise and fall when she breathes. She's beautiful, even after working a long shift, even with God knows what staining the front of her shirt. She's even more beautiful than usual because she's all worked up, pissed off at me, and God help me, I like it.

"I was going to say, you need to do something about it," she admits, her voice small. "You know how I feel about you. There's no point in my explaining it. But I don't know how you feel about me."

"I care about you, El. You're my fri—"

She shakes her head, the look on her face making me snap

my lips shut. "We have more than friendly feelings toward each other, and you know it. Admit it."

I remain quiet. To admit what I feel for her could change... Everything.

The silence stretches, and I can feel her withdrawing. I don't want that. I want her into this. Into me. Yes, I care about her. Yes, she's my friend. I've thought about more with Ellie before. Of course I have. And the way I feel about that little prick coming around her is confusing. My raging emotions have me tied up in knots.

So tight, I'm afraid the only one who can untangle them is her.

"Make a move, Jackson," she says softly. "Or let me go forever."

I stare at her, frozen, her words on repeat in my brain.

Make a move? Yeah, no. I remember what Chuck told me. What I've told myself. This is a girl I shouldn't mess with. No matter what she says, I know in the end...

I will hurt her.

"Well?" She lifts her chin, her dark eyes blazing into mine. "What's it going to be?"

The words flicker through my brain at the same exact moment my lips find hers.

Fuck it.

CHAPTER 16

ELLIE

O h God, Jackson is kissing me. What I said to him actually worked. I figured he'd bail as usual and I'd be left all alone with my thoughts, bitterly disappointed in him yet again.

Instead, his mouth is on mine. Hungry. Insistent. I'm pressed in between the door and his muscular body, and there is nowhere else I'd rather be. He kisses me stupid, his tongue searching my mouth, his hand dropping from the door to land on my hip, pulling me closer to him.

I can feel what I'm doing to him. Wait a minute. Is that his—

Oh my God, it's *huge.*

He winds his arm around my waist, his hand finding my butt and holding me close. A whimper sounds, and I realize it's me.

I'm whimpering.

Without hesitation, I sling my arms around his neck. Bury my fingers into the silky soft hair at his nape. Return his kiss with all the enthusiasm I've kept pent-up inside of me. He won't let up, and I'm not even sure how we're breathing, but I don't want this moment to end.

I'm consuming him as he's consuming me.

He wraps his other arm around me as well, and somehow, he lifts me, my legs automatically going around his waist. He pins me to the door, pressing his denim covered erection right against the spot where I ache for him the most and oh my God, when he does that, I see stars.

We let our mouths and hands do all the talking. Words ruin everything, especially between us. He finally breaks the kiss, only to run his hot mouth down my neck. Licking. Nibbling. His hands are sprawled across my butt, pulling me into him as he rubs against me. I grind against him right back, letting my body take over and do its thing. An incessant throbbing starts between my legs, making me feel greedy. I want more.

More, more, more.

"Let's go inside," he whispers against my lips, just before he resumes kissing me. This goes on for minutes. Hours. I don't know. I've lost all track of time thanks to Jackson. "Show me your bed."

It's the way he says *show me your bed* that brings me back to reality. I press a hand to his chest, pushing a little. He breaks the kiss, lifting his head so our gazes meet, our heavy breaths mingling.

"I don't know," I tell him.

He frowns, lowering his brows. "What do you mean, you don't know?"

"What's going to happen if I 'show you my bed'?"

"I'm going to make you feel good," he says, his voice full of promise as he leans in to kiss me again, but I keep my arm extended so he can't.

I know he can deliver on that promise. I'm just not sure if I'm ready to go there yet. I talked a good game just now, but I know myself. I feel too much.

For him.

"And after that?" I'm shaking. I don't know why. Nerves maybe? I'm definitely not cold. I feel like I'm burning up.

"I don't know. Does there have to be an after that? Can't we just let it play out?" he asks, sounding pained.

"With me and you? Yes, there has to be an after that. Letting it play out might end up a total disaster." I nod, proud of myself that I said it.

He needs to know he can't just fuck me and forget me. Not that I think he would, but knowing Jackson, if we did actually have sex? Afterward, he'd avoid me.

For months, even years, if things got awkward.

Knowing us, they'd get mega awkward.

He leans his forehead against mine, closing his eyes. "You think too much."

"It's my best and worst trait." I touch his face. His achingly beautiful face. I run my fingers along his jaw, committing to memory the agony in his gaze as I touch him.

He's affected by me. He can say and do whatever he wants, but he cares.

He just doesn't know what to do with those feelings yet.

And that's the only reason I'm letting things go this far between us in the first place. Deep down, I *know* Jackson has feelings for me. He's just afraid. Of me. Of us.

Of everything.

"Are you going to let me come inside?" he asks.

"I shouldn't," I tell him truthfully.

"Come on, El. Let me." He grips my hips again, his touch and tone persuasive. "I'll stop if you want me to."

See how he knows we're going to do something that I might want to stop? Besides, it's Jackson.

I won't want him to stop. I didn't want him to stop just now. I had to get my feelings out first. But did he actually hear me? I don't know.

"Okay," I whisper like an idiot.

He lifts his head from mine, his smile triumphant while

carefully setting me on my feet. We don't say a word as I finish unlocking the door and slowly open it, letting him in first. It's dark inside, not even a lamp left on, which is fine. I have my flashlight on my phone and I can make my way around the place without running into furniture.

I'm still not that familiar with my new home, but I'm getting there.

It's a four bedroom, and I have three other roommates. All girls I don't know, but so far, we get along okay. I'm not necessarily close to any of them yet, and the arrangement we have is nice, since we don't share a bedroom, so at least we each have some privacy.

Tonight, in this very moment, I'm very, very glad Jackson and I will have privacy. Otherwise, it wouldn't be happening.

I shut and lock the door before I lead him to my bedroom upstairs. The townhouse is tri-level, with two bedrooms on the top floor, the common living space on the second, and two other bedrooms on the bottom. Jackson follows me up the stairs closely, nearly bumping into me, and I wonder if he's just eager, or only trying to remind me that he's there. Maybe a combo of both?

Or maybe I'm just overthinking things as usual.

Cracking open my door, I'm about to quietly sneak inside, but Jackson pushes at the door instead, making us both barrel in. He shuts the door for me and turns the lock, an ominous sound in the otherwise quiet room.

I swallow hard when he hits the light switch and the overhead light comes on. The hungry expression on his face as he studies me, and I feel decidedly lacking.

"Uh, I need to change first." I glance down at my dirty clothes.

"You won't need to change," he says with a wicked smile.

"Can I at least shower?"

"Did you dip yourself into a vat of barbecue sauce?" he asks. "Or maybe ranch? Spill a gallon of beer on your shirt?

"What?" I frown. "No. Well, maybe a half gallon of beer."

He laughs, and it is the best sound. "Then you don't need to take a shower."

"I might smell," I tell him as he makes his way toward me.

"I'm willing to take my chances."

"You should turn off the light."

His gaze darkens. "I want to see everything."

Oh. Shit.

I mean, I want to see everything too. It's Jackson, after all. But I'm nervous. Self-conscious.

"Please?" I whisper.

He stops in front of me, huffs out a breath and goes back to the door, where the light switch is. He hits it again, shutting the lights off before he walks past me and turns on the lamp that sits on my bedside table.

"Compromise?" he asks, lifting his brows.

I give a jerky nod, fighting the nerves that suddenly swarm me.

After I drop my keys and my phone on the bedside table, he wraps me up in his arms and just holds me for a moment. The two of us standing beside the bed, not saying anything. I cling to him because I can, absorbing his heat and his scent and his strength. Everything about him, I want.

I'm nervous though. So nervous. And worried. Having him in my bedroom is sending a message. Things are going to another level between us, and I hope I don't regret it.

God, I'm so scared I'll regret it.

His lips touch my forehead. My temple. He's breathing me in; I can hear him inhale. I tighten my arms around him, taking advantage of this position, enjoying the sensation of his strong arms wrapped around me. I could stand like this for hours and not complain.

He reaches for me, his fingers coming under my chin, exerting gentle pressure. I lift my head up to find he's already watching me. His eyes aren't so full of hunger anymore.

There's something else there. I can't quite figure out what it is. Maybe nerves, like me?

Doubtful. Again, this is Jackson. He's done this sort of thing a million times before.

But he's never done them with me.

His hand shifts to my cheek, cradling my face, his gaze never straying from mine. We're still not speaking. I also still stand by my assessment that words tend to ruin everything between us. As in, we say all the wrong ones, and make each other mad.

Right now, the silence is perfect. His actions are telling me what he wants.

Me.

Dipping his head, he brushes my mouth with his own in the softest of kisses. The moment our lips touch, I melt. Without thought I reach up, my hand sliding around the back of his neck, holding him to me. His mouth is on mine again. And again. I open to him, his tongue a tease, sliding into my mouth. Quickly retreating.

The way he kisses me is perfect. Dreamy. I want more.

I tighten my fingers around his nape, indicating just that and he deepens the kiss. His arm squeezes me closer, pulling me into his long, hard body and I wish we were already on the bed.

Where I could rub my body all over his.

But I'm getting ahead of myself. Right now is for kisses. Sweet yet slightly filthy kisses that are full of tongue and soft moans and low groans. Testing and teasing, trying to figure out what the other likes. Wants. Needs.

I like, want and need all of it.

We kiss each other as if we're ravenous. As if we've been holding back for so long, and we're finally giving in to our urges. This is how I feel, at least. I've been pent-up, longing for this boy, this man, for what feels like forever. He's shown me so many pieces of himself, but never this. This is the one piece he's kept hidden away from me. It feels like a triumph, that his hands are finally on me, and his mouth is fused with mine.

Like I've won the grand prize.

My phone starts to buzz from where I left it on the bedside table and I ignore it. The buzzing stops, only to start up all over again.

"Maybe I should get that," I say against Jackson's lips.

"No," he says, just as he devours me again.

I forget all about the buzzing, consumed by Jackson consuming me. That deep ache is back between my thighs, reminding me that I want more. The longer he kisses me, the lower my inhibitions become. I can feel the urgency grow until it's a steady, demanding beat.

My phone buzzes again.

"I need to see who that is," I say after I rip my lips from Jackson's.

He breathes deep, his arms springing away from me as he lets me go. I check the phone and see it's Ava trying to Face-Time me.

At ten thirty at night.

I send Jackson a helpless look. "I should answer it."

He nods. Swallows hard. "Go for it."

Not caring that she'll see us together, I answer the call, my image popping up in the camera as I wait for Ava to appear and Jackson's nowhere in sight, completely out of view. I look a mess. Thoroughly kissed, my lips swollen, my eyes bright. I run a hand over my hair, tucking the strands behind my ears and finally, Ava's face appears.

It's soaked with tears.

"What's wrong?" I say, my heart freezing in fear. "Is everything okay?"

She sniffs. Dashes a hand under one eye, then the other. "I hate it here," she wails.

I collapse on the edge of my mattress, my own heart

breaking at seeing my best friend so upset. "Aw, you'll get used to it."

"I miss everyone. Why did I leave? What was I thinking? I miss my mom and dad, and Beck. I miss Eli so much. I miss you." She starts to actually cry. "I miss everyone. I have no friends. My boyfriend is going to break up with me, I just know it."

"Wait, what?" I shoot a look in Jackson's direction, who just shrugs in reply. "What do you mean, Eli is going to break up with you? Did he say something?"

"No, not at all. I'm just worried. How did my sister make her long-distance relationship work with Ash? I don't get it. I want to fling myself off a bridge, I'm so miserable," Ava says.

"Hey, don't say stuff like that. You're scaring me," I tell her, dead serious.

"Oh, like I'd actually do that. You know I wouldn't." She sniffs. Wipes at her face with one hand, her eyes bloodshot. "I'm sorry I'm calling so late. Eli was exhausted. We talked for two hours tonight, and he was falling asleep right in front of me. I miss him so much."

"I know he misses you too. I also heard he's going to San Diego to play your school," I say. "Doesn't that make you happy?"

"Yes, at least I'll get to see him, but it won't be enough." She sniffs yet again, clearly feeling sorry for herself. "I'm coming home during his bye week."

"When is that?"

"First week in October. I can't wait. I'll get to see you too." She offers me a weak smile. "What are you up to?"

Uh, about to mess around with Jackson? We might even have sex?

Yeah. Can't say that. Especially in front of Jackson. "I just got off work. Was about to go to bed."

"You like working there? At Doghouse?" she asks.

Clearly, she wants to have a conversation.

I send Jackson a sympathetic look and he plops down on my bed, stretching out his long legs toward me, his head propped on my pillows. He slips his arms behind his head, watching me with a smirk on my face as I listen to Ava. She's lonely, I can tell. I would be too if I were her, missing all of us, who are all still pretty much here together.

So I let her talk, and tell her that I miss her when she starts to wrap the conversation up.

"You should come to San Diego too," she suggests.

"I wish I could, but I'm working this weekend," I say. "Plus, my car is at the shop. It needs a new alternator."

"Oh no," she says. "What happened?"

And that turns into an additional five-minute conversation. I glance up to check on Jackson to see he's lying there, the smirk gone, his eyes closed.

Damn it, he's going to fall asleep.

We talk some more, because screw it. Jackson is sleeping. I can tell by how deeply he's breathing. And he's so cute. He looks so young when he's asleep. Like a cute little boy.

Who can kiss like a demon and from what I can tell, has a monster dick.

Oh geez, where did those thoughts just come from?

Blushing, I maintain a normal conversation with Ava and never once bring up Jackson. Not even in regards to the car repair. We end the call with lots of I love yous, I miss yous and hope to see you soon.

I carefully set my phone on the bedside table and watch Jackson. He's still asleep. Dead to the world.

Since nothing is currently happening, and I don't want to disturb him, I decide to take a shower.

It feels good to wash the slime of my evening off of me, and actually, I'm really glad Ava interrupted us. I did not want to have one of my first sexual experiences with my dream man happen while I smell like the Doghouse Grill.

Gross.

I wash my hair and lather my body in my favorite body scrub that leaves my skin feeling smooth and soft. Once I'm done, I dry off, use my favorite scented lotion, put on a cute pair of short pajamas I bought at Target a few weeks ago, and then open the bathroom door to see—

Jackson is still asleep. This time lying on his side, his mouth partially open, the occasional huff of sound coming from his lips.

Like a snore.

I cover my mouth to stifle any noise I might make. Like laughter. I creep around the bed to the other side and make sure my phone is charging before I turn off the lamp. Then I return to the empty side of the bed and carefully lie down next to him, on top of the covers. My eyes slowly adjust to the darkness, so I can barely make out his features. Unable to help myself, I reach out and touch him. Trace the length of his strong nose. One sharp cheekbone. Then the other. His lips.

His eyes snap open at the same time his fingers circle around my wrist, stopping my progression. "Gotcha."

My heart trips over itself. "You scared me. How long have you been awake?"

"The entire time," he says.

"No way." I don't believe him.

"You came out of the bathroom." He sniffs the air, scooting closer, his face right in my damp hair. "You took a shower."

"I did. Now I don't smell like a grill anymore," I say.

"Yeah, you smell way fucking better." He releases my wrist to scoop me up, pulling me into his body. "Is Ava okay?"

"No," I say. "She says she hates it there."

"She's homesick. Seeing Eli this weekend will make her feel better." He dips his head, his mouth on my neck. "You should come to San Diego."

Is he inviting me to watch him play? Maybe spend time with him? Or is it only for Ava's sake?

Probably the latter.

"I can't." I close my eyes, my hands going to his shoulders. "I have to work."

"You always have to work." He drops kiss after kiss on my sensitive skin, making me shiver. "Trade shifts with someone."

"I need the money. That's why I always work."

He says nothing. Just continues to kiss me. Nuzzle me. Lick me. Oh God, when he uses his tongue, my imagination explodes. I wonder what else he can do with it.

Many, many wonderful things, I'm sure.

His head lifts and his mouth is on mine. The kiss goes instantly deep, and I pull him to me so I'm on my back and he's above me. His hands are on my waist, and he slips them beneath my T-shirt, skimming my sides, gooseflesh rising in their wake. When his hands find my breasts, they come to a stop.

"No bra?"

I shake my head. What was the point? At the time, I was hopeful. Plus, I don't wear a bra to bed. I rid myself of that thing as much as possible.

He cups my breasts, his thumbs streaking across my nipples, making me hiss in a breath. "Let's take this off."

Jackson helps me take off my shirt. Somehow, his disappears too. And when he returns to kiss me yet again, I nearly want to cry at how good it feels to be with him, skin on skin. His is hot and smooth and hard, with soft hairs on his chest, right in the center. I run my hands over his broad shoulders, clutching him to me as we kiss and kiss, our legs tangling together.

His hands race over my skin, searching everywhere he can reach. One hand slides over my stomach, heading south, fingers toying with the waistband of my sleep shorts. His other hand cupping my breast before tracing circles around my aching nipple. His mouth is still on mine, our tongues dancing. I'm overwhelmed with sensation. His hands are literally everywhere, his tongue and mouth stealing my breaths, my thoughts. I'm shaking. Nervous. Excited. Anticipating what's going to happen next.

When he slips his hand beneath my shorts, I don't stop him. When he encounters nothing but bare flesh, he makes an appreciative sound. And when his hand dips further, his sure fingers finding my pussy, I moan into his mouth, encouraging him.

Oh God, that's exactly what I want.

Those expert fingers begin to move, parting me. Searching. Sliding over my wet skin. A choked sound escapes me when he finds my clit and strums it, his rhythm slow at first, picking up quickly. I cling to him, my entire being focused on that one spot between my legs as I hold my breath. He removes his mouth from mine, shifting to my ear and whispering, "Relax," right before he sinks his teeth into my ear lobe.

It stings. It feels good. So good. I move my hips with his hand, straining toward it, wanting more. He withdraws his fingers to get rid of my shorts, fumbling as he yanks them down. I help him, kicking them off, desperate for him to put his hand back on me and then his fingers return, making me cry out in relief.

"Shh," he murmurs, his mouth hovering above mine. "Don't want to wake up the roommates."

He kisses me before I can say anything, his fingers busy, his tongue thrusting. I cling to him, gasping into his mouth when he slips a finger inside of me.

This is the absolute farthest I've ever gone with a guy. He's going to make me come. I can feel the orgasm looming, building with his every stroke. He increases his speed, pulling out to rub my clit, and I grab hold of him tightly, a frustrated cry falling from my lips.

I'm so close. Desperate to fall over that edge.

He kisses me. Softer this time. His fingers slow, the intensity lessening. I feel like I'm floating on a cloud, lost in the delicious sensation his fingers are drawing out of me. I'm so wet, I can hear them search my folds, gliding over me, and I lie there, solely focused on his fingers. My throbbing clit. His mouth on mine. His tongue.

The intensity slowly returns, but it's somehow smoother. Not as frantic, but still consuming. My breathing increases with his every stroke, his thumb pressing against my clit and from out of nowhere, it hits me.

I'm coming.

My body is consumed with shivers, a soft cry falling from my lips that Jackson swallows. Time stops, but he never stops touching me, kissing me, and the orgasm feels as if it could go on forever. My heart feels as if it could beat right out of my chest and I arch my back, my hips lifting, seeking his fingers. Not ever wanting him to stop.

Until it's over, and I'm practically begging him to stop. It's too much. My skin is too sensitive. It's literally throbbing in time with my heartbeat.

I can't say anything. I'm too focused on calming my heart rate, my still rattled body. He shifts away from me, his hand still on my hip, his head dipping to draw my left nipple into his mouth. He sucks it deep, making me wince in pain. In pleasure. I rest my hand on his shoulder, gently pushing him away and he stops.

"You okay?" he murmurs against my temple as he drifts the back of his hand across my stomach.

I nuzzle against his bare chest, my mouth brushing against his hot skin as I speak. "Yeah."

"Was it good for you?" I can hear the humor in his voice. I think he already knows the answer to my question.

"Yes," I say.

He kisses me, so tenderly I almost want to cry. It's like that orgasm brought all of my emotions to the surface, and I'm barely hanging on. Especially since I'm experiencing all of this with Jackson. It's like a dream come true. "You should go to sleep. I bet you're tired."

"But what about you?" I try to look up at him, but he's holding me too tight.

"I'm fine," he says.

I can literally feel his erection between us. He is far from fine.

"Jackson..."

"Stop." He kisses my forehead again. "Let me take care of you."

I remain quiet as he crawls off the bed, watching him as he pulls back the comforter and sheet to tuck me beneath it. I see his unmistakable erection tenting the front of his shorts and I'm so tempted to touch it. Stroke him. See what he does.

I'm also afraid he'll reject me, so I keep my hands to myself.

He pulls the covers up to my chin, smiling down at me before he kisses me on the lips. It's chaste. Sweet. He smiles. Rises to his full height and grabs his T-shirt that is lying on the end of my bed, ready to slip it on.

"Are you leaving?" I ask incredulously.

He frowns. "You don't want me to?"

I shake my head. That he even has to ask blows my mind.

"Stay for a little bit," I whisper.

He drops his T-shirt where he found it and climbs into bed with me. Pulls me close. Holds me tight.

I fall asleep immediately.

CHAPTER 17

JACKSON

S hit.

I can't sleep. My mind is racing over what I did to Ellie. Jesus.

I stripped her naked. I made her come with my fingers. In the scheme of sexual things, it shouldn't be that much of a big deal. What's a finger bang in the scheme of life? It's no biggie.

But with Ellie, this has been building up between us. We've just changed…

Everything.

I know she has to be a virgin. She's never said it out loud, but come on.

It's Ellie. She's definitely a virgin. The fictious three other guys she made out with besides me did not do what I just did to her.

Nope. No way.

I'm still as hard as a rock. And she's been asleep for the last ten minutes at least. Maybe longer. I've lost track of time. All I can focus on is her hot little naked body smushed up against mine. Her ass rubbing my dick. No wonder I'm hard.

A sigh leaves her when I squeeze her closer. It would take

nothing for me to get rid of my shorts and boxers and slide into her welcoming heat. When I slipped a finger inside her earlier, she'd been so tight. Squeezing around me like a vise. That's why I didn't use a second finger. I was afraid I might hurt her.

Virgins aren't my style. I like my women experienced. Up for anything and everything. Hell, I usually like the foreplay stuff better than the actual act, because with actual sex comes so much more than I can deliver.

Expectations. Commitment. Even if it's committing to another hookup the next day, the next week, the next month, I usually avoid that sort of thing. One and done is my mantra.

A mantra I live by.

Until this moment. I can't imagine trying to give the one and done treatment to Ellie. She'd hang me up by my balls, all her girlfriends gleefully helping her do it. I can imagine the blood thirsty grins on their faces. Ellie. Ava. Hayden and Gracie…

I shudder at the thought.

So what do I do now? How do I handle this? I still need to help her out with her car situation. I need to pick her up from work tomorrow night. Probably the night after that too. What are we going to do? Come back here and mess around some more?

My dick twitches. I guess that's its way of saying yes.

Damn it, I think I've fucked everything up.

It takes me a while, but I eventually fall asleep. And dream, of course. Scary ass dreams of Ellie in a hideous, bright white wedding dress, chasing after me down an endless aisle, her friends—the bridesmaids all wearing matching hideous yellow dresses—chanting my name over and over again. Until I'm suddenly at a concert, on stage, ready to perform. But every girl watching me in the audience looks exactly like Ellie in that damn wedding dress. Haunting me.

Taunting me.

My eyes snap open and I blink the room into focus. Ellie is still nuzzled up against me, her back to my front. Dim grayish light is filtering through the blinds and I try to roll over as slowly as possible, so I don't wake her up.

It works. I roll right out of bed and check my phone. Just past five.

I need to get the hell out of here.

I slip my shirt back on and step into my slides. Grab my phone and wallet from where I left them, along with my keys. Go back to the bed and drop a light kiss on Ellie's forehead before I exit her room. I make my way down the stairs and am just about to open the front door when I hear a rustle in the kitchen, an unfamiliar girl standing at the counter, dressed in workout gear and a banana in her hand, watching me with her mouth hanging open.

"Ellie's boyfriend?" she asks me, her voice squeaky.

I smile at her, unlocking the door. "Sure."

I don't say anything else as I slip through the door and quietly shut it behind me.

———

I do terrible on the psych test, but I don't even care. It's only twenty points and it's still early enough in the semester that I can pick up my grade, no problem. Once I'm done with the two classes I have in the morning, I go in search of Caleb, who also has an hour break in between classes. We usually grab something to eat on campus and chill.

Caleb is a great guy. He's also a complete horn dog. Women are his main focus of study on campus, and what I mean by that is he thinks about them constantly. As in, he wants to conquer as many as possible during his college years. He has this giant fear of becoming complacent once he graduates. He thinks he's going to end up exactly like his father, which isn't necessarily a bad thing. His dad seems like a cool enough guy. Works hard, been married to Caleb's mom for over twenty years. They live in a small house. Caleb had a relatively simple life growing up, but they seem like happy, well-adjusted people.

Why Caleb acts the way he does, I don't know. I don't question it either. He confuses me. You'd think he'd want to be like his parents eventually.

Caleb is also a lot more introspective than any of us give him credit for. When Tony was going through his issues with Hayden, it was Caleb who gave him solid advice, surprising all of us.

I guess I shouldn't be surprised then, when he sees me as I approach him in front of the on-campus Starbucks, that he says, "What the hell is wrong with you?"

Settling in the chair across from his, I pull my sunglasses out of my backpack and slip them on, staring up at the sky. "Nothing. Didn't sleep much."

"Why? Banging some hottie?"

We have that in common—always in search of girls. We might've also gone out on the prowl together a time or two. I'm the last one standing beside him, he always says. It's just the two of us who don't have a girl attached at our side all the time, which Caleb thinks is absolute bullshit.

I never remind him of how he still hooks up with Baylee on occasion. Girl has crushed on him for what feels like forever, according to everyone else. She's the girl he kept as a secret side piece the last two years they were in high school. She took all of his shit, and still came back for more. I don't know if that means she sees the potential in Caleb, or she's a complete idiot.

"Not really," I hedge, not sure if I want to tell him about Ellie.

Everyone in our friend group knows that Ellie has crushed on me for a long time. At first, they assumed we would end up together. At one point, I wondered if it would happen as well. But I resisted. I kept on resisting. Eventually, everyone figured that it wasn't going to happen. The guys felt sorry for Ellie because she was still hung up on me. The girls thought I was leading her on, and told me privately I was an asshole who needed to make it happen or cut ties.

That last bit was brought to me by the ever unfiltered, tell it like it is Ava Callahan.

I get why she said that. She's Ellie's best friend. She wants to protect her.

Which makes me think of that FaceTime call last night, and how Ellie never mentioned I was there. Not once. And I spied on that conversation openly until I eventually fell asleep. I'm fairly confident she never mentioned my name while I was sleeping either.

Interesting.

"Not really, you didn't hook up with someone, or not really because you did, and you don't want to talk about it?" Caleb asks, always curious.

"I don't want to talk about it." I keep my head tilted back, still facing the sky, but I'm giving Caleb serious side-eye.

He grins. Literally rubs his hands together. "Come on. Spill. I need deets. Was it filthy hot and you want to keep her to yourself? Afraid she'd see me and dump your skinny ass?"

Caleb is bigger than me, and he never lets me forget it.

"Nah, that's not it," I tell him, keeping my expression neutral.

"You're embarrassed because she's your secret ho and you don't want us to know who you're fucking on the low?"

Shit. That is scarily accurate. Though Ellie isn't a ho. Far from it. "We're not fucking."

Yet.

That sends a shiver down my spine.

"Jackson. Come on. Be a homie and tell me what

happened last night." He pauses for a second, that grin still on his face. "And with who?"

I turn to look at him, slowly shaking my head. "Nope. No way. No deets. You'll tell people."

"Who the hell would I tell? And who would care? Everyone we know is all lovey-dovey and getting fucked on the daily by their significant other." He sounds so annoyed, his smile long gone. "Please don't tell me you're keeping this under wraps because you're going to end up like the rest of them."

I frown. "What do you mean?"

"Tied down at the tender age of nineteen and in a committed relationship." He rolls his eyes. "Seriously, what the hell is going on with everyone? Why are they wanting to get so serious, so fast?"

I shrug. "Sometimes you just know when you've found your person, I guess."

"You've been spending too much time with the girls," he mutters, shaking his head. "You sound just like them."

"I sound just like who?"

"Hayden. Ava. Ellie." He waves a hand. "Ugh, Jocelyn. She's the worst when it comes to believing in true love and all that shit."

"Caleb. You sound crazy right now," I tell him, not holding back. "So down on our friends' relationships."

"You're usually down on them too." He reaches over and nudges me in the shoulder.

"Where did you go? I want my friend back."

"It's still early. Plus I'm tired," I admit.

His grin returns. "Right. Banging your secret hottie. Give me deets when you're ready to reveal. You know I'll be sitting here waiting impatiently to hear what's going on and with who."

Yeah. Not going to happen for a while. Once they find out I'm messing around with Ellie, the shit is going to hit the fan.

And splatter everywhere.

I go about the rest of my day in somewhat of a fog. Tired from lack of sleep. Confused over what I did with Ellie. Confused more by my feelings for her.

As in, I'm not sure how to feel. Where to go next with this. And why can't I stop thinking about her?

By the time we're wrapping up practice and in the locker rooms, I'm moving slow, going through the motions, and not talking much. I'm eager to get out of here, go straight home and collapse into bed.

But I can only take a nap, because I still need to pick up Ellie after she gets off work. Not that I've confirmed this with her. Like a complete shithead, I haven't texted her all day. And she hasn't said anything to me either. Haven't seen her around on campus, though I never really do, unless we all plan to meet up, which hasn't happened since school started.

Does this make me an asshole for not contacting her? I am the one who slipped out of her room in the early morning hours without a word or a note or a text. She's probably pissed at me.

What else is new?

"Wanna go grab dinner?" Diego asks us as he slips a shirt on over his head.

"Don't you have to run home to wifey?" Caleb asks, taunting him as usual.

"Jocelyn and Gigi are with her mom and sister. They're shopping, having dinner, whatever. Addie got her braces off today so they're celebrating," Diego explains. Addie is Jocelyn's little sister.

"So you're a free man for the night?" Caleb offers up his hand and Diego slaps it. "Let's go."

"I'm fucking starving, so I'm down," Eli says, his gaze cutting to mine. "How about you?"

I should say no. I'm tired. I could go back to our apartment and get a few hours of sleep under my belt before I have to go pick up Ellie.

But my friends are watching me with hope in their eyes. They want me to go with them, and I can't resist these fuckers.

"Sure," I say easily. "I'm hungry."

"Let's go to Doghouse Grill," Eli says, and they all nod in agreement.

Except for me. Shit. I don't want to go there. Not tonight. Really don't want the first time I see Ellie after what happened last night to be witnessed by my friends.

They'll give us endless shit, especially if Ellie reacts negatively toward me, which she has the potential to do. I am the asshole who hasn't reached out to her after I reached between her legs.

If she's mad and acts rude toward me, they'll ask what I did to piss her off, and what can I say?

No big deal. We kissed. I took her to her bed. Stripped her naked. Touched her everywhere. Fingered her until she came. Held her close and slept with her for a few hours until I snuck out of her bed without a word. And that was it. Big mistake, am I right?

That I even thought of the words *big mistake* makes me feel like a complete dick.

Everyone else agrees that we're going to Doghouse Grill, so I have to agree, too. Which I do with a barely there shrug. Eli catches my gaze, frowning in question, and I just shake my head.

"You're riding with me," he says, pointing his finger at me.

Great. Now I'm going to have to explain myself. I'd love to avoid this conversation.

Looks like I'm not gonna.

Once we're in Eli's Charger and he's fired up the engine until it roars, he pulls out of the parking lot and immediately starts talking.

"What is your deal? Why didn't you want to go there to eat? Does it have to do with Ellie?" Eli asks.

He's far more aware of the Ellie thing than anyone else, only because we lived those moments together during our senior year. When he was in hot pursuit of Ava and Ellie became my new adoring fan.

"She might be mad at me," I say.

"Why?"

"We might've done something last night."

Silence fills the interior of the car, making me squirm.

"What exactly did you two do?" he asks carefully.

"You can't tell anyone. Especially Caleb." He will never let me live this down.

Let's be real. None of them will let me live this down.

"Dude, just spit it out," Eli says impatiently.

"We hooked up."

More silence as Eli absorbs what I just said.

"Really? How was it? Did you fuck her? Please tell me you didn't fuck her," Eli says, keeping his gaze on the road.

"I didn't fuck her. But we did other stuff." I don't need to go into detail.

"Damn bro. I never thought you'd actually go for it." He shakes his head. "How was it?"

It's none of his damn business, but I guess I need to give him something. "It was—good."

"Want more?"

"Yes. No. I don't know." I shrug. "I don't normally return for seconds. Or if I do, it's only because I know I'll never see her again."

"You're probably going to see Ellie a lot over the next few years," Eli reminds me.

"I know," I say miserably, hating that I sound so down and out. "I fucked up."

"Maybe. Maybe not," Eli says.

"What do you mean?"

"Keep it light. Keep it casual. See what happens. Ellie might be down. She's eager to take any bit of attention you toss her way, I know that," Eli explains.

"You make her sound desperate," I say, my voice edged with steel. I don't like hearing him talk about her like that. "She's not."

He actually laughs, the fucker. "Simmer down. I'm not knocking your girl. I'm just stating facts. This is a girl who's been worshiping the Jackson Rivers shrine for a long ass time. She'll do whatever she can to keep you."

"Eli, what the fuck are you saying? I don't want to string her along. She's the serious type. You know this," I point out.

"Right. You're right. But she might be the nonserious type too. You'll never know until you talk to her." He turns onto Shaw Avenue and we're only minutes from the restaurant. "I say you go for it."

"Are you giving me permission?"

"If that's what you need, then yes." He grins. "Do it. Do her. Do her all night long, for as many nights as possible. Let it happen. See where it takes you."

"If Ava heard you say this about her best friend, she'd kick your ass," I remind him.

The look of terror on Eli's face almost makes me laugh. "You can't tell her. She'll kill me."

"You'd deserve to be killed." I finally do laugh, but it's brief. "I can't use Ellie like that."

Eli exhales, shaking his head. "I know. I was just talking out my ass. She's a good girl, Jackson."

"I know. She's one of the best." The absolute best. So responsive. So pretty. So sweet. All mine.

Yeah, no. Those last two words don't apply. Well, they do. She could be all mine. All I have to do is say the words and I could make it happen.

Egotistical of me to think, but it's true. She wants me.

Damn it, I want her too.

Could I keep it casual with Ellie? Probably not. She'd be in way too deep. She probably already is.

The problem? I don't want pressure and commitment. I just want more.

More Ellie.

CHAPTER 18

ELLIE

've walked around in an orgasm-induced fog for much of the day. Silly, right? Jackson makes me come once and I can't stop thinking about it. How perfect the moment was—at least for me. I'm sure it would've been better if he'd let me do something for him, but of course, typical me, I was too scared to push.

As I go about my day, I become more and more confident. I'm not even mad that he slipped out of my bed God knows when and didn't leave a note or text me. He hasn't texted me all day. And that's all right. I'm cool with it. I'll see him again tonight, when he picks me up after work, and then...

Then I'll jump him.

I'm downright giddy at the thought.

I take the bus from campus back home after class so I can get ready for work. I really miss my car. Maybe I should text Jackson and ask if he's talked to the mechanic yet? I don't want to seem pushy...

Ugh, I hate how I second-guess myself.

Entering my apartment, I find my roommate Alaina sitting on the couch, watching TV. She glances in my direction when she hears the door open, her face lighting up.

"Ellie! Hey, hi!"

I shut and lock the door before I turn to face her, confused by her enthusiasm. She's been the least friendly of my three new roommates. Not that she's been mean or anything, but she hasn't been especially nice either.

"Hi. How are you?"

"Good. Great! How are *you* is the question." The sly look she sends my way has my mind going blank. She's watching me as if she knows all of my secrets.

But what could she know?

"I'm good," I say carefully as I enter the living room, clutching the strap of my backpack. "It's a Wednesday, you know? Closer to the weekend."

Which I still have to work, so a weekend doesn't equate days off for me. I do have Sunday off though. Friday and Saturday night are both going to be busy, though not as much as usual since the football team is playing an away game.

"Yes. Right. The weekend. I'm guessing you'll be spending it with your boyfriend?" The pointed look she sends me, along with her words, makes me realize that she probably saw Jackson.

But when? Not when we arrived. The house was quiet. They were asleep.

Maybe this morning when he left?

"Um, I don't really have a boyfriend," I admit.

"That's not what he said." Her tone is knowing and when I continue to stare at her helplessly, she throws her hands up. "Girl, you've been keeping secrets! That boy is *gorgeous*."

"Oh. Uh, yeah."

"Having middle of the night hookups with a complete hottie." Alaina shakes her head. "I must've seen him around campus before. He's really familiar. And really hot, too. I didn't know you had it in you."

"What do you mean, had it in me?" Now I'm vaguely offended.

"That you could snatch up a guy like that. Whew." She fans herself. "I about died when I saw him sneaking out of the house this morning."

And there's my confirmation. "What time was that at exactly?"

"Little after five. I like to get up early and go running, remember." Alaina is a running freak. She owns so many pairs of running shoes, it's borderline obsessive. She showed us her collection when she first moved in, and even admitted she didn't bring half of it.

What she did bring seemed pretty excessive.

"He was about to leave when he glanced over at me standing in the kitchen, eating a banana. I about swallowed my tongue when I saw him." She's staring at me in amazement. "Please tell me you two hooked up."

What I really want to tell her is that what Jackson and I did is none of her business, but I don't have it in me to be that rude. I just smile and nod, trying to look mysterious, not saying a word, but she won't let me get away with it.

"Come on," she says. "You have to tell me."

I don't have to tell her anything. "He's an old friend," I finally say. "We've known each other since high school. He's a year older though."

"He said he was your boyfriend," Alaina says.

I frown. "Really?" I find that hard to believe.

She nods. "Well, I asked him if he was your boyfriend, and he said yes. Maybe you two need to have a little talk. Define what you guys are doing."

Alaina grins. I scowl. I don't understand where she's going with this. Or why she cares so much. Maybe she just likes to gossip. Or maybe she's digging for info on Jackson because she's interested in him too.

I look at her—as in, I really take note of her features. Long brown hair. Pretty face—not outrageously gorgeous or anything, but she's really cute. Slender figure. Tall. Extremely fit. Eats well, a vegetarian who's considering going full vegan. She's probably Jackson's type.

But does he even have a type? To me, he seems to appreciate all females, which is so freaking frustrating.

I'm selfish. I want him to only appreciate me.

"Like I said, we're just friends," I tell her, deciding to remain honest. "Maybe there's potential for more, maybe not. We'll see."

"I love your attitude, Ellie. I wish I could be more like you. When I meet a guy I like, I go all in—and somehow, I always mess it up." Her compliment makes me feel bad for judging her earlier and looking at her as competition. "I wish I was more casual with my feelings like you. I'd give anything to be able to keep an open mind and not fall so hard for someone that I can't even see straight."

I mull over what Alaina said to me as I get ready for work. She thinks I'm super casual over this situation with Jackson, when that's the furthest thing from the truth. I'm not casual at all. I am in love with stupid Jackson Rivers and I have been for over a year. I've let him keep stringing me along like the complete dumb girl I am.

And now when he gives me a crumb—okay, it was more than a crumb—of attention, I've got stars in my eyes all over again and orgasms on the brain. As in, when can he give me another one?

What if he never gives me another one? He could totally freak out. That's his way. He's not one to stick with a girl for very long. He can't commit. And according to Caleb, I have commitment written all over my body like invisible tattoos.

He told me that once last year at a party when he was drunk and annoyed with women in general. I adore Caleb most of time, and at one point in my life had a major crush on him, but he can say some really awful things.

I suppose it's part of his charm.

Hayden texts me as I'm doing my hair, pulling it into two

tight braids so that'll it stay out of my face completely tonight. I don't care if I end up looking twelve.

Hayden: **I can't take you to work, but Gracie can!**

Me: **Oh no! Are you okay?**

Hayden: **Turns out I have a dentist appointment I completely forgot about. They called me and left a voice-mail confirming it yesterday and I didn't check my voice-mail until an hour ago. Oops. I'm sitting in the waiting room now.**

Me: **Is Gracie cool with taking me? I could find another ride if I have to.**

Hayden: **No, she's fine with it! She adores you. You know this.**

I smile. I suppose I do. I adore Gracie too. I adore the both of them.

Me: **Have fun at the dentist!**

Hayden: **It's just a cleaning but ugh. LOL See ya sweetie!**

I can't help but think I have good friends.

I'm bounding down the stairs when I get a text from Gracie.

Gracie: **I'm in your apartment parking lot, ready to take you to work.**

Me: **You're the best! I'll be right out.**

I grab my purse and leave the apartment, glad no one is around that I have to talk to so I can escape quickly. As I make my way toward Gracie's Honda Civic, I contemplate what I should say. If I should tell her about what happened between Jackson and me last night. Though she might imme-diately assume he's going to do something terrible, which we all know he's capable of. And he's capable of doing some crappy stuff. Like possibly ignoring me.

God, I hope not.

Why am I thinking such negative thoughts anyway? Gracie will be excited for me. And neither of us should automatically assume he's going to do something terrible. He's not a horrible human.

Most of the time.

Ha.

I've never really talked to Gracie alone for a long period of time. It's always Hayden and Gracie together. The drive to Doghouse Grill isn't long. Ten minutes if traffic is bad. But we're early, and we have time to chat in her car if she wants to.

I might want to.

As I get closer, Gracie spots me and waves, hitting the unlock button so I can open the passenger side door. I slide into her cool vehicle and shut the door, smiling over at her.

"Thank you so much for driving me to work."

"It is no problem." She glances around, peering out the windshield. "This complex is so nice."

"Thanks. I like it here. I feel safe."

"I love that it's gated. Our complex isn't. My mom had a fit about that, but we're on the second floor, so that calmed her down some." Gracie rolls her eyes as she puts the car in reverse and backs out of the parking space. "She's super over-protective sometimes, and I'm almost twenty-one for God's sake."

"My parents are really overprotective too," I admit, gnawing on my lower lip, dying to blurt out that I messed around with Jackson last night.

But I keep the words locked in, waiting for the right moment.

"They can't help it, I guess." She glances over at me as she waits for traffic to pass before pulling out onto the street. "You like working at Doghouse Grill?"

"It's okay. Great tips. Really fast-paced, which helps the time fly by. I see lots of college students," I tell her.

"Cute boys?"

"Yes," I say with a smile. "Lots of those."

"I should hang out there for a while tonight then. I need a new man in my life," she says with a sigh.

"What happened to Franz?" He seemed sweet. Not very talkative, though. Tall, with a hint of dork. I love that Gracie doesn't discriminate when it comes to guys. She's attracted to all types.

"We were bored with each other," she admits. "We couldn't really make conversation. And yes, sometimes I'm not in a relationship for conversation, but I do want to be able to talk to the guy before and after the good stuff, you know what I mean?"

I have zero experience with that, but I nod like I do.

"Were you attracted to him sexually?" I ask.

"Sort of. He was a decent kisser. But that's about as far as it got before I realized maybe he wasn't the guy for me." She sends me a quick look. "Hayden says I'm addicted to the chase. Once I catch them, I'm over it."

"Maybe you are," I say gently. I definitely think Hayden is onto something.

"That sucks. Makes me sound shallow."

"I'm thinking it's more you just haven't found the right guy yet," I say, not wanting her to believe she's shallow. She's not. Gracie has substance. She's smart and fun and she wants to be a teacher and work with little kids. That's awesome. So what if she hasn't figured out what she wants in a guy? This is why she keeps dating all sorts of them.

She's trying to find the perfect man for her.

"I suppose," she says, sounding weary. "My mom says you have to kiss a lot of frogs before you find your prince."

"Sounds like your mom is wise." I pause. "Or she really likes clichés."

Gracie laughs. "Both. I don't know. I'm starting to think I need to go on a man ban and focus on my path to discovery. A little self-help is always good for the soul."

"A man ban?" I laugh. "I like the way that sounds."

"You should join me. I'm sure you'd benefit from a man ban too, since Jackson always strings you along." She presses her lips together, regret on her face. "That sounded mean. I'm sorry."

"No, it's true." Until last night. "Here's where I say I have something to tell you."

"Oooh, what is it?"

"You can't tell anyone."

She holds up her hand. "Scout's honor."

"Not even Hayden."

"What? I don't like keeping secrets from her! More like it's impossible for me to keep secrets from her."

I sigh. "Seriously, Gracie. This is big. And I want to be the one who tells Hayden."

I'm terrified of what Hayden might say though. And Gracie too. But the cat is halfway out of the bag so I don't have a choice.

"What is it?"

Here we go.

"Jackson came over to my apartment last night and…" I don't finish the sentence.

Gracie's quiet for a moment. The silence is a killer. I'm literally squirming in my seat.

"And what?" she finally asks.

"We kind of…hooked up."

She squeals. So loud, I wish for the silence again. My ears are literally ringing.

"Are you fucking serious?" she screeches.

"Yes! Can you believe it?" I shout, then immediately clear my throat. I need to calm down. "We did."

"What happened?"

"Um…" It's hard for me to say the words out loud.

"P into V?"

"No."

"Mouth on P. BJ."

I shake my head.

"Ooh, mouth on V." Her smile is dirty, there is no other way to describe it.

"I wish," I say on a sigh.

"Did he finger you, Ellie?" I slap my hands over my face and she bursts out laughing. "Oh my God, he did! He finger-banged you!"

"I've always hated that term. It's so…crass."

She laughs some more. "Please tell me he made you come."

"Uh…yeah."

"Nice! Did you give him a hand job?"

"No."

"No?" She sounds almost alarmed.

"He said he wanted to take care of me," I admit.

Another sigh leaves her. "He's got a serious hero complex with you. Hayden is right. He has a thing about always rushing in to take care of you."

"Why do you think he does that?" I ask, genuinely curious. I've tried to figure him out, but I'm at a loss most of the time.

"He's put you on a pedestal. A lot of men do this. I think it's called the Madonna whore complex? Like, he desires you, but you're his friend and he respects you too, so in his head, he shouldn't fuck with you," she explains, frowning. "I'm messing this up. But I think you know what I mean."

"I do," I say, glancing out the window. "I don't want him to see me as some sort of Virgin Mary he can't touch."

"*Are* you a virgin, Ellie?"

"I am." And I'm not even embarrassed by it. I'm only eighteen. I've never really had a serious boyfriend before. Last night with Jackson is as far as I've ever taken it.

But I'm ready to do more.

"That's a lot of responsibility for a guy like Jackson," she says. "He seems the type to always want to play around and never commit."

"I know. He's afraid of commitment. His parents had a nasty divorce." And he told me about it too. How it messed with his head. Made him realize he didn't want to get married. He even said he doesn't want kids.

I thought at the time he just hadn't found the right woman yet. Like Gracie and her endless dating. But maybe he's telling me the truth. Maybe he really has no desire to get married and have children. He wants that rock star life, where he's free to do whatever he wants with no responsibilities.

"That can mess with people's heads, witnessing the fallout of their parents' relationship," Gracie says. "But hey, this is progress in your relationship with Jackson. Have you talked to him? You two been texting all day?"

I slowly shake my head. "We haven't talked."

"At all?" She sounds incredulous.

"Not at all. He's supposed to pick me up from work tonight."

"And you haven't texted him to confirm that?" She makes a noise. "That is the perfect excuse. You need to text him right now. Pronto. Ask him if he's still getting you."

"Okay, okay, but he's at practice right now. He won't answer me." It's almost five o'clock. He's still on the field.

"Whatever. He'll get the text when he's done and answer you. If he doesn't, though..." She shakes her head firmly. "What a dick! You'll know where you stand."

Uneasiness fills me at the idea of him not responding. I would be devastated. "It won't be too pushy?"

Ugh, I need to stop being so insecure. Two seconds ago I was feeling on top of the situation. I *am* on top of it. And Jackson is finally giving me what I want—his attention. Himself. I need to stop worrying over every little thing and stand up for myself.

I've got this.

"Push as hard as you want! It's your right. He had his fingers between your legs last night. He's seen your O face. Don't you want to see his O face?" she asks.

Yes. Yes, I do.

"Right. Your lack of answer is a yes. Text him right now."

I send him a quick text.

And hope I get to see his O face tonight.

CHAPTER 19

JACKSON

We enter the Doghouse Grill and stand in line, the guys joking and giving each other shit while I remain quiet. They ignore me, and I wonder if they can feel the tension radiating off of me in waves. I'm a strung-out mess.

All over seeing Ellie.

I need to get a fucking grip.

She's not at the counter taking orders, which is something she does on occasion. It's some other cute girl who is flirtatious with every single one of us, including me.

"Aren't you Jackson Rivers?" she asks me before I even give her my order.

I can hear Eli snickering behind me. The asshole.

"Yeah." I smile, not in the mood to lay on the charm, as usual.

"I love your songs," she says, snapping her gum. "I listen to you on Soundcloud."

"I'm on Spotify too," I tell her.

"Yeah, but you've got a couple of covers on Soundcloud that you don't have on Spotify. I like the covers a lot. Your Nirvana remakes are amazing." She grins.

I check her out. I can't help it. She's cute. Tight little body. Nice smile. Good lips. Decent tits.

Not interested.

"Thanks," I say. "I want a cheeseburger."

I give her the rest of my order and pay before heading for the soda dispenser. Caleb is waiting for me, a mystified expression on his face.

"That girl was all over your stick," he says.

"She was not," I say irritably, as I fill my cup with ice and then add Cherry Pepsi.

"She so was. Flirting hardcore and you didn't even notice." I can feel him watching me. "What the hell is wrong with you?"

"Nothing," I say with a shrug as I snap a lid on my drink and grab a straw. "I'm not going to fuck around with some girl who works with Ellie, Caleb. I'm not stupid."

"Oh. Good point. I would've jumped all over it and then fucked everything up." Caleb frowns.

Sounds about right. But I don't say that out loud.

Caleb doesn't think before he leaps. He just jumps—consequences be damned. I'm pretty much the same way, so I really have no room to talk.

We find a table and wait for our food, and I keep watch for Ellie to appear. I don't know where she's at, but I know she's here. I got her text when we finished with practice, asking if I was going to pick her up tonight. I said yes, and now here I am, way earlier than planned, which might throw her.

But then again, maybe she'll be glad to see me.

The double doors that lead to the outside patio swing open and she appears, a big smile on her face as she carries a tray of empty glasses with one hand, balancing it with ease. Oh damn, she looks fine as fuck in those short shorts and the navy Bulldogs T-shirt that clings to her chest perfectly, her dark hair in two braids that hang long past her shoulders, showing off her adorable face.

"Ellie!" Diego shouts, and she stops, pivoting toward our table when she sees us all.

Though I'm fairly certain she hasn't noticed me yet.

They all greet her when she stops by our table, making idle conversation as she nods and smiles at each of us. Her gaze settles on me and her smile becomes knowing. As if we share a little secret.

Which we do.

I can't help but smile at her. It's automatic. Like breathing.

"Hey, Jackson." Her voice is completely normal.

I almost sag with relief.

"Ellie. Looking good." I nod toward her, unable to help myself.

Her cheeks turn pink. "Thanks. You're still picking me up tonight, right?"

"You didn't get my text?"

"I haven't had a chance to check it yet. Been on duty."

"I'm coming back to get you," I confirm.

"You can come in early and hang out with Chuck again if you want," she says with a shrug.

"Is he working?"

"Sure is."

"I might do that. Kind of tired though. Was up late last night," I say.

"Oh?" Her eyes are wide. Her cheeks now blazing red.

The guys swivel their heads from me to her and back to me again.

"Yeah. Might take a nap before I come back here."

"Okay. Sure." She nods. Swallows hard. "See ya."

She leaves.

They all look at me.

"What the fuck was that about?" Caleb asks, always the no nonsense one.

"Just their usual banter and shit," Eli says, rushing to my defense. "No big deal, right, Jackson?"

"Right," I say, taking a giant drink of my Cherry Pepsi.

But they're probably all on to me. Fuck it.

I sort of don't care. Would they really give me a bunch of shit if they found out Ellie and I have hooked up? Maybe. Caleb would for sure, but only because he doesn't want to lose me as his last single friend.

We talk. About all sorts of things. Mostly football. I don't say much. Just nurse my Cherry Pepsi, my eyes tracking Ellie's every movement when she comes into view. She's helping customers. Bringing them whatever they requested. Clearing their tables. Laughing and joking with a group of guys.

That makes the hair on the back of my neck rise up.

My number is called first and I go to the counter to pick up my food, waiting as they grab a couple of containers of ranch for me.

I smell Ellie before I actually see her.

"Didn't expect you to come in so early," she murmurs as she sidles up next to me.

I flash her a quick smile. "The guys wanted to come."

"And you didn't?" The disappointment on her face is obvious.

I hate that I put it there.

"Like I mentioned earlier, someone kept me up late last night." I reach out, tugging on the end of her braid, my fingers brushing against her chest.

The disappointment is gone, just like that. "I'd tell you I'm sorry, but I'm not."

"Aren't you feisty tonight?"

She grins before she turns and walks away, leaving me hanging. I watch her go, my gaze on her ass. I need to get a better look at that ass. Naked. Maybe tonight.

"Hey! Your ranch?"

I glance over at the guy behind the counter who's holding

out two small containers toward me. I take it from him and set them on my tray. "Thanks."

I head back to the table in a daze, Eli walking in the opposite direction, passing by me to get his food. He sees my face and starts laughing, the prick.

"You're so fucked," he calls to me.

Damn. I think he's right.

It's when we're almost finished with dinner that I spot Carson, the fucker, here eating again. He was just here last night. Why is he back?

I know why. The second he leaves the counter after making his order—and he came by himself—he's cruising straight toward Ellie, who's on the far side of the restaurant, cleaning a cluster of tables after a big group left. I watch him touch her arm to get her attention, my blood heating when she turns to face him, a smile on her face when she realizes it's him.

My gut churns, watching them talk. Ellie seems pleased to see him. He says something and she smiles. He says something else and she laughs.

What the fuck was that all about?

"Hey." Eli nudges me in the ribs to get my attention. "You all right?"

I jerk my gaze away from Ellie and Carson, the dick, to smile tightly at my friend. "Never better. What's up?"

"What's up with you? You looked ready to chew through steel just now," Eli says, his brows lowered in concern.

"I'm fine," I say with much more assuredness than I mean. I don't feel fine though. I'm ready to fuck someone up. He *touched* her.

Touched her.

And she didn't stop him.

"Jackson, what's going on with your music right now?" Diego asks me. "Playing any shows soon?"

"I'm on hiatus during football season," I tell him. "School

and football don't leave me much time to do anything else. I've written a couple of songs though."

"That's so cool," Diego says, nodding. "You have options, and both are pretty great."

"The football thing is going nowhere," I say with a self-deprecating chuckle. "I suck."

"No, you don't," Eli says, immediately rushing to my defense. "You just haven't had a chance yet to show them what you can really do."

I completely ignore what Eli says. "I look at it like a vacation. I'm getting a little time off right now with my ass warming the bench."

They all laugh, including me, and yeah, I'm trying to make light of it. I've tried to act like it's no big deal all season, but I'm starting to feel a little low. Like, why am I even doing this? I enjoy being with my friends and being part of a team, but if I can't get on the field, then what's the point? I always bring my all during every practice, and the coaches lavish on the praise when I do something exceptional, which is more often than me screwing up. But they never put me out there during a game.

If this keeps up, I'm out. Seriously. I'm starting to feel like a complete loser, while the rest of my friends are actually playing. Even Caleb is out on the field during games.

We talk more about football and the upcoming game this Saturday. We're flying to San Diego, so at least we're not stuck on a bus for hours. Granted, it would be a nice bus, but still. My gaze slips to Ellie every time she passes by, lingering on her until she's out of my line of vision. Carson is now sitting at a table, eating his food by himself. She stops by every few minutes to say something to him.

Yet, she's never come back over to our table to say something to *me*.

What the hell kind of game is she playing? Does she need

a reminder of who made her come all over his fingers last night?

Determination filling me, I rise to my feet, without saying anything, about to leave the table when Caleb pipes up.

"Where you goin'?"

"Gotta piss," I lie.

I make my way toward Ellie, who is currently at a table near the back of the restaurant, close to the bathrooms. She's cleaning off a table, stacking empty beer glasses in a tub when she sees me. She stands up straighter, wiping her hand on a dishtowel as I approach.

"Hey," she says.

"Chat for a minute?"

"Uh—"

I grab her elbow and steer her toward the bathrooms, not giving her a chance to answer. I pull her into the short hallway, tucking the two of us into the farthest, darkest corner, her back to the wall, me standing directly in front of her.

"Jackson," she hisses. "I'm at work."

I kiss her, effectively shutting her up. She responds immediately, her arms coming around my neck, her lips parting for my invading tongue. I plunder her mouth, sending her the reminder she needs.

I'm the one she wants. I'm the one she's kissing right now. And I'm determined to make her forget that little fuck Carson is trying to make a move on her.

When I finally end the kiss, we're both breathing hard, and she's gazing up at me with wide, dazed eyes. Reaching out, I trail my fingers along her delicate jaw, ignoring the swarm of confusing emotions that swirl within me.

"What was that for?" she asks, breathless.

"Just wanted to kiss you." I do it again, keeping it light and quick. "I really like the braids." I tug on the end of one, unable to resist.

"I look like a child." She rolls her eyes.

"No, you definitely do not." I rest my hand on her curvy hip, giving it a squeeze. "What did Carson want?"

She contemplates me, her lips curling into a barely there smile. "He wanted food. That's why he came here."

"Looks like he might've wanted something else." I grip her hip, determined to act like I don't give a shit.

Of course, this too perceptive girl sees right through me.

"Uh huh. Well, we were supposed to go on a date a few days ago, remember." She presses her fingers against the back of my skull, giving me no choice but to dip my head and find her lips.

"Don't tell me he asked you on another date." I gently bite her bottom lip, making her sigh.

"He didn't." Her arms drop from around my neck, and she presses her palms against my chest, giving me a light shove. "But he still might."

I stare at her, incredulous. "You're going to tell him no, right?"

"I don't know. Why should I? I'm not with anyone currently." She exerts more pressure, giving me no choice but to back away from her. "I have to get back to work."

"Ellie," I say to her retreating form, still standing in the darkness. She glances over her shoulder at me, her expression questioning. "You're really going through with it?"

"Going through with what? Nothing's happened." A devilish grin appears. "Yet."

And with that, she saunters away.

Fuck. Guess I deserved that.

CHAPTER 20
ELLIE

Pure joy streams through my veins, warming my entire body as I walk through the restaurant, smiling at everyone I pass. Oh, that little moment with Jackson just now was one I never, ever want to forget. The possessive gleam in his eyes when he tugged me back into the hall. His devastating kiss. The oh so not casual way he asked me about Carson.

He's jealous. Unbelievable. I had no idea I could make him feel this way, and it's an…exhilarating experience.

What a moment to be alive.

I didn't expect Jackson to show up here tonight with his friends. But more than anything, I didn't expect Carson to show up either. Alone. I thought he'd order his food to go, but he stayed, and he keeps trying to talk to me. Completely oblivious to the death glares Jackson keeps sending his way.

Once I make my way out into the restaurant, I gather up the rest of the dishes and glasses and take them back to the kitchen, whistling the entire time.

I never whistle. I don't think I've ever whistled like this my whole life.

I leave the kitchen and head straight for Carson's table;

he's currently watching me with a sweet smile on his face. I don't want to use him. That's not my plan. I actually like this guy, and if Jackson wasn't in the picture, I would go all in with Carson.

Jackson is in my life though, and for some reason, he still wants me, which I cannot deny, is thrilling. But it's also fleeting. He won't be around forever. Eventually he will ditch me, and while I can prepare my mind and heart and body for this, I'll still be devastated.

Maybe it will be easier, knowing I can have Carson to potentially comfort me.

Ugh, I am playing a twisted game, and I need to make sure no one gets hurt, including myself. And Carson. I'm already in over my head…

"How's your food?" I ask Carson, noting the mostly empty basket in front of him.

"The cheeseburger was great." He leans back in his chair and pats his flat stomach. "I keep coming around here every night, I'll need to exercise more to work this off."

I laugh. "The food here is sinfully good."

"Yeah." He smiles, his gaze skimming down the length of my body, settling on my legs. "It is sinfully good."

Um, I don't think he's referring to food.

My gaze lifts to find Jackson's. He's already watching me with Carson, his hand clutched into a fist, resting on the table in front of him. Oh, he looks furious.

Sexy.

All that fury pointed straight at me, though I'm not his target.

That's Carson.

"Can I get you anything else? Take anything away for you?" I ask Carson, my tone light and flirtatious.

"You can agree to go out with me next week? When you're free?" Carson asks, sounding hopeful.

I appreciate how straightforward he is. There's no games

with Carson. He's interested. He doesn't hold back with me, which I like. He's confident. So is Jackson, but that's a whole other level of confidence.

Carson reminds me, yet again, that he's more my speed. But...

"I don't have my work schedule for next week yet," I tell him with a slight frown. Which is true, but I can almost guarantee my days off will be Monday and Sunday, as usual. Sometimes my manager changes it up, but rarely. She knows I need as many hours as I can get, and since I've started here, she's made sure I get them.

"When do you find out?" he asks.

"Tomorrow night."

"Well, let me know Friday in class, okay? If you want," he adds, some of that fear of rejection slipping into his request.

I smile at him reassuringly. "I'll let you know."

"Cool. Glad I came in tonight so I could see you." He nods and smiles.

"You see me every single day in class," I remind him.

"Maybe I want to see you more." His cheeks turn ruddy and he takes a sip from his mostly empty cup before awkwardly jumping to his feet. "I'll see you tomorrow?"

"For sure," I say. "Bye, Carson."

"Bye." He steps toward me. Then steps back, indecisiveness written all over his face, until finally, he practically lunges forward and pulls me into the quickest hug.

I rest my hands on his shoulders briefly—they're not as broad as Jackson's, not even close—before Carson lets me go, turns and exits the restaurant without a backward glance.

Okay. That was kind of nice, but odd. I think he worked up the guts to do it and then bailed in embarrassment?

Boys can be so weird.

And speaking of boys...

"When you gonna slip us a free basket of fries with our order, Ellie?"

I turn to see Diego, Eli, Jackson and Caleb standing there. It was Caleb asking for the free fries.

"Ask me next time you come in and I'll see what I can do," I tell him. I can totally get them a free basket of fries. I'd just use my employee discount and cover the cost, which is minimal. "How was your dinner?"

"Delicious as usual," Eli says, his brows furrowing as he studies me. "Hey, I wanted to ask if you're sure you can't come to San Diego this weekend to see Ava?"

My heart drops and I slowly shake my head. I wish I could. "I have to work Friday and Saturday, so I can't. I'll see her when she comes during your bye week, though. Tell her I said hi. Give her a big hug from me."

"I will. For sure." He nods. Gives me a quick hug because Eli and I, we have an understanding. A mutual love for our girl Ava. I didn't necessarily approve of their relationship at first, but I know how much he loves her, and how much she loves him. They're perfect for each other.

"I'll hold you to the fry promise," Caleb tells me before he pulls me in and smothers me against his chest. I shove him off. "See ya, squirt."

Not the best nickname, but whatever.

Even Diego hugs me. "You should come over sometime. I know Jocelyn would love to see you."

"I'll text her," I say, smiling at him. I miss Jocelyn too. I saw her more last year when I didn't go to Fresno State, which makes no sense, since we're both here now.

My time is filled up with other things lately.

Jackson stops in front of me, his expression like stone. Oh, he seems so angry still. At me? He has no reason to be. "See you later?"

"Yes," I say with a firm nod. "What time are you coming back?"

"Around nine-thirty? Or is that too early?"

"You don't want to hang out with Chuck?" I frown.

He shakes his head. "I'm taking a nap when I get home. I'm dead on my feet."

"Oh. Okay." I nod. "Get here around nine-forty-five, okay? We probably won't be here much past ten."

"Okay. Cool. See ya." He doesn't hug me, which only makes it more obvious that something is going on between us.

The jerk.

"Jackson, wait," I call to him.

He stops and turns to face me. "What's up?"

"Did you call the mechanic today?"

"Actually, yeah I did. He said your part is coming in tomorrow, not sure when though. And the car should be done by Friday."

"I hope so, since you're leaving."

"I can always leave you my car if yours isn't ready." He shrugs.

"No way. I am not driving your fancy Mercedes," I tell him.

"Afraid you'll wreck it?" He raises his brows.

I nod. I don't want that responsibility.

"You'll be fine." He winks. On anyone else it would look cheesy. But not Jackson. "See ya later, El."

I watch them leave, letting the promise of what might unfold later tonight swirl around me.

I can't wait.

———

It's almost ten, and Jackson still isn't here to pick me up.

I text him repeatedly. Call him. No answer. No response.

I'd bet money he's dead to the world and fast asleep, and I get it but...

How could he forget me?

Annoyed, I contemplate who I could ask to come get me. I

hate to reach out to Gracie or Hayden. They've already done so much for me, and I don't want to take advantage of their friendship. Any of the guys who were just here would probably come get me, but I don't want to ask any of them either. They're probably too busy or sleeping or whatever.

I don't know. I'm being ridiculous.

Instead, I call up my new friend, who answers on the first ring.

"Ellie, hey. What's going on?" Carson asks, sounding wide awake, thank God.

"Um, my ride didn't show up and I'm stuck at work, needing to get home," I tell him.

"Say no more. I'll come get you." I can tell he's getting up from whatever he's doing and walking around. "I can be there in ten minutes. You're not stuck outside waiting, are you?"

"No, not yet," I tell him, glancing around the quiet restaurant. We're pretty much done. Most everyone who worked has already left for the night. I'm just waiting for my manager to wrap things up before she leaves for the evening.

And then I'll have to wait outside.

"I'll be there soon, okay? Hang tight." He ends the call before I can respond.

Three minutes later and my manager, Donna, is exiting her office, pulling the door shut and locking it, a cash bag in her hand. "I thought you already left," she says when she spots me.

"My ride never showed up," I tell her with a shrug.

"Oh no. I can take you home after I drop this off at the bank," she says, waving the deposit bag at me.

"Thank you, but I called someone else. They should be here any minute." I glance toward the front windows and out at the parking lot, but no cars have showed up yet.

"I'll wait in here with you until they arrive," Donna says.

"I can wait outside," I start, but she shakes her head.

"No way. I'm not leaving you alone in that parking lot," she says firmly. "I don't mind."

"Thank you," I say with relief, grateful that Donna is so kind. "I appreciate it."

"Not a problem. Perfect opportunity for me to tell you what a great job you've been doing since you started working here. You fit in perfectly, and everyone really likes you," she says. "Which isn't always the case. They can be kind of cliquey here sometimes."

"Aw, thank you. I like everyone here too. It's a great place to work," I say, meaning every word. No one acted unfriendly or rude toward me when I started. Everyone was very welcoming.

A car pulls into the lot and I smile in relief at Donna. "That's my ride. He got here fast."

"Perfect."

Donna and I exit the restaurant, me standing with her as she locks the doors. I turn to see another car pull into the lot and realize in a panic the first car that showed up is Jackson.

It's Carson who only just arrived.

Oh. Shit.

I pull my phone out of my purse to see I have a text from Jackson.

Sorry I fell asleep. I'll be there in 5 min

Damn it!

Donna must see the stress on my face. "Everything okay?"

"I think I have two rides," I say with an awkward shrug. "Not sure which one I should get rid of."

My heart wants to get rid of Carson; my head says I should tell Jackson to get the hell out of here.

Jackson climbs out of his car, striding straight toward me. He's clad in a pair of gray, low hanging sweatpants that show off the waistband of his boxers—classic Calvin Klein—and no shirt.

No. Shirt.

My brain scrambles at his seeing his bare chest.

"El, I'm so sorry. You haven't been waiting long, have you?" He jogs toward me, reaching out his hand to touch my elbow. His gaze cuts to Donna. "Hey. Thanks for waiting with her."

"Of course," Donna says, sounding amused. "See you tomorrow, Ellie."

She leaves, heading for her car parked near the back.

Jackson frowns at me. "Wait, that isn't her ride?"

He nods toward Carson's car.

"No, that's—"

The driver's side window slides down, revealing Carson's face. "Hey, Ellie."

Jackson's entire demeanor goes cold. His hand drops from my elbow. "What the *fuck?*"

"You didn't respond to my texts and calls," I tell him, my voice low. "I panicked. I thought you forgot about me."

"I would never forget you, Ellie," he says, his tone fierce.

"You did tonight," I point out.

"I'm here now, aren't I? Jesus." He runs both of his hands over his head, his fingers sliding through his hair. In this position, the muscles in his arms bulge and flex, his biceps huge.

Regret slams into me, hard and swift. I should've never called Carson. I should've called Eli and told him to wake up Jackson. I totally messed up.

"I honestly didn't think you'd show up," I whisper, wincing when I hear Carson's car door slam.

Oh God, I really hope this doesn't turn into a confrontation.

"Ellie," Carson says, hurriedly walking over to where Jackson and I are standing. "You okay?"

He glares at Jackson, who glares right back.

Carson has balls. Jackson is clearly taller and bigger, his muscular chest on complete display. Which is a total distraction for me, I have to admit. I keep sneaking glances at him.

He's all rumpled and sexy, like he just rolled out of bed, which he totally did. If I could rewind the last fifteen minutes and change how this has all unfolded, I so would.

But I can't. I've created this big ol' mess and now I have to clean it up as best I can.

"I'm great. Uh, just a miscommunication." I smile at Carson before I turn my gaze to Jackson. "He can take me home."

"The fuck he will," Jackson growls as he goes to stand behind me, his hands curling around my shoulders. "I'll drive her home."

His commanding voice tells me—and Carson—that he's not going to back down.

I whirl on him, giving him a shove. "Stop being a macho asshole. I'm going home with Carson."

"Ellie, come on," he starts, but I shake my head.

"Nope, I'm riding with Carson. You can go home." I flounce away from Jackson before he can say another word, my entire body shaking. I follow Carson to his car, opening the passenger door and climbing inside. He drives a silver Chevy Malibu. A nice, practical car.

For a nice, practical guy. How fitting.

"That's the guy from the party, right?" Carson asks, once he's in the driver's seat and about to back the car out of the lot. "Is he actually your ex or something?"

"He's just a friend. He was supposed to pick me up, but he forgot," I say nonchalantly, like it's no big deal.

"Oh." Carson nods, still a little confused. "Okay. He seemed kind of mad."

Major understatement, but I don't correct him.

"He's fine." I wave a hand. "Don't worry about him."

The thing is, Jackson didn't actually forget me. He just fell asleep, like I originally thought. And he seemed really pissed that Carson was here to get me. I probably shouldn't have gone with Carson, but I felt bad for dragging him out here.

Plus, I was still mad, thinking Jackson forgot about me, and then he showed up. Enraged and hot and bossy...I just reacted. I wanted to hurt him like he hurt me. Which is silly and petty but...

I've made my choice, and I sort of regret it. What I've actually done is made everything worse, but it's too late now.

We make idle small talk while Carson drives me home, but I'm distracted. I swear to God, we're being followed. By Jackson. And maybe we are.

Or maybe I'm reading too much into things. He wouldn't follow me. He doesn't care that much.

By the time we're at my apartment complex, I'm exhausted. "Thank you for coming to my rescue," I tell Carson. "Sorry that was such a pain with Jackson."

"It's cool. Tell him I didn't mean anything by showing up," Carson says, ever the polite one.

I smile and climb out of his car. "I owe you."

"You don't owe me anything. I didn't mind coming to get you. I swear," Carson says.

"You're the best," I tell him with a weak smile. "See you tomorrow."

I shut the door and he watches me approach my apartment building, only leaving when I wave, and he must view it as me reassuring him I'm safe.

What a nice guy. He's such a good guy.

Seriously, what am I doing, wasting my time with Jackson?

Another car pulls into the lot, and I immediately recognize it. A Mercedes. Jackson, of course. As if he's been lying in wait for Carson to leave before he makes his approach. Anger courses through my veins and I march back out to the parking lot, heading straight for Jackson's car. He climbs out of the driver's side, his expression thunderous as he slams the door as loud as he can.

"You followed us? I knew it!"

"Why did you leave with him? Huh?" He throws his arms out, impressing me momentarily with his wingspan. Oh my God, if I could punch myself in the face right now, I so would. "You knew I was coming."

"That's the thing. I had no idea if you would show up or not. You never responded," I remind him.

"I did respond. I was a little late, but damn it, I showed up. You gotta have more faith in me, El. Like I said, I will always be there for you," he says.

"Why? Am I your charity case, Jackson? You always want to run to my rescue. My knight in shining armor. Your job isn't to save me, I hope you know," I retort, crossing my arms.

"I don't think of it as a job. I always want to help you. What the hell is wrong with that? You're making it into an accusation, like it's a character flaw," he says.

"It is! You want to be my hero, and I don't need one. I just want you to be my friend," I throw at him.

He stops short, his hands on his hips, his gaze dark. "Just my friend?"

I sink my teeth into my lower lip, releasing it quick when his gaze drops to my mouth. "Y-yeah."

"You don't sound too sure of that." He takes a step toward me. Then another one. I'm frozen in place, my breaths coming too fast, my heart in my throat. He stops directly in front of me, so close he's practically standing on top of my feet, but I keep my head bent. Too scared to look in his eyes. Or stare at his chest. It's a fabulous chest. One I want to rest my head against so I can listen to his heartbeat. "That's all you want from me?"

"What do you want from me?" I ask the ground, hating how shaky my voice is.

His fingers slip beneath my chin, tipping my face up. His eyes are blazing with a mixture of emotions, none of them familiar. His expression is pained. He seems tortured. Confused. Mad.

Hungry.

I feel all those same emotions as I wait for him to say something. Anything.

"I don't know," he whispers, dipping his head so his mouth hovers just above mine. "I know I want to kiss you so fucking bad right now. I want to sprawl you out on the hood of my car and strip you naked. I want to put my mouth on you and make you come. Make you forget that little asshole, once and for all."

I'm speechless, my gaze ensnared in his. I can visualize everything he just described perfectly, and I want that.

All of it.

Every last little bit.

"Why do you do this to me?" he asks after I haven't responded.

"Do what?" I whisper.

"Make me want things I shouldn't." He lightly strokes my chin with his fingers. "Tell me to go home."

"Why?" I frown.

"If you invite me into your room, I might do something we'll both regret," he admits.

I cannot begin to imagine he'd do anything I'd ever regret. Not when it involves me with him.

God, he's confusing.

"Maybe I want it," I tell him, feeling bold.

He smiles. Kisses me. Far too quickly for my liking. "You don't," he whispers against my lips. "I'm in a bad mood. I might take it too far."

A shiver slips down my spine at the promise in his voice. I have a feeling I'd like it when he takes things too far. "You don't scare me, Jackson."

"I should." He takes a step backward, as if he needs the distance. "You should go to bed, Ellie."

My heart rattles in my chest, as if it's trying to escape its cage. I'm so turned on, I can barely think straight. "You're coming with me?"

He shakes his head slowly. "Not tonight, sweetheart."

"Oh." The disappointment is real. Slowly, I turn and start walking toward my apartment. I can feel Jackson's heavy gaze on me the entire way, and it's only when I'm actually at the door, my key in the deadbolt and turning it, that I glance up to find him still watching me.

I offer up my hand in a little wave.

He nods.

Climbs into his car.

And drives away.

CHAPTER 21

JACKSON

I never thought I had it in me, but seeing Carson show up to drive her home, knowing Ellie lost all faith in me and actually had a backup plan, left me feeling out of sorts.

And that's putting it mildly.

Truly? I became an enraged asshole.

This is where I admit I'm a jealous fuck. Girls don't normally make me feel like this either, with the exception of…

Ellie.

Watching her talk—watching her flirt—with Carson right in the middle of the restaurant drove me out of my mind with jealousy. That she would act that way right in front of me after what we did the night before?

Fucking unbelievable. Didn't know Ellie had it in her. That she actually had it in her to drive me out of my mind with lust.

I'd felt like such a dick when I woke up, realizing I was late to get her from the restaurant. Seeing all those texts and missed calls had sent me into overdrive, speeding like a maniac to get to her as fast as I could.

Only to find she'd called Carson when I didn't respond.

She'd lost all faith in me, just like that, though I guess I can't blame her. I disappointed her.

Yet again.

I'd followed Carson to her apartment, deranged. Angry. Ready to beat some skinny freshman ass. Ellie confronting me threw me for a loop. What threw me even further?

How badly I wanted to fuck her. Seeing her angry, yelling at me, the little argument we had outside had turned me on and made me hard.

What the hell is wrong with me?

I went home and jerked off to thoughts of Ellie just as I described her: naked and sprawled out on the hood of my car, my mouth on her pussy, driving her wild with my tongue, just before I plunged my dick into her tight, wet heat. I came in an instant, as if I had no control over myself.

I fell asleep with her on my mind. Woke up with her there too. Before I went to class, I called the mechanic, who informed me the part came in and they were working on her car this morning. It would be available to pick up later this afternoon.

"I have to be somewhere by four and so does Ellie," I told the guy, not one hundred percent sure when Ellie starts work but close enough. "Can we pick it up before then?"

"I will make sure it's ready by three," the mechanic promised me.

I ended the call and contemplated how to approach her. Calling her is out of the question. Pretty sure she has class. She's more of an early bird than I am. I decide to text her instead.

Texting is safe. It's our normal mode of communication. Always has been.

Me: **Your car will be ready today by three.**

She doesn't immediately respond. I go about my business, getting dressed. Gathering up my shit. Making myself a bowl of cereal in the kitchen and eating slowly, staring at my phone as I scroll through Instagram.

Still no response from Ellie.

Shit.

I dump the leftover milk out into the sink, the spoon falling with an extra loud clatter and I turn on the water, rinsing everything before I snap the faucet off with a low growl.

"What the hell is up your ass this morning?"

I turn to see Eli standing there glowering at me. He's the one who's been in a bad mood lately, missing his girl like the pussy-whipped fucker he is.

"Didn't sleep well," I lie. I slept fine. I don't want to admit my feelings for Ellie are leaving me on edge.

As in, I don't quite understand what I'm currently feeling, but I know I don't like it.

"Grumpy fucker," he mutters, shaking his head as he shuffles deeper into the kitchen.

"You're the one who's been grumpy for a solid month," I remind him, leaning against the counter and watching as he grabs a mug out of the cabinet, goes to the Keurig he brought with him when we moved in together, and loads it with a coffee pod.

"Yeah, because I miss Ava. Knowing I'm gonna get laid this weekend is making me feel a lot better," he admits truthfully. He sends me a look. "Is that your problem? Maybe you just need to get laid."

That is definitely my problem, but the only person I want to have sex with at the moment is Ellie. No one else will do.

No one.

"Probably," I bite out, glaring at him, even though I'm not mad at him. I'm just mad in general. "I should get to class."

Eli checks his phone. "Can't you wait a few? We usually head over there together."

"We're going to have to drive separately today. I have to

take Ellie to the mechanic shop to pick up her car this afternoon," I explain.

He crosses his arms, studying me intently. "You are all torqued up, and I don't get it. Did something happen between you two last night? I saw the way you were watching her when she talked to that guy she brought to the party a few weeks ago."

I'm instantly filled with low-key anger at the thought of Carson. He needs to keep his hands off of her. His eyes off her too. "She's playing us both."

"Ellie?" He starts to laugh, shaking his head. "That's not her style and you know it."

"Maybe she's changed."

"You're the true player, and now you're getting played?" He laughs harder. "Oh, this is some shit right here."

"What the hell are you talking about?"

"Are you sprung on her? Is that your problem? Jealous over the fact that she's talking to someone else while also messing around on the side with you?" Eli nearly doubles over in laughter. "This is fucking fantastic."

"How is it fantastic? What the hell, Eli? I thought you were on my side." I clasp the back of my head, the muscles straining in my arms. I want to hit something. Maybe Eli's smiling smug ass face, I don't know.

"You like her." He shakes his head, chuckling. "And you don't know what to do with yourself."

"I've always liked her," I say defensively.

"Not like this. You have actual, real feelings for her." He points at me. "And you don't know what to do with them."

"I *do not* have actual, real feelings for her." I am lying through my teeth. I do have feelings for her, and I don't know what to do with them.

"Sure you don't." He doesn't believe me.

"I'm just sexually frustrated. Like you said," I continue.

"Uh huh. Can't stop thinking about her?" He lifts a brow,

grabbing his finished coffee and dumping a bunch of sugar and creamer in it.

"I *can* stop thinking about her," I say defensively.

"Right. Is she on your mind now? Can't wait to see her? Ready to destroy that fucker who put his hands on her last night right in front of you?"

My hands curl into fists and he notices. Of course he does. He's deliberately provoking me. "That fucker showed up after work to drive her home."

Eli frowns. "Thought that was your job."

I explain to him what happened and by the time I'm finished, he's laughing all over again. "She actually thought I forgot about her."

"Wouldn't be the first time," he reminds me.

Now I'm frowning. "What do you mean?"

"You used to ignore her all the time. Listen, you never mentioned it to me much, but Ava gave me all the deets, thanks to Ellie sharing them with her. You two talked allllllll the time online. And then you'd see her in person and ignore her. Or act like she was your buddy, and that was it. It twisted her up inside. Made Ava mad too," Eli explains.

"Ellie is easy to talk to," I admit. "But then I'd see her and she'd give me those heart eyes and I…I couldn't take it."

"Yeah, well, now you're the ass with heart eyes and she's giving you a taste of your own medicine," Eli says, sipping from his extra hot coffee. He winces. "Fuck, I burned my lip. Gotta keep these babies pristine for Ava this weekend."

"You're fucking ridiculous," I mutter, my mind filled with thoughts of Ellie. How much I must've hurt her in the not so distant past. Her adoration was a heavy responsibility, one that I wasn't up for.

"No, you're ridiculous for not just—going for it. Ellie's a cool chick. She's tolerated your ass for this long, and she's still around. You need to jump on that. Jump on her, before you lose her," he says.

Fear makes my heart feel like it's in a stranglehold. "You think I could lose her?'

He shrugs. "If that other guy is making moves that are working, then yes. You have the potential to lose her. She's finding other options instead of just being stuck on you."

Shit, shit, shit.

"Just don't make a move for only selfish reasons," Eli adds.

"What do you mean?"

"Make sure you're doing this because you really do care about her. That it's not just some ego thing. If that's all it is, that's some straight-up bullshit," he says. "You like her, you want more with her, cool. You just want to fuck her to see what it's like? Not cool."

I've always appreciated how my friends don't hold back, especially Eli. He tells it like it is, and a lot of the time, I need that.

Like now. Now, I really need it.

It's only when I arrive on campus and am walking to class that I finally get a response from Ellie. Seeing her name flash on my phone screen makes my heart leap.

Who am I right now?

Ellie: **OMG YAY! Thank you for letting me know.**

I respond to her immediately.

Me: **What time do you have to be at work?**

Ellie: **Four. I can pick it up before that, and then drive straight over to work.**

Me: **What time do you want me to get you?**

Ellie: **Um, I don't know. I'm done with school by two. What time works for you?**

Me: **I'll pick you up at three.**

She goes quiet for a while, leaving me on edge. I stomp across campus with determined steps, glowering at people who dare to make eye contact with me. Even the girls.

I'm a fucking mess.

By the time I'm settled in my chair in class, I get a text from her.

Ellie: Sounds good! See you at three.

I smile. Contemplate sending her a heart. Even add one to the chat, ready to send it, but I chicken out at the last minute.

Like a heart emoji is going to make all the difference in the world. Like we're in fucking middle school or something. I need to get over my damn self.

If I was smart, I'd get over Ellie. But I guess I'm not smart.

So I'm going to keep this going instead.

———

I'm done with my last class for the day and am headed toward the parking lot when my phone rings. I don't even bother checking to see who it is. I just answer like a dumbass.

"Jackson. Thanks for picking up the call," an overeager male voice greets me.

I glance at the screen, seeing that it's an unfamiliar number. Great.

"I don't have a car warranty that expired. And I own a Mac, not a PC," I tell him, just about to end the call when I hear him frantically trying to get my attention.

"Jackson, don't hang up! My name is Rick and I'm with Evergreen Records! I've been trying to get a hold of you for weeks!"

I come to a stop near a bench, my interest piqued. "Keep talking."

"A scout from my company saw you perform this summer in Seattle. She said you were amazing," he says, his voice overly enthusiastic.

They always talk this way, trying to ramp up my excitement. I get why. They want to entice me, but I always play it cool. You give yourself away and suddenly, it's on their terms.

I want to always keep it on my terms.

"I had a good summer," I agree.

"I'm sure you did. I was hoping we could set up a meeting," he says. "And if I have to, I'll come to you."

Interesting. Usually it's a phone call meeting first. Zoom next. By then, they're mentioning terms and sending over contracts, which are never in my favor. That's when I bail.

No one's come to meet me in person, face-to-face before.

"I know you perform locally a lot," Rick says. "Have any shows coming up that I can attend?"

"No. Football season is keeping me busy," I answer.

"That's right. You're a rock god and a jock." Rick chuckles. "What a combination."

"It's not that big of a deal," I tell him. "I'm just keeping my options open."

"Yes, versatile. I fucking love it," he gushes. "I'm thinking I can be up there in about two weeks. How's your schedule for the beginning of October?"

"My bye week is the first weekend in October, so your timing is perfect," I tell him.

"Fantastic. Maybe you can book a last-minute gig too. I'd love to see you perform. I'll be bringing a few of my executives with me. We'd all love to meet with you," he says, just before he rattles off my email address. Would love to know how he got that. "Can I send some information over? And as we get closer, I can also send you an itinerary."

"Sounds great," I tell him, because why not? I like to entertain these offers, even though I never accept them.

"Looking forward to meeting with you. Can't wait to see you perform, too. I have a feeling we'd be great partners for each other," Rick says, just before we end the call.

This feels almost serendipitous. Too easy, even. And while I'm all for easy, my guard will still be up. I'll have to drag my father into this too. He's a shark, and he doesn't fall for a bunch of pretty lies and empty promises. Plus, he has one of the best lawyers in the area. She's the one who looked over my previous contracts, finding fault in every single one of them. Record companies aren't in the business to make a musician rich, is what my dad's attorney told me, and she's right.

They're in the business to make money for themselves. Period.

I'll talk it over with Ellie too. I always like to get her opinion. I value it. When she speaks, I listen. When she does anything lately, I'm right there, watching. Waiting. Hanging on every word.

Clearly, I'm a mess when it comes to her. I need to figure my shit out.

Soon.

CHAPTER 22

ELLIE

I lucked out when I texted Hayden and Gracie, asking if they'd be on campus around lunch time today. They both were, and so we agreed to meet up.

I couldn't keep what happened with Jackson to myself. I had to fill Hayden in on everything—I stunned her silent, which I don't think happens very often—and then I let them know what went down when Jackson showed up with his friends. And later, when he magically appeared to pick me up. How I rode home with Carson instead.

How growly and sexy Jackson was after he followed me home. His voice rich with promise, the words he said to me. When he kissed me—a minor kiss in the scheme of kisses, but the words he said and the way he acted touched me deep.

I'm still not over it.

When I finally finish my story, my friends are watching me with surprise etched on their faces, their eyes wide. They don't say a word.

"Well?" I urge, desperate for their opinions. "What does that all mean?"

"He wants you," Hayden says. "I don't doubt it at all."

"That was kind of hot." Gracie fans herself. "He actually said he wanted to put you on the hood of his car?"

I nod. I didn't hold anything back. Gave them pretty much every bit of info he detailed. "He was so—fierce."

"Hmm, an alpha. I love it," Gracie says, dreamy-eyed.

"I just don't want him to be all hot for you because he doesn't like seeing you with someone else," Hayden says.

"Why not?" Gracie asks, nudging her. "A little jealousy never hurt anybody. I love it when they get all caveman and grunt *mine* while slinging you over their shoulder," Gracie says.

"I have never had that happen to me," Hayden says to her best friend.

"Well, neither have I," Gracie agrees, both of them casting me a look. "Has Jackson done that to you?"

"No." I shake my head. "Not that I necessarily want him to."

"Oh, give it up. It would be totally hot if he did that," Gracie says.

Hayden sends her a look, effectively shutting her up, before she turns her attention to me. "What are you hoping to get out of this with Jackson?"

"What exactly do you mean?"

"Are you wanting a long-term relationship with him?" She cuts right to the point.

I nod. Nibble on my lower lip. "That's what I've always wanted."

"Do you like this Carson guy?" Hayden asks.

Gracie makes a face, but I ignore her.

"He's so nice. If Jackson wasn't in my life, I would totally go for him. He's definitely more my type. Jackson is more like my dream guy," I admit.

"Sometimes, we get our dream guy," Hayden says. "Tony is mine, and I love him so much. He feels the same way. And even though we're two years apart, and we're still young, I can totally see a future with him."

Gracie is furiously shaking her head. "I know you both are big believers in true, lasting love, but it doesn't always have to be like that. You can find yourself in a relationship that is totally enjoyable for the two of you, and not be committed to each other forever."

"Says the woman who doesn't last past a month with a guy," Hayden says, jabbing her thumb at Gracie.

"Hey, don't knock it until you try it," Gracie says.

"I did, and I didn't like it," Hayden reminds her.

I smack the table lightly, getting their attention. "I know what you guys prefer in your relationships, and I appreciate the encouragement, but I don't want a short term anything with Jackson. If I take it any further and then he dumps me? I'll be devastated."

And that's not even an exaggeration.

They both give me sympathetic looks and I sigh deeply. I don't want their sympathy. Not right now. I need help. Assistance. I need to make myself so desirable to Jackson, he'll never look at another woman again.

I have no idea how to do that. Or if I can even make it work.

"I don't have any major advice," Hayden says, her voice soft, a faint smile on her face. "Just be your sweet, normal self. He's drawn to you. Now more than ever. And he's jealous of Carson. Maybe that's the kick in the ass he needs to make a move."

"I totally agree," Gracie says with a nod.

"So you don't think I need to do anything different to try and get his attention?" I ask, wanting to be sure.

"No," Hayden says. "Just—keep being you, while he spirals out of control and completely falls in love with you."

My heart flutters at her words, and I tell it to calm down. "I don't want to get my hopes up."

"You're not misreading him. Don't think that you are," Hayden says.

"He's picking me up at three to take me to the mechanic shop," I reveal. "My car will be ready by then."

"Aw, so he won't have to pick you up after work?" Gracie looks disappointed.

I shrug. "Guess that obligation is finished."

"He can still come by after work though," Hayden says with a sly smile.

"Booty call!" Gracie says, and they give each other a high five.

I scowl at them, but they just laugh at me. Until I'm laughing too. Worry nags at me though. What if this doesn't work out? I'm a planner. I normally like sure things. Whatever is happening between Jackson and I can't be described as one, not in the least. He doesn't come with guarantees. Most people don't.

Seriously, what the hell am I doing? Is it a mistake, believing I can have something real with the boy who used to avoid me in public places, yet told me all of his deepest secrets in private? Should I even trust him?

My heart tells me yes. My logical brain?

Is screaming at me, *nooooooo.*

We chat a while longer and then Hayden agrees to drop me off at my apartment, which is a big help. She gets me home earlier than normal so I take a shower and get ready for work, taking my time so I look the best that I can.

By the time it's close to three, I'm a nervous wreck. My stomach is twisted up in knots and my hands are shaking as I apply a coat of lip gloss. When I'm finally done, I rub my lips together and take a step back, contemplating myself. I look no different. My hair is curled, so that's nice. I turn to the side, smoothing my T-shirt over my stomach. At least it's not stained, and I'm wearing my best bra so my boobs look good.

There's a knock on the door and I run down the stairs,

slowing as I get to the bottom, and taking a deep breath. I need to remain calm. Unfazed.

I approach the door, exhale slowly and turn the lock, opening the door and smiling at Jackson, who is standing on my doorstep, sexy as can be.

Black T-shirt. Light gray basketball shorts. Socks covering his feet with Nike slides. The typical stuff I see boys wearing on campus. Jackson just looks a little sexier with it. Maybe it's the longish blond hair that flops over his forehead. The chain around his neck. The look in his eyes when his gaze meets mine, the faint smile curling his lips.

"Hey," he says, his voice low and a little gravelly. "Can I come in for a minute?"

"Sure." I open the door wider and he walks inside.

"I wanted to get here a little early because I hoped I could talk to you," he says as I shut and lock the door. He stops in the middle of the living room, glancing around. "This is nice."

"You've been here before," I remind him.

"Yeah, when it was pitch black and I couldn't see anything." He smiles.

I blush, remembering that night.

I need to keep it together. Not get all flustered over him, which is far too easy to do.

"What did you want to talk about?" I ask, needing to change the subject.

"I wanted to apologize for what happened last night," he says, his expression solemn. "I acted like a complete asshole."

"Oh. It's okay." What does he mean, he acted like an asshole? Yes, I'd been mad at him for thinking he forgot me, but I got over that fast.

"I never want you to think I'd forget you. I was so tired. I just—when I fall asleep, sometimes I sleep hard. And that's what happened. I didn't mean to be late." He takes a step toward me, his hand reaching out, but he lets it drop before he makes actual contact. "And then I acted like a dick toward you. And your—friend."

There it is. That tiny glimpse of jealousy. I'm tempted to smile. Worse, I'm tempted to ask him about it, but I keep that particular question to myself. "He's fine. Don't worry about him."

"If you say so." He doesn't sound so sure. "Are we fine?"

"What do you mean?"

"Me and you." He takes another step closer, and this time, his hand makes contact with my arm, his fingers warm on my skin. "I don't want to fuck this up."

"Fuck what up?" I ask, suddenly breathless.

"I don't know. Whatever it is we're doing right now." His hand drops from my arm to my waist, pulling me in until we're flush against each other. "Your roommates home?"

I shake my head. "No—"

He kisses me before I can finish the sentence, and I'm lost. To the sensation of his mouth moving on mine, his tongue searching. His hands gripping me close. I wrap my arms around him and hang on for the ride, never wanting this to end. I could drown in him, in this, in us so easily. But I need to keep my head. I have to remain smart.

I don't want to get hurt.

We kiss like this for minutes. Until I'm finally pulling away, needing to breathe, to gather my thoughts. "We should probably get going."

"Yeah." He exhales loudly, leaning in, pressing his forehead to mine. "I don't want to though."

Excitement races through me at his confession. "We're running out of time."

"You're right. Practice starts at four." He releases me and takes a step backward, running his hand through his hair. Trying to regain his composure. "You ready?"

I go to the mirror that's on the wall right next to the front door, checking my hair. I run my fingers through it, noticing there's not a bit of gloss left on my lips. I chance a look at Jackson, who is currently sporting a few flecks of glitter on his pretty mouth.

Ha. I marked him.

"Let's go," I say.

———

Once Jackson settles up with the mechanic, we go out to the parking lot and I climb into my car to test it. The engine starts right up, and I reach out to pat the dashboard, murmuring, "Good girl," under my breath, feeling completely ridiculous, but serious.

I *need* this car. It's practically my lifeline. The only thing I own and I can't lose it. And now I'm completely in debt to Jackson since he just forked over almost nine hundred dollars to fix it.

The car probably isn't even worth that much.

"Engine sounds good," Jackson tells me when I roll down the window and offer him a thumbs up.

"It does. Thank you again for paying for the repairs," I say, my voice sincere, my gaze never straying from his. I wonder if he knows how much it means to me, what he did. "I want to pay you back."

"Ellie. I know you don't have a lot of money." His smile is sweet. "I don't mind."

"I do, though. That's the thing. And I don't want to feel like I owe you so much money. I'd rather pay you back. In small chunks, because that's the only way I can manage it," I explain.

"Whatever makes you happy," he says, his entire demeanor easygoing. "That's all I want."

I take his words to heart. And of course, my heart soars, because it's stupid and a big believer in true love.

"Have fun at practice," I tell him, not wanting him to leave.

"Have a good night at work," he says, acting like he doesn't want to leave me either. "Since we're leaving tomorrow for the game, I probably won't see you until Monday."

My soaring heart crashes, just like that. I momentarily forgot that they're leaving. I suppose I could invite him over to my place after work. I should.

I totally should.

"Good luck at your game," I say, instead of inviting him. "I'm sure you guys will do great."

"They'll do great," he says, his voice light, his gaze full of disappointment. He blinks and it's gone. "While I'll sit on the bench."

He hates that. I know he does, and there's nothing I can do to fix it for him. "You'll get your chance."

"Maybe. Maybe not." He shrugs one broad shoulder. "See you Monday?"

I nod, fighting the sadness that threatens to overtake me. "Be safe."

His gaze softens. "You too."

I watch him walk to his car, wishing he would've at least kissed me goodbye. Said something growly and sexy like he did last night. We may have had a mini make-out session at my apartment, but it wasn't much, and I wanted more.

With Jackson, I always want more.

Right now, we're acting...normal. Like we're not trying to be anything other than friends.

And that's depressing.

CHAPTER 23

JACKSON

The next few weeks pass by in a blur. Two away games in a row. Plenty of practices leading up to them. Lots of travel that leaves us exhausted but luckily enough, we win both games.

Not that I had anything to do with it.

Now it's the long awaited first week in October—bye week for the Bulldog football team. It's a relief to not have a game to play this weekend, and our practices so far aren't nearly as intense. Which is good because I have other things happening.

Like a performance Thursday at Strummers, just for Rick and the execs at Evergreen Records. All of my friends are going as a show of support. I warned Caleb he can't yell anything obscene, and he seemed disappointed. He might've also pouted like a little baby. Tough shit. I'm not going to let him make fun of me while I'm on stage.

I have people to impress.

Ellie will be there too, of course. Speaking of her...

We haven't seen each other much these last couple of weeks. She's always working. I'm in class—she's in class. Or I have football. I leave for an away game. We haven't been able to connect except through text, and I miss her.

I told myself not having her around would be a sign. Maybe even help me realize I don't need her in my life like I thought I did. I was acting like a possessive fuck around her, and I didn't like it. That's not me.

But absence can make the heart grow fonder, and that's exactly what's happening with me when it comes to Ellie. I miss her so damn much it feels like there's a hole in my heart, which is some dramatic, sappy shit. Just call me John Mayer because I'm writing songs about it, too. Emotional ones that are about her smiling face and other parts of her I want to explore.

I'm debuting a song Thursday night. Hopefully she won't be too offended.

More than anything? Hopefully she'll realize the song is about her.

After practice Wednesday night—our last one for the week, thank God—we head over to the Doghouse Grill for dinner, and I'm pretty sure Ellie's working. I'm not even that hungry, but I'm glad we're going there. Eli is in the best mood I've seen him in a long time, and that's thanks to Ava arriving tomorrow.

"Smiling because you know you're getting some pussy tomorrow?" Caleb asks Eli as we walk toward the restaurant entrance.

Tony slaps him on the back of the head. "So crude."

"Sorry, Dad." Caleb glares at Tony. I laugh. Eli just shakes his head.

"I'm glad she'll be here tomorrow," is all Eli says. And that's all he has to say. We know he's glad. He's been missing his girl something fierce.

I think about me and Ellie. If she left and went to school somewhere else. Or if I left for another tour. Moved to Los

Angeles to pursue this music career thing for real. What would I do? How would *we* do?

Frowning, I shake my head. Why am I even thinking like this? We're not actually together. I'm still as free as a bird. So is she. If I moved, we'd both have to move on. There would be no other choice.

I rub my chest absently, my heart aching just thinking about it.

Yep. I am in way too deep. I need to get over myself. Stay strong. Remember she's just a girl. A girl I like. A good friend. That's it.

We enter the restaurant and stand in line, and I spot Ellie working behind the register, taking orders with a cheerful smile on her pretty face. Her long dark hair is in braids again. Looking cute as can be. My once aching heart now thumps in excitement at seeing her, and I tell it to calm the hell down.

We haven't even done anything yet, and look at me. I fingered her *once.* We've kissed a few times. And here I am, like a lovesick puppy dog.

"There's your girl." Tony jabs me in the ribs with his elbow. "Hayden mentioned you two haven't seen each other much lately."

"We're both busy," I say with a shrug.

"You're not leading her on, are you?" he asks.

I glance over at him, scowling. "No. I don't know what we're doing, if you want me to be real."

"Yeah. Just asking. Hayden is worried. So is Gracie," Tony says.

Great. That makes me feel terrible. I don't like it when those chicks gang up on me. They're fiercely protective of Ellie.

"Gracie is what?" Caleb asks, always nosy when her name pops up.

"Ready to beat your ass," I tell him.

He frowns. "What did I do now?"

"What do you always do?" Tony asks him, going along with it. "She's sick of your shit."

"She can suck my dick," Caleb says cheerfully, just before his expression turns serious. "Actually, I really wish she would."

Eli shoves Caleb, so he topples over a little bit. "You need to learn how to respect women."

"I do respect them! I love my mama," Caleb says, his expression wounded as he rubs his arm.

Lately we've all been giving Caleb endless shit, and it's fitting because that's usually his job. He's been more subdued lately and none of us are quite sure why. He's still seeing Baylee on the side, here and there, which is messed up, but I have no room to judge or talk, so I keep my mouth shut. He's also working hard to get into Gracie's panties, and while she plays a good game of *stay away from me* when it comes to Caleb, I don't know if she actually feels that way.

I think, deep down, she's attracted to him.

"Leading on one girl while trying to get with another isn't cool," Eli says.

"I'm not doing that," Caleb says defensively. "Gracie and I, we're just joking around with each other. And Baylee knows where we stand."

"Uh huh." This is from Tony.

We're all looking at Caleb as if he's full of shit.

"Hey, I'm not being any worse than Ellie." Caleb jabs his finger into my chest. "You know she's still seeing that Carson dude."

"What?" All the hairs on my body seem to stand on end. I glance in her direction once again, and as if she can feel me looking at her, she meets my gaze, offering me a sweet smile and a little wave.

I lift my chin in greeting before looking away.

"She is," Caleb says, his expression smug. "I see the two of them together on campus all the time."

"They have classes together," I say in her defense. I do not want to go down this path. I don't want to get jealous and act like a dick. I'm not that guy. I'm not.

I don't want to be, at least. But it's like I can't help myself when it comes to Ellie.

"Yeah, keep telling yourself that. Pretty sure they've even gone on an actual date," Caleb says, stressing that last word extra hard, so it'll punch me right in the gut. Gee, thanks, my friend.

"Bro, why you gotta be like that?" Eli says to Caleb, coming to my defense. "Are you purposely trying to rub it in his face?"

"Caleb," Tony says, sending him a dark look. "Why are you starting trouble?"

"Why are you all on my jock? I'm not trying to start trouble. I'm just stating facts," Caleb says with a shrug. "I heard the girls talking a few nights ago. Ellie went to the movies with that guy."

What the fuck? The movie date finally went down? Though I guess this is what I get. I'm too busy and don't make time for her, like maybe I should. He persists because he's not stupid or hesitant, and she goes on a date with him.

I'm instantly pissed.

And insanely jealous.

By the time we make it to the counter to place our orders, we're all not talking, too busy glowering at each other. Caleb claims he didn't mean to start shit, but come on. He totally did. He wanted the heat off him, and now I'm the one who's pissed off.

"Don't you guys look menacing," Ellie greets us, her smile fading as she takes us all in. "Okay. Who wants to order first?"

"I will." Caleb flashes her that charming, 'I don't give a shit' smile and tells her what he wants. Tony is next. Then Eli. And finally.

Me.

"Hi," she greets me with one of those breathless smiles of hers. The ones that usually make me want to discover other ways I can leave her breathless. "I'm so glad you came in tonight. I've been thinking about you."

"Really? Did you think about me when you went to the movies with Carson?"

The words fall from my lips without thought. They're just out there, bouncing between us, and her mouth drops open as she scrutinizes me.

I snap my lips into a straight line, hating that I said that. Hating that I look like a territorial dick. Hating worse that I'd love nothing more than to piss a circle around where she stands so I can tell that Carson kid to back the fuck off, once and for all.

Disgusting but true.

"Um, are you okay?" Her smile is fake. Frozen in place. Like she doesn't know what to say.

"I'm fucking great." My smile is just as fake as I make my order.

She gives me my total. "Maybe we could talk later? After I get off work? I close tonight. As usual."

"You don't have plans?" I ask pointedly as I hand over my credit card.

Ellie sends me a questioning look. "No. Do you? Look, I know we've been super busy lately, but—"

I rudely interrupt her. "I'm available."

That's all I say. I can barely look at her. I can barely see straight, I'm so jealous. Which is stupid. We're not together. Ellie is always just...there, and I took advantage of that. Expecting her to wait for me. Knowing deep down, I could never be what she needed.

Maybe that's not true, though. Maybe I do want her. I sure as hell don't want her with anyone else. That's some straight-up bullshit. I can barely handle the thought of her being with another guy, like that wimpy Carson. He seems nice enough, but fuck that. He doesn't know her like I do. He doesn't understand her like I do either.

"I'll text you when I'm off work." She hands me the credit card slip and a pen and I scrawl my signature across the piece of paper, thrusting it toward her.

"You do that," I bite out, storming away from the counter before she can even hand me my receipt. I head for our table, glancing over at the bar, where Chuck stands. He waves at me and I do the same, the need for alcohol suddenly consuming me. I wish I was twenty-one. I wish I could order a beer. A couple of shots. What the fuck ever I can get my hands on.

"We got alcohol at the house?" I ask Eli when I join them at the table.

Eli shrugs. "Maybe a couple of beers?"

"I do," Caleb says. "The girls left behind some cheap ass tequila from that party they had at our house."

Tony sends him a look, but otherwise remains quiet.

"I'm coming straight over then after we're done here," I tell them, sipping from my boring ass soda cup.

"I take it your conversation with Ellie didn't go over so well," Eli says.

"Your observation would be correct." I scowl in her direction, my gaze dropping to the perfection that is her ass.

I look away before I become too fixated on it.

"Coming over to our house to get blindingly drunk won't help matters," Tony says, ever the logical one.

"It'll help me cope," I say with a halfhearted smile.

"Do you really need alcohol to cope, Jackson? If that's the case, you have a bigger problem than just Ellie," Tony continues.

"I don't need you giving me shit tonight," I mutter, glaring at the table. If I look at Tony too long, I might get pissed at him, and I don't want that. I like the guy. It's not his fault I'm in such a foul mood.

My bad mood is like a wet blanket draped over all of us. We're downright somber as we wait for our food and I blame myself, though I'm also blaming that dick Caleb for bringing up Ellie's date with Carson in the first place. Deep down, I know I'm just shooting the messenger or however that saying is supposed to go. I shouldn't be mad at Caleb for telling me.

I should be upset with Ellie that she went on a date with someone else.

Though really? I guess I shouldn't. We've never once defined what we are. Currently, we are friends. Who kiss on occasion. I gave her an orgasm once. I'd like to give her a bunch more, and I'd love it if she gave me a few as well. Could that ever happen?

I'm hopeful. But she might let my ass down easy tonight. She might like Carson, and want to pursue something with him. He's the better guy for her. I know this. I can't guarantee shit. I have too much going on, and I'm anti-commitment, while she is the poster child for a long-term relationship. You look up commitment in the dictionary and there's a photo of her above the definition with the caption, 'This is the type of girl you look for as a wife'.

Yeah. That's Ellie. She doesn't want a one-night stand or a couple of quick hook ups. She's the real deal.

By the time we get our food, we're a little more talkative, though we're consuming food at an efficient rate so not much is being said anyway. Caleb takes off to go flirt with a girl who's in one of his classes and the second he's gone, I breathe a sigh of relief.

"I'm pissed at him," I tell my remaining friends.

"You shouldn't be," Tony says in defense of Caleb. "I hate how he said it, like he wanted to taunt your ass, but I'm pretty sure he's telling you the truth."

"Yeah, he wouldn't lie about that," Eli adds.

I stare at Eli hard, but he won't look me directly in the eyes.

Hmmm.

"What do you know?" I ask him.

His gaze barely meets mine before he looks away again. "Nothing."

"Liar," I murmur, lightly pounding my fist against the edge of the table. "Tell me, Eli. Did Ava say something to you?"

He sighs. Shakes his head. Takes a sip of his drink. Stalling like crazy. I practically growl in frustration before he finally opens his damn mouth.

"Fine. What Caleb said was true. Ellie did go out with that guy to the movies. It happened Monday," Eli confesses.

I frown. "A few days ago?"

He nods. "All the girls encouraged her to go, including mine. Ava told me about it last night."

"And you didn't think you should tell me?" I ask incredulously.

"I didn't want to, because I knew you'd act like this," Eli says. "You're all pissed off, but come on. You two aren't actually together. You hooked up with her once and haven't really talked to her much since. She figured you lost interest."

Say the fuck what? "When did I ever act like I've lost interest? I've been busy. Just as busy as the rest of you." My gaze scans the table, and Tony and Eli just shrug. "I've been talking to her at night. We text almost daily."

"Right. Like usual. Like you used to. She truly believes she's been regulated back to her old position in your life. The girl 'good enough' to be friends with, but 'not good enough' to date or whatever." Eli waves a hand, his expression vaguely disgusted. "I sound like a girl. I need to stop hanging out with them all the time."

When is Eli hanging out with them all the time? He makes no damn sense.

My gaze switches to Tony, who's watching us with an impassive expression on his face, still eating. Quiet as usual, the broody motherfucker. "What do you think about all of this?"

He swallows his food down before he says, "I think you need to make a move, son."

My brows shoot up. I expected some long, thoughtful observation, which is Tony's normal style. "On Ellie?"

"No, on some other random girl. Yes, *of course* on Ellie. Haven't you wasted enough time? She's been patiently waiting for you, and when you finally realize you might have feelings for her, you toy with her for a little bit, and then you back way off." He shakes his head, setting down his sandwich. "I know it's some scary shit, committing yourself to one girl, but you can do this. It's not so bad. It's actually pretty fucking amazing when you find the right one."

I contemplate the two of them. My two closest friends who have girlfriends. Who are perfectly happy being with just one woman. One is so over the top in love with his girl, he acts the fool over her most of the time. And the other one is calm and cool, and only ever seems truly happy when she's in his presence.

That wouldn't be so bad, right? Why am I being such a dumbass about this?

"Because you're afraid to love," Tony says, as if he can read my mind.

Or maybe I said that last part out loud. Yeah, that must've been it.

My mind drifts to Diego, the most committed one of all. He has a kid for the love of God, and he's happy. Perfectly content playing house with Jocelyn and their baby girl. That is some overwhelming shit right there, but he's never questioned it. Was never tempted to back out either. He wanted it. Wanted her and the life they now have. He seems happy too.

"I'm not afraid to love," I scoff, leaning away from the table. My appetite evaporates. Actually, my stomach is twisted in knots, and that can't be good. "I just see no reason to tie myself down at this age."

"You won't look at it as tying yourself down if you actually fall in love with her," Eli says, sounding logical for once in his damn life. "Look, I'm ridiculous when it comes to Ava. I love that girl more than anyone else in the world, and it's killing me that we're not living in the same area code right now, but I fucking love her. And I will do whatever it takes to keep loving her, even if we're apart. It sucks, but she's worth it."

Ellie comes into view, striding across the restaurant with purpose, her gaze going to our table every few seconds. Enough times that our gazes finally snag. Catch. She smiles at me, heading toward the back of the restaurant and, without thought, I rise to my feet.

And follow after her.

My steps determined, I'm directly behind her in seconds. Close enough that I can reach out and touch her.

So I do.

She whirls on me, my fingers still clasped loosely around the crook of her elbow. She tilts her head back, her expression neutral, reminding me of a queen.

"If you're mad at me, I can't get into an argument with you right now, Jackson. I'm on the clock," she says haughtily.

Huh, so now she's mad too? Okay, I can play this game.

"I don't want to argue," I say, which is the truth. "I just want to know something."

"Oh." She seems surprised. "What do you want to know?"

"Is it true? You went on a date with Carson?" I keep my voice level. Calm. Inside, I'm anything but. My thoughts, my emotions are in chaos. Just having her this close, barely touching her, is sending me into a tailspin.

A sigh leaves her and she drops her head, staring at her feet. I wait for her to say something, the blood roaring in my ears, drowning out all other sounds. She is taking way too long to answer a simple question.

"Yes," she tells her feet. "I couldn't put him off forever, waiting for you to make a move. So I went out with him."

She was putting him off for me? Yeah right. "How was it?"

She shrugs one shoulder but says nothing.

I crowd her, until her back is against the wall and I've got my hand braced above her head, leaning into her, my other hand playing with the end of one of her braids. "How was it?" I repeat. "Did you enjoy yourself?"

"The movie was good," she whispers.

"Did he touch you?" I have no business asking her this. What does it matter if he touched her? She's not mine.

Yeah, the little voice inside my head says. *Keep telling yourself that.*

"He held my hand afterward," she admits, her voice soft. "When we walked through the parking lot to his car."

I tamp down the overwhelming emotion that threatens to take over. So what if he held her hand. It's no big deal.

But it makes me angry, thinking of him touching her. Worse?

It fucking hurts.

"Did he kiss you?" My voice is raw, and I clear my throat, hating how fucking needy I sound. Like if she admits that they kissed, I'll fall apart.

Her gaze never straying from mine, she slowly shakes her head.

Relief floods me and I nearly sag. But I keep myself upright. Act like none of this shit is bugging me.

I can't resist touching her though. My fingers find her chin. Trace her jaw. She closes her eyes and swallows hard, and I'd give anything to kiss her. Reassure her.

Reassure her of what? That I still want her? Pretty sure it's fairly obvious.

More like I need the reassurance she still wants me.

My hand drops and I back away from her, giving her space. Giving me space. "Do you like him?"

"Who?" She frowns. "Carson? I mean, he's nice. He really likes me. And he doesn't mind letting me know that either."

Ouch. Fucking direct hit.

Ellie, one. Jackson, big fat zero.

"Do you want to be with him?" I brace myself, waiting for her answer.

"Do you want to be with me?" she throws back in my face.

"You answer first," I say, sounding like a little kid.

"I don't know." She pauses. "Maybe."

A growl leaves me and I thrust my hand into my hair, gripping the back of my head. "What the fuck, Ellie?"

"No. You don't get to act like this. I should be the one who's saying 'what the fuck'." She reaches out, pushing at my chest, sending me stumbling backward. "What are we doing, Jackson?"

"What do you mean?"

"Me and you. What are we *doing?*" A ragged exhale leaves her and she shakes her head. "I promised myself I wouldn't have this conversation with you right now."

She tries to leave and I grab hold of her arm, stopping her. "We're having it."

"I'm working," she reminds me.

"You started it."

"I did not!" She's positively indignant.

"You did," I say, immediately realizing we're just going round and round.

"You never answered my question," she says. "Do you want to be with me?"

I do.

The two words come to me, unbidden. Automatic. That's what I want to say, but fuck.

Should I say that? She could reject me for that Carson

dude and I'll be left standing here with my heart in my hands, and she'll shove it back at me a broken, shattered mess.

Jesus, I really have turned into fucking John Mayer. I love that guy. He's a great song writer, but sappy as shit sometimes.

"Well?" she says, her tone hostile.

I bite back the words I want to say. Out of habit. Out of self-protection. I want to admit to her what I want. But it's like…

I can't.

"That's what I thought," she says after too many beats of silence. "I can't keep chasing after you, Jackson. And you have to stop counting on me always being there for you. There's nothing in it for me. You get it all."

"Ellie—"

"No." She shakes her head. "There's no point in us talking tonight. You can figure out your shit on your own. I'm tired of trying to help you. Of being your support system all the time, when it's like you can't even see me. And you don't get to be jealous of a guy when you won't ever make a move on me. Your arrogance is—annoying."

"Annoying?" I laugh. I can't help it. "You don't think I see you? I see you every goddamn day, Ellie. You haunt my thoughts. You're in my dreams. I think about you when I jerk off, for Christ's sake. I see you. I see *all* of you."

I'm breathing hard. So is she. Her gaze drops to my mouth, as if she wants me to kiss her, and so I give in.

I kiss her.

Like I can't help myself.

The moment my lips crash down on hers, she responds. Her hands curl into the front of my T-shirt, trying to pull me closer. I give her what she wants, pressing her against the wall, my body flush with hers, our mouths fused. Hungry. Tongues tangling. I touch her face. Her hair. Her shoulder.

Her chest, cupping her breasts. She fits perfectly in my palm and I press harder, making her moan into my mouth.

Just as fast as I kissed her, I back away, ending it all. Her eyes open and she watches me warily, her chest rising and falling at a rapid pace. She says nothing.

"I see you," I repeat. "But my question is, do you really *see me*, Ellie?"

She doesn't answer.

So I walk away.

CHAPTER 24
ELLIE

"Are you excited about Jackson's show tonight?" Ava smiles at me in the mirror, her entire expression joyful. She's so glad to be home. With us. With Eli. I'm glad she's here too. I've missed her terribly.

But my mood is terrible. I can't stop thinking about my little argument with Jackson last night. The words we said to each other. The way he kissed me.

I wasn't that mad about our not seeing each other much over the last few weeks. I get it—we're both busy. But I hated how jealous he got over Carson. Yes, I can admit it didn't feel right going on that date with him. I shouldn't have done it at all. Carson is sweet. He's a good guy.

I just don't think he's the guy for me.

Even though I went on a date with him, it doesn't give Jackson the right to act like a jealous asshole and demand I stop seeing Carson. Not that he ever said stuff like that. But his obvious jealousy infuriates me. If he wants to actually be with me, he needs to tell me. He needs to do something about it. Maybe I made things worse, but I don't know.

I feel like we both made things worse, and now I'm nervous. Maybe we're not made for each other after all.

Maybe this will never work.

"Are you okay?" Ava asks when I still haven't said anything. "You seem down."

"I'm fine." I turn to face her, a weak smile pasted on my face. "I'm so glad you're here. I've missed you."

She pulls me into a tight hug. "I've missed you too. And I've known you long enough to know there's something bothering you. What's wrong?"

I pull away from her, waving my hand dismissively. "I'm fine. I don't want to ruin your mood."

"If you're not happy, I'm not happy. End of story." She grabs hold of my shoulders and gives me a gentle shake. "Is it Jackson?"

I nod, exhaling loudly. "He's such a prick."

"Is he now?" Ava arches a brow, sounding amused. "So tell me. Have you seen his prick yet?"

I laugh. That was just the thing I needed to hear. "No. But I've felt it."

She gapes at me. "You haven't seen it?"

"We haven't done much." I shrug.

"You said you hooked up. He fingered you."

I hate how my friends say fingered. It's kind of—ick. "I never did anything to him."

"What? Unbelievable." Ava shakes her head. She and Eli have been sexually active since they were sixteen. Those two go at it all the time. "Jackson needs to make a move."

"That's pretty much what I told him." I explain everything that's happened between us to Ava. Like break it all down, right there in the middle of my bathroom while we get ready for Jackson's performance at Strummers tonight. I wanted to back out, but it would look weird if I didn't show when all the rest of our friends will be there. Diego and Jocelyn even got a babysitter for Gigi so they could go. If I didn't show my face, the gang would know something's up.

"Maybe you overreacted," Ava says when I finish speaking.

"Nope. I didn't." I shake my head, not about to take responsibility for the blow up. "He's the one with jealousy issues, yet he never tells me that he actually wants to be with me. If I give him a piece of myself and then he dumps me for some other random girl to hook up with after a performance or game or whatever? Forget that. I don't want to be just another girl added to his list."

"You're already on the list," she reminds me gently.

"I've never allowed his P into my V, as Gracie says." I roll my eyes while Ava laughs. "And that P is coming nowhere near me if he can't tell me, *Ellie, I want to be with you*. He couldn't manage it last night. What's going to change?"

Ava's laughter dies and she sends me a sad smile. "Are you going to be okay at Strummers?"

I shrug. "I don't know. Probably. I've done this sort of thing before. Watched him with adoration in my eyes while hundreds of girls and Caleb scream his name."

We both smile, thinking of Caleb fangirl screaming.

"I heard Caleb isn't allowed to scream his name tonight. Not with those record execs coming to watch him perform," Ava tells me.

Right. The record execs. Jackson told me about his call with the guy from Evergreen last week. I hope it works out for him, though he'll probably tell them no anyway.

And I'm sad no one told me about Caleb not being allowed to scream how hot Jackson is like he usually does. But I haven't been hanging around any of them lately. I've been too busy. And okay...maybe I'm distancing myself from the gang. They all surround Jackson continuously, keeping us linked. I might need to break that connection.

Sooner than I thought.

"I'll go tonight, but if he acts like a jerk, forget it. I won't stick around," I say.

"We're all going to hang out at Eli and Jackson's apartment after the concert," Ava says, reaching out to gently touch my arm. "I want you there."

"And I would love to be there, but I can't go." I shake my head, anxiety filling me just at the thought of being there. "I have to protect myself."

"I get it. I do." She hauls me in for another hug. Ava is never one to avoid her emotions. That's one of my favorite things about her. "He's a fucker."

"Who? Jackson?" I start to laugh.

She pulls away from me, her expression fierce. "He is. A complete motherfucker. Why does he have to toy with your emotions like this? Why can't he just give in and tell you what you want to hear?"

"Because maybe he doesn't feel that way about me. I don't want him saying those things if he doesn't mean it." My words are logical, as are my thoughts. And I tell myself it's okay if he doesn't actually feel that way about me.

But it hurts. It hurts like crazy because why else would he get jealous over Carson? Is Jackson that much in denial? Or is he one of those assholes who doesn't want me, but doesn't want anyone else to have me either?

I'm guessing the latter. So many guys are like that. It's such bullshit.

"It's okay if that's the case," I continue since Ava hasn't responded. "I can move on. Eventually."

"Yeah, I know you can," she says softly, her eyes glowing. "You're such a good person, Ellie. And you have such a big heart. If Jackson can't see your worth, another guy will, and he'll give you the proper treatment you deserve."

"I know. You're right. Thank you." We hug again. Her words are reassuring. They make me a feel a little better. Though deep down inside...

All I want is Jackson.

———

We arrive at Strummers thirty minutes before they open the doors. The line is wrapped around the building, nothing but teenaged girls as far as the eye can see. I rode over to Strummers with Eli and Ava, feeling like a complete third wheel. They are all over each other, Eli acting like he can't take his eyes or hands off of her, and by the time we're out of the car and headed for the venue, I'm walking far ahead of them so I don't have to witness their slightly sickening display of affection toward each other.

It's definitely a me problem and not a them problem, that's for sure.

I spot Diego, Jocelyn, Gracie, Hayden, Tony and Caleb already standing in line, and I rush toward them, laughing with Gracie and Hayden as they wrap me up in a group hug.

"We haven't seen you in forever!" Hayden says, squeezing me extra hard. "Are you avoiding us?"

I am going to miss them so badly. I don't want to end our friendship, and I won't. But I'm definitely going to keep them at arm's length for a little bit while I work on getting over Jackson.

"I'm not avoiding you," I tell them both with a smile. "I've just been really busy. Working a lot."

"God, I know. School is such a grind," Gracie says, rolling her eyes. "I'm ready to graduate."

"G, we have two more years," Hayden reminds her. "Well, a little less than that, but still. Buckle down, babe. We've got a long way to go."

We talk about school. Classes. Tony joins our conversation, wrapping his arms around Hayden from behind and holding her close. Eli and Ava arrive long minutes later, which makes me wonder what they were up to. Probably making out. Now they're hanging all over each other and everyone greets them enthusiastically, especially Ava. Caleb hangs back from the group, on the complete opposite side from where Gracie's standing, and I wonder if those two have had another spat.

I feel for them. I really, really do.

Once the doors open, it's a mad rush to get inside. Normally by this point in the night, I'd be texting Jackson, wishing him luck. Gushing over his potential performance and reassuring him that he's going to do great. But I do none of that. I don't text him at all, because damn it, I want him to miss me.

I want him to miss me so badly, he'll realize he needs me in his life after all.

The inside of Strummers is jam-packed with people. Jackson is the main attraction tonight. There's a band opening before him, and I feel sorry for them. These girls aren't here to see them. They're all Jackson Rivers' fangirls, just like I used to be.

Used to be. Ha.

Still am.

Caleb worms his way through the crowd of overexcited females, indicating that we should all follow after him. We make a human chain, linking hands as we move through the thick clusters of people, trying to get closer to the stage. There's no advanced admission tickets at this place. It's first come, first serve and the floor is open. This is where I'm grateful for the big football players in our group. They just push their way through the crowd, Caleb always being the most aggressive of the bunch.

We're closer to the stage, but there are still a few rows of people ahead of us. The lights go down, girls start screaming, and when the curtains lift, a band is on stage. All of them young, baby-faced cuties.

The girls start shrieking as soon as they launch into a fast-paced song.

"Who are these guys?" Ava shouts into my ear.

I shrug. "I don't know."

"They're Cupid's Bow," Gracie yells at us with a big grin on her face. "Aren't they adorable? They came up with the name because one of their moms told them they look like a group of cherubs, since they have such pretty faces."

I want to roll my eyes, but I keep myself in check. I pay close attention, the way they smile out at the crowd, pointing and winking at girls. Making it seem like they're singing at one girl in a particular. There are two guitarists and a bassist, and they're not bad. Their voices are a little shaky, but I've heard worse. And their enthusiasm makes up for any lack of skill. They look like they're truly enjoying themselves. And from all the incessant screaming, I'd guess the majority of the audience enjoys them too.

Hmm, maybe they all aren't here just for Jackson. Maybe this band is attracting a bunch of groupies too. Smart to put them together.

The set goes on for over a half hour and it's continuous teeny bop sounding rock music. I could easily imagine these guys on the radio. I find myself moving to the music. Gracie and I dance around each other in circles, laughing as Gracie sings along with the chorus. Someone is clearly a fan.

This is what I love about Gracie. She embraces everything and everyone. She's interested in all sorts of different things, and she's open to everyone. She's not afraid to say what she feels either.

I could take lessons from her. In fact, I have been, and she's been a big help. Showing me how much stronger I can be.

That's what I need. To be stronger. To stand up for myself. To ask for what I want, instead of expecting someone to figure it out on their own.

Like Jackson.

The band ends their set with a ballad, and all the girls sway with their arms up in the air, clutching their phones with the flashlight on, brightening the room. The couples I'm with are all cuddled up with each other, while Gracie, Caleb and I stand together, me in between them. I catch Caleb glancing in Gracie's direction what feels like every few seconds, and I wish these two would either make it happen or give up. He also needs to do that with Baylee. Either tell her he wants to be with her, or cut her loose.

He's not good enough for her. She's put up with that shit way too long. Longer than I have with Jackson. I've gone to school with Baylee for what feels like forever. I've never really gotten close to her though. She moved in a different circle than I did, plus she's a year older than me. And while she's hung out with our group a few times, Caleb doesn't bring her around that much. He actually told us he didn't want to put ideas in her head by letting her hang with us.

That's kind of messed up. But that's exactly what the two of them are.

Like Jackson and me.

He put way too many ideas in my head, and now look at me. Pissed and hurt, ready to walk away for good. I'm even willing to give up my friends, so I don't have to deal with his dumb ass anymore.

That's actually infuriating.

When Cupid's Bow finish their set, the curtains drop and the girls are left screaming at nothing. Once the regular lights come up and background music starts, some of the crowd thins, giving us more room to inch closer to the stage.

"Hope he brings it tonight," Caleb says, shaking his head. "That band wasn't so bad."

"You're into the One Direction sound now, hmm?" Gracie teases.

"That shit went a lot harder than 1D," he scoffs, shaking his head. "Besides, I happen to like Harry Styles. That fucker does whatever he wants and no one judges him for it."

"Are you serious?" I ask him, shocked. I don't think I've

ever heard a guy admit he likes Harry Styles. Not even Jackson, and he appreciates all kinds of music. Even boy bands.

"Sure. Why not? He sings and girls drop at his feet. They lose their fucking minds over that guy. To have that kind of power…" His voice shifts and he shakes his head. "Must be mind-blowing."

"Ask your friend. I'm sure he knows all about it," Gracie says, her gaze immediately going to mine. "Oops, I didn't mean anything by—"

"No, it's okay. Jackson does have a pretty big fan club," I reassure her.

"Yeah, but you're still his number one fangirl, right?" Gracie's brows shoot up.

I slowly shake my head. "I don't think so. Not anymore."

And that makes me sad. Worse, it kind of hurts. It's for the best though. I need to move on.

I have to.

We all chat while we wait for Jackson's performance. It's so hot in here, I'm sweating. Thank god I put my hair up in a high ponytail and am only wearing a cute camisole I bought at the end of summer. The straps are thin, as is the fabric, showing off plenty of skin. I wish I would've worn shorts because these jeans are confining, but whatever. Ava and I were going for a look, and we sort of match, like we're still in middle school.

It was fun, getting ready with her earlier. Like old times.

The music stops. The lights shut off, and the crowd goes silent while we wait. I'm breathless, knowing what's about to happen, but still excited over it anyway.

This is what Jackson does to me.

A single spotlight clicks on, shining on the stage, and there he is. Sitting in his ornate throne, his guitar in his lap, wearing jeans and a black tank. He leans in close to the mic, flicking his head to get the strands of his long blond hair out of his face. "Good evening. I'm Jackson Rivers."

The crowd goes wild. Including me.

He launches into a song that is vaguely familiar, but I can't quite place it. He usually kicks off every performance with a cover song, and it's normally Nirvana.

But this isn't Nirvana. I'm not sure who it is, but I can't help swaying to the beat, letting it take over my body. Jackson's voice wraps all around me, his fingers plucking the guitar strings nimbly, creating a bluesy sound. It dawns on me who the song reminds me of. I'm not a huge John Mayer fan, though my mom used to be, but the song has a Mayer feel and I'm thinking that's who it is.

Hmm. Not what I would consider Jackson's normal style, but I'm digging it.

Once the song is over, everyone claps and shouts. Jackson's smiling, his gaze scanning the crowd. I keep myself tucked behind Caleb, not wanting him to see me enjoying this. Maybe I shouldn't be enjoying it.

But it's like I can't help myself. I love the way he performs, his songs, his voice, his charisma on stage.

The curtains lift, revealing the band behind him, and he jumps out of the giant chair, leaving his guitar behind as he goes over to the microphone stand and clutches the mic with both hands. "I have a new song I'm debuting tonight. Wanna hear it?"

All the girls scream *yes* as loud as they can, including Caleb. Jackson sends him a warning look, and I can't help but smile.

I love how Caleb gives him endless shit, and Jackson just takes it.

"Wanna know what it's called?" Jackson asks, his gaze zeroing in on me and never straying.

Yes! They all scream again, except for me. I can't speak.

All I can do is stare helplessly at this man I am hopelessly in love with.

He waits until they quiet down, licking his lower lip in

this sexy way that probably has half the girls in the room melting as he murmurs close to the mic, "The song is called 'Pink'. Here we go."

The band starts playing, Jackson nodding his head to the beat. I'm breathless with anticipation, waiting to hear him sing and when he starts, I'm riveted.

When I first met you, I didn't know what I had
 You were loyal and true, yet I treated you so fuckin' bad
 You should've walked, when I proved who I really am
 Yet here you still are, and you're taking a stand
 There are things I've done, words I can't take back
 That hurt you, destroyed you, and I'm a complete dick
 But now I'm here with my heart in my hands
 Eager and willing to make you understand
 That every single part of me aches for you
 Do you ache for me too?

Oh shit. I think this song is about…me.

Gracie and Hayden send me knowing looks. I can only shake my head helplessly, my eyes wide, my heart thumping wildly. I glance back at the stage, Jackson's eyes finding mine once more as he launches into the chorus.

Pink
 Like the color of your perfect lips
 Pink
 That smile of yours
 could sink a thousand ships
 Pink
 Are your cheeks
 when you think

of all the things I can do
Pink
Is my favorite place to touch you

The guitarist plays, and Jackson points at the crowd, his index finger aimed right at me.

There's no other place I'd rather be
*   Than in the pink of you, surrounding me*

"What the hell?" Caleb swivels his head in my direction, gaping at me. "Is he singing about your ah...vagina?"

Gracie slaps his arm. Hayden starts to laugh. Ava is suddenly behind me, gripping my shoulders, her mouth at my ear.

"Pretty sure this song is for you," she whisper-yells.

Yeah. I'm pretty sure it is, too.

CHAPTER 25

JACKSON

played my fucking heart out tonight. Not for the fans, not for my friends. Not even for Rick and his people from Evergreen Records. Tonight wasn't for any of them.

Tonight was for Ellie.

After our stupid argument the night before, I went over to Caleb and Tony's and got shit-faced drunk. I couldn't stop laughing at one point and they all got really pissed at me. They sat me down and gave me a talking to, and after I calmed down, I actually listened. I got real quiet as their words sunk in.

So did Ellie's.

I'm a selfish dick. And I know it. I've been in denial, but my feelings for Ellie have been hiding in plain sight. I was just scared. Scared of fucking up. Scared of hurting her. Scared of getting myself into a situation I didn't want to be in.

How bad could it be, being with Ellie? I have fun with her. She's my friend. Even better, I want her. I'm attracted to her. I care about her. We have serious chemistry. I don't know why I couldn't admit this to myself sooner.

At least I've realized how much she means to me before I

fucked it all up for good. Now I just need to convince her that I know what I want.

And that's her.

I saw her hiding behind Caleb when I first started performing. She didn't want me to see her, but like I told her last night, I do see her, all of her.

Everywhere she goes.

Pink is, of course, just for her. An ode to Ellie, and everything that she is. Every pretty little part of her, including the pink between her legs. Crude, yes, but fuck it. The words are all true. There is truly nowhere else I'd rather be, than sinking in the pink of her and feeling her surround me.

I performed for over an hour, and before we went on stage, I told the bodyguard who's on duty backstage tonight that I didn't want any girls back there except for the list I gave him. No random women sneaking into my dressing room fawning all over me and hoping for a hook up. I'm over that shit. No liquor in my room either. I need to keep a clear head so I can talk to these record people and see what they have to say.

I did some research on Evergreen and I like the company's message. They seem selective on who they sign, and they have a couple of up-and-coming superstars on their roster. They have big dreams and lots of plans, just like I do. I don't think I'd get lost in the shuffle with them. They're not too big of a machine yet.

They're exactly what I'm looking for. Now here's hoping the terms are agreeable.

Once I do a couple of encores—what the fuck is this life—I find my way backstage, collapsing in the chair in my dressing room and going through about two and half water bottles before I finally feel like I've got enough fluids in me.

There's a knock at the door before it cracks open, Stu, the bodyguard, peeking his dark head inside. "Your friends are here."

"Let them in," I tell him, anticipation thrumming hard through my veins.

They burst into the dressing room seconds later, noisy as fuck, giant smiles on their faces as they greet me. They all embrace me, even Ava, who gives me a big hug and calls me a sexy rock star.

"Hey, don't call him sexy," Eli protests, yanking her into his arms. He glares at me as if I'm going to try something with her.

I just bark out a laugh. He's crazy.

"I'd say about two thirds of that crowd were creaming their panties over you," Caleb says to me as we perform a complicated handshake we made up recently. "Though that band before you was a tough act to follow."

"It was my idea for them to open for me," I say. Cupid's Bow are all barely out of high school, like me, and they're trying to make it big. Also like me. They're all a bunch of pretty boys who are playing up their looks over their talent, but I get it. They're not bad, but they look way better than they sound.

"You're fucking crazy. They about stole the spotlight," Caleb says truthfully.

I'm not worried about it, but I appreciate his concern. So I just slap him on the back, my gaze snagging on Ellie, who is currently chatting with Gracie and Hayden, glancing over at me what feels like every five seconds.

I don't stop looking at her either, and when her gaze finally meets mine, I crook my finger at her, silently calling her over.

She doesn't even hesitate. Just glides right on over to me, her expression wary, though her eyes are clear as she studies me.

"What did you think?" I ask as I grab a towel from the counter and wipe the sweat off my forehead. I'm still amped up. A little shaky even. Adrenaline coursing through my veins after such an epic performance. I need a shower. Wouldn't mind fucking all of this energy out of me either.

Wonder if Ellie's game, because she's the only one I currently want to fuck.

Her smile is small. As if she's trying to contain it. "You were—good."

"That's it? That's all I get?" I raise my brows, wanting more.

I always want more when it comes to her.

"I'm supposed to be mad at you, Jackson," she says, though she doesn't sound that mad at all.

"Yeah, I know," I say like a smug dick, but fuck it. "What did you think of your song?"

"*My* song?"

"Pink," I tell her with a dirty grin. "That was all about you."

She's quiet. Everyone else is talking, laughing. They're loud. Obnoxious. Happy. But the sounds fade, and all I can do is focus on Ellie and what she's about to say to me. I'm in suspense, worried she might've hated it.

"Were you actually referring to my—" She waves a hand in the direction of her lower body.

Unable to resist, I sneak my arm around her waist and pull her in close, dropping a kiss on her surprised lips. "Yes," I murmur against her mouth. "All of those words were true. I'm a dumbass, El."

"Oh, I know you are." She gently sets her hands on my chest, as if she's going to push me away.

I can feel her touch right down to my bones. Deeper. I want those hands all over me. Taking off my clothes. Stroking me. Guiding me home. To the spot between her legs where I know I'll fit perfectly.

She doesn't push me away. She pulls me in instead, slipping her arms around my neck, her fingers toying with the hair at my nape. "You're a pain in my ass, Jackson Rivers."

"I know. I'm a stupid fuck. But come home with me tonight and I'll show you how much you mean to me," I murmur, just before I steal a kiss.

"What the fuck? Now you two are together?"

This comes from Caleb.

Ellie pulls away from me, her cheeks flushed as she laughs. "We don't know what we are, Caleb."

"I know what we are." I slink my arm around her shoulders, pulling her into my side. "She's mine."

They all say "ooooh" at the same time, the fuckers. Every single one of them.

Ellie's cheeks turn pink. I glare. They all laugh at us, just as we start laughing too.

I am on top of the world right now.

On top of the fucking world.

There's a loud knock at the door, just before Stu barges inside. "There's a group from Evergreen Records here to talk to you, J. What do you want me to tell them?"

I glance around at my friends. "Time to leave, folks."

Complaining groans fill the air, but they all file out of the room, offering their congratulations to me as they pass by. Ellie tries to make her escape with them, but I keep my arm firmly around her shoulders, not letting her go until they're all gone and I've sent Stu away to bring Rick and his cronies back to the dressing room.

"Give me a kiss for luck," I tell her, feeling cocky.

"You don't need it." She gives me a sweet peck on the lips anyway, pulling away before I can demand more. "Good luck. You've got this."

"This one feels right to me," I tell her, suddenly nervous.

Scared.

Damn it, I've never been scared talking to any of these record label people. Not once. I'm the one who always acted like I've got nothing to lose, and they've had everything to gain. But right now, I'm worried I'll somehow mess this up.

And I don't want to. Not with this label.

Ellie's expression turns serious too. As if she understands how important this is to me, even though I haven't said that out loud yet. The girl can read my mind. She's so attuned to me. Just like I'm tuned in to her.

"You're going to be fine. I'm sure they already love you," she whispers, patting me in the center of my chest. She curls her fingers around the chain dangling from my neck, pulling on it so I have no choice but to meet her lips one more time for a gentle kiss. "Just be yourself, Jackson. They won't be able to resist you."

I blow out a harsh breath, leaning my forehead against hers for a beat as I gather my thoughts and nerves. "Right. Okay. You coming back to my apartment? We're having a small get-together. I want you there."

"I wasn't planning on it," she admits, biting her lower lip in that way of hers. I want to be the one who bites that lip. "I was kind of mad at you."

"You still mad?" I hang on her every word, praying she doesn't reject me.

"A little." She shrugs. A small smile tickling the corners of her lips. "How can I stay mad when you write me dirty songs?"

"Then it worked." I squeeze her hand as she slowly pulls away from me. "I won't be too long, I don't think. I'm not sure how this is going to go."

"It'll be great." She smiles.

I wish I had as much faith in myself as she has in me.

I watch her leave the room, my gaze glued on her ass, exhaling loudly with relief that she's not completely pissed at me. The minute she's gone, three dudes and an extraordinarily beautiful woman stride into the dressing room, all wearing matching cool smiles on their faces as they study me with undisguised interest.

It's a little creepy. I feel like an animal locked up in a zoo.

The one in the expensive suit steps forward, his hand thrust out toward me. "Jackson, a pleasure to meet you. I'm Rick."

I shake his hand. "Nice to finally meet you."

"Terrific performance tonight. Really enthusiastic crowd," he says, nodding as he glances around the cramped dressing room. "No alcohol to celebrate?"

"Wanted to keep a clear head," I tell him truthfully.

"Got it. Well, we think you're fabulous. Amazing. Such a unique sound, considering the market currently. Great rendition of Vultures. Mayer is a lyrical genius," Rick gushes.

"Thanks." I'm suddenly filled with the need to have a shot to calm my nerves.

"And that new song. 'Pink'? That's a hit in the making right there," Rick continues. "A little fine tuning is all it would take to turn it into a chart topper."

"No shit?" I rub my jaw. I wrote it for Ellie, never thinking it could be an actual hit. I just wrote it to work my feelings out.

"Very racy," the attractive woman says with a faint smile, her gaze meeting mine. Her eyes are ice blue, her hair platinum blonde, her skin is smooth as silk, and her tits look ready to bust out of the low neckline of her shirt. "Lots of innuendo."

"More than innuendo. We can all figure out what you were singing about." Rick laughs. "Though you don't come right out and say it."

"Yeah." I smile, glancing around at each of them. "I'm glad you enjoyed the performance."

"We did. We did. We're, uh, we're also very interested in the band that opened for you. Cupid's Bow." Rick shakes his head, rubbing his jaw with his hand. "Those boys were something else."

My stomach sinks. "Did you talk to them?"

"We did. We did." He nods repeatedly, overly enthusiastic. "We set up an appointment with them next week."

"Great. They're an awesome bunch of guys," I say, fighting disappointment.

Rick keeps rambling, and the other guys chime in, introducing themselves to me, though I immediately forget their names. The woman eyes me like a piece of meat she wants to consume. They talk and talk, but they don't say anything of substance, and that's when it hits me.

They're not going to offer a meeting to me. I know it. I can feel it in my bones. And I did this shit to myself. It was my idea to have Cupid's Bow open for me, and look what it got me.

Straight out of a record deal.

CHAPTER 26
ELLIE

The moment Jackson walks into the apartment, everyone starts cheering. Calling his name and clapping, Caleb whistling so loud it makes my ears hurt. I clap along with them, my excitement dying the moment I see the look on Jackson's face.

He's not happy. Not at all.

Oh, he's smiling and nodding and holding his hand up, so his friends can slap their palms together. He graciously hugs Ava and Jocelyn, who are both gushing over his performance. Diego gives him a hug too, just before the couple slips out, having to get home so they can relieve their babysitter, which is Jocelyn's mom and sister.

But I can see it in his eyes, in his entire demeanor. Things didn't go the way he wanted them to with the record label, and my heart aches for him.

He takes the beer Eli offers him and polishes it off in a couple of gulps. Caleb gives him another beer as I wait for him to come to me, my eyes never straying from him as he moves about the apartment.

It takes him a while to notice me, but I'm not offended. I can tell he needs their accolades. He was feeling down and they're treating him like the man. I totally get it. I'm just sitting here, listening to Gracie go on about how she got the Snapchat handle from one of the guys in Cupid's Bow, and how she's totally going to hit him up.

Finally, Jackson notices me, and the relief that crosses his face when our gazes meet sends a little thrill deep inside me. I sit up straighter, on the edge of the couch, pleased when he settles directly beside me and leans in for a kiss.

I give it to him, right in front of everyone, pleased that he's not holding back. I'm so used to him doing that. When we were both in high school, he would talk to me for hours on Snap, and then pretend I barely existed in person. It devasted me.

To have him kissing me in front of everyone, not giving a crap who sees, is what I've wanted for what feels like years.

"Are you all right?" I whisper when he pulls away.

His smile stays firmly in place as he slowly shakes his head. "Not really. We can talk about it later though."

I touch his cheek, wishing he wasn't so down. "It's going to be okay."

"With you?" He raises a brow.

I nod.

Jackson presses his cheek against mine, his mouth at my ear. "I wish we could go to my room."

"I wish we could too," I whisper in return. "But they want to spend time with you." I wave my hand in the general direction of our friends.

"I'll give them thirty minutes," he says, as he reluctantly pulls away from me.

"That's definitely not long enough." I laugh when he scowls. "Ninety minutes."

"No fucking way," he practically growls. "An hour."

"Perfect. An hour." Anticipation races through me when I see the dirty gleam in his gaze as he studies me. I know what he's thinking about.

I'm thinking about it too.

"Countdown is on," he says, just before he leaps to his feet. "See you in an hour. I need to go make the rounds with my people."

I giggle, waving at him. Fighting the combination of nerves and excitement that fills me at what we're about to do. At what epic line we're going to cross in our relationship.

The moment he's gone, Gracie says something. And I'd sort of forgotten she was sitting there on the couch.

"What was that all about?" The sly look on her face tells me she already knows.

"Nothing," I say, trying to infuse my voice with an air of mystery, but Gracie isn't buying it.

"Uh, huh. Are you two making sex plans for later?" She crosses her arms, waiting for my answer.

I can't hide it from her. I'm too excited. "Yes," I say with a giant grin. "We are."

"Make sure he's gentle with you." When I frown, she rolls her eyes, lowering her voice. "You're a virgin, Ellie. It's going to hurt."

I don't want it to hurt. I want it to feel amazing. I want him to feel amazing too. I'm sure he's used to being with women who aren't virgins. Who are adventurous and willing to do anything. I'm definitely willing when it comes to Jackson, and I'm sure I'll be bold, especially when it has to do with him, but I don't want to be in pain or cry over it.

"Won't it hurt no matter how we approach this?" I ask her.

"Yeah. I mean, the intensity level could fluctuate," she says, her expression thoughtful. "Make sure you're good and lubricated."

Ha. I sort of want to die of embarrassment over this.

"I don't think that'll be a problem," I say, trying to keep a straight face.

Just before we both burst into giggles.

I spend the next hour enjoying my time with my friends, soaking up Ava's bubbly good mood, laughing with her and the rest of the girls as she tells us stories about her time so far in San Diego. The weather is perfect, she spends a lot of free time at the beach and she's become friends with her dorm roommate.

"But she'll never replace you," Ava says to me at one point, which makes me misty eyed.

"She better not," I say gruffly, just before I pull her into a hug.

I'm hugging on a lot of people tonight. It doesn't help that I've had a couple of shots. A giant margarita made by Caleb, who's on bartending duty tonight. I don't even ask where the liquor comes from. They just always seem to magically have it, I'm guessing thanks to older friends.

Oh wait. Caleb keeps mentioning his fake ID. That's where they're getting it.

"There's a party at my frat tomorrow night," Caleb says. "You should all come."

"Yes!" Ava shouts, smiling at all of us. "I'm there."

"What if I want to keep you to myself?" Eli asks her as he approaches her from behind, slinging his arms around her waist.

"We can hang out at the party for a while," she says. "And then you can have me all to yourself."

A happy sigh leaves me as I watch them, feeling sappy. Gracie sighs too.

"They're couple goals," she says.

"So are Hayden and Tony," I add.

"Right? He would do anything for her. He's so good for her. They're good for each other." Gracie slowly shakes her head. "It feels like I will never find that."

"You will," I tell her firmly. "He's out there, just waiting for you."

"Really? Because I'm starting to think a guy like that

doesn't exist for me." Her gaze goes to Caleb, as if she can't help herself.

"You like him?" I ask.

"Not particularly," she says with a sigh. "I find him attractive. I'm drawn to his pretty face and his fucked-up mouth. I bet he's amazing in bed. Or wherever else he likes to have sex."

"I had a huge crush on him in middle school. When he was in the eighth grade and I was in the seventh," I admit.

Her eyes widen. "Really? Do tell."

I shrug. "It's like a rite of passage at my school for every girl to have a crush on Caleb Burke at some point in their life. He's just so attractive and flirty. He always has been. He makes every girl feel like she matters, even though, deep down, he doesn't really give a shit."

"I don't think he doesn't give a shit," Gracie says, actually defending him. "It's more like he just really likes women. All sorts of them."

Sounds familiar, is what I want to tell her. Gracie really likes men—all sorts of them. "He'll be a hard man to tame."

"Maybe he shouldn't be tamed. Maybe he should run wild and free," Gracie says, sounding thoughtful.

I think of Jackson. He's a little wild and free himself. And if he really pursues the rock star life, is that something I want to deal with? It's one thing to be one of his adoring fans. His good friend.

I'm pretty sure I'm about to step into the next level and become his actual girlfriend. How will I deal with those adoring fans? Can I handle them? Will I want to? And what if his career actually takes off? Will I end up getting left behind?

All things I really don't want to focus on right now.

Long minutes later, I'm in the kitchen, munching from a bag of tortilla chips, when I feel someone approach me from behind. A very tall, broad someone, who slowly wraps his arms around my waist and presses his body to mine.

"Time's up," Jackson whispers in my ear. "It's been an hour."

"No way." I'm still munching on the chips, shivering when he nuzzles his nose against my neck.

"It's true. It's actually been over an hour. I got stuck in a conversation with Eli and Caleb about our game next week." His lips move against my sensitive skin when he speaks. "I don't give a shit about football."

"You don't?" I frown, settling my hands over his.

"Don't really give a shit about the music either," he adds, his teeth grazing the spot just beneath my ear.

"You're lying." I melt against him when he shifts his arms lower, his fingers slipping beneath the hem of my shirt, touching my bare skin.

"It's true." His mouth is at my ear once more, his husky voice making me throb between my thighs. "The only thing I care about right now is you."

I slowly turn within his arms, so I can face him, my expression somber. The effects of the alcohol I consumed earlier have seemed to wear off. I am completely sober. "Do you really mean that?"

He grabs my hand, resting my palm against the center of his chest. I can feel his rapidly beating heart. "Feel that?"

I nod.

"That's what you do to me." His fingers encircle my wrist and he shifts my hand lower, to the front of his jeans. "Feel that?"

I curl my fingers around his erection, hoping no one is paying attention to us.

"You do that to me too. Now let's go to my room," he says, his expression, his tone so, so serious.

Only his eyes are lit with a fire that I recognize.

The same fire that burns inside me.

We don't say anything to announce our departure. We just leave, Jackson leading me down the short hall to his bedroom. We slip inside the room, Jackson reaching over and turning on the lamp that sits on top of his dresser before he pulls the door shut and locks it. I glance around his room, taking it all in, since I've never been here before. It's clean, nothing cluttered on top of every available surface like my space. His bed is neatly made, and I go to sit on the edge of it, anticipation curling through me at what is about to happen next.

Along with a healthy dose of fear.

He must've taken a shower before he came home, because he's wearing shorts and a T-shirt, his tank and jeans long gone. I watch as he toes off his shoes, kicking them to the side. He whips his shirt off next, pulling it off with one hand in that casual way guys do. My mouth goes dry at the sight of his bare chest. It's lean. Sculpted with muscle that stretches smooth and taut. A flat belly with a golden trail of hair that leads from below his navel and far past the waistband of his shorts.

"I realized that last time I got to see you naked, but you've never seen me naked," he says, his voice casual. Like it's no big deal, that the man of my dreams is stripping in front of me. "Figured you were curious."

I say nothing. My voice has completely left me.

He rests his hand against the center of his chest for a brief moment before it goes sliding down. Over the flat terrain of his stomach, until his fingers are toying with the waistband of his shorts. "Do you like watching me, Ellie?"

I realize I do a lot of that. Watch Jackson. When he's out on the football field. When he's on stage. He's my favorite thing to look at, bar none.

"I do," I whisper.

His hand slips beneath the front of his shorts, and he palms himself. I wish I could see everything. Witness him stroking himself. What a sight to see. So much on display for me to look at, I don't know where to look first.

So I watch his busy hand moving beneath his shorts, and I fantasize what he looks like naked.

He must see the need on my face, because he gets rid of the shorts, kicking them away when they fall to his feet. He's just in his boxer briefs now. They cling to him like a second skin, the pale gray fabric outlining everything.

Everything.

Jackson walks toward me, leaning over as I tip my head back, our lips meeting in a deliciously dirty, open-mouthed kiss. His tongue plunders, wrapping around my own, his hand sliding into my hair, gripping the back of my head, fingers tugging on the strands. It hurts, but I like the sting, the hungry way he kisses me, how he's not holding anything back. I can feel his energy washing over me, making me hungry too and I reach for him, my hands landing on hot, bare skin, my fingers immediately exploring.

I want to explore every inch of him.

He abruptly pulls away, his hands at the side of his briefs as if he's going to pull them down at any second. "Want to see?"

"Yes," I whisper without hesitation.

He smiles. "Show me what you've got first. Let me see you, El."

I take my camisole off, revealing my lacy bra. My nipples poke against the fabric, hard and tingling, and I reach behind my back, undoing the hook so they spring free. I discard the bra, letting it fall to the floor and I sit in front of him, naked from the waist up.

His gaze never straying from my breasts, he murmurs, "Show me more."

As if in a trance, I rise to my feet and undo the snap of my jeans, sliding the zipper open before I push the denim down my legs, kicking them off. My panties are pale yellow and cheeky and I hesitate, not about to show him all the goods, even though he's already seen them.

"Your turn," I tell him, my voice husky.

"At the same time?" he asks.

I shake my head. "You go first. You've already seen me."

"Got me there," he says with a closed-lipped smile, right before he sheds the briefs.

Revealing himself in his full naked glory.

And what a sight it is to see. His cock is huge. Pointing in an arc, the head toward his flat stomach, the muscles in his thick thighs defined. My mouth pops open, I can't help it, and I stare at him for a little while, caught up in all this male beauty on display just for me.

"You're making me nervous," he says after too much silence.

I lift my gaze to his. "You're beautiful," I say truthfully.

He reaches for me, the two of us toppling on top of the bed, his mouth finding mine as his hands find my breasts. He strokes and teases, his fingers and his tongue, trapping me by slinging a heavy leg over mine, so I can't move away.

Not that I would. I want this. I want him. His hands on me, his mouth on me. All over me. His hot skin pressing into mine. He rolls me over on my back, hovering above me, the heavy weight of his cock resting against my stomach, leaving a wet spot. Feeling brave, I reach for him, circling my fingers around his thick girth, giving him an experimental stroke.

Jackson moans into my mouth, his kisses turning ravenous.

Bolder, I do it again, eliciting another agonizing groan. I pick up my pace, confidence racing through my veins as I stroke him in earnest. His hips start to move as he devours my mouth and I want to laugh in triumph, I feel so good.

He wants this. He wants me. All these years I didn't think I mattered to him and look at him now. All over me, his cock in my hands, his mouth locked with mine. I always fantasized about this moment, never truly believing it would happen. And look at us now. We're finally doing this.

It's happening. And it's everything I could've ever dreamed.

"Fuck," he rasps against my lips, shifting his pelvis away from my seeking hand. "You keep that up, I'm going to come all over your fingers."

"I want you to," I say, sounding greedy—because I am. "Please."

He lifts his head, staring down at me with a knowing glint in his gaze. "How about you come all over my face instead?"

I should be embarrassed. Tell him to stop. But I don't. I nod eagerly instead, smiling up at him. "Okay."

He laughs, shifting down my body, blazing a trail of hot kisses all over my skin. I lie there and take it, my body seemingly melting into the mattress, resting my hand on top of his head, threading my fingers through his hair. He kisses and licks at my breasts, drawing one nipple into his mouth and sucking, his cheeks hollowing out. I watch, fascinated, breathless as he takes his time, lavishing equal attention upon both of my breasts, every pull of his mouth causing an answering pull between my thighs.

He moves lower, his lips skimming my stomach. A shaky sigh leaves me and he glances up, those blue eyes seeming to penetrate my soul as he stares at me, his hands reaching for my panties and tugging downward. He pulls them off my legs, and without warning, his fingers find me, parting my folds, stroking my delicate wet skin. A choked gasp sticks in my throat.

"So wet," he whispers, just before he ducks his head and continues on the journey he started at my chest.

I part my thighs, eager to feel his mouth on me. He settles himself in between my legs, searching me with his fingers, his eyes never straying from the spot he sang about onstage mere hours ago.

"Just as pink as I remember," he murmurs, his warm breath wafting across me, making me jump. I'm dying to feel his mouth on my flesh and I close my eyes, taking a deep breath as I try to calm my racing heart.

His lips touch me. Gently at first. Exploring. I slowly open my eyes to find he's still watching me, the lower half of his face buried against my pussy. All I can see are those beautiful blue eyes watching me, making me feel beautiful too.

I see him.

And he sees me too.

He licks me. Laps at me gently, searching, teasing. A tremor moves through me when he flicks at my clit with his tongue, reminding me I'm already so close to the edge, and it would take nothing for me to fall. I reach up behind me, wrapping my arms around a pillow to anchor myself, but it doesn't help. I'm floating. Rising above the bed, my entire body made of air, my heart racing so hard I'm scared it'll fall out of my chest.

At the same time he wraps his lips around my clit, he pushes a single finger inside of me. A low moan fills the room, and I realize it's me. I'm moaning as he begins to thrust. In and out. Over and over. Driving me wild with his tongue and lips, that finger.

Oh shit, that finger.

"Tight," he whispers, slowing his movements. "I don't want to hurt you."

"You're not—" a whimper leaves me when he sucks hard on my clit, "—hurting me."

He lifts away from me completely, his finger still inside my body, his knowing gaze watching me carefully. His lips and chin are shiny with my juices and he seems very, very pleased with himself. "You close?"

I nod. "I-I think so."

He smiles. Sticks his tongue out and laps at me, the gesture lewd. Dirty. Leaving me breathless. "You like it when I do that?"

"Yes," I whisper, closing my eyes so I can savor the sensations racing through me. Opening them once again so I can watch him.

I always want to watch him.

"I'm going to add another finger," he tells me, just before he does. I squirm, the stretch stinging only for a moment before my body relaxes. I start to move with his hand, enjoying the rhythm. Chasing it. He rises up, his fingers still between my legs, his mouth finding me as we kiss sloppily, his tongue thrusting into my mouth. I suck on it eagerly.

"That's what you taste like," he says after he breaks the kiss, his molten gaze making me shudder.

I'm probably going to hell for enjoying this so much, but it's too late for regrets now. And when he resumes his position between my legs, diving in once more to eat at me hungrily, I'm all in. Grinding against his face, reaching for that orgasm that hangs just out of reach. Desperate to come. I lift my hips, my feet flat on the mattress so I have better leverage. He slips a hand beneath me, clutching one ass cheek to him as he continues his assault with his tongue and fingers, his lips and tongue working a delicious rhythm.

It slams into me out of nowhere. Everything stills. My breath. My heart. My entire body. Just before I fall completely apart, a shaking, gasping mess as the orgasm sweeps over me. He holds me to him, never letting up, his mouth a form of exquisite torture as he draws out the climax as long as possible. Until I'm pushing him away, my body too sensitive, my pussy literally throbbing from all of his devoted attention.

"Holy shit," he says after he slides up the mattress to pull me into his arms. He holds me close, his hands running up and down my back as I press my face to his chest, trying to calm my agitated heart. "You came hard."

It's all because of him. All of my feelings, my emotions that have been wrapped up in him for all these years just came flowing out of me. It was amazing. Almost scary.

I want to do it again.

CHAPTER 27

JACKSON

She's so damn beautiful, lying in the middle of my bed, completely naked and so open. Watching her come was a sight to see. One I want to witness on repeat.

But my body is aching. My cock fucking throbbing, eager to get inside her. I've been ready to fuck since the performance. Even after the disappointing meeting with the record label, I was able to put that all out of my mind, knowing what was possibly going to happen tonight with Ellie.

My gorgeous, sweet Ellie. Watching me with glowing eyes, smiling at me as she drifts a hand down her front. She touches herself between her legs, her teeth sinking into her lower lip and I stare, fascinated as she strokes herself. She's so wet, I can hear her busy fingers, and I clasp hold of her wrist, stopping her as I lean in to kiss her.

"I can do that," I tell her, slipping my fingers between her thighs once more. "But you have to return the favor."

She eagerly reaches for my cock, her fingers wrapping tightly around me. Whatever she lacks in experience, she makes up for with enthusiasm. She's eager. Ready and willing. Surprisingly not shy. I never want her to stop touching me.

"You have condoms?" she asks at one point, just before she shoves at my shoulder so I land on the bed on my back.

"Yeah," I say, waving a hand toward the bedside table. "A couple in the drawer. A box in the bathroom."

"Aren't you prepared." She climbs on top of me, shocking the shit out of me as she starts kissing my chest. "Your skin is so smooth."

I lay there and let her have her way with me. She kisses me everywhere she can reach, her tongue toying with my nipples, making me jump. Her hair dragging against my skin, tickling me. She rains kisses on my rib cage. My stomach. Her mouth draws closer to my dick, and I tell myself not to push. Not to ask for it. Maybe she's not ready for that. She hasn't done much. I need to remember that.

She wraps her fingers around the base of my cock, dips her head and draws me into her mouth, so deep I groan. Loud enough for everyone that's still in the apartment to hear me. She licks and sucks. Strokes. Wraps her lips so tight around the head that I almost explode.

"Stop, stop," I tell her, not wanting to come in her mouth. She lifts away from me, and I roll toward the bedside table, fumbling with the drawer. Her hands don't leave me as I find a condom and tear the wrapper open, pulling the circle of rubber out and waving it at her.

"Let's put this on," I say roughly, my entire body feeling as if it's being pulled taut, strung out with tension. One wrong move and I could come. And I'm not ready. I want to draw this out. For her and for me.

She watches me roll the condom on with an eager gaze, practically pouncing on me once I'm done. We kiss and kiss, our movements sloppy. Reckless. Desperate for connection. I didn't know it could be like this. Feel like this. As if I'm addicted and she's the only drug that can satisfy me. I'm not bored or impatient. Ready to end it so the girl will leave and I can be alone. That's how it's been before with others. Quick and fast and get the fuck out.

Not with Ellie. I want to savor her and I can tell she feels the same.

I position her so she's lying on her back, me hovering above her, my knees on either side of her hips. I stroke myself, watching her watch me with lust-filled eyes, her lids at half-mast. Releasing my grip, I reach between her legs, testing her. She's wet. I slip a finger inside her, feeling her tense up.

Tight. So fucking tight.

"I'll go slow," I promise, removing my finger from her pussy so I can angle my cock right at her entrance. "I don't want to hurt you."

She takes a deep breath, her entire body rigid. "I'll be fine."

I stroke her skin, rising up so I can drop a soft kiss to her lips. "Relax, baby. It'll hurt worse if you're all tense."

She nods. I can feel her trying to forcibly relax her muscles. Her shoulders. Her arms. Her legs. I rub her pussy with the head of my dick, back and forth, lingering around her clit, my mouth never leaving hers, and she relaxes more, seeming to sink into the mattress.

This is when I try and sink inside of her.

Slowly, I push in. Inch by inch, stretching her wide. Her eyes open, her pupils blown as she blinks up at me. Her mouth hanging open as I push my way in farther. There's a hitch in her breath and she stills, making me pause too. Waiting her out.

She exhales, her eyes falling closed, and I go farther. Deeper. It's excruciating, how slow I have to go. How snug and hot she feels around my cock. I'd fuck her hard and fast if I could, but I restrain myself. I want to make this good for her.

Another slow, gentle thrust, and I'm fully inside of her

body. Her belly rises and falls with her deep breaths, brushing against me. I have to be hurting her.

And that fucking kills me.

"Are you okay?" I whisper, curling my arm around the top of her head, my fingers in her hair.

She nods, pressing her lips together. Her eyes open as she breathes out, and I swear to God that sends me even deeper, making me moan.

"Does it hurt?" I ask, not wanting to move yet. She's so hot. Tight. Gripping me like a goddamned vise.

"Stings a little," she says, shifting beneath me.

I kiss her. Lick at her mouth. Suck on her lower lip as I very slowly start to move. Pulling myself almost all the way out, before I push back in, keeping it nice and slow. Jesus, that feels good.

So damn good.

She moans with every slow thrust, lost in the sensation of my body inside hers. I stay at the same pace, languid. Lazy. Thrusting in and out of her, noting how her body relaxes, making it easier.

Soon I'm moving faster, my orgasm looming, but I remind myself to take my time. I need to make this good for her.

I want to make her come again.

Rising up, I reach between us, my fingers finding her clit, brushing against it. She hisses in a breath, her body moving beneath mine so I don't have to do anything at all. She's riding my dick, sliding up and down, my fingers toying with her clit, making her increase her pace. Panting, whimpering breaths leave her again and again as I press and twist, fingers circling. Her tits bounce with every movement and I watch, fascinated, afraid I'm going to blow before she does and she suddenly arches her back, her tits thrust into the air, her head hanging back as a choked cry falls from her lips.

And then she's coming, her inner walls squeezing around my cock again and again, milking me. Sending me headlong into my orgasm within seconds after hers ends. I still above her, my entire body shaking, her name falling from my lips before I collapse on top of her, jolts of sensation skimming all over my body over and over.

Again and again.

Fuck me.

I don't think I've ever come so hard in my life.

She runs her hands up and down my back, soothing me as the shaking slowly subsides. I cling to her, my mouth at her temple, her warm, pliant body shifting beneath mine and I realize I have to be crushing her. I start to move away, but she tightens her arms around me, not letting me leave.

"Don't go," she whispers. "Not yet."

I remain where I am, directly on top of her, my cock softening, trying to keep most of my weight from crushing her into the mattress. Those hands of hers are wandering everywhere, making gooseflesh rise.

Making other things start to rise too.

I can't go there yet. Her body is probably too sore for a repeat performance. She was a virgin for God's sake.

A virgin.

I'm Ellie's first. And you never forget your first.

The enormity of that weighs on me, making me realize how serious this moment is for her. She's been hung up on me for a while. For years. And while I've cared about her too, I'd never let myself go there. Too worried I'd fuck it up—fuck her up—and make her hate me forever. Our friendship was too valuable to me.

But look at me now. Wrapped all around her after having the best sexual experience of my life. With my best friend.

"I'll be right back," I tell her, kissing her forehead before I withdraw from her body and make my way over to the connected bathroom. I dispose of the condom in the trash, take a piss, and wash my hands before I make my way back to my bed. Ellie's slipped under the comforter, her hair a mess, her eyes big as she watches me return.

I stop at the end of the bed, resting my hands on my hips, studying her in return. "You look freaked out."

"I'm not used to you walking around naked." She averts her gaze for a moment, waving a hand in my direction.

"You don't like it?"

She turns towards me once more, a faint smile curling her lips. "I, uh, I love it. It'll just take some getting used to."

I go to the other side of the bed and crawl under the covers, slipping my arms around her from behind and hauling her body in close. She's warm and fragrant and soft. So soft. I drop a kiss on her shoulder. Another one. Yet another one, my lips traveling, finding her neck. She arches her head back, giving me better access, and I kiss and lick her there, unable to stop.

It's like I can't get enough of her.

"Are you sore?" I murmur against her cheek.

She shakes her head, her hair rustling against the pillow. "No."

"Full of regret?" I kiss her earlobe. Bite it.

"Absolutely not," she says without hesitation. There's a pause. "Do you regret it?"

Her voice is so small. And her body is tense, as if she's bracing herself for me to say something shitty.

"The only thing I regret," I start, using my hand to turn her face more towards mine, "is that we didn't do this sooner."

The relieved smile is a sight to see. I kiss her, making it disappear. I can't stop kissing her. My cock stirs to life, eager to get back at it, and I'm afraid he's going to be disappointed when nothing else happens.

Ellie reaches for me, her fingers clasping my dick firmly, giving me a stroke that makes me groan. "Again?" she asks, sounding amused. "Already?"

"You're probably tired," I say. "Sore. It's okay—"

"I'm fine," she interrupts. "I'm up for anything."

"Really?" My hands wander, finding her breasts. I tease her already hard nipples with my fingers, feeling her melt against me. "I don't want to push."

"I don't want you to stop," she admits, a soft sigh falling from her lips when I pinch her nipple. "Don't ever, ever stop."

"Okay," I whisper. "I won't."

True to my word, we don't stop.

Not for the rest of the night.

CHAPTER 28

ELLIE

I wake up in a room that's not mine, with strong arms wrapped around me, holding me close to a very hot, very hard body. There's also something very hot and very hard poking insistently against my backside.

Hmm. Pretty sure I was awoken by Jackson Rivers' erection. What a way to start the morning.

The man is insatiable.

But then again, so am I.

Smiling, I slowly grind my butt against him, his erection trapped between us. He groans. In his sleep? I'm not sure. I keep my eyes closed, savoring the feeling of being in his arms. Naked. In his bed. With him completely surrounding me. Holding me close. Snuggled up behind me, spooning me. It's downright romantic.

I knew Jackson was a romantic soul. It shows in the songs he writes, and sometimes in the way he acts. He's actually very sweet. Oblivious sometimes, but I can forgive that.

Now that I'm in his bed, I can forgive him for pretty much everything he's ever done to me. All the years of torture and ignoring me. The denial. Oh, he was in such strong denial.

He's mine now. And I'm his. It's going to work out between us.

I just know it.

I wriggle against him again, just because I can, and his arms tighten around me, trying to keep me still.

"Don't you have class?" he growls against my ear, trying to sound grumpy, but I can't help but find that growl extremely sexy.

I laugh. I can't keep it in. I'm too happy. "Yes."

"Won't you be late?"

"I'm skipping today," I admit, stroking his forearms. They're strong. A little hairy. I think of all the girls screaming for him last night. A few of them said some pretty vulgar things. What they wanted to do to him. What they wanted him to do to them.

Look at me now. I'm the one who's in his bed this morning. And we did all sorts of vulgar things throughout the night.

These giddy feelings, just how perfect this moment is, could go straight to a girl's head.

"You're going to skip class?" He sounds shocked. "Damn, I didn't know you had it in you."

"Well, I had something—or someone—in me all night long, and now I never want to leave this spot," I confess with a smile.

He slowly thrusts against me. He's relentless. "You're a dirty girl, Ellie."

"You should know," I say lightly. "You're the one who corrupted me."

"Best thing I've ever done, for sure." He squeezes me tight. "I think I'll skip class today too."

"We should," I agree. "We can skip together. Hang out all day. Go to breakfast. I never go out for breakfast. Should we do that? Oh my God, I'm so hungry. Though it's a little late. It's close to ten already, huh? We could have brunch. Do they call it brunch on Friday?"

"Yes." He kisses me, silencing my rambling words. I don't know why I just did that. Maybe I'm afraid he'll turn me down? That he'll have something better to do than hang out with me? "They call it brunch any day of the week. And we should definitely go to brunch. I need to shower first though."

"I should shower too," I say, closing my eyes when he nuzzles my neck. He's so snuggly and warm. Do we have to get out of this bed? I'd rather stay here all day, in our own little bubble, keeping reality where it belongs.

Out of our lives. At least for a little while longer.

"Let's conserve water and shower together," he suggests, his lips tickling my skin.

"You want to take a shower with me?" I squeak, sounding dumb.

"I want to do everything with you," he admits, just before he turns me over and kisses me senseless.

———

We end up at a restaurant not too far from campus, a quaint little breakfast place that is mostly empty, thanks to the late hour. We sit outside on the patio, the breeze ruffling Jackson's dark blond hair, making a mess of it. Making him look adorable and sexy and all I can think about is the fact that I have now had sex with him.

I've had sex. With Jackson Rivers. Something I never thought would happen.

I also can't stop staring at him as we sit at the table, my menu open, though I'm not looking at it. I'm so hungry I could probably eat the actual menu, but I can't concentrate on what I want to order. All I can do is stare at this boy sitting across from me, who's completely rocked my world in the best possible way. How did I get so lucky?

I have it so bad for him. He could take advantage of that

too, if he wanted to. I need to remember that. Jackson is capable of that sort of thing. He takes without thinking. He's done it to me before, and I gladly let him do it, like a complete idiot. I need to remember to stand up for myself more. Hayden and Gracie taught me that. So did Ava. Jackson might not like it, but too bad.

Hmm. Maybe we're not out of the woods yet.

Ugh, I hate feeling doubtful. It's the worst.

"What are you getting?" he asks.

I snap out of my Jackson-induced daze and concentrate on the menu once more. "I'm not sure. Bacon and eggs?"

"I thought you liked sweet stuff. Pancakes. Waffles," he says.

That he noticed shouldn't thrill me so much, but it does. It means he pays attention to me. "You're right." I close the menu, my gaze meeting his. "I'm having French toast."

He smiles. "Will you share?"

I slowly shake my head, teasing him. "Nope."

Jackson mock pouts. "Come on. So selfish."

"Says the king of selfish," I tease back.

His mock pout disappears, hurt filling his gaze. "You're right. I am the king of selfish. Always taking advantage of you."

"I didn't mean it like that—"

"Yeah," he cuts me off. "You did. And it's cool. I get it. I've been oblivious to you for so long. Taking advantage of your friendship. Of you always being there. I counted on you, when you couldn't always count on me."

I didn't want to start such a serious conversation between us the morning after we had sex for the first time, but here we go. "It's partially my fault too."

He literally scoffs. "That I took advantage of you? How?"

"I shouldn't have been such a doormat," I say with a shrug. "I was weak when it came to you."

"You're my weakness now. You always have been," he says, his voice low.

My heart leaps at his admission. Is he for real? The sincerity in his gaze, on his face, tells me, yes. "I kept waiting and waiting, hoping you'd notice."

"I noticed," he says immediately. "I just—I was in denial."

"Okay, then I was hoping you'd finally realize," I amend.

His smile is slow. Sexy. "I did. Finally."

"Yes." My answering smile is slow as well. "You did."

The server appears at our table with the vanilla lattes we ordered when we first arrived, and Jackson orders for himself and for me, taking charge. I sit back and watch him, yet again unable to tear my gaze away. I think about what we did earlier, when we took a shower together. We lathered each other up, soapy bubbles everywhere, making our skin slick. Fingers seeking and finding all of our secret places, where we like to be touched the most. Mouths locked, kissing hungrily, as if we couldn't get enough of each other. We didn't have actual sex, but we got each other off, and it was…fun.

Lots and lots of fun.

"What are you thinking about?" he says after the server leaves.

"The shower." I grin, my cheeks growing warm.

"It was all right," he says nonchalantly with a shrug, barely holding back a smile. Now he's the one teasing.

"You were the one shouting my name earlier, so I'm guessing it was more than all right for you," I return.

"Got me there," he says, stroking his jaw, looking thoughtful. "Heard from any of our friends this morning?"

I shake my head, trying to take a sip of my drink, but it's still piping hot so I set it back down. "Have you?"

"Caleb texted me. Wanted to know if we're going to the frat party tonight," he answers.

"Are we?"

"Do you want to?" he asks.

"Probably. Ava wants to go, and I want to spend as much time with her as possible before she leaves," I say, pausing for a moment before I continue. "And did Caleb really ask if *we* were going?"

"Yes, he did." Jackson thrusts his phone out toward me, the text exchange with Caleb pulled up. I squint as I read it, seeing that, yep, Caleb asked exactly that.

Caleb: **You and Ellie coming to the party tonight? Or will you two still be too busy coming in your room?**

I roll my eyes and laugh when I read the text. "He's so crude."

"I mean, I'd rather do the latter, but if you want to go to the party, we can," he says. "I know you want to hang out with Ava, though Eli is going to monopolize as much of her as he possibly can. He's so glad she's here."

"I know he is. They've missed each other. She complains to me all the time how much she hates being down there when we're all here," I say.

"They'll make it work," he says firmly, and I love that he believes in them as much as I do. "And the party tonight should be fun. I haven't been to one since last year."

"Are you still active with the frat?" He joined his freshman year but hasn't really mentioned anything about it at all lately.

"Didn't I tell you? I dropped out," he says. "I had too much going on. They want you fully committed, and I just couldn't manage it."

"You do have a lot on your plate," I murmur, just before I sit up straight. "Oh! You never told me what happened with the guy from Evergreen last night!"

The look on Jackson's face tells me what I'd assumed yesterday. He doesn't have good news. "They liked Cupid's Bow better."

My mouth drops open. "*What?*"

He nods. "They set up a meeting with those guys for next

week. The lead singer texted me earlier, thanking me for asking them to open for me. And that's what sucks the worst —I did this to myself."

My heart breaks at seeing the miserable expression on his face. He's never really cared about the record deal offers before, but I'm guessing this is the one he'd finally set his hopes on. "I'm so sorry, Jackson."

"It's okay." He waves a hand, smiling faintly, but it seems forced. "They liked my song, though. Pink."

"They did?" I smile, thinking of it. How he wrote it for me.

"Yeah. That Rick guy was really laying it on thick last night. Gushing over me. They all were. He had a team with him. But they never asked to set up a meeting, so I figured they weren't interested," he says. "Guess they'll sign Cupid's Bow instead."

"They might still be interested in you," I suggest, not wanting him to give up yet. "You never know."

"I know," he says firmly. "I can tell. And it's okay. I'm still not ready to do this, I don't think. Especially now."

"Why especially now?" I ask with a frown.

"Because I've got you." He reaches across the table, settling his hand on top of mine. "If I were to make a record, I'd probably have to leave the football team. Eventually even drop out of school. Record. Tour. Make publicity rounds. Appearances. Whatever. It would take up all my time. I'd never see you."

I frown. It's his secret dream, becoming a recording artist. A rock star. Playing music for a living. He's told me that more than once. I don't want to be the one who crushes his dreams. "We could make it work."

"Could we, Ellie?" His tone is serious as he links his fingers with mine. "We're finally really together, and you'd be perfectly okay with me leaving for months at a time? While you're here at school? We'd be living separate lives."

No. I wouldn't be okay with any of that, but I'd figure out a way to deal with it. "I don't want to be the reason you give up."

Just like I put so many expectations on him, I don't want him to put a bunch on me either. The pressure would be too much. Being responsible for his future is a lot. Watching him give up on something he's worked toward these last few years isn't what I want for him.

Not even close.

"You're not. I've come to realize I'm just not that good," he says, his voice light. As if it's no big deal. But it is. This is a huge deal. And I don't believe him. I think he's just trying to convince himself. "I don't necessarily fit a certain mold. I'm just doing my own thing, and I don't think I'm marketable."

"You had other record labels wanting to sign you," I remind him. "They thought you were marketable. Because you're unique. You're not the same old pop star. You have a little more edge."

"You're just saying that because you're my biggest fan," he says with a smile. "And did they really believe I'm marketable? Or were they momentarily caught up in the hype?" He shrugs, pulling his hand away from mine. "Maybe I'm already a 'has been' at nineteen."

"Jackson…" I start, but he shakes his head.

"I still need to process this," he says, his voice firm. "And I really don't want to talk about it anymore. Okay?"

I slowly nod, trying not to frown. I can tell he's upset, and I don't want to make it worse. He's struggled the last year with all of this. The sudden local fame, and how fast it grew. The attention from social media, and the record companies. How he turned them all down when his friends—including me—thought he was crazy. Why not jump on the opportunity when it's being presented? He should've.

He'd never say it out loud, but I think he's almost—scared of fame. Scared of the responsibilities. The expectations. The pressure. He's not one who deals well with pressure. Not at all.

And maybe now he's regretting his life choices, and I wonder if that includes me.

No, not me, I think as he watches me, his eyes full of emotion, his perfect lips curled into this knowing half-smile. I can't help but smile in return, the both of us barely looking away from each other as the server arrives with our meals. He's happy with me.

I can tell.

CHAPTER 29
JACKSON

"I don't want her going back to school," Eli says to me as we watch Ava and Ellie sitting together outside at Ava's parents' house. We were all invited to the Callahans' home Saturday afternoon for a barbecue and it feels like *everyone* is here, except Jake and his girl and Autumn and Asher Davis.

Ash went pro. Autumn is the newest Instagram sensation, gathering lots of followers as she documents her new life as the fiancée of a future quarterback superstar. Jake is too busy kicking ass on the USC football team. Hannah is in art school, doing what she loves.

I'm jealous of all four of them. I can admit it. They're doing exactly what they want, and enjoying every minute of it. While I'm stuck in between two worlds, not sure where I fit in. I love football, but I'm not getting the chance to play. I love making music, but I'm starting to realize I was a damn fool for thinking I could actually be successful at it.

It was a mistake, not agreeing to one of those contracts when they were offered. Now I've got nothing.

Well, I've got my friends. And Ellie.

Ellie.

My gaze lingers on her, how she throws her head back and laughs at something Ava says. Jocelyn is sitting with them, as well as Baylee, who Caleb brought with him. For whatever reason, they're all getting along perfectly well, which is shocking considering Baylee's association with the awful Cami Lockhart. That girl destroyed more relationships than she actually had herself during her time in high school.

Wonder where she's at now?

Best if I don't ask, especially Eli, who had his own run-in with her. Multiple times.

"I don't blame you," I finally say to him, glancing over at him. His expression is grim, his jaw tight, his lips thin. He doesn't look happy, when he should be soaking up these last hours with his girlfriend. "What's wrong with you?"

"Long distance relationships are bullshit," he mutters fiercely. "Having her here this weekend is reminding me why I hate them. I don't want to let her go."

"Yeah." I sip from my water bottle. I'm glad the Callahan family invited us to their house, and I'm having a good time, but we're keeping it clean. Ava's parents don't let us drink in front of them, not like my dad, who would provide me with plenty of alcohol and weed any time I asked for it. He'd leave me a stash of both, since he was always working or out of town. This is why I was always partying in high school. Kind of fucked-up, but back then, I thought it was great.

We all did.

"You and Ellie for real now?" he asks me out of nowhere.

I shrug. "We haven't actually talked about it and made it official, but I think so."

"She can't quit looking over here at you," he observes.

"I'm doing the same thing to her," I say, smiling at her when our gazes lock. She returns the smile with a shy one of her own before she resumes her conversation with her friends.

"You've got it so bad," Eli says, shaking his head. "Finally."

"I shouldn't have led her on like I did for so long," I admit, suddenly feeling down on myself. An emotion I've been battling with all weekend.

The disappointing meeting with Rick and his people won't leave me, and it's colored my mood. Even having Ellie all to myself for the entire weekend since she took the time off for Ava's visit hasn't completely lifted my spirits, though it's been the perfect distraction. Just the one I needed.

I'm happy with her, I really am. We can't get enough of each other, and she's surprisingly wild in bed. Girl does not hold back, and I appreciate that.

A lot.

But I'd hoped to not only be having the time of my life with her, I'd fully expected to have something lined up with Evergreen. My future, solidified.

Instead, I feel like I'm floundering more than ever.

"You were blind," Eli says, as if that's explanation enough. "You didn't see what was happening right in front of your eyes. Not like I did with Ava. I took one look at her, and I fucking knew. I had to have her."

"Yeah, I wasn't as sure as you were," I say, thinking back on those days. When I would host parties out at my uncle's abandoned cabin by the lake, playing my guitar around the fire and singing songs, with Ellie always by my side. Gazing up at me with those big eyes, looking at me as if I could change her entire life.

God, I was such a dick.

"Just don't fuck it up," Eli says, his tone turning serious. "Ellie is a sweet girl. I'd hate to see you hurt her."

"I don't plan on hurting her," I say defensively.

"I know, but you probably could with little effort. You're kind of an ass sometimes. A little selfish," he says.

I start to laugh. "That's pretty funny, coming from you."

He frowns. "What do you mean?"

"You're a selfish ass, Eli. You strut around wherever you're at, thinking you're king of the goddamn world. It's the Eli Bennett show and we're all just living in it," I say, sounding bitter. Sometimes his cocky attitude makes me angry. Defensive.

It's an emotion that's been bubbling just beneath the surface for days.

Eli glares at me, not saying a word. His entire body seems tense.

In fact, he looks pretty fucking...mad.

Shit.

"You really think that?" He sounds offended.

I shrug, most likely needing to back pedal, but not necessarily in the mood for it. Maybe I want to hash it all out with my best friend. Get out my frustration. "Sometimes, yeah."

"You're just mad because it's not always the Jackson Rivers show either. I think it pissed you off that all those girls weren't just there for you Thursday night. They were also screaming over that boy band. Is that what set you off? Made you act like such a grump? You're finally getting Ellie's pussy and look at you. You're still not happy," he throws at me.

Anger suffuses me over his comment about Ellie. "Don't say that about my girl."

"Why? Does it bother you? Sick of it being the Eli Bennett show? Wish it was the Jackson Rivers show instead?" He stands, his body vibrating from barely restrained anger.

I stand too, my hands clutched into fists.

As the silence continues, the tension mounts between us. I'm tall, but he's taller. The glower on his face says he means business, and damn it, I mean it, too. He can't just say those kinds of things about Ellie. And he sure as shit can't try and get me all riled up over something so fucking stupid.

Yet here I am, all riled up over something really fucking stupid. Worse? I'm the cause of this in the first place.

"Hey!" Ava calls from where she's sitting.

We both swivel our heads in her direction, matching shitty expressions on our faces.

Ava frowns. So does Ellie.

"Everything okay over there, boys?" Ava calls.

"Sure," Eli says, cutting a glare in my direction before he returns his attention to his girlfriend. "We're fucking great, babe. Oops, sorry, Coach."

"Watch your mouth, Bennett," Drew Callahan says from where he's manning the barbecue, his wife Fable right beside him, carefully watching us both.

Great. We're causing drama and that is the last thing I want.

"Bro," I tell Eli, giving him a nudge. He glares, not giving an inch. "This is stupid. I don't want to fight with you."

"I don't either. But you're kind of acting like a dick."

"And you're tense as shit over your girlfriend when, like I said, you should be over there sitting with her right now, clutching her tight." I tilt my head in Ava's direction. "Go to her. Tell her you love her. Tell her you'll miss her when she's gone."

"I already have," he says, sounding miserable, the tension slowly leaving him. "I'm a needy little fuck."

"She likes your sorry ass, so don't even worry about it. Go." I gently shove his shoulders, pushing him forward. "And I'm sorry. I didn't mean to start shit."

"I'm sorry too. But you need to get out of your funk. Stat," he says, shooting me a smile before he strides over to where Ava's sitting. He literally picks her up, making her shriek, before settling on the couch and pulling her onto his lap. She wraps her arms around his neck, delivering a smacking kiss on his lips, and they're immediately lost in each other.

No one else matters.

That's all the girls'—including Ellie's—cue to leave them alone. They all get up from where they were sitting, leaving

Eli and Ava alone. I wait, watching Ellie as she approaches me, and I pull her into my arms when she gets close, giving her my own version of a smacking kiss.

Not as much smacking. And with a little tongue.

"You two seemed mad at each other," she says when the kiss ends.

"We were. I thought we were going to come to blows," I admit.

Ellie frowns. "What in the world? Why?"

"He's tense over Ava having to leave tomorrow. And I'm tense about…other stuff," I say, knowing she won't let me get away with a vague answer.

"Like what?" Her frown deepens.

"I don't want to talk about it here." I drop another kiss on her lips. "We can discuss it later."

"It's not anything about us or—me, is it?" She sounds so concerned. I hate that.

"No. Not at all. I'm dealing with my own stupid shit." I thought I'd be over it by now, but I'm way too much in my head over this Evergreen Records' thing. I feel like I fucked up my entire musical career, and I have no one to blame but myself.

That sucks. Hard.

"Your stupid shit is mine too, you know." She rests her hand on my chest, her fingers curling into my T-shirt. "I want to help you."

The sincerity in her voice tells me she means every word she says. This girl has always wanted to help me. Support me.

"I know you do." I kiss the tip of her nose. "I appreciate it. I appreciate you."

She slings her arms around my shoulders, clinging to me. "This weekend has been the best one I've had in a long time."

"Me too." I slip my arms around her waist, pulling her in closer. "I'm glad you didn't have to work."

"I have to go back tomorrow though." She mock pouts. It's cute. "I work all week."

"We have an away game next Saturday," I remind her. "Pasadena."

"Who are you playing?" she asks with a frown.

"UCLA." I grimace. "Probably going to have our asses handed to us."

"I don't know. I've heard their season hasn't been that great," she says.

I'm surprised. "You keep up with college football? Besides just the Bulldogs?"

"I work at a sports bar. We have ESPN on the big screen TVs at all times. It's not like I'm purposely keeping up. I can't help but absorb all of that information when I work there practically full-time," she explains.

I laugh, squeezing her tight. "I love that you know what's going on in college football."

"I like to know what's going on with all aspects of your life," she tells me, patting my chest. "Everything," she stresses.

She wants to ease my burden by taking some of it on herself, but how can I explain to her what's going on inside my head when I can't fully figure it out myself? I'm still working through this, and what I need from her right now, more than anything else, is patience.

Lots and lots of it.

We stay at the Callahans' house long into the night, until we all finally leave in a caravan of vehicles to head back down the hill for Fresno. Ava and Eli ride with us back to our shared apartment, the girls chatting away while us guys interject here and there. We didn't make it to Caleb's frat party after all, which Ava points out midway through our drive, but Ellie reassures her that there are plenty of other frat parties for us to go to in the future.

I realize this is what I missed out on when we were in

high school. We could've double dated with Eli and Ava all the time, and it would've been fun.

But I would've most likely fucked it up. She would've dumped my ass, and been completely out of my life in a flash. Maybe I did the right thing, not getting with her when we were younger.

Maybe there's a reason we waited.

By the time we arrive at the apartment and we're all tucked away in our respective bedrooms, I decide to tell Ellie about my earlier thoughts.

"You know, we probably wouldn't be here right now if we'd gotten together when we were both still in high school," I say as we lie on my bed in the dark.

"You really believe that?" she asks, her voice soft, her head nestled on my shoulder.

"Yeah. I was thinking about it on the ride home. I would've done something stupid, and you would've dumped my ass," I say.

"Probably."

"And then our friendship would've been ruined. We couldn't get it back. We'd be out of each other's lives for good." I turn to her, touching her cheek. "So in a way, I'm glad I was an idiot and took this long to finally realize how I feel about you."

She laughs. "Nice way to justify your feelings, Jackson."

"I'm being serious." Her laughter dies. "I know it sounds like an excuse, but all those 'what ifs' are in my brain. High school relationships rarely last."

"We're surrounded by high school relationships that are still lasting," she points out.

"Yeah, but for how much longer?"

Ellie gasps. "Are you saying they're all going to break up with each other?"

"I don't know. The chances are high. And maybe...maybe we will break up too." Fear seizes hold of my heart and I take deep, even breaths, mentally calming myself. I don't want that. I don't want to lose Ellie.

She's quiet for a moment. "I hope not. We only just started this thing. We're not even officially together."

Something comes over me at her words. I take another deep breath and say what it is. "I want you to be my girlfriend."

More silence. It's unnerving, how quiet she is. Does she really have to think about this? There was no hesitation on my end, but I guess I deserve her momentarily considering my offer. I mean, I've been a complete dumbass for the last two years so—

I hear a sniff. Another one. And I realize.

Oh shit.

She's crying.

"El. Baby." I pull her into my arms, hating how she cries against my chest, her shoulders shaking. "What the hell? Why are you crying?"

She pulls away, so she can look up at me, her eyes shining with unshed tears. "I'm just s-so h-happy."

"You don't act like it," I say, smoothing her hair away from her face. "You're killing me right now."

"You don't think we're moving too fast?" she asks, her voice shaky.

"I'm saying I didn't move fast enough. I could've lost you," I tell her, leaning in to lightly kiss her lips.

She starts to cry harder, too overcome to form words, I guess.

"Ah shit." Unwanted emotion bubbles up in my chest and I close my eyes, tucking her close to me. "Don't cry. I'm not worth your tears."

"See, that's the thing, Jackson." She snuggles close, her arms wrapped tightly around me. "You are."

CHAPTER 30

ELLIE

'm at work, busting my tail as I hustle around the restaurant, trying to keep up with cleaning tables among the influx of customers. We're always super busy on Thursday nights, thanks to NFL football. The game is currently on every TV in the building, and every table in the place is full, bursting with people.

Ash Davis is playing tonight, and all of our customers want to cheer on the hometown hero.

I'd love to tell people that I went to the same high school as he did. I want to tell people my best friend is his fiancée's little sister, but I keep my mouth shut. Most likely no one would believe me, so what's the point?

Instead, I bask in the glory that is Ash's local fan club.

At the top of the fourth quarter, Hayden and Gracie walk in, ordering a late dinner. They beckon me over to their table when they see me, and I go to them, telling my manager as I walk by her that I'm taking a quick break.

"Go for it," Donna says. "You've been on your feet all night."

I gladly settle into the booth seat next to Gracie, smiling at

Hayden who's sitting in a chair across from us. "What are you guys doing here? It's Thursday Night Football."

"I knew the restaurant would be packed with guys, so here I am," Gracie says with a dazzling smile, just before she scans the room.

Hayden laughs. "I'm her wing-woman. We tried to get Tony to come with us, but his eyes were glued to the television at his place. Said he couldn't risk leaving. The score could change and he'd miss something."

"They have a pretty solid lead," I say, glancing at one of the TVs to check the score.

"He would've killed my vibe," Gracie says. "I don't need Tony here cockblocking me."

I laugh. She's probably right.

"Enough about cockblocking and football," Hayden says, leaning across the table, her gaze never leaving me. "We haven't talked. Like, really talked in *days*. We need to know—what's up with you and Jackson?"

"We're good," I say, barely containing the smile that wants to stretch across my face.

That is the understatement of the year. We had the best weekend ever. This week has been amazing too. Unfortunately, he left early for the away game this weekend. Had some plans come up, he explained, being very mysterious.

I have no idea exactly what's going on, but when I pressed him about it, he said he'd be able to explain everything to me when he gets back Sunday.

Eeep, I hate secrets, but this isn't a bad one. He seemed a little excited. He couldn't stop smiling.

And last night, when he stayed over with me, he kept me up for half the night, driving me out of my mind every time he touched me. It's getting better and better between us. I miss him so much now that he's gone. There's a hole in my heart just knowing how far away he is from me right now.

I hate it.

But I love him. So much, it's overwhelming.

Does he feel the same way? Probably not as intensely as I do…

"Good?" Hayden's brows shoot up. "That's it? That's all we get?"

"We need more details," Gracie adds.

I laugh and launch into a story about the weekend first, and everything we did—without sharing many details at all, much to their disappointment. I wrap up that particular story with Jackson asking me to be his girlfriend.

"Aw, so you two are official already?" Hayden clasps her hands together in front of her chest. "That's so sweet."

"And quick," Gracie says. "I'm surprised he moved so fast. I guess you two wanted the label?"

"There's nothing wrong with labels," Hayden says in defense of me, before I can even speak.

"Says the woman who claims relationships are bogus and didn't want to call Tony her boyfriend at first," Gracie throws back at her. She glances my way. "I have zero issues with you two moving fast. I'm the queen of moving fast."

"You're also the queen of can't commit," Hayden points out.

"Stop it, both of you," I tell them. They love nothing more but giving each other crap. "Let's talk about me for a few more minutes."

"Ah, I love this. Ellie standing up for herself, and getting demanding," Hayden says, sitting up straighter. "Tell us— how is Jackson in bed?"

"I'm sure he's perfection," Gracie says, lifting a single brow. "I'm also positive he has a giant dick."

"You guys." My cheeks go hot. "He's…good. With his hands. With all of his parts, really. But don't forget, I have nothing else to compare him to."

"I doubt he's bad at sex, so we won't focus on that." Gracie laughs. "And how's the equipment?"

"Sufficient," is all I can manage before they both burst out laughing.

I laugh with them too. It feels good to talk to them about this. To laugh and joke with my friends and savor the fact that I actually have a boyfriend. One who seems really into me.

Finally.

We rehash everything that happened during the weekend, including Jackson's concert. The song he wrote that everyone figured out was about me. It *was* fairly obvious from the way he sang it right to me.

"Oh my God, I never did hear what happened with the record company people," Hayden says. "Did they make an offer or whatever?"

"Oh yeah." I wince. This is a touchy subject, one that Jackson still doesn't want to talk about. "They um...they seemed more interested in Cupid's Bow, according to Jackson. They set up a meeting with them and everything."

"Get the heck out," Gracie breathes, her eyes wide. "No kidding? They were pretty awesome."

"I think Jackson was disappointed they didn't even want to sit down and talk to him," I say.

"But why?" Hayden frowns. "He's turned down every record deal that's been made to him so far. I thought he wanted to keep his freedom—his musical integrity or some such bullshit like that."

Gracie giggles, but I don't. I'm hurting for him, just like he's hurting over this.

Not that he likes to talk about it.

"I think he really liked Evergreen Records and assumed they'd offer him a contract. When they didn't—when they showed interest in the group he asked to open for him instead of him—I think it crushed him. He doesn't want to talk about it though. He's pretending it never happened, but I think he's down about it."

"That sucks," Gracie says, frowning. "I feel bad for him."

"So do I," Hayden adds. "But he'll come around. At least he has you there supporting him."

"True." He's always had me supporting him.

"Hey, whatever happened to Carson? Did you tell him you were with Jackson now? Of course you did. Did he take it well?" Gracie asks, her brows shooting up. "He's such a sweetheart. Cute too."

"Don't get any ideas," Hayden warns her.

Gracie rolls her eyes in response.

"I talked to him Monday after class. I told him I thought we were better off as friends," I explain, my heart momentarily heavy. I saw the disappointment flicker in Carson's gaze when I talked to him, and I felt bad, but it was the right decision. I'm not interested in him like that, and it wasn't fair of me to use him like I did, even though that's not what I meant to do. He's a good guy. He deserves someone who's totally into him.

I'm not that person.

"Did he take it okay?" Gracie asks.

"I know he was disappointed, but he'll get over it. There are so many girls on this campus for him to choose from," I say.

"But you're special, Ellie." Hayden smiles at me. "You care so much. About everyone."

"I care too much," I stress, sighing as I lean back against the seat. "I should go back to work."

The crowds coming in have slowly diminished, but the restaurant itself is pretty full, despite the late hour. Meaning I have lots of tables to clean still, and plenty of customers to help.

After I hug the girls and tell them to enjoy their dinner, I make the rounds before heading outside to the patio to clear off a few tables. It's starting to cool down more in the evenings, and the breeze sweeping through the outside area is chilly. I shiver, dumping all the dirty dishes in a tub so I can take them back to the kitchen, not bothering to check on who's sitting outside.

That's my first mistake.

"Hey cutie."

I ignore the slurring male voice, thinking he must be talking to someone else.

"Sweetheart. Come over here," the same voice asks a minute later. There's pounding on the table, making the glasses rattle. "I have a question for you."

Okay. Pretty sure he's talking to me.

I glance over my shoulder to see an older guy sitting alone, a few empty beer glasses sitting on the table in front of him. He tips to the side on his stool, almost falling off of it, and I'd make the assumption that he's pretty drunk.

Ugh.

"Can I help you?" I ask, pasting a polite smile on my face.

"Damn, you're pretty." He blinks at me, as if he's trying to bring me into focus. "Wanna come sit with me? Chat for a few?"

"I'm working," I say, my voice flat. God, I really hate creepers.

"Yeah, whatever. Think you're too good for me, don't ya? Get me another one of these then." He waves his index finger at the empty glasses. "And hurry. I've been waiting fifteen minutes for that asshole bartender of yours to bring me my order."

"Give me a few minutes," I tell him as I quickly wipe down the table I'm standing next to.

"I've already been waiting. Knowing that guy, he's gonna come over here and kick me out. It's happened before." He barks out a laugh, then burps.

Ew.

With my smile frozen in place, I tell him, "I'll be right back."

I hurriedly leave the patio area, bursting through the

double doors into the restaurant and stopping by the bar to let Chuck know the guy outside wants another beer.

"The dark-haired guy sitting alone? Yeah, he already tried ordering another beer, and I told him no." Chuck shakes his head, his expression disgusted. "I refuse to serve him. He's drunk as hell and belligerent. Had to kick him out of here myself last week. He was picking fights with other customers."

"Oh." My smile fades. "Well, maybe you could go tell him that you won't serve him? I think he's expecting you."

"Ha, I bet he is. I'd be glad to." Chuck wipes his hands on a clean, dry rag before tossing it down. "And if I have to kick him out again, so be it. We don't get a lot of asshole drunks in this place, but he more than makes up for it."

"Thank you, Chuck, for taking care of him," I say. "I appreciate it."

By the time I'm coming out of the kitchen, Chuck and another guy that works here are personally escorting the rowdy customer out of the restaurant, each of them holding one side of the guy, practically dragging him out. The customer is grumbling and carrying on, and when he spots me, he points a finger straight at me, his face bright red.

"It's all your fault they're kicking me out! You bitch!"

Everyone inside the building goes quiet, swiftly looking from him to me.

Oh God. This is so embarrassing.

"Come on, jackass," Chuck mutters, jerking hard on the man's arm. "You're out of here."

"I'm a paying customer! You can't kick me out!" the man yells. "Don't listen to that little bitch! I'm not drunk!"

I never said he was, though it's fairly obvious. That was all Chuck.

Donna comes to stand beside me, slinging her arm around my shoulders. "Come on, let's go to the back."

I follow behind her to her office, feeling numb. I can't

believe that guy made such a scene. Worse, I can't believe he dragged me into it, when I had nothing to do with what was happening.

Such a jerk.

"Are you okay?" Donna asks once we're tucked away in her tiny office. "Do we need to write up a report about this guy?"

"What? No, I don't think so. He's just really drunk," I tell her.

"Yeah well, he's caused trouble here before. Tried to grab one of the girls last week. Chuck tossed him out, but he wouldn't leave, so I had to call the cops," Donna explains.

"Oh no." At least he didn't try to grab me. "He only said some stuff to me. Nothing too crazy."

"He did call you a bitch," Donna reminds me with a sigh as she walks over to her filing cabinet and pulls open the top drawer. "I'm going to have you fill this form out, just to document what happened. That way we're all covered."

"Covered for what?" I ask as she hands me a form.

"In case he decides to come back again. He's a frequent customer, but I'm banning him. We need documentation," Donna explains.

I start to fill it out. Gladly.

———

I'm leaving the restaurant along with Donna and a couple of other coworkers. Chuck already took off after surveilling the parking lot, looking for our troublesome customer. Once he declared the coast was clear, Donna let him go.

My car starts up with ease—it's always a little nerve-wracking since the alternator went out. I still don't quite trust it. I wave at Donna, who zooms out of the parking lot as if her tail is on fire.

I'm sure she's tired. We all are. It was an extra busy night.

I put the car into reverse and start to back out of the parking spot when the engine stalls. Sputters.

Dies.

My heart squeezes as I put the gear into park, the car lurching forward. I attempt to start the car, the engine trying, but it doesn't quite make it. I sit there for a moment, thinking about what I should do. Who I can call.

God, this stupid car. I absolutely cannot afford for it to go out on me again. I'm already in debt to Jackson, and whatever else is wrong with it, it's probably a really expensive fix. I wish I could get a new car, but that costs money.

Money I don't have. I'm only eighteen. I'm sure I wouldn't qualify for a loan, and it's not like I can afford a monthly car payment. My budget is pretty tight already.

Telling myself I don't need to send myself into a worse panic, I pull out my phone and bring up my messages, hating that Jackson isn't here to come to my rescue. He'd drop whatever and come running. I know he would.

But he's gone. I can't rely on him all the time.

I'm just starting to type out a text to Hayden when there's a rapid-fire knock on my window, startling me so badly, my phone slips from my fingers, falling onto the floorboard. I glance up to find the drunk customer standing there, an evil grin on his face.

"What's wrong, pretty girl? Car trouble?" he yells, his voice muffled.

Shit, shit, shit! What is he doing here?

I reach down, scared to take my eyes off of him, my hand scrambling, in search of my phone, but I can't find it. It must've slipped under the seat and out of my reach.

He bangs on the window again, harder this time. "You're a bitch, you know that? Ruining my good time. Why are you all bitches, huh? What the fuck do you want from us?"

He's angry at women in general, I guess. Lucky me.

And oh God, he looks furious. His face is red, his eyes

wide and blazing. Has he been hanging around here all this time? Why didn't Chuck spot him? Was he hiding behind a tree? There are no other cars in the lot. This is why we felt safe. Why Donna let Chuck and the other guys who work with us leave earlier.

Big mistake. Huge.

"Go away!" I scream at the guy, which only infuriates him. I take my gaze away from him long enough to try and grab my phone, my fingers curling around it. Finally.

I pull it out, finishing the sentence I started to Hayden.

Me: **Hey! Can you come get me at the restaurant? My car broke down again and there's a guy**

The man reaches for the door handle, lifting up on it. My automatic locks don't work all the time, and the door actually swings open, letting in a gust of cool air and an overwhelming scent of beer mixed with sweat.

And the man. The man barges into my car, lunging for me. I scream as loud as I can, the phone falling from my hand again. I hear it land with a clatter, and I have no idea if the text actually sent to Hayden or not. I try to fight him off, struggling beneath him, but he's so heavy. And smelly.

He grabs hold of my shoulders, giving me a shake. "Shut up! Quit screaming!"

I scream even louder. I have no idea what he wants from me, but I'm terrified. He lets me go to smack me across the face with his fist, so hard my ears ring and the scream dies in my throat.

"That's it. Be a good girl. Don't yell," he tells me, his voice calmer. Quieter. "Be nice, and I'll be nice too."

Anger and a massive dose of adrenaline floods me, drowning out the fear. Until all I can think about is hurting him. Destroying him. It's the only way I'll get out of this alive, I think.

I'm in pure fight or flight mode.

I'm ready to fight.

Ignoring the pain in my throbbing face, I concentrate on bending my knee beneath him, my foot falling to the floorboard, giving me good leverage. I aim straight at his crotch and with a grunt, I swing up my knee with all my might.

Nailing him right in the balls.

"Fuck! You bitch!" he groans, tipping over in agony with so much force his forehead smashes into my nose.

Plunging me into complete darkness.

CHAPTER 31
JACKSON

didn't want to tell Ellie why I came to Los Angeles a day before I had to, and without the team. I had to get special permission from the school, and the coaches gave their approval after I explained what my plans were.

Rick at Evergreen left me a voicemail Wednesday morning, saying he felt like an ass that they never scheduled a meeting with me. They wanted to talk. They're interested in me, he said. Could I come to Los Angeles in the next few days?

I played that message over and over, excitement rising within me. I didn't want to jinx anything so I told no one about this meeting I was able to schedule. Not even Ellie.

I wanted to ensure I could make this happen first, before I told people. I didn't want to let them down—didn't want to let myself down either.

I'm going to his office first thing. I couldn't sleep last night. I was too excited, too nervous, too agitated, all of it. So I gave up trying and stayed up till four in the morning writing a song.

Another one for Ellie.

I tried texting her to let her know I'm thinking about her,

but she never answered, so I figured she was sleeping. I know she had to work, so I left her alone, and eventually fell into a deep, dreamless sleep myself that almost had me missing my alarm this morning.

Lucky for me, I woke up with a few minutes to spare for a quick shower before I gathered up my shit and hopped into my car, making my way toward Evergreen's offices in downtown Los Angeles. I stayed at a hotel nearby, because I wasn't about to let the traffic fuck with this appointment. It still takes me longer than I predicted to get there, so when I'm finally pulling into the parking garage, I've only got a few minutes to make it up the elevator and into their offices to be on time.

"Park it for me, will you?" I ask as I climb out of my Mercedes, leaving the engine running. I throw my keys at the valet dude and he catches them with one hand, tearing off the slip I need to collect my car later. I exchange it for two twenties, pressing them into his palm.

"Thanks, man," he says, shoving the bills in his pocket. "I'll take good care of it for you."

"Thanks," I tell him as I dart into the building, running toward the elevators. By the time I'm strolling into the lobby of Evergreen, it is exactly nine o'clock on the dot.

Perfect timing.

My phone is buzzing in my pants' pocket, but I ignore it, flashing a charming smile at the pretty woman sitting behind the counter.

"Here for my nine a.m. with Rick," I tell her, sounding way more confident than I feel.

She glances at her computer screen before smiling up at me. "Jackson Rivers?"

"That's me," I say with a nod.

"Go ahead and sit down. He'll be right with you," she says. Her voice and her smile are flirtatious, and I wink at her in return, making her smile grow.

I mean nothing by it. She doesn't interest me. I have a

pretty girl sitting at home waiting for me, and I'm pretty sure she could be the love of my life.

I practically collapse in the chair the moment the realization hits me.

Yes. I love her. I do. And not just as a friend, though I've loved her like that for well over a year. I was just flat out in denial over it, over *her*. But here I sit, in a total daze, after staying up half the night working on a song that's all about her. While I have the biggest opportunity of my life waiting to happen in one of those nearby offices, all I can do is think about her.

And wish I was sitting with her right now. Holding her close and telling her I love her, right before I kiss her.

Fuck. I'm such a sap. But only for her.

My phone starts buzzing again and I pull it out of my pocket to see I have a call from Hayden. I answer it, my voice low.

"Thank God you answered. Where are you?" she asks, sounding frantic.

"I'm about to go into a meeting," I tell her, turning away from the reception desk. "Can I call you back after it's done?"

She ignores my question. "Are you on campus right now?"

"No, I'm in L.A." I hesitate for only a moment, my heart sinking as I hear noises in the background. The quickened sounds of her breathing. None of this feels right.

It doesn't feel good either.

"Jackson, you need to come home. Ellie—she's been hurt."

"What?" I practically yell, leaping to my feet. "What do you mean?"

"She's in the hospital. She's okay," Hayden rushes to say before I can interrupt her. "They kept her overnight for observation, but she's fine."

"Wait a minute, she was in the hospital overnight? Are you saying something happened to her yesterday? What the hell? And why the fuck didn't someone call me sooner?" I glance over at the receptionist, who's watching me with wide eyes. I send her a pleading look and point toward the door, letting her know where I'm going before I exit the offices completely, standing out in the corridor.

Jesus, I'm probably fucking this up with Evergreen, but I don't really give a damn.

"It all happened so quickly," Hayden says, and I realize she sounds exhausted. Worried out of her mind. "I got a text from her, asking me to pick her up, and I went there. To the restaurant. I brought Gracie with me, and we found Ellie in her car."

"What do you mean? Was she in a car accident?"

"Someone—a guy—" She goes silent for a moment and fear seizes my throat. I stop breathing, waiting for her answer. "She was attacked, Jackson."

"What? Is she okay? Did he—" I close my eyes, pressing my forehead against the wall. My knees are weak. Like, I feel as if I could collapse to the floor. My mind can barely wrap itself around the terrible things that might've happened to her.

I can't even say the words out loud.

"No, no. He didn't rape her or anything like that. He was really drunk. A pissed-off customer, I guess? That's what her boss told me. Everything happened so fast, and it became chaotic, really quick, especially after Gracie called 9-1-1. We've been sitting in the hospital all night, and I didn't even think to call you until now. I didn't even call Tony until an hour ago," Hayden says. "I'm so sorry."

My mind is racing. I need to get out of here. Go home. Go to Ellie.

I turn to look through the window, spotting Rick standing next to the reception desk, watching, waiting for me with a frown on his face. I hold up a finger at him, hoping he'll give me a minute, before I turn away.

"Is Tony with you?"

"Yes. Well, he's coming to the hospital right now. Gracie's still here with me too. The hospital was able to call Ellie's parents and they're coming to get her. It was so crazy, Jackson. Everything happening all at once," Hayden says.

"Is she going to be okay?" My voice is hoarse and I swallow hard. I feel like I'm going to be sick.

"Yes. He broke her nose when he knocked his head into hers. That's why they kept her overnight. She took a pretty hard hit to the head," Hayden says.

"I'll be right there. I'm leaving now." I don't even have to consider where I need to be. I'm going home to Ellie.

"She's woken up once, but only for a few minutes. She was groggy. I think they're keeping her sedated." Hayden's voice lowers. "It was so scary, Jackson. I feel so terrible, but I didn't see her text until I got out of the shower, and that was like fifteen minutes later. I think about if I'd been any later, what would've happened? When we got there, I found him on top of her in the car. He was crying, saying he didn't mean to—to kill her. She was passed out, but I didn't know, and I became hysterical. God."

Hayden chokes on the last word and starts to cry. I close my eyes, hating this. Hating that I'm not there.

"I'll call you back in a few. Let me hop in my car," I tell her, ending the call before I walk back in to speak with Rick.

"Jackson." Rick smiles, approaching me with his hand out. "So glad you're here. Ready to talk?"

"No," I tell him gruffly, noting the surprise in his gaze. "I have to go. Something came up."

Rick frowns. I'm sure he doesn't get turned down often. "Jackson. I rearranged my *entire* schedule to fit you in this morning. And I don't know if I'm going to be able to fit you in again." He pauses. "Do you understand what I'm saying?"

"I do, I understand." I tell him with a firm nod. "And I get it. Sorry to waste your time, sir, but my girlfriend is in the hospital. I gotta go."

Before he can even say anything, I'm tearing out of his office, my mind going a million miles a second, telling me I need to leave.

I need to get to Ellie.

————

By the time I'm driving through the south end of Fresno—in record fucking time I might add—I receive a call from Tony.

"What's up?" I answer, knowing he's been with Hayden this morning at the hospital.

"They released Ellie. She's going home with her parents," he says.

"How is she?"

"She's okay. Awake at least. Tired."

"How bad is it? Tell me the truth. Don't sugarcoat it," I demand.

"Her nose is swollen and she has two black eyes," he says.

"Fuck. I'm going to murder that guy," I say through clenched teeth.

"He's in jail," Tony says. "Got arrested for public intoxication and assault. Maybe a few other charges. Not sure."

"Where is she now? At her apartment?" I can't even compute exactly what Tony is telling me. I don't know how to feel about it. I don't know what to do. My emotions are everywhere. I feel helpless. Disappointed in myself. When things got rough, I wasn't there for her. And if I plan on having any sort of career in music, I won't be here for her most of the time.

Which makes me feel like absolute shit.

"Her parents took her home. She's with them," Tony says.

I punch the steering wheel, frustration rippling through me. "I'm going up there. I'm calling her right now."

"I don't think she has her phone on her, but she told us she wants to see you," Tony says.

"Where the hell is her phone?"

"It got lost in the car, I think? I have no idea. The police might have it. The car was taken in for evidence," he says. "Or it was just towed? Not sure. It broke down on her last night in the parking lot at the Doghouse Grill. That's how the guy caught her in the first place."

"*Fuck.*" I pound the steering wheel again, so hard it hurts my hand. "I hate that fucking car. She needs a new one."

"She can't afford one," he reminds me.

"I'm buying her one. Fuck this. I'm tired of it. I'll trade in this shitty Mercedes and get Ellie something that's dependable. I can drive whatever." I don't care. I was a pretentious little shit in high school, but I'm realizing that material things don't mean shit if you don't have the one you love sitting beside you.

"You're going to actually buy Ellie a car?" Tony sounds amused.

"How can you laugh at a time like this, huh? Fuck, she almost died!"

"Jackson, calm down. She didn't die. That's the best thing about this. And you don't realize that because you haven't seen her yet. Yeah, she's sore and she looks like hell, but she has a pretty good sense of humor about it."

"A sense of humor? Some asshole *attacked* her," I stress, barely able to wrap my head around those words.

"A drunk loser who's upset because his wife left him. That's what the police officer told Hayden when he talked to her earlier this morning," Tony explains.

A ragged breath escapes me. I won't be able to calm down until I see Ellie for myself and know she's okay. I need to hear her say those words. Until then, I'm in pure freak out mode. "I'll be at her parents' house in an hour. Probably less."

"You know where they live?"

I hesitate for a moment. "Uh, no."

"I'll text you the address. Oh, and Jackson?"

"Yeah?"

"She'll be all right. Really. She's a lot stronger than everyone thinks she is," Tony says before we end the call.

His words are supposed to be reassuring, but it doesn't work. I'm stressed the entire drive, gripping the steering wheel so tight, my fingers are fucking cramping up. I have to shake them out every few minutes, which isn't good for my game or my guitar playing. I need to fucking relax.

But when the girl you care about more than life itself is suffering, you can't. It's just that simple.

By the time I make it, I'm a rattled mess. Still running on adrenaline, and ready to tear that drunk asshole completely apart. Not that he's going to cross my path anytime soon. He better hope not, because I will fuck that guy up, and then I'll end up being the one sitting in jail.

I knock on the door, pacing the front porch. It swings open immediately, and an older version of my girlfriend is standing on the doorstep, blinking up at me before she breaks out into a gentle smile that has me staring mutely at her.

Ellie looks just like her. It's uncanny, the resemblance.

"You must be Jackson," she says. "I'm Renata. Ellie's mom."

"Nice to meet you—" I start.

She jerks me into a hug, surprisingly strong for such a small woman. I return the hug, finding comfort in the tight grip of her arms. The way she holds me, like a mom should. Something I don't get much of. I'm not close to my parents at all. Since I've been in college, I rarely see my dad, and I used to consider us close. I appreciate how welcoming Ellie's mom is. "It's so nice to meet you too," she says after she releases me, looking a little flustered. "Come in, come in."

I walk inside the house, glancing around. It's small but clean, and I can smell a candle burning. It's homey looking, the furniture a little worn, but I bet that couch is comfortable. I glance to my left, spotting a photo of Ellie on the wall right next to where I'm standing. She's young, like in elementary school, her hair in two ponytails on either side of her head, and she looks absolutely adorable. I smile as I study it.

"She's in her room," her mother tells me, her voice soft. "I insisted she come home for the weekend, so I can take care of her."

"How bad is it?" I ask, my voice grave. I don't want any bullshit. I need someone to be straight with me.

"She looks—terrible." She tries to smile, but it wavers, and she gives up. Her face appears ready to crumple at any second, and I really hope she doesn't start to cry. I don't do well with women and tears. They make me uncomfortable. "But my girl is strong. I'm so proud of her. She tried her best to fight that guy off."

"I bet she did," I murmur, never doubting Ellie's strength for a second. "Do you mind if I go see her?"

"Oh, of course. She wants to see you. She keeps asking about you. Her room is the last door on the left," her mother says, shooing me down the hall. "Would you like anything to drink?"

"I'll be fine," I reassure her as I make my way down the hall. I slow down as I approach the door, hesitating in front of it. It's partially open, but I hear no noise coming from within the room, and I wonder if she's sleeping.

I don't want to disturb her.

But I'm dying to see her.

Slowly, I open the door to find her in bed lying on her back, her head propped up on a stack of pillows. Her eyes are closed, and her face…

Holy shit her *face*.

Tony didn't lie and neither did her mother. She looks fucking awful. Two black eyes have caused dark purple and yellow bruising. There's a bandage across the bridge of her swollen nose. She looks like she got into a fight and lost.

Rage fills me and I clutch my hands into fists, wishing I could hit something. Someone. It hurts me to see her hurting. My chest aches. My heart pounds. That asshole tried to hurt her, and for no real reason. He could've done serious damage to my girl. I'm just grateful she's still here. Alive.

She must hear me because her eyes crack open and she studies me from where I'm standing across the room.

"Jackson. You made it." She tries to smile, but she winces, giving up. I'm sure she's in pain. "I look terrible."

"Yeah," I croak before I slowly make my way toward the bed. "But what's the other guy look like?"

"Terrible. Even worse because he's in jail." She closes her eyes, lying still for a moment as I carefully settle onto the edge of the bed beside her. "I did my best to beat him up."

"I bet." I drift my fingers down her arm and she smiles, her lips barely turning up at the corners. "What the fuck, Ellie? Tell me what happened."

She explains everything that occurred last night. How the guy was a drunk asshole and got kicked out of the Doghouse Grill. How he blamed her for getting escorted out, yelling at her in front of everyone. How her car wouldn't start and then he magically appeared. Her car is old, and the doors don't always automatically lock and that's how he was able to get inside. How he jumped her and hit her.

"He *hit* you?" I see red. I want to tear him from limb to limb.

Ellie nods. "It was so shocking. It stunned me more than anything else. I've never been hit like that before."

I can't stop touching her, but I don't want to hurt her either, so I keep stroking her arm, needing the connection. "Do you remember what happened next?"

"I kneed him straight in the balls," she tells me, her voice edgy. As if she's mad, reliving the moment. "It all happened so fast. His head snapped forward when I hit him, and he nailed me right here." She reaches up to demonstrate, pointing at her nose and the spot between her eyebrows. "He smacked me so hard with his forehead, I passed out. That's why they kept me for observation last night. They were worried over how hard the impact was. He gave me a concussion."

"But you're okay," I say, needing to hear her say the words.

"I'm okay," she whispers, nodding. She smiles, her eyes swollen little slits when she does. "I look terrible."

"You're beautiful." She is. It doesn't matter if she was toothless and bald, I would still think she's stunning, because she's mine. Because I care about her so damn much. "I'm just glad you're okay."

"I'll get better. This is temporary." She grabs my hand, squeezing it. "Where were you? You were so mysterious about going to Los Angeles. What happened?"

"It was nothing," I say dismissively. "I had an appointment with Evergreen earlier this morning, but I bailed on him the moment I found out what happened to you."

Her mouth drops open and she snaps it shut quickly. "Jackson. Don't tell me you left without talking to him because of me."

"Yeah. I did. I had to. None of that shit matters, El, if I don't have you in my life. Can't you see that?" I lean forward, dropping the softest kiss on her upturned lips. God, I don't want to push, but I want to show her how much she means to me. "I freaked out. I didn't know what happened to you."

"I'm okay," she whispers. "You should call him. Try to meet with him again."

This is such typical Ellie behavior. Thinking of me when it should be all about her.

"It doesn't matter," I repeat, pulling away so I can look at her. I'm completely in awe of her. She acts like what happened last night was no big deal. All she can do is worry about me, and I don't deserve it. Shit, I don't deserve her. "I think I ruined that chance for good."

She keeps her gaze downcast, plucking at the comforter that covers her. "I hate that I made you leave your meeting." Her frown is killing me. Seeing her like this is killing me, and I hate it.

I want her to feel better. I want to be the one who makes her smile. Makes her happy. Makes her forget what she's suffered through.

"You didn't make me do anything. It was an automatic reaction. My girl is hurt, I come running. My girl needs me, I'm there. And that's what upsets me the most," I say, emotion welling up, threatening to consume me.

She frowns. "What do you mean?"

"I failed you, El. That fucking tears me up inside, you know that? I had no idea what was going on, and it kills me that I was so far away." I touch her hair, careful not to touch her face. I don't know how much pain she's in, and I don't want to make it worse. "I'm down in Los Angeles, fucking oblivious, wrapped up in my own bullshit while some asshole is attacking you…"

I get choked up, and I can't continue. Seriously, I'm going to fucking bawl like a baby, so I close my eyes, breathing deep. Trying to calm my riotous emotions, when she's the one who's been through hell and back.

Yet I feel like I've been through it with her. *Fuck.*

Tentative fingers stroke the top of my hand and I turn it palm up, interlocking our fingers together. "I'll be okay, Jackson. Really. Don't get so upset. It was scary. I can't lie. I panicked, and it was truly the most terrifying moment of my entire life, but honestly? He wasn't mad at me. He was just drunk and mad at his ex. The cops came to my room earlier and explained everything before I left the hospital. He wasn't in the right frame of mind. He's been threatening his ex since they broke up."

"I'm not in the right frame of mind either." I crack open my eyes to find her watching me. "If I got the chance, I'd kill him."

Her expression is full of doubt. "You would not."

"I would," I say fiercely. "Anyone who lays a hand on you, doesn't deserve to live."

She squeezes my hand, saying nothing. Just smiles that patient smile at me while my emotions threaten to spill out all over the place.

So I let them.

"I'm in love with you, El. Took me a while to come around and realize this, but I am. You mean more to me than anything else in this world. I don't give a shit about school or music or football, or anyone else. None of it matters if I can't have you by my side," I confess, my throat raw.

Fuck, saying those words feels scary. My confession leaves me vulnerable. I feel exposed. As if I tore into my guts and completely revealed myself, just for this girl. No hiding behind my charm or whatever the fuck else I used to get by. I'm just me, standing with my heart in my hands like a goddamned John Mayer song, offering it to Ellie.

The girl who gives me life. Gives me love. Gives me everything I could ever want.

I look at her. Really look at her, and see that there are tears leaking out of the corners of her eyes. Damn it, I made her cry again.

"Ellie. Baby." Agony fills my voice. "Why the tears?"

"You're crying too," she says, sniffing. "Don't get all accusatory."

I can't help it, I laugh. Then wipe at my eyes, feeling the tears there. "You're right."

"I know." She pauses. "I'm in love with you too, Jackson.

I've been in love with you since the first time I saw you, I think."

"You giving me some Eli Bennett bullshit right now?" I ask her, making her giggle. "He says the same thing about Ava."

"Well, I feel that way about you, so yes. I'm giving you some Eli Bennett bullshit right now," she says as she works to sit up straighter, trying to get closer to me I suppose, but she grimaces in pain.

I move toward her instead, my face in hers, trying to ignore the horrible black and purple bruising beneath her eyes and around her nose, but it's hard to avoid. She looks terrible.

Beautiful.

More than anything, she looks like mine.

"I don't deserve you," I tell her. "I want to be a better man for you, Ellie."

"You're already a good man," she says, reaching up to touch my cheek. "And you're only going to get better."

"With you be my side," I add, turning my face so I can drop a kiss on her palm.

"Of course," she says firmly. "I can't believe I'm having the most romantic moment ever and I look like this."

"You're beautiful."

"You're blind," she says with a laugh.

"Blind with love," I amend, making her laughter die.

But her eyes still sparkle. Despite the bruising and the swelling, she's watching me with those all-knowing blue eyes and I understand in this moment…

I will *never* find another girl like my Ellie.

CHAPTER 32
ELLIE

S *pring*

I can't take my eyes off of Jackson as he paces back and forth out on the back patio of his apartment, talking on the phone. I wish I was out there, blatantly spying on his conversation, so I could hear every word he's saying, but I'm not. I gave him privacy because I'm a considerate girlfriend, but damn, I'm dying to know what's happening right now.

Eli strides into the living room, stopping short when he sees Jackson outside, still pacing. Still talking. I'm pretending to be scrolling on my phone, but I'm bored. Anxious.

"What's going on out there?" Eli asks me. "He looks serious."

I want to say, *oh you know, our entire future is on the line, and he's trying to figure out what's happening next,* but I don't.

"He's on the phone with Rick," I say instead.

"Ah. Evergreen Rick."

I nod. Don't really say anything else because what else is there to say?

My man ended up taking a record deal with them. He skipped the spring semester on campus, opting to take four classes online, so he could be at the studio down in Hollywood, working on tracks, creating an album long into the night, while catching up with his classes during the day. It's been intense, his schedule has been heavy with obligations, but he's fulfilled every one of them.

I'm so proud of him. All of his hard work is paying off.

Originally, he didn't even want to meet with them yet again. But when Rick called around a month after Jackson ran out of their meeting, confessing that he couldn't stop thinking about him and his music, Jackson went back to Evergreen Records.

And they came to an agreement.

He wanted me to go with him down to Los Angeles, but I couldn't. I have a lease at my apartment I can't break, and a job and school. My friends, and my family. We've changed some safety procedures at work so an incident like what happened to me won't ever occur again. Donna felt so guilty over leaving me behind that night, but I told her it wasn't her fault. She didn't know.

That guy was going to do something, it didn't matter to who. I was just the unlucky one.

I healed nicely. Both inside and out. The bruises are gone, and my nose is a little crooked, but nothing major. I'm okay. Mentally, I feel even stronger. Like I struggled and fought, and came out the other side a better person. Pain is a true learning experience. You can grow from it, and I feel like I've grown a lot this year.

I've also been considering some things. About my life, and what I want from it. I'm going to make some changes. Do something different this summer, and next year too.

So is Jackson. I can feel it. The best part?

We're going to do everything together.

I can tell the conversation is coming to an end. I see the

smile on his face. The way he's nodding again and again, his dark blond hair bobbing across his forehead. A giant smile stretches across his face and I hear him laugh, the sound causing joy to bubble inside of me.

It was good, their conversation. He's going to give me good news.

He ends the call, reaching for the handle on the sliding glass door and pulling it open so he can enter the apartment.

"Well?" I ask after he closes the door but still hasn't said anything. "What did Rick say?"

He grins and scoops me up right from the couch, swinging me around and around, making me laugh. "It's official. Pack your bags. We're going on tour, baby."

"Yes!" I wrap my arms around his neck and squeeze him tight, bringing his mouth to mine for a too-quick kiss. "I can't wait," I say, pressing my forehead to his.

"Wait a minute," Eli says from behind us.

We both stop twirling, turning to look at Eli, who's watching us with his hands on his hips and a frown on his face.

Oops. I sort of forgot he was there. I bet Jackson didn't even see him.

"What?" Jackson asks him.

"You're going on tour again this summer?" Eli asks.

Jackson nods, smiling down at me. "Yeah. For longer though. And I'm bringing Ellie with me."

"What about the groupies?"

I roll my eyes. "Eli."

The guys love to give Jackson crap about the groupies.

"Fuck the groupies. I've got everything I want right here." Jackson kisses me again, his mouth lingering on mine.

"Ha, I was giving you shit." Eli shakes his head, his hands still on his hips. "You're not coming back to school, are you?"

"I don't know, man. I get the feeling my entire life is about to change, so maybe not," Jackson says, that grin still stretching his mouth wide. Like he can't stop smiling. I can't stop smiling either. "They're bumping up the schedule, too. We're dropping the first single in two weeks."

"Pink?" I ask excitedly.

"Yeah. They wanted me to debut with a banger. The ballad will come next."

"I See You." The ballad he wrote for me after what happened in the parking lot that night. It's such a beautiful song, filled with so much emotion. It makes me want to tear up every time I hear it.

Jackson's face lights up. "Oh and get this. Fucking Cupid's Bow is opening for me through the summer."

"No way," I breathe, laughing. "I love it!"

"Remember how jealous I was over them?" Jackson shakes his head as he laughs too.

Of course I do. He was so down, and it was all for nothing. Look how well they're both doing. Together. And with the same record company, too. Now they're going on tour together. I love it.

Life has a way of working out perfectly sometimes, I swear.

"You're really going on tour with him all summer, Ellie?" Eli asks me, pulling me from my thoughts.

Jackson finally sets me down on my feet, releasing me and I smile at Eli. "I am. I already warned my boss I was probably quitting. She promised me if I ever came back, she'd rehire me."

"If?" Eli's eyebrows rise.

I shrug, excited about the unknown. "Yeah. I don't know what's going to happen. I kind of like the idea of being the boho girlfriend of a famous rock musician. Going on tour with him. Traveling the country," I say.

"Maybe the world," Jackson adds.

"Yeah. It'll be fun. We're only young once, right?" I glance over at Jackson, smiling tenderly at him. He sends me the same look, and I remember the conversation we had last night, when the scheduled call with Rick still loomed over his head and Jackson wasn't one hundred percent sure if we were touring or not.

"Promise you'll come with me, El. I don't want to do this life alone. I know school is important to you, but you don't even know what you want to do yet. We have the rest of our lives to figure that shit out. Just—come with me. Be my support, my muse. Travel the country with me, baby. Let me see it all through your eyes too," he said, his gaze never straying from mine.

How could I resist that?

I agreed. I'll take a semester off. So will he. He won't be playing football for the Bulldogs any longer, but it doesn't matter anymore. He went after what he really wanted, and now he's got both. His music career.

And me.

———

"We need to start packing," Jackson says much later, when we're in bed and snuggled up together. We went out to dinner to celebrate, bringing everyone along with us. They were all happy over Jackson's news, though I saw the faint judgment in Caleb's eyes. The guy is still miffed he's now the only single man standing. He can't fathom how Jackson is going on tour, performing music for screaming women for months, and that he's taking his girlfriend along with him.

Ah, poor Caleb. He has no clue what it's like, to really love someone. He'll figure it out someday.

"I have to get all of my stuff out of the apartment before we leave," I tell him. The lease is up in July, but we're leaving the beginning of June. I plan on paying the remainder of my rent before I leave the apartment for good. I never did really make friends with my roommates. They were nice enough;

we just all had such different schedules and we never really saw each other. Plus, I didn't spend much time there.

"What about your place here?" I ask him, my fingers skimming his bare chest, my head propped on his shoulder. "What's Eli going to do without you?"

He chuckles, his chest vibrating with the sound. "Get this. Tony and Hayden are moving in together when school's over. He told me that at dinner."

"No way." I haven't talked to Hayden in a few days. Guess she's been holding out on me. "What about Gracie?"

"She's moving in with—are you ready—Eli and," he pauses, "Caleb."

"Noooo…" I close my eyes, pressing my face against his chest. "That sounds like a disaster waiting to happen."

"I already warned Eli that living with those two is going to be trouble. He's game for it, though. He says they can squabble all they want, but he's not worried about it." Jackson slips his arm around my shoulders, pulling me in for a kiss on the lips. "Can you see the three of them living together?"

"No. It sounds like a nightmare." I give a little shudder.

His expression turns serious. "You okay with going on tour with me?"

I smile. "Yes. Of course I am."

"You sure? It's going to be a grind, El. Lots of traveling. Sleepless nights. I'll be on stage a lot of those nights, while you're watching from the wings. You might get bored or pissed at me. I don't want you thinking I'm ignoring you."

"I know you won't be ignoring me. You'll be working. It'll be fun. An adventure," I tell him, shifting so I'm lying half on top of him, my face in his. He's in his boxers. I'm wearing panties and a tank. Easy-to-get-rid-of clothes, since we do that a lot once we're in bed together. Get rid of our clothes.

"I'd rather be bored out of my skull with you on tour, than all by myself, missing you *and* bored out of my skull."

"I bore you?" he asks with a faint smile, though his brows are furrowed.

As if he really thinks he bores me.

This man sometimes still has doubts when it comes to me and our relationship. Like he can't believe I'm in love with him, when I'm the one who harbored feelings for him far longer than he ever did.

Maybe he was experiencing them too, he just didn't know how to label them. Or recognize them.

It doesn't matter anymore. All that matters is we're together. Our life is going to be good. Amazing. Epic.

Together.

It's all that matters.

"That's what you got out of what I just said? That you bore me?" I roll my eyes before I dip my head down and kiss him. "What I'm trying to say is that no matter where I'm at, I'm going to be happy because I'm with you."

"Oh. Yeah." He wraps his arms around me, his hands landing on my butt, his fingers slipping beneath my panties. "That's better. I can go along with that."

"Figured you could." I kiss him again, my lips lingering. He deepens the kiss in an instant, his tongue parting my lips, tangling with mine. "I'm so excited," I say when we end the kiss moments later.

"So am I." He thrusts his hips against me, so I can feel his excitement, literally.

I laugh. "I'm not talking about that kind of excited, though I suppose I am."

He shifts, slipping his hand between us, his fingers diving beneath my panties to test me. "Yep. You're definitely excited."

We stop talking after that, getting lost in each other. Found in each other. Our hands wandering, dispensing each other of any remaining clothing, our fingers seeking. Stroking. I grab a condom and roll it onto his thick erection, just before he takes over, flipping me onto my back and sliding inside of my body with ease, all the way to the hilt. He holds himself there, hovering above me, that chain he's always wearing dangling from his neck. The necklace he gave me when he came back from last summer's tour is around my neck as well, a symbol of his love for me, even when he didn't realize it yet.

"I love you," he whispers as he slowly starts to move.

I move beneath him, hooking my legs around his hips. "I love you too."

"Even though I'm an egotistical shit?"

"Especially because of that," I say with a smile. He hits a particular spot deep within me and I close my eyes on a moan. "Oh my God, don't stop."

He hits that spot again and again, increasing his pace, and I can already feel it coming. My orgasm pressing down on me. Until it's all over me, and I whisper his name, my body shaking, my inner walls squeezing him tight, choking the orgasm right out of him mere minutes later. Until we're both a trembling, panting heap of tangled limbs and quivering parts, clinging to each other.

"That was almost embarrassingly fast," he says after he's found his voice.

"Mmm. I didn't mind." I snuggle closer, but he gently pushes me away, getting up so he can dispose of the condom. When he comes back into the bedroom, I'm already sitting up, the sheets falling to my waist, exposing my upper body to him. Of course his gaze drops to my chest, lingering there. "I want to get on the pill before we leave."

He raises a brow. "Really?"

I nod, bringing my knees up to my chest and hugging them to me. "I'm tired of condoms."

Jackson grins. "Me too."

"We should get rid of them for good."

"I agree." His smile fades. "I've never had sex without one before."

"That's reassuring," I tease him.

"You trust me? Is that what you're saying?" he asks as he comes back to the bed and climbs beneath the covers, pulling me to him.

"I trust you. I've always trusted you." I kiss his jaw. His chin. His lips. "I love you, Jackson."

"I love you too, baby. You and me? We're going to conquer the world together," he says with all that Jackson Rivers' confidence I love.

"We are," I agree, settling in next to him.

Right where I belong.

EPILOGUE

JACKSON

Summer

Adrenaline races through my veins as I stand on the sidelines of the stage, listening to the crowd. They're chanting my name over and over again, wanting me to come back out and perform one last time for them. Some of them sound desperate, high-pitched female voices yelling, "Jackson, *please!*"

Ellie always tells me she can feel their pain. She knows what that's like, wishing I would notice her. Really notice her. And I tell her what I say in the song that I wrote just for her. The one that's currently racing up the Billboard charts, which is fucking unbelievable. "Pink" did well, but "I See You" is already doing better. Rick swears it's going to outperform the first single.

He says it's going to hit number one.

"They want you," Ellie says, sliding her hand into mine. This is our ritual. One we started early on in the tour. Now it's late August. She says this to me every time they're out there chanting my name and we're backstage, tucked in close together.

She supports me. Loves me. Encourages me. And I do the same for her. At the beginning of the summer, she started a YouTube channel about our travels and exploits, and she's gained lots of followers fast. Rick wasn't thrilled I was bringing my girlfriend on tour at first, but now he loves it. He loves all the attention Ellie's social media brings to us, to me. She's completely blown up. She even has sponsors now.

It's fucking wild. Our lives have taken a total turn, and it's amazing.

I couldn't do any of this without her.

"Do you want me?" I ask. This is also part of our ritual. I know what her answer is going to be. It never wavers.

"More than you'll ever know." She tugs on my hand, pulling me down to kiss her lips. I linger there, drinking from her, not wanting to stop, but she gently pushes me, giving me no choice.

"Go out there. Show them what you've got," she murmurs.

I lift my brows. That line is new. Usually she says, *Go out there. Show them that you're mine.*

She smiles serenely, making me think of a queen. She's transformed this summer. I love the woman she's becoming. "You don't belong to just me anymore, Jackson. You belong to all of them too."

Ellie points at the screaming crowd.

"Not true—" I start, but she shakes her head.

"It's okay. They can have a piece of you, but not all of you," she says. "I'm the one who's in your bed every night. That's all that matters to me."

Ah fuck. This girl. Her confidence in herself and me is astounding. She's changed so much. All for the better. I'm in awe of her.

"Love you." I kiss her again. "I'm gonna go make girls cry now."

She giggles. "Have fun."

I run back out on stage, my bandmates following after me. The crowd roars their approval as I sling my guitar strap around my neck and approach the mic, strumming the guitar a couple of times to tune it. I stand there, quiet, surveying the audience and how deep it goes. How many people came out tonight to support me. To listen to my songs. They grow with every venue, I swear. This venue is outside, so there are a ton of people here. I see more male faces than usual out there, which is surprising.

Not that I don't appreciate my female fans, but I don't want to be labeled as a teen heartthrob and that's it. Though Rick tells me there's worse things that could happen to my career.

I suppose he's right.

Once the crowd is mostly silent, I start to play, my acoustic guitar so much softer than the electric guitar, of course. I don't play acoustic nearly as much as I used to, and I miss it. Miss my fucking chair too. It was part of my schtick, but Rick told me I needed to try something new, so here I am.

Standing. Smiling out at the crowd before I speak.

"This song is for my girl," I say, my voice husky. I glance to my right to see Ellie standing in the wings, a giant smile on her face as she watches me. "She's the love of my life. And she better never forget it."

The crowd goes nuts. Ellie mouths *I love you* to me. Her words are like an adrenaline shot straight to the heart.

Damaged. Broken. Blind and stupid
Looking for girls. Losing myself. Drinking too much
Finding happiness in things that don't matter
Yet there you stood, always by my side. Never wavering

How much did you endure while I was fucking around?
Yet you never left me, yeah you stood your ground

I strum the guitar, tapping my foot, thinking of that night, and how I started writing this song while she was being attacked. And how far we've come since then.

When it's dark and cold, and you're feeling lonely just know
    I see you
    When we're miles apart you've still got a piece of my heart
    Yeah
    I see you
    Even before when I took advantage of your faith in me
    I saw you
    And now we're together, we're so much in love, you always know
    I see you
    I see you

The crowd in front of the stage is swaying back and forth, singing along. I start playing with them, not saying the words but they always scream them back to me, loud and clear.

I see you
    I see you

I finish the song, overwhelmed with emotion, which is my usual state lately. I feel like a giant baby, which is not normal. But I'm embracing it, because fuck, I'm feeling everything, and it's so damn good. I didn't know my life could be like this, and it's all thanks to my girl.

My Ellie.

She changed me in so many ways. I was running away from my feelings because they scared me. Ellie made me see that. A relationship doesn't destroy you. If you're in the right one, with someone you love and who supports you, it lifts you up.

It makes you a better person.

That's what Ellie has done for me.

I start to wrap up the song and I glance her way, waving my hand toward her, beckoning her onstage. Her eyes go wide and she shakes her head, but I keep waving at her, mouthing to her *come here.*

She walks on stage, slowly approaching me, looking so incredibly nervous. But she's got nothing to fear. The crowd starts screaming. Some of them say her name, which startles her. Of course, they know who she is. We're a package deal.

The moment she's close, I launch into a repeat of the chorus, wanting to say the words directly to her. Wanting everyone to see how much this girl means to me.

How much I love her.

"And now we're together, we're so much in love, and you always know. I see you," I tell her, not even singing anymore. I stop playing the guitar, too caught up in the shine of unshed tears in her eyes. "I see you. I love you, baby."

Swear to God, a collective sigh rises from the crowd.

Just as I end the song for good.

And kiss her.

PLAYLIST

"Rockstar Knights (with Tripple Redd)" -
Kid Cudi, Tripple Redd
"notice me (feat. BENEE)" - ROLE MODEL, BENEE
"affection" - BETWEEN FRIENDS
"telepatia" - Kali Uchis
"WHY AREN'T WE HAVING SEX?" -
Liza Owen
"Pink + White" - Frank Ocean
"blushing!" - BETWEEN FRIENDS
"Kiss U Right Now" - Duckwrth
"Vultures - Live at the House of Blues, Chicago" - John Mayer

Find the rest of The Sophomore playlist on Spotify: https://
spoti.fi/3fGY64d

ACKNOWLEDGEMENTS

It was a true joy to write Jackson and Ellie's story, though the music lyrics tripped me up some. I don't consider myself poetic, so I had to channel my inner Drew Callahan (if you read One Week Girlfriend, etc. you know what I'm talking about) to come up with (hopefully) passable lyrics. I hope you enjoyed reading this book as much as I enjoyed writing it. Their story was a long time coming.

I want to thank everyone at Valentine PR, including my precious Nina and the rest of the gang. You all make my life a lot easier. I also want to thank Michelle Lancaster for the fabulous photo of Lochie (he is such a great Jackson!) and Hang Le for the magnificent cover. Thank you to Rebecca and Sarah for slapping my book into shape, as well as Brittany for the excellent beta read and notes. You are all the BEST.

And as always, thank you to the readers, bloggers, reviewers, etc. who read my books and share them everywhere. I seriously cannot do this job with you!

p.s. - If you enjoyed this book, I would greatly appreciate it if you left a review on the retailer site you bought it from, or on Goodreads. Thank you so much!

ALSO BY MONICA MURPHY

LANCASTER PREP

Things I Wanted To Say (but never did)

A Million Kisses in Your Lifetime

Promises We Meant to Keep

WEDDED BLISS

The Reluctant Bride

The Ruthless Groom

The Reckless Union

COLLEGE YEARS

The Freshman

The Sophomore

The Junior

The Senior

DATING SERIES

Save The Date

Fake Date

Holidate

Hate to Date You

Rate A Date

Wedding Date

Blind Date

THE CALLAHANS

Close to Me

Falling For Her

Addicted To Him

Meant To Be

Fighting For You

Making Her Mine

A Callahan Wedding

FOREVER YOURS SERIES

You Promised Me Forever

Thinking About You

Nothing Without You

DAMAGED HEARTS SERIES

Her Defiant Heart

His Wasted Heart

Damaged Hearts

FRIENDS SERIES

Just Friends

More Than Friends

Forever

THE NEVER DUET

Never Tear Us Apart

Never Let You Go

THE RULES SERIES

Fair Game

In The Dark

Slow Play

Safe Bet

THE FOWLER SISTERS SERIES

Owning Violet

Stealing Rose

Taming Lily

REVERIE SERIES

His Reverie

Her Destiny

BILLIONAIRE BACHELORS CLUB SERIES

Crave

Torn

Savor

Intoxicated

ONE WEEK GIRLFRIEND SERIES

One Week Girlfriend

Second Chance Boyfriend

Three Broken Promises

Drew + Fable Forever

Four Years Later

Five Days Until You

A Drew + Fable Christmas

STANDALONE YA TITLES

Daring The Bad Boy

Saving It

Pretty Dead Girls

ABOUT THE AUTHOR

Monica Murphy is a New York Times, USA Today and international bestselling author. Her books have been translated in almost a dozen languages and has sold over two million copies worldwide. Both a traditionally published and independently published author, she writes young adult and new adult romance, as well as contemporary romance and women's fiction. She's also known as USA Today bestselling author Karen Erickson.

- facebook.com/MonicaMurphyAuthor
- twitter.com/msmonicamurphy
- instagram.com/monicamurphyauthor
- bookbub.com/profile/monica-murphy
- goodreads.com/monicamurphyauthor